AT NIGHT
WE WALK
IN CIRCLES

AT NIGHT
WE WALK
IN CIRCLES

DANIEL ALARCÓN

FOURTH ESTATE • London

Fourth Estate
An imprint of HarperCollins*Publishers*
77–85 Fulham Palace Road,
London W6 8JB
www.4thestate.co.uk

First published in Great Britain by Fourth Estate in 2013
First published in the United States by Riverhead Books in 2013

1 3 5 7 9 10 8 6 4 2

Some of this work has been previously published in *The New Yorker*,
in slightly different form, as 'The Idiot President'.

A catalogue record for this book is
available from the British Library

Hardback ISBN 978-0-00-751739-8
Trade paperback ISBN 978-0-00-751740-4

Book design by Gretchen Achilles

Printed and bound in Great Britain by
Clays Ltd, St Ives plc

FOR CAROLINA, LEÓN, AND ELISEO

The spectacle's externality with respect to the acting subject is demonstrated by the fact that the individual's own gestures are no longer his own, but rather those of someone else who represents them to him. The spectator feels at home nowhere, for the spectacle is everywhere.

—GUY DEBORD, *The Society of the Spectacle*

BÉRENGER: [*who also stops feeling the invisible walls, greatly surprised*] Why, what do you mean?

[*The* ARCHITECT *returns to his files.*]

In any case, I'm glad my memory is real and I can feel it with my fingers. I'm as young as I was a hundred years ago. I can fall in love again . . . [*Calling to the wings on the right:*] Mademoiselle, oh, Mademoiselle, will you marry me?

—EUGÈNE IONESCO, *The Killer*

PART
ONE

1

DURING THE WAR—which Nelson's father called *the anxious years*—a few radical students at the Conservatory founded a theater company. They read the French surrealists, and improvised adaptations of Quechua myths; they smoked cheap tobacco, and sang protest songs with vulgar lyrics. They laughed in public as if it were a political act, baring their teeth and frightening children. Their ranks were drawn, broadly speaking, from the following overlapping circles of youth: the longhairs, the working class, the sex-crazed, the poseurs, the provincials, the alcoholics, the emotionally needy, the rabble-rousers, the opportunists, the punks, the hangers-on, and the obsessed. Nelson was just a boy then: moody, thoughtful, growing up in a suburb of the capital with his head bent over a book. He was secretly in love with a slight, brown-haired girl from school, with whom he'd exchanged actual words on only a handful of occasions. At night, Nelson imagined the dialogues they would have one day, he and this waifish, perfectly ordinary girl whom he loved. Sometimes he would act these out for his brother, Francisco. Neither had ever been to the theater.

The company, named Diciembre, coalesced around the work of a few strident, though novice, playwrights, and quickly became known for their daring trips into the conflict zone, where they lived out their slogan—Theater for the People!—at no small risk to the physical safety of the actors. Such was the tenor of the era that while sacrifices of this sort were applauded by certain sectors of the public, many others condemned them, even equated them with terrorism. In 1983, when Nelson was only five, a few of Diciembre's members were harassed by police in the town of Belén; a relatively minor affair, which nonetheless made the papers, prelude to a more serious case in Las Velas, where members of the local defense committee briefly held three actors captive, even roughed them up a bit, believing them to be Cuban agents. The trio had adapted a short story by Alejo Carpentier, quite convincingly by all accounts.

Nor were they entirely safe in the city: in early April 1986, after two performances of a piece titled *The Idiot President*, Diciembre's lead actor and playwright was arrested for incitement, and left to languish for the better part of a year at a prison known as Collectors. His name was Henry Nuñez, and his freedom was, for a brief time, a cause célèbre. Letters were written on his behalf in a handful of foreign countries, by mostly well-meaning people who'd never heard of him before and who had no opinion about his work. Somewhere in the archives of one or another of the national radio stations lurks the audio of a jailhouse interview: this serious young man, liberally seasoning his statements with citations of Camus and Ionesco, describing a prison production of *The Idiot President*, with inmates in the starring roles. "Criminals and delinquents have an intuitive understanding of a play about national politics," Henry said in a firm, uncowed voice. Nelson, a month shy of his eighth birthday, chanced to hear this interview. His father, Sebastián, stood at the kitchen counter preparing coffee, with a look of concern.

"Dad," young Nelson asked, "what's a playwright?"

Sebastián thought for a moment. He'd wanted to be a writer when he was his son's age. "A storyteller. A playwright is someone who makes up stories."

The boy was intrigued but not satisfied with this definition.

That evening, he brought it up with his brother, Francisco, who responded the way he always did to almost anything Nelson said aloud: with a look of puzzlement and annoyance. As if there were a set of normal things that all younger brothers knew instinctively to do in the presence of their elders but which Nelson had never learned. Francisco fiddled with the radio. Sighed.

"Playwrights make up conversation. They call them *scripts*. That crap you make up about your little fake girlfriend, for example."

Francisco was twelve, an age at which all is forgiven. Eventually he would leave for the United States, but long before his departure, he was already living as if he were gone. As if this family of his—mother, father, brother—mattered hardly at all. He knew exactly how to end conversations.

No recordings of the aforementioned prison performance of *The Idiot President* have been found.

By the time of his release, in November of that same year, Henry was much thinner and older. He no longer spoke with that firm voice; in fact, he hardly spoke at all. He gave no interviews. In January, in response to an uprising by inmates, two of the more volatile sections of Collectors were razed, bombed, and burned by the army; and the men who'd made up the cast of *The Idiot President* died in the assault. They were shot in the head or killed by shrapnel; some had the misfortune to be crushed beneath falling concrete walls. In all, three hundred forty-three inmates died, vanished; and though Henry wasn't there, part of him died that day too. The incident garnered international attention, a few letters of protest from European capitals, and then it was forgotten. Henry lost Rogelio, his best friend and cell mate, his lover, though he wouldn't have used that word at the time, not even to himself. He did not take the stage again for nearly fifteen years.

But a troupe must be bigger than a single personality. Diciembre responded to the curfew, the bombings, and the widespread fear with a program of drama-based bacchanals, "so drunk on youth and art" (according to Henry, a notion echoed by others), "they might as well have been living in another universe." Gunshots were deliberately misheard, interpreted as celebratory fireworks, and used as a pretext to praise the local joie de vivre; blackouts put them in the mood for romance. In its glory days at the end of the 1980s, Diciembre felt less like a theater collective and more like a movement: they staged marathon, all-night shows in the newly abandoned buildings and warehouses at the edges of the Old City. When there was no electricity—which was often—they rigged up lights from car batteries, or set candles about the stage; barring that, they performed in the dark, the spectral voices of the actors emerging from the limitless black. They became known for their pop reworkings of García Lorca, their stentorian readings of Brazilian soap opera scripts, their poetry nights that mocked the very idea of poetry. They celebrated on principle anything that kept audiences awake and laughing through what might have otherwise been the long, lonely hours of curfew. These shows were mythologized by theater students of Nelson's generation; and, if one searched (as Nelson had) through the stands of used books and magazines clogging the side streets of the Old City, it was possible to find mimeographed copies of Diciembre's programs, wrinkled and faded but bearing that unmistakable whiff of history, the kind one wishes to have been a part of.

By the time Nelson entered the Conservatory in 1995, the war had been over for a few years, but it was still a fresh memory. Much of the capital was being rebuilt. Perhaps it is more correct to say that the capital was being *reimagined*—as a version of itself where all that unpleasant recent history had never occurred. There were no statues to the dead, no streets renamed in their honor, no museum of historical memory. Rubble was cleared away, avenues widened, trees planted, new neighborhoods erected atop the ashes of those leveled in the conflict. Shopping malls were planned for every district of the capital, and the Old City—never an area with exact boundaries, but a commonly employed shorthand referring to the neglected and ruined center of town—was restored, block by block, with an optimistic eye toward a UNESCO World Heritage designation. Traffic was rerouted to make it more walkable, dreary facades given a dash of color, and the local pickpockets sent to work the outskirts by a suddenly vigilant police force. Tourists began to return, and the government, at least, was happy.

Meanwhile, Diciembre's legend had only grown. Many of Nelson's classmates at the Conservatory claimed to have been present at one or another of those historic performances as children. They said their parents had taken them; that they had witnessed unspeakable acts of depravity, an unholy union between recital and insurrection, sex and barbarism; that they remained, however many years later, unsettled, scarred, and even inspired by the memory. They were all liars. They were, in fact, studying to be liars. One imagines that students at the Conservatory these days speak of other things. That they are too young to remember how ordinary fear was during the anxious years. Perhaps they find it difficult to imagine a time when theater was improvised in response to terrifying headlines, when a line of dialogue delivered with a chilling sense of dread did not even require acting. But then, such are the narcotic effects of peace, and certainly no one wants to go backward.

Nearly a decade after the war's nominal end, Diciembre still functioned as a loose grouping of actors who occasionally even put on a show, often in a private home, to which the audience came by invitation only. Paradoxically, now that travel outside the city was relatively safe, they hardly ever went to the interior. Was this laziness, a reasonable response to the end of hostilities, or simply middle age blunting the sharp edge of youthful radicalism? Henry Nuñez, once the star playwright of the troupe, all but withdrew from it, attributing the decision not to his time in prison but to the birth of his daughter. After his prison home was razed, almost in spite of himself, he fell in love, married, and had a daughter named Ana. And then: life, domesticity, responsibilities. Before Diciembre consumed him, he'd studied biology, enough to qualify for a teaching position at a supposedly progressive elementary school in the Cantonment. The work appealed to his ego—he could talk for hours about almost anything that came to mind and his students would not complain—and in his hands biology was less a science than an obsessive branch of the humanities. The world could, in fact, be explained, and he found it miraculous that the students listened. For extra money he drove a taxi every other weekend, crossing the city end to end in a serviceable old Chevrolet he'd inherited from his father. Though he hadn't been inside a church since the mid-1980s, he put a bright red "Jesus Loves You" sticker in the front window to make potential passengers feel at ease. It was therapeutic, the mindlessness of driving, and the blank, sometimes dreary streets were so familiar they could not surprise him. On good days he could avoid thinking about his life.

Henry kept a giant plush teddy bear in the trunk, bringing it out for his daughter to sit with whenever he picked her up from her mother's house. The bigger she grew, Henry told me, the more his ambition dulled. Not that he blamed her—quite the contrary. Ana, he explained, had saved him from a mediocre sort of life his old friends had suffered to attain: painters, actors, photographers, poets—collectively, they are known as artists, just as those men and women who train in spaceflight are known as astronauts, whether or not they have been to space. He preferred not to play the part, he said. He was done pretending, a conclusion he'd come to in the aftermath of his imprisonment, after his friends had been killed.

But in late 2000, some veterans of Diciembre decided it was important to commemorate the founding of the troupe. A series of shows was planned in the city, and a Diciembre veteran named Patalarga even suggested a tour. Naturally, they called on Henry, who, with some reluctance, agreed to participate, but only if a new actor could be found to join. Auditions for a touring version of *The Idiot President* were announced for February 2001, and Nelson, a year out of the Conservatory at the time, signed up eagerly. He and dozens of young actors just like him, more notable for their enthusiasm than for their talent, gathered in a damp school gymnasium in the district of Legon, reading lines that no one had said aloud in more than a decade. It was like stepping back in time, Henry thought, and this had been precisely his concern when the proposal was first floated. He sighed, perhaps too loudly; he felt old. Since his divorce, he saw eleven-year-old Ana on alternate weekends. His students were his daughter's age; they completed science "experiments" where nothing at all was in play, where no possible outcome could surprise. Lately this depressed him profoundly, and he didn't know why. Whenever Ana came to stay, she brought with her a bundle of drawings tied with a string, all the work she'd done since they'd last seen each other, which she turned over to her father with great ceremony, for critique. Unlike his old friends, unlike himself, his daughter was not pretending: she *was* an artist, in that honest way only children can be, and this fact filled Henry with immense pride. They would sit on his couch and discuss in detail her works of crayon and pencil and pastel. Color, composition, stroke, theme. Henry would put on his most elegant, most highfalutin accent, and describe her work with big words she didn't understand but found delightful, funny, and very grown-up—*poststructuralist, antediluvian, protosurrealist, aphasic.* She'd smile; he'd rejoice. *The anthropomorphic strain running through your oeuvre is simply remarkable!* More often than not, hidden within his daughter's artwork, Henry found a terse note from Ana's mother, which was, in content and tone, the exact opposite of Ana's lighthearted drawings: a list of things to do, reminders about Ana's school fees, activities, appointments. Words free of warmth or affect or any trace of the life they had once attempted to make together. The playfulness would cease for a moment as Henry read.

"What does it say, Daddy?" Ana would ask.

"Your mother. She says she misses me."

Henry and his daughter would dissolve into fits of deep-throated laughter. For a girl her age, Ana understood divorce quite well.

The revival of Henry's most famous play was timed to coincide with the fifteenth anniversary of its truncated debut and the twentieth anniversary of the founding of the company. When he told Ana's mother the idea, she congratulated him. "Maybe you can get locked up again," his ex-wife said. "Perhaps it will resurrect your career."

A similar notion had crossed his mind too, of course, but for the sake of his pride, Henry pretended to take offense.

Now, at the auditions, his career felt farther away than ever. Whatever this was—whether a vice, an obsession, a malady—it most certainly was not "a career." Still, this dialogue, these lines he'd written so many years before, even when recited by these inexpert actors, provoked in Henry an unexpected rush of sentiment: memories of hope, anger, and righteousness. The high drama of those days, the sense of vertigo; he pressed his eyes closed. In prison, Rogelio had taught him how to place a metal coil in the carved-out grooves of a brick, and how to use this contraption to warm up his meals. Before that simple lesson everything Henry ate had been cold. The prison was a frightful place, the most terrifying he'd ever been. He'd tried his hardest to forget it, but if there was anything about those times that had the ability to make him shudder still, it was the cold: his stay in prison, the fear, his despair, reduced to a temperature. Cold food. Cold hands. Cold cement floors. He remembered now how these coils had glowed bright and red, how Rogelio's smile did too, and was surprised that these images still moved him so.

For their part, the actors were mostly too nervous or excited to notice Henry's troubled, uneasy countenance; or if they did, they assumed it was in response to their own performances.

Some, it should be noted, had no idea who he was.

But Nelson did recognize Henry. He'd heard him on the radio that day, and not long after, decided to become a playwright. All these years later, and in many ways, it remained his dream. What did he say to Henry?

Something like: "Mr. Nuñez, it's an honor."

Or: "I never thought I'd have the chance to meet you, sir."

The words themselves aren't that important; that he insisted on approaching the table where Henry sat, absorbed in dark memories, was enough. Picture it: Nelson reaching for his hero's hand, his eyes brimming with admiration. A connection between the two men, the mentor and his protégé.

When we spoke, Henry dismissed the idea.

I insisted: Did the playwright see something of himself in the young man? Something of his own past?

"No," Henry responded. "If you'll pardon my saying so, I was never, ever that young. Not even when I was a boy."

No matter. On a Monday in March 2001, Nelson was summoned to rehearsals at a theater in the Old City, a block off the traffic circle near the National Library, where his father had once worked. After a dismal year—a breakup, a protracted tenure at an uninteresting job, the disappointing aftermath of a graduation both longed for and feared—Nelson was simply delighted by the news. Henry was right: Nelson, almost twenty-three, had a backpack full of scripts, a notebook jammed with handwritten stories, a head of unruly curls, and seemed much, much younger. Perhaps this is why he got the part—his youth. His ignorance. His malleability. His ambition. The tour would begin in a month. And that is when the trouble began.

2

NORMALLY, Nelson would have shared news of this sort with Ixta. Now he doubted himself. She'd been his girlfriend until the previous July, and they'd parted ways, not amicably, on a day that Nelson considered to be the dead heart of winter. Ghoulish clouds, a fine, gray mist. It was entirely his doing—he wanted freedom, he said. She scoffed, "What am I, your jailer?" and in response, selfish but authentic tears bubbled in his eyes. He was going to the United States and couldn't be beholden to her or anyone in pursuit of his future. They didn't speak for three months, during which time he made no plans and took no steps toward this supposedly brave and life-changing move.

In early October, Nelson and Ixta met for a coffee, a tense affair which led, nonetheless, to another meeting, a few weeks later. Quite unexpectedly, midway through this second encounter, he found himself laughing. And Ixta laughing too. It wasn't tentative, or self-conscious, or polite. And this shook him, the realization that, had he more nerve, he could reach across the narrow table that separated them, and—in front of all these

strangers—casually lay his hand upon hers. No one would notice or think it odd. They might even smile at the sight, or say to
themselves something like:

Oh, what a handsome young couple!

He didn't, of course—not that day—but he did make some
progress. Slowly. Patiently. At the steady rate of an ant gathering
food, or a bird building a nest. And it paid off: by the start of the
Christmas season, they were sleeping together again. It happened almost by accident at first, but the second time filled him
with hope. They began meeting every two weeks or so, more if
Mindo, Ixta's new boyfriend, was working nights. These en-
counters were the source of both happiness and torment for
Nelson, but he was, in any case, unable or unwilling to push
things any further. In their nakedness, they talked about everything except what they were doing together, the future, and
somehow the vagueness of their new relationship was why it felt
so very adult. Ixta never asked if he still intended to leave for the
United States, nor did he mention it. He would—someday soon,
he felt certain—tell her he loved her, that he missed her, that he
was sorry for everything, and that they should be together, if not
forever, then at least for now. Afterward, things would be clearer.
He hadn't written the scene out—he didn't do that sort of thing
anymore—but he had projected himself into it, rehearsed a
speech or two in his head. As it turns out, Ixta was expecting
this as well. She didn't know how she'd respond, but she was
waiting. There was only the small issue of his not having said
anything.

In March, when he heard the news about Diciembre, Nelson

considered all they'd been through, what surely lay ahead, and decided it was correct to call her *first*. Her place in line was a nod to their past, to their imagined future. The phone rang twice, a curt hello. Ixta let him talk, and congratulated him, drily. He listened: it was the voice she used when Mindo was in the room.

Nelson and Ixta were both actors, though, so this fact hardly precluded conversation; in fact, it was more important than ever to behave naturally. Just two friends talking. The subterfuge was part of the attraction, one imagines. Ixta played her part: the news was grand, she told him. "How long will you be gone?"

"A couple of months, maybe three."

There was a certain sadism to his announcement. "I felt abandoned," Ixta said to me later. "Again."

She kept this confession to herself, and instead offered: "You always did want to travel."

"It could even go for longer, if we're well received."

"One hopes."

Nelson waited for her to go on, but she didn't. She'd gifted him these two words, but they were impossible to interpret. One hopes for what?

In the background: "Who's that, baby?"

Nelson flinched, but refused to back down. Later, he'd wonder if he'd been reckless. But really: what if they *were* caught? Shouldn't he *want* that to happen?

"Shall we celebrate?" he asked.

In his mind, the fact that they were lovers—and only lovers, for now—was a relief to Ixta. He imagined her grateful that he placed no pressure on their future, did not demand a label for this new iteration of their relationship. He imagined her impressed by his maturity, by his willingness to share her with another man. But this formulation was partial. It did not take into account the fact that she'd loved him, or that he'd broken her heart. It did not consider that her heart might be broken still, or that every time they slept together, it broke a little more.

"I don't know," Ixta said. "I'm busy this week."

"I thought you'd be happy for me," Nelson said, and immediately regretted it. He sounded so plaintive, so self-involved. There were certain traits he'd been careful not to manifest since their reconciliation, but here they were, slipping out into the open, naked. He wanted to be a better person; and if that were not possible, at least to seem like one.

"I *am* happy for you," she said. "Thrilled."

He doubled down: "I'd like to see you."

Ixta sighed: talking to herself now, in a rapid clip that tumbled the conversation to a close. "Sure. Yeah. Okay. Great. Talk soon." He could almost hear the man lying next to her, eyes half-closed, wrapping Ixta's brown hair casually around his finger.

Nelson held the phone a little while longer, for no good reason.

THE SECOND PERSON to hear the good news was his mother, Mónica, who'd been widowed three years prior, and whose capacity for joy had been greatly diminished ever since. That phrase is hers: "capacity for joy," she said to me, as one might describe the potential speed of a four-cylinder engine, or the memory inside a new computer. When this was brought to her attention, Mónica laughed. "Too many years as a bureaucrat," she said. "Imagine the life I could have had!"

But the truth is she'd liked her life just fine until her husband died. The house she and her younger son shared was strange to them now; and both spent as little time there as possible. The first year, Nelson often heard his mother crying very late at night. Francisco would sometimes call from California, and stay on the phone with her for long spells. The melancholy chatter emerging from the other room lulled him to sleep. He slept quite a bit in those days. Mónica was better now. She still kept her husband's pajamas under his old pillow, and respected the notion that one side of the bed was his. It was only right she feel her husband's absence like a wound.

Mónica went to the movies a great deal, American mostly. She'd developed a taste for action films and thrillers. The more explosions and special effects, the better; if the movie involved aliens or submarines, she privately rejoiced. She even tried to explain this new interest to her sons, separately, with varying results. Predictably, Nelson (for whom the storytelling aesthetic was not a matter of taste but a deeply held conviction) was less than supportive. Francisco, on the other hand, regarded it as comical, and somehow in keeping with his mother's other eccentricities; she made origami swans from tea bag wrappers, flocks of them appearing in the house's odd corners: in a little-used kitchen cupboard, behind the fine china; in the dining room, seated at the head of the table; or perched on windowsills, facing the street. She never threw away a magazine without cutting a pretty picture or two out of it first, their refrigerator door becoming the de facto gallery space for these images, a collage of faces which had made Nelson and Francisco feel, as children, that they were part of an eclectic and impossibly large family. And since Sebastián had passed, Mónica had picked up one of his old habits: writing letters to the newspapers, for example, complaining about potholes, traffic jams, rising crime, the lack of green space. These she wrote in Sebastián's name, under his signature, faithful to her husband's acid and erudite style. Whenever one was published, Mónica felt a pang, a sense of accomplishment, a confirmation of her solitude. She'd save the clippings in a folder, and sometimes read them before bed, as Sebastián had often done when he was alive.

About the movies, Mónica felt neither of her sons understood. It wasn't the stories she liked but the atmosphere that came with them. She'd find herself in line in front of the theater, surrounded by mad swarms of teenage boys, behaving as teenage boys do: badly. They were manic, poorly dressed, unnecessarily loud. I accompanied her to one of these films, and saw firsthand her unmistakable joy. The worse the film was, the more mindless, the happier Mónica became: her new peers talked back to the screen and cheered every explosion, creating a cacophony nearly equal to that of the film itself. It was a surprise to her too, she told me, but in their company, she felt peace. Comfort. A reminder that she wasn't dead yet.

The night Nelson received the news about Diciembre, it so happened that both mother and son were home at dinnertime and that neither had eaten. He'd intended to mention it in a slapdash, toss-away sort of comment that might require a quick hug and little else, but that's not how things turned out.

"Do you remember the audition?" he asked, "from last week?" And without waiting for an answer, he blurted it out: He'd gotten the part. He'd be going on tour.

Mónica was a small, proud woman; both smaller and prouder, in fact, in the years since Sebastián had died. Now, though she tried to hide it, Mónica began to cry.

Nelson protested: "Mom."

"I'm happy for you," she said. "That's wonderful!"

Her voice cracked. She asked for details, but had to sit to hear them. Her legs felt weak. He told her what he knew: They would leave the capital in April, head up into the mountains. As many shows as they could manage, perhaps six or seven a week. In most every town, they'd begin with a negotiation, for a space, for a time. They had contacts, and Diciembre was respected and fairly well known, even now. If the town was big enough, they'd stay awhile, until everyone had seen them perform. The circuit was sketched out, but subject to improvisation.

"Of course," Mónica said.

He went on. Roughly: San Luis (where one of the traveling members of Diciembre had a cousin), a week and a half in the highlands above and around Corongo (where the same man was born, and where his mother still lived), Canteras (where Henry Nuñez himself had lived from age nine until he ran away to the capital at age fourteen), Concepción, then over the ridge to Belén, and into the valleys below. Posadas, El Arroyo, Surco

Chico, up toward San Germán, and then the coast. A dozen smaller villages in between. An undeniably ambitious itinerary. The heart of the heart of the country. It was the tour Diciembre had intended to do, fifteen years earlier, until Henry's arrest scuttled those plans.

By this point, Mónica was sobbing.

"What a beautiful trip," she said, "just beautiful." And though she meant these words, perhaps it's worth noting that she'd never heard of most of the towns her son listed, and could hardly connect an image to their names. She confessed it to me: They weren't, in her mind, specific places but ideas of places. Notions. Echoes. The fact that one could even go to the interior still amazed her: during the war much of the country had been off-limits, far too dangerous for travel—but now her son would board a night bus and think nothing of it. It was astonishing. In 1971, on their honeymoon, she and Sebastián drove her father's car out of the city, into the fertile valleys that tilted toward the jungle, to picturesque riverside towns with cobblestone streets and thatched-roof adobe houses. Complex, unpronounceable names, which ten years later, during the war, would be synonymous with fear. But not then. If some of the names had been forgotten, everything else she recalled vividly: the bright, clean water; the thick, humid air; the magical feeling of levity; and this man—her husband—all to herself. Her body ached at the memory.

"What's the matter?" Nelson asked, sitting beside his mother as she wept. "It's only a couple of months."

Mónica couldn't explain, or preferred not to. Where to begin?

"I haven't eaten, I'm just a little light-headed," she said, and tried to remember the last time she'd cried. Like this? Weeks—no, months! Later she told me: "I was frightened. I'd be left alone, completely alone. I was certain I'd lose him. I don't know how, but I just knew."

THE ONE PERSON Nelson didn't share his good news with was his brother, Francisco. They weren't talking much in those days. Francisco's occasional e-mails went unanswered (Nelson didn't take this form of communication seriously and thought of it as a fad); and whenever he called from the United States, it seemed his younger brother had just stepped out. In all, they spoke perhaps three times a year, never for longer than ten minutes. The crushing, but entirely logical, result of so much distance was this: the less they spoke, the less they had to talk about.

Nelson's childhood can be divided roughly into two parts: before Francisco left for the United States and after. Until age thirteen, Nelson lived with Francisco, sharing a room, all manner of confidences, and a certain conspiratorial tension. To be sure, there was a hierarchy: when Francisco bullied Nelson, Nelson admired his brother's strength; when Francisco made fun of him, Nelson marveled at his brother's wit; when Francisco tricked him, Nelson appreciated his brother's cleverness. It would be unfair to say they didn't get along—though they argued a good deal and even fought on occasion, that's only part of the story. It's more accurate to say Nelson looked up to his brother without reservation; that he—like younger brothers

throughout the world, since hominids organized into families—
was born into a cult. That Francisco was, until he left, and for a
good while afterward, the model of everything Nelson wanted
to be.

Mónica and Sebastián moved together to Baltimore in 1972,
to study. They'd married the year before, and once in the United
States decided it was time to start a family. Sebastián, when he
was alive, explained the decision this way: having an American
baby was like putting money in the bank. Francisco was born in
1974. Mónica worked toward her public health degree at Johns
Hopkins, Sebastián for his master's in library science. While his
parents studied, Francisco observed the interior of their small
apartment in the company of a talkative American nanny. So
talkative, in fact, that in the interview, Mónica and Sebastián
had hardly been able to get a word in. They hoped some of this
woman's English would stay lodged in their son's brain, where it
might be useful later.

Francisco's linguistic education was cut short, however,
when the government back home was ousted three months before his second birthday. The news was spotty, but Sebastián and
Mónica soon gathered a few salient facts. The most important:
the new leaders were not on friendly terms with the Americans.
The response came soon enough: the family's visas would not be
renewed. Appeals, they were told, could be filed only from the
home country. The university hospital wrote a letter on Mónica's
behalf, but this well-meaning document vanished into some bureaucrat's file cabinet in suburban Virginia, and it soon became
clear that there was nothing to be done. Rather than risk the

undignified prospect of a deportation (or more unthinkable, staying on, and living in the shadow of legality) Sebastián and Mónica chose to pack their things and go; just like that, their American adventure came to a premature end. Still, the accident of his place of birth gave Francisco an important practical and psychological advantage, something which shaped his personality in the years to come: a U.S. passport, and all that it represented.

Nelson was born in 1978, when Francisco was four. The armed conflict began two years later, in a faraway province to the south of the capital, a place so remote the war was almost three years old before anyone took it seriously. Five before many people knew enough to be afraid. By 1986 though, everything was clear enough, even to Sebastián and Mónica's two young boys. Throughout their childhood, as the war tightened its grip on the city, as the economy began to wobble, Francisco taunted Nelson with his remarkable travel document. It was the equivalent of a magic carpet, the possibility of escape implicit among its powers, somehow always present in conversations between the brothers. It was expected that Francisco would emigrate as soon as was feasible, and bring his younger brother with him at the first opportunity. Francisco finished school, studied for the TOEFL, and as the date of his eventual departure drew near, lorded this good luck over his increasingly frightened younger brother. Nelson did Francisco's laundry, made his bed, fetched things for him from the store—an endless number of petty errands, all under threat of a withheld visa. "What a shame," Francisco might say, shaking his head sadly as he observed a messy stack of poorly folded clothes. "I'd hate to have to leave you here."

(Remarkably, this scene, recounted to me by a shamefaced Francisco in January 2002, also appears in Nelson's journals. In that version, Francisco's quote is slightly, albeit crucially, different: "I'd hate to have to leave you here *to die*.")

Whatever the exact words, regrettable episodes like these were forever imprinted on Nelson's consciousness, the threat of being left behind reiterated so often and with so many harrowing overtones that it began to sound like a ghost story, or a horror film, in which he, Nelson, was the victim. At the time Francisco had no understanding of what he was putting his brother through. Whatever cruelties he committed in those years were a function of his impatience and immaturity. His ignorance. He was eager for his own life to begin far from the crumbling, violent city where he lived. Though he never admitted it, not to his younger brother or to anyone, Francisco was also afraid: that it was all a dream, that he too would be condemned to stay; that someone at the airport in Miami or New York or Los Angeles would take a look at him, at his passport, and laugh. "Where'd you get this?" they'd ask, chuckling, and he'd be too startled to answer. He knew nothing, after all, about being American. He was hungry for experience of the kind he could only have far from his family and their expectations. Land of the free, etc. In this regard, Francisco was an ordinary boy, with ordinary ambitions.

In spite of it all, the two brothers were close, until January 1992, when Francisco, age eighteen, boarded a plane and disappeared into the wilds of the southern United States to live with some friends of the family. In the months and years that followed, he wrote letters and called from time to time, but began nonetheless to drift from Nelson's memory and consciousness. Nelson entered a kind of holding pattern: an American visa would soon arrive, or so he'd been told, to whisk him away toward a new beginning. His early adolescence coincided with the hard bleak years of the war, when life was strangled by violence, when families went about their routines in a state of constant apprehension. Things were at their worst that year Francisco left; and Nelson, like the rest of his traumatized generation, spent a lot of time indoors. (As did I, for example.) Instead of venturing out into the unsafe streets, Nelson read a great deal, and watched television with a kind of studiousness his mother found alarming, a rigor occasionally rewarded with a glimpse of topless dancing women, or a lewd joke worth repeating at school, or the sight of a normally stoic reporter buckling before the weight of some new and terrifying announcement.

The news in the late 1980s and early 1990s never failed to supply a somber, cautionary anecdote starring families just like one's own, now mired in unspeakable tragedy. Men and women disappeared, police were shot, the apparatus of the state teetered. This last phrase was heard so often, whether in adult conversation or on the radio, that Nelson began to take it literally. He would imagine an elegant but precariously built tower, swaying in a rising wind. Would it fall? Of course it would. The only question serious people asked was who would be crushed beneath it.

For Nelson, for his family, for most of the city's alarmed residents, the calculus was fairly simple: those who could leave, would. If Nelson, the boy, grew fond of escapism, he was merely a product of his time; if he found little use for homework, for education as it is traditionally and narrowly defined, it was because he reasoned it was of little use—he'd soon be starting over anyway; if he daydreamed of a life in the United States, he did so at first with a whimsical ignorance, his imagined USA requiring little detail or nuance to serve its comforting spiritual purpose. As for his current reality, Nelson chose to think of himself as passing through; and this allowed him to withstand a great deal, content in the notion that all his troubles were temporary. For a while, it wasn't a bad way to live.

I'll go on, though everyone knows I'm writing about a country so different now, so utterly transformed that even we who lived through this period have a hard time remembering what it was like. The worse the situation at home, the more comfort Nelson took in his eventual emigration; each May he expected to celebrate his birthday with his brother in the United States, but unfortunately, each year it was postponed. Francisco did not complete the required paperwork. He did not submit to the interview. He did not petition for his little brother to join him in the United States when he had that responsibility and that right; when he could have done so as soon as 1994. For this negligence, Francisco blames his youth, though he is self-aware enough to be a little embarrassed by his lack of consideration. In his defense: he was discovering his new country, attempting to become what his blue passport had always said he was—an American.

He didn't have the time or the inclination to consider what his equivocating might mean to Nelson, how it might affect his life and worldview. It's really quite simple, when one considers it: Francisco didn't want to be in charge of his young brother. He was only twenty years old, enjoying himself, working odd jobs, and moving often. He didn't want the responsibility. Sebastián and Mónica nagged and pestered their older son, even shamed him, but it would be years before Nelson's paperwork finally went through.

Meanwhile, Nelson's obsession with the United States animated his teen years. With the help of his father's library access, he learned a more than passable English (though his accent was described by a former teacher with whom I spoke as "simply horrific"), and even a basic familiarity with American history. He studied the geography, and followed his brother's itinerant journey across the country, placing himself alongside Francisco in each and every one of these towns: unglamorous places like Birmingham, Alabama; St. Louis, Missouri; Denton, Texas; Carson City, Nevada. He'd read his brother's letters, and begun to engage in a kind of magical thinking.

At first, filled with hope, he thought: That could be me.

Then, with a hint of bitterness: That should be me.

Sometimes, just before sleeping: That is me.

In interviews, an interesting portrait emerges: Nelson telling friends his residency papers would soon come, that he'd soon be off, even bragging about it, his imminent departure a matter of pride. One wonders how much of this he believed, and how much of it was posturing.

"He could be a little smug, honestly," said Juan Carlos, a young man who claimed to have been Nelson's best friend from 1993 until 1995. "At the end of every school year, he'd say good-bye, letting it slip that he probably wouldn't be back the following term. He'd shrug about it, feigning indifference, as if it were all out of his hands. He was going to study theater in New York, that's what he always said, but the next year, he'd be back, and if you ever asked him about it, he'd just ignore the question. He had this skill. He was very good at changing the subject. It was something we all admired."

The much-promised and much-delayed travel document finally arrived at the American embassy in January 1998, three, or even four years late. The war was over, and the country was beginning to emerge from its depression. Nelson sprang into action. He was entering his third year at the Conservatory, and began to study his options with a seriousness his parents found impressive: as a playwright and actor, New York was naturally his preferred destination, but he would also consider Los Angeles, Chicago, and San Francisco. His brother was living across the Bay in a city called Oakland, tending bar and working alongside a kind older gentleman named Hassan who owned a clothing store. (All of which was a great disappointment to Mónica and Sebastián, though mostly to Sebastián, who'd wanted Francisco to have a different sort of career.) In those months, the two brothers spoke often and enthusiastically about Nelson's plans, discussing the future with an excitement and optimism Nelson would later think of as naive. Francisco went along, even going so far as to visit a few local drama schools in the Bay Area, asking of the admissions officers the precise questions that Nelson had dictated to him over the phone: What percentage of students continue to further study? Who are your most successful alumni? Who is your typical alum? What percentage of the incoming class has read Eugene O'Neill? What percentage has read Beckett?

When Sebastián died suddenly in September 1998, these plans, those conversations, and that intimacy vanished.

No one had to tell Nelson that he could no longer leave. It was never discussed. He understood it very clearly the instant he saw his mother for the first time, in the hospital, immediately after Sebastián's stroke. He found her facing the window at the end of the hall; she was backlit, but even in silhouette, Nelson could tell she was shattered. The hallways of the clinic smelled like formaldehyde, and as he walked, Nelson could feel his feet sticking to the floor. Mónica's neck was tilted in defeat, her shoulders slumped. When he reached out to touch her, she startled.

"It's me," he said, somehow expecting, or perhaps only hoping, this might calm her down. It didn't. Mónica collapsed into his chest.

Nelson thought: She's mine now, she's my responsibility.

And he was right.

Francisco returned in time for the funeral, dismayed to find his mother so broken and his brother so distant. He felt tremendously guilty (even tearing up when he recalled it to me), and Nelson, being Nelson, opted not to make things easier. Perhaps that's uncharitable; perhaps Nelson simply *couldn't* have made it easier for his remorseful brother. Perhaps he didn't know how. They hadn't seen each other in more than five years, and hardly knew how to be in the same room anymore. Nelson didn't cry in his brother's presence, something Francisco found disconcerting, since his every inclination in those first days home was to weep. He'd never wanted to come back like this; now he hated himself for having postponed a visit home for so long.

Mónica's two sons spent most of their time sitting on either side of their mother, receiving guests. The condolences were torturous. Francisco and Nelson both cursed this tradition. When they found themselves alone, they spoke in hushed tones about their concern for their mother, but not about their own feelings. ("Numb," Francisco told me. "That's what I felt. Numb.") There were some unpleasant postmortem details to handle—closing certain accounts, going through their father's desk in the basement of the National Library, etc.—tasks which they performed together.

After much insistence from Francisco, they finally went out one night, just the two of them. Mónica's sister Astrid had offered to keep their mother company. Nelson drove his father's old car, which still smelled of Sebastián, a fact which was obvious to him, but not to Francisco, who'd been gone too long to remember something as important as how their father had smelled. The evening was cold and damp, but Francisco had scarcely left his mother's side in the week he'd been home, and the very idea of being out in the streets of the city filled him with wonder. He asked Nelson to drive slowly; he wanted to see it all. It had been only six years, but nothing was as he remembered—

it was like visiting the place for the very first time. He marveled at the brightly lit casinos lining Marina Avenue, neon castles built as if from the scavenged ruins of foreign amusement parks. There was a miniature Statue of Liberty, slightly more voluptuous than the original, smiling coquettishly and wearing sunglasses; there was a replica Eiffel Tower, its metal spire glowing amid klieg lights. A few blocks down, a semifunctional windmill presided over a bingo parlor called Don Quixote's. On a windy day, Nelson explained, this attraction might even rotate, albeit very slowly. It was not uncommon to see young couples posing for pictures with the windmill, turning its blades by hand and laughing. Sometimes they wore wedding clothes. It was impossible to say when, how, or why this place had become a landmark, but it had.

Francisco noted each as they passed. "How long has this one been there?" he'd ask, and Nelson would shrug, because he had no answers and little interest. He found his brother's curiosity unseemly. He'd long ago decided not to pay attention, because it was impossible to keep up with anyway. Maps of this city are outdated the moment they leave the printers. The avenue they drove along, for example: its commercial area had been cratered by a bomb in the late eighties—both Nelson and Francisco had clear memories of the incident—and the frightened residents had done what they could to move elsewhere, to safer, or seemingly safer, districts. Its sidewalks had once been choked with informal vendors, but these were run off by police in the early nineties, and had reconvened in a market built especially for them in an abandoned lot at the corner of University Avenue.

Now the area was showing signs of life again: a new mall had been inaugurated, and some weekends it was glutted with shoppers who had money to spend, a development everyone, even the shoppers themselves, found surprising.

They found a restaurant along this renovated stretch of gaudy storefronts, a loud, brightly lit creole place, whose waiters hurried through the tables in period dress, evoking not so much a bygone historical era but the very contemporary tone of an amateurish theater production. Everyone is acting, Nelson thought, my brother and I too—and the idea saddened him. They ordered beers, and Francisco noted that they'd never had a drink together in their lives. They clinked bottles, forced smiles, but there was nothing to celebrate.

Francisco knew Nelson's plans had changed, but he thought it was worth discussing. He was only desperate to recover something of that optimism, that closeness he'd felt with Nelson as recently as a month before. He found it hard to believe it could disappear so quickly, and so completely.

Nelson didn't accept the premise. When Francisco asked, Nelson's face screwed into a frown. "I don't have plans anymore."

"You don't have plans? No, what you mean is—"

"You've seen her. You've seen how she is. I'm supposed to leave now?"

"I'm not saying *now*. Not immediate plans."

Nelson rolled a bottle cap between his fingers, as if distracted. He wasn't. "When will it be okay, do you think, to abandon my mother?"

Francisco sat back.

"I mean, let's just estimate," Nelson said. "Three months? Six months? A year?"

He fixed his gaze on his brother now.

"That's not fair," Francisco protested.

"Isn't it?"

"Dad wouldn't want you to . . ."

There was something steely and cold in Nelson's eyes that kept Francisco from finishing that sentence. He never should've begun it, of course, but perhaps the damage was already done. Perhaps the damage had been done earlier, in 1992, when he left the country and his brother behind. Perhaps there was no way to repair it now. The two of them were silent for a while, which didn't seem to bother Nelson at all. In fact, he seemed to be enjoying himself. He drank his beer unhurriedly, with an amused nonchalance, as if daring his older brother to speak.

A few days later, Francisco was on a flight back to California. Neither the future, in the general sense, or Nelson's plans in particular, were mentioned again.

3

THE THEATER SAT AT THE EDGE of the Old City, in a rough, lawless neighborhood of decrepit houses, narrow streets, and metal gates held closed by rusting padlocks. It had once been known as the Olympic, the city's premier stage for many years, though its glory days were long past. Nelson's parents had taken in a show there once, when they were dating, an evening notable because it was the first time Sebastián ran his fingers along the inside of his future wife's thigh. That night, Mónica sat almost perfectly still through the performance, widening her legs just enough to let him know she approved. 1965: the theater was in its prime; Sebastián and Mónica were too. Onstage, there was a comedy, but Nelson's father paid no attention to the actors, imagining only the skin of his Mónica's magnificent thighs, remembering to laugh only because those around him did.

The Olympic's brightly lit marquee had once meant something; "A palace of dreams," one of the founding members of Diciembre called it, remarking on the pride they felt the first time they performed there as a troupe, in 1984, two years before

Henry's arrest. But for Nelson and actors of his generation, it was simply a second-rate porn theater, frequented by old men, sad drunks, and prostitutes. Together, the worn-out members of these various tribes gathered to watch grainy films of blow jobs and acrobatic threesomes, projected out of focus on the yellow screen, sometimes without sound. Nelson didn't know his parents' story, but he had his own. Before this rehearsal, he'd been to the Olympic exactly twice: the first time, at age thirteen, with a few friends, when we'd pretended to be horrified and uninterested. A couple of months later, he returned, alone. That day he sat, as his father once had, thinking of flesh. Unlike his father, Nelson jerked off furiously and violently; one might even say ecstatically. (One assumes his father would have done the same, only *after*, in private.) To Nelson's credit, he had enough presence of mind to avoid staining the pants of his school uniform, a fact noted with pride in his journal, entry dated September 2, 1991. He emerged from the darkened theater with a feeling of accomplishment.

In a sense, the Olympic had been a palace of dreams for Nelson as well.

Then, in 1993, there was a small fire, which caused just enough damage to shut down the porn operation. The Olympic was abandoned. Five years later, Patalarga took the money he'd made from his leather business and bought it from the city for a song. His wife was opposed to the purchase, but he insisted. The Olympic sat, mostly unused, for three years while Patalarga figured out what to do with it.

It was this man, the owner, who opened the door when Nelson arrived for the first rehearsal. He was short; dark-skinned; neither heavy nor thin, but stout; with full cheeks and wide, green eyes. His black hair was cut short and combed forward, and he wore a cell phone the size of a woman's pocketbook clipped to his belt.

They shook hands; they introduced themselves.

"Patalarga?" Nelson asked, just to be certain he'd heard correctly.

This man had another name, a long, multisyllabic given name, known only to a handful of close friends, and which no one used regularly anymore but his elderly mother. When Patalarga was a child, his mother had used that birth name in a variety of ways, with different intentions, intonations, and gravity, depending on her mood, or the weather: to curse her absent husband, for example, to remind Patalarga of his heritage, or to evoke the passing of the years. In his hometown, or what remained of it, that name still had resonance, and there were those who could read his past and predict his future by the mere sound of it. Of course, that's precisely why Patalarga had left that town and why he stayed away. When he was older, in the city, he'd shed that name as a snake sheds its skin, and felt nothing but relief.

"That's right," he said now. "Just Patalarga."

The two men stood for a moment, something unspoken floating between them. The wood floor was dusty and cracked; the theater's ticket booth, which had once represented so much possibility for Nelson and his father, was covered with a slab of pressboard. Nelson looked up at the ceiling of the ruined lobby: even the chandeliers seemed poised to fall at any moment.

"We've never met before?" Patalarga asked.

"At the audition."

"Besides that."

"No."

Patalarga stepped closer. He could sense the young man's doubts. Nelson was half a head taller, but still Patalarga managed to throw an arm around the actor, and dropped his voice to a low rumble. "Have you been here before?"

"No," Nelson lied.

"Do you know Diciembre? Do you know what we do?"

Nelson said he did.

Patalarga shook his head. "You think you do."

"I know this is where you put on *The Idiot President*. I've read Mr. Nuñez's work."

Patalarga smiled. "Good. Make sure you tell him how much you like it. He's not well these days."

Then he led Nelson into the theater, through the foyer (strong smell of bleach, threadbare carpet worn to a shine), and past the doors, to the orchestra. The brass-plated seat numbers had mostly been stolen, pried off, sold for scrap at some secondhand market on the outskirts of the capital. Some rows had seats gone as well, recalling for Nelson the proud, gap-toothed grin of a child. He searched involuntarily for the spot where he'd sat that second time—"my triumph over shame," he'd written in his journal—as if one could remember that sort of thing. The carpet had been pulled up in certain places, and the cement floor below was adorned with overlapping oil stains, evidence of some carelessly attempted, and casually abandoned, repair.

The playwright sat at the foot of the stage, a script in his lap, his legs dangling off the edge. He seemed rather small, even childlike, the domed roof of the theater rising high above him. He didn't look up when Nelson appeared, but instead kept on reading inaudibly to himself. It was his own script, naturally; and as he read, he marveled, not at its quality (which in truth he found suspect) but at its mere survival. His own.

Patalarga was right; Henry was not well. The playwright explained it to me this way: that week, and in all the weeks since that first rereading of his old script, even his daughter's artwork had been unable to shake him from this melancholy. He'd begun to think very deeply and with some clarity about his time in prison. Who he was before, whom he'd become after, and how—or even if—those two men were related. There were many things he'd forgotten, others he'd attempted to forget; but the day he was sent to Collectors, Henry told me, was the loneliest of his life. He realized that day that nothing he'd ever learned previously had any relevance anymore, and each step he took away from the gate and toward his new home was like walking into a tunnel, away from the light. He was led through the prison complex, a vision of hell in those days, full of half-dead men baring the scarred chests to the world, impervious to the cold. He'd never been more scared in his life. One man promised to kill him at the first opportunity, that evening perhaps, if it could be arranged. Another, to fuck him. A third looked at him with the anxious eyes of a man hiding some terrible secret. Two guards led Henry through the complex, men whom he'd previously thought of as his tormentors, but who now felt like his protectors, all that stood between him and this anarchy. Halfway to the block, he realized they were as nervous as he was, that they, like him, were doing all they could to avoid eye contact with the inmates that surrounded them. At the door to the block, the guards unlocked Henry's handcuffs, and turned to leave.

The playwright looked at them helplessly. "Won't you stay?" he asked, as if he were inviting them in for a drink.

The two guards wore expressions of surprise.

"We can't," one of them said in a low voice. He was embarrassed.

Henry realized then that he was alone, that these two guards were the only men in uniform he'd seen since they'd left the gate. They turned and hurried back to the entrance.

An inmate led Henry inside the block, where men milled about with no order or discipline. He remembers thinking, I'm going to die here, something all new inmates contemplated upon first entering the prison. Some of them, of course, were right. Henry was taken to his cell, and didn't emerge for many days.

He had mourned when the prison was razed, had even roused himself enough to participate in a few protests in front of the Ministry of Justice (though he'd declined to speak when someone handed him the bullhorn), but in truth, the tragedy had both broken him and simultaneously spared him the need to ever think about his incarceration again. No one who'd lived through it with him had survived. There was no one to visit, no one with whom to reminisce, no one to meet on the day of their release, and drive home, feigning optimism. In the many years since, there were times when he'd almost managed to forget about the prison completely. Whenever he felt guilty (which was not infrequently, all things considered), Henry told himself there was nothing wrong in forgetting; after all, he never really belonged there to begin with.

Ana's mother, now his ex-wife, had heard the stories (some of them), but that was years before, and she was no longer capable of feeling sympathy or solidarity toward the man who had betrayed her. Besides Patalarga, few people were, at least not by the time I became involved. Henry's colleagues at the school where he taught were jealous because the director had granted him leave for the tour. If they'd known his controversial past, they likely would have used it as an excuse to be rid of him forever. His old friends from Diciembre were no better—their constant refrain after his release was that Henry should write a play about Collectors, something revolutionary, a denunciation, an homage to the dead, but he had no stomach for the project, had never been able to figure out how or where to begin.

"It will be therapeutic," these friends of his argued.

To which Henry could only respond: "For whom?"

Now that it was all coming back to him, he had no one to talk to. For years, he'd been losing friends and family at an alarming pace, in a process he felt helpless to reverse. He said offensive things at parties, he hit on his friend's wives, he forgot to return phone calls. He stormed out of bad plays, scraping his chair loudly against the concrete floors so that all could turn and see the once famous playwright petulantly expressing his displeasure. (Later he felt guilty: "As if I never wrote a bad play!") Sometime in the previous year he'd even offended his beloved sister, Marta, and now they weren't talking. Worst of all, he couldn't even remember what he'd done.

Patalarga interrupted this reverie. "Henry," he said. "This is Nelson."

The playwright set aside his old, imperfect script, and looked up, squinting at the actor: the young man's features, his dumb grin, his unkempt hair, his pants in need of a hem. Of the audition Henry could recall very little. The handshake, yes. And that this boy had read the part of Alejo, the idiot president's idiot son, with a preternatural ease.

"You're perfect," Henry said now. "You're, what? Eighteen, nineteen?"

"Almost twenty-three," said Nelson.

Henry nodded. "Well, I'm the president."

"Yes, sir."

"The idiot president," Patalarga added.

THEY WENT TO A BAR to celebrate; it felt good to drink in the middle of an afternoon. They got a table in the back, far from the windows, where it was almost dark. The heat faded after the first pitcher. Someone sang a song; a couple quarreled—but what did it matter? "Soon we'll be off, into the countryside!" Henry proclaimed, glass held high, his head light and his spirit charged. He felt better than he had in weeks. Optimistic. Patalarga seconded the notion, with similar enthusiasm; and the two old friends reminisced aloud for Nelson's benefit: past tours, past shows, small Andean towns where they'd amazed audiences and romanced local women. Epic, week-long drunks. Fights with police, escaping along mountain roads toward safety. Everything got stranger once you rose beyond an altitude of four thousand meters, that supernatural threshold after which all life becomes theater, and all theater Beckettian. The thin air is magical. Everything you do is a riddle.

"I've never been off the coast," Nelson admitted.

They pressed him: "Never?"

"Never," Nelson repeated, his face reddening. It was shameful, in fact, now that he thought about it, though he'd never had occasion to feel ashamed of it before. His family's few trips out of the city had always had the same unfortunate destination: Sebastián's coastal hometown, a cheerless stop along the highway south of the capital. He felt something like anger now when he thought of it: He'd seen nothing of the world! Not even his own miserable country!

Henry said, "Ah, life in the mountains! Patalarga can tell you all about it."

"Pack your oxygen tank," warned Patalarga. "We'll be going there in a few weeks."

Henry whistled. "Four thousand one hundred meters above sea level! Can you imagine the trauma? His brain has never recovered."

"What was it like?"

Patalarga shrugged. "Bleak," he said. "And beautiful."

They refilled their glasses from the pitcher, and called for another. Nelson wanted to know about the play. He still hadn't seen a full script, had never found one in any anthology, though he'd checked them all, even the most obscure volumes his father had dug up in the National Library. Of course he remembered the controversy, he said, everyone did (a gross exaggeration), and Nelson even told them the improbable tale of how he'd heard Henry on the radio, interviewed from prison. "You sounded so strong," Nelson said.

Henry frowned. "I must have been acting." He didn't remember the interview. "In fact, if you want to know the truth, I don't even remember writing the play."

Nelson did not believe him.

The only solid proof of his authorship, Henry said, was that he'd been imprisoned for it. "The state made no mistakes during the war—surely you must have learned that in school."

Patalarga laughed.

"I didn't do well in school," Nelson muttered, and dropped his chin. He'd drunk more than he realized. Suddenly his head was swimming.

Patalarga allowed himself a moment of vanity: "I was assistant director," he said, though it wasn't clear to whom he was talking.

Henry's eyes were bright and enthusiastic now, but Nelson could see behind them a deep tiredness, a distance. Deep creases formed around his mouth when he smiled. When they'd met an hour ago, at the Olympic, he'd seemed about to cry. Henry continued: "Patalarga would have liked to have been arrested too.

44

He's always been a little jealous of my fame, you understand. Perhaps if he finishes that pitcher, he'll be drunk enough to admit that what I'm saying is true."

Patalarga glared at Henry, then poured what remained of the pitcher into his glass. He drank it down greedily, wiping his mouth on the sleeve of his shirt. "Henry hasn't been the same since he left the prison. Still, he's my friend. We tried to help, tried to get him out."

"They *did* help," said Henry matter-of-factly. "They *did* get me out. I'm here, aren't I?"

He pinched himself, as if to further underline the point.

"Yes," Patalarga said, nodding. "That's what I've been telling you for years."

They'd chosen a place well known to Nelson, a bar called the Wembley. At least once a week, after school, Nelson would meet his father at the National Library, and then they'd come to this bar together. It never changed. There were then and are now black-and-white photos of garlanded racehorses and women in wide, billowing dresses carrying parasols, men in dark suits and dark glasses who do not smile, and behind them, the barren hills that were once the frontiers of this city. The streets in the pictures are hardly recognizable, but if you look closely you can make out the vague outlines of the place the city has become. The people from the photos are rarely seen now, but every so often, they stroll into the Wembley as if they have just come from the racetrack, or stepped off a steamer ship, or attended a baptism at the cathedral around the corner. Sebastián might have been one of these men had he chosen something more lucrative to do, something besides library science, but even so, he would have joined them just as their power and relevance were waning. The wealthiest left during the war for reasons of security, the most daring thinkers faded into a protective invisibility, and the once large middle class is poor now: having once owned the city, indeed the country itself, all that remained of their vast holdings were bars like the Wembley, thick with the musty air of a rarely visited provincial museum. In the old days, if a gentleman happened to run out of cash, he could leave his jacket at the coat check, and receive credit based on the quality of the fabric, the workmanship of the tailor. It was simply assumed that a man wearing a suit had money to spare. Those times were long since extinguished, and still, Nelson's father had loved the place. He'd eat a hard-boiled egg, drink one tall glass of beer, and quiz his son on what he'd learned in school that day. When he was finished, they'd catch the bus home.

So when Henry ordered a hard-boiled egg to go along with his glass of beer, Nelson felt a shock, something within him shifting. He watched Henry eat, his smacking jaws and lively eyes, and compared this new face to the one he remembered as a boy: his father, who spent the war years smuggling dangerous books out of the library before the censors could destroy them. Here, at this very bar, Nelson's old man had revealed his secret treasures: pulling from his briefcase Trotsky's theories on armed insurrection, or a hand-printed booklet containing eulogies for Patrice Lumumba, or a chapbook of Gramsci's outlandish poetry. And the years aged him: his gray hair thinning to a dramatic widow's peak, a system of minute wrinkles adorning his face. The last time Nelson saw him, at the hospital, he'd looked like a fine pencil drawing of himself. Nelson wondered if he would look like that too, when he was old.

"What?" Henry asked now, because the boy was staring. "Shall I order you an egg?"

They spent the rest of the afternoon discussing the play itself: its rhythms, its meaning, its wordplay. Nelson jotted down notes as Henry and Patalarga spoke, considering the script's inflection points, the breaks in the action, and the malaise that ran deep beneath the text, a gloom which Henry described as "indescribable."

Indescribable, wrote Nelson.

"Why are you writing this down?" Patalarga asked. It wasn't an antagonistic question; he was only curious.

Nelson shrugged. "Is something the matter?"

"We never wrote things down."

"Didn't we?" Henry asked, because the truth was he didn't remember.

The plot of *The Idiot President* centered on an arrogant, self-absorbed head of state and his manservant. Each day, the president's servant was replaced; the idea being that eventually every citizen of the country would have the honor of attending to the needs of the leader. These included helping him dress, combing his hair, reading his mail, etc. The president was fastidious and required everything follow a rather idiosyncratic protocol, so the better part of each day was spent teaching the new servant how things should be done. Hilarity ensued. Alejo, the president's son, was a boastful lout and a petty thief, who remained a great source of pride for his father, in spite of his self-evident shortcomings. The climactic scene involved a heart-to-heart between the servant, played by Patalarga, and Nelson's character, after the president has gone to sleep, wherein Alejo lets his guard down and admits that he has often thought of killing his father but is too frightened to go through with it. The servant is intrigued; after all, he lives in the ruined country, subject to the president's disastrous whims, and furthermore has spent the entire day being humiliated by him. The president, whose power seems infinite from a distance, has been revealed to the servant as he really is, as the play's title suggests. The servant probes Alejo's doubts, and he opens up, voicing concerns about freedom, about the rule of law, about the suffering of the people, until the servant finally allows that, yes, perhaps such a thing could be done. Though it would be daring, maybe it wouldn't be such a bad idea. For the sake of the country, you understand. Alejo pretends to mull it over, and then kills the startled manservant himself, as punishment for treason. He picks the corpse clean, pocketing the man's wallet, his watch, his rings, and the play ends with him shouting toward the room where the president is sleeping.

"Another one, Father! We'll need another one for tomorrow!"

If one recalls the times, it's easy enough to understand why *The Idiot President* was so controversial during the war. The play debuted a few months after the inauguration of a new head of state, a young, charismatic but humorless man acutely lacking in confidence. Though Henry maintained during his interrogation that the piece was written with no specific president in mind, this new president was simply too self-involved to accept such a possibility. It's as if he thought he was the only president in the world. Henry's protests mattered not at all: he was sent to prison; his release seven months later was as arbitrary as his initial arrest. Meanwhile the country was speeding toward a precipice. The fall began in earnest soon after.

Other topics covered that first evening at the Wembley: Henry's daughter and her artistic gifts; Patalarga's opinionated and talented wife, Diana, who'd played the role of Alejo in the first production of *The Idiot President* ("That's how we met," said Patalarga), but who'd wanted nothing to do with the revival, and had gladly made way for the new member of the troupe; Patalarga's first cousin Cayetano, whom they'd meet on tour, and who'd spent many nights at the Wembley carving poetry into the scarred wooden tabletops with his penknife; and finally, the delicate negotiation a man makes with his ego in order to teach elementary school science when he is actually a playwright.

On this last point, Nelson found he had a bit to say. Henry, according to Nelson, should not be working in an elementary school. Or driving a cab, even if he claimed to enjoy it. If Henry taught at all, it should be at the Conservatory. But in fact, if the world were fair, he would be abroad, in Paris or New York or Madrid, where his work could be appreciated. He should be overseeing the translations of his plays, winning awards, attending festivals, giving lectures, etc.

In the entire country there was probably no one who admired Henry's work as much as Nelson. He might have gone on, but noticed his friends shaking their heads sadly. Nelson stopped, and watched them watching him.

"Oh, the feeble, colonized mind," said Henry.

"We thought you were different," Patalarga said.

"More enlightened."

"It's just pitiful."

Henry and Patalarga, he would discover, often fell into these rhythms, one of them finishing the other's thought. Nelson wasn't the only one who found this tendency off-putting. Now, as Patalarga called for a new and final (or so he promised) pitcher, Henry explained their objection. In their day, there was an illness—"Would you call it that, my dear assistant director?" and Patalarga nodded lugubriously—yes, a syndrome, endemic to his generation. Young people were led to believe that success had to come in the form of approval from abroad. Cultural colonialism—that's what it was called back then.

"I thought," declared Patalarga, "that we had rid ourselves of this."

They had drunk a good deal, perhaps too much, or perhaps only too much for Nelson. He didn't know what to say. He began to explain. His point had simply been that Henry's work deserved wider recognition; his mind was neither colonized nor feeble. If anything, he was more skeptical of the United States than the rest of his generation. Why wouldn't he be? His older brother had all but abandoned the family to make his life there.

Francisco would not have agreed with this point, but let's limit ourselves, for the moment, to Nelson: he'd been employing his older brother as a straw man for years, to suit whatever narrative purpose his life required at any given moment. A hero, a lifeline, an enemy, or a traitor. Now, when a villain was called for, Francisco once again obliged.

"Really?" Henry asked.

"There was a time when I idolized him. When I would have given anything to go. But then . . . I don't know what happened."

"It passed?" Patalarga said.

"You outgrew it," said Henry.

Nelson nodded. He raised the glass of beer to his lips, as if signaling an end to his confessions. Just like that, he'd updated his story for this new audience, something closer to the truth. His friends from the Conservatory would have been surprised.

It was early, not yet nine, when they left, but they'd been drinking for what seemed like an eternity. The long summer day slid toward night, the sky shaded pink and red and gold; a sunset made to order, splashed across the horizon. Patalarga sprang for a cab, and the three of them headed south from the Old City. Henry rode up front, declaring it a relief to be in the passenger seat for once. He chatted with the uninterested driver, suggesting a scenic route. "It'll cost more," said the driver.

"What is money? We have to see it all," Henry answered. "We're leaving soon, and heading into *exile*!"

He shouted this last word, as if it were a destination, not a concept.

They drove past the National Library, past the diminished edge of downtown, through the scarred and ominous industrial flats, past trails of workers in hard hats trudging the avenue's gravel-lined shoulder; then along the eastern boundary of Regent Park, where the vendors packed away their wares, bagging up old magazines and books, sweeping away the remains of cut flowers and discarded banana leaves, stacking boxes of stolen electronics into the beds of rusty pickup trucks. Nelson sat by the window and watched his city, as if bidding farewell. It wasn't an unpleasant drive: at this speed, along these roads, beside these fallen monuments, the capital presented its most attractive face: that of a hardworking, dignified metropolis, settled by outcasts and opportunists; redeemed each day by their cheerless toil and barely sublimated willingness to throw everything away for a moment's pleasure.

"Isn't it lovely?" Henry asked from the front seat.

Patalarga had fallen asleep; Nelson was lost in thought. The city *was* lovely. There could be no place in the world to which he belonged so completely.

That was why he'd always dreamed of leaving, and why he'd always been so afraid to go.

4

IN EARLY 1998, Mónica secured funds to pay for a public health theater troupe in the city. She would hire a group of actors to perform plays about unwanted pregnancy, teenage depression, sexual health, et cetera, before audiences of local public school students. Nelson had just finished his third year at the Conservatory, and it briefly occurred to him that he might get a job within this farsighted (and therefore doomed) government program, but Mónica wouldn't even consider it. "Nepotism is the lowest and least imaginative form of corruption," she told him, as if her objection were purely a matter of aesthetics. Nelson must have given her an odd look, because she added, rather halfheartedly, "Not that you aren't qualified."

He let the issue drop, and a few weeks later she asked him to help oversee the auditions, as an unpaid adviser. This was how he met Ixta.

The troupe was to be modeled on a similar program based in Brazil. Each week the Brazilians sent Mónica a package containing proposals, planning documents, full-color graphs charting the rise and fall of the teen suicide rate in the infinite slums of Rio de Janeiro. Except for the reports to European and American donors, which were in English, these materials were all in Portuguese, including the scripts, which would eventually prove to be something of an inconvenience. Mónica's supervisor—a natural-born bureaucrat, if ever one existed—was ambivalent about the whole enterprise, and for weeks he dithered, neglecting to approve the cost of translation in time for the auditions. He claimed it was a mistake; insults were traded, but in the end, Mónica had no choice but to make the best of it.

The day of the auditions arrived, muggy and warm, and they gathered in a conference room on the third floor of the Ministry of Health. Because of an architectural defect, the windows would not open, and the temperature in the room rose slowly but relentlessly, so that by lunchtime, both mother and son were sweating profusely. One after another the actors came in, took a look at them, at the script, and then scratched their heads. At first it was all very funny: Mónica apologized; the actors apologized. They squinted at the pages, then read phonetically, and everyone laughed. Some of the actors translated as best they could, Mónica and Nelson listening with some amusement as the Portuguese was rendered haltingly into stiff and lifeless Spanish. If there was any acting happening, it was hard to tell.

Nelson took notes, but as the heat intensified, as the monologues became increasingly predictable and maudlin, his mind drifted. The soporific heat, the grating sound of broken Portuguese, and these disappointing actors—his friends, many of them—it was all too much. More than a few gave up and walked out. They blamed the heat; they blamed the script; they blamed the Ministry of Health and the entire hapless government.

Ixta was different. They'd already been at it for three and a half hours when she walked in. She wasn't pretty but had what one might call "presence": the set of her jaw, perhaps, or her pale, powdered skin, or the bangs that fell precisely before her eyes, so it was difficult to guess what she was thinking or what she was looking at. And she'd dressed the part, wearing a schoolgirl's uniform, right down to the white knee-high socks and shapeless gray skirt. With a few quick steps she carved out a space that became hers, transforming the carpet into a stage. She took the pages they'd given her, and flipped through them very quickly, nodding. She handed the pages back to Mónica, and promptly crumpled to the floor. It happened very fast.

"Is everything all right?" Mónica asked.

Ixta looked up for a moment, and shook her head. It was a hideous, pitiful face: battered and young and streaked with tears.

"How can everything be all right?" she muttered. "How can it?"

Mónica looked on with a raised eyebrow.

"What happened?" Nelson asked, playing along.

"The girls at school. You know the ones. They say things."

Ixta sat up, rolled her head around, so that her bangs fell back, and Nelson caught, briefly, a glimpse of her red, swollen eyes. Then she stood slowly, unlocking each of her joints one by one. When she was on her feet, she slouched and crossed her legs, scratching her face and mumbling a few words neither Mónica nor Nelson could make out. Something about the cliques that ran the school and a boy she'd liked.

"He said he wanted to kiss me," Ixta whispered, "but then he didn't."

Mónica remembers the audition well: "The girl exuded so much vulnerability it felt indecent just to watch her." After a while, she asked Ixta to stop. They still had six or seven actors waiting, she explained; and Ixta nodded, as if she understood, then all but ran from the room into the hall. She hadn't even given them her contact information.

"Go on," Mónica said, turning to her son. "Go after her."

Nelson found Ixta sitting by the elevators, legs crossed, head drifting into her chest, back against the wall. The rest of the actors eyed her with a mixture of curiosity and dread.

He knelt beside her. "You all right?"

Ixta nodded. "It's hot in there."

"You did very well."

She bit her lip, looking straight ahead at the elevator door, as if she could see through it, into the shaft and farther, into the metal cage that rumbled invisibly through the old ministry building. "I suppose you're going to ask me out now."

"I was going to ask you for your information, actually," Nelson said. "For the play. In case we need a callback."

"Sure," she said, unconvinced. "For the play."

He gave her a piece of paper, and Ixta wrote down her full name and telephone number. Her letters were rounded and bubbly. It was the handwriting of a teenage girl. She was still in character.

"Don't call after ten," she remembers saying. "My father doesn't like that."

So Nelson called her the very next night, at precisely nine-thirty.

Their first days were, by all accounts, magical. I find even this simple declarative statement difficult to write without feeling a small pang of jealousy. Friends describe Nelson as smitten, Ixta light as air. That summer and into the fall, neither of them made it anywhere on time, not to work nor to class nor to rehearsal. They were seen at the hothouse parties in the Old City, dancing like lunatics, or at one of the local theaters, registering their distaste by leaving loudly in the middle of the first act (a petulant gesture in the finest spirit of Henry Nuñez). They spent many nights in Nelson's room, with the door closed, talking and laughing, making love and then talking some more, so perfectly entwined in spirit, mind, and body that Sebastián and Mónica tiptoed around their own house, afraid to disturb the young couple.

Ixta, Nelson told his father one night, was like a riddle he felt compelled to solve.

Sebastián nodded. Though the metaphor concerned him, he kept his reservations to himself. Nothing is more deserving of one's respect, he told Mónica that night, as they lay in bed, than two young people who've found each other.

Nelson was as charming as he was clumsy, and Ixta liked

this about him. Sometimes he read her his plays, texts he'd never shared with anyone. They were very good, she tells me, experimental, odd. One piece, a political parody clearly influenced by the work of Henry Nuñez, was set in the stomach of an earthworm: the cabinet of an ungovernable nation convenes to discuss the country's future, their conversation periodically interrupted by giant waves of dirt and shit passing through the digestive system of their host. First, the bureaucrats' professionalism fails them, then their courage. The stage fills with shit, and over the course of the play they slide gradually into despair. How exactly something like this might be staged was unclear, and in fact, when Ixta asked, it was obvious that Nelson hadn't thought too much about it.

"Isn't that what producers, directors, and stage managers worry about?" he asked.

Ixta remembers telling him to do animations instead. She laughed at the memory, because he didn't appear to understand that she was joking. He just stared at her, confused. "He asked me if I was making fun of him," she told me. "He couldn't draw more than stick figures."

In any case, Nelson had other plays that were perhaps less challenging logistically: a comedy dramatizing the story of Sancho Panza's birth, for example. Or a murder mystery set in a futuristic brothel, where male robot-human hybrids paid extra to sleep with that increasingly rare species, the pure human female. He'd intended the piece to be a comment on technology, but also erotic.

Nelson worked two mornings a week at a copy shop in the

Old City, spending his afternoons at the Conservatory. Ixta was three years older, and set to graduate that year. She took every opportunity to make light of his youth. She liked to pretend she was abusing him. He was game. They went to hotels that rented by the hour, places in the seedy backstreets of the Monument District, creating elaborate scenarios drawn from plays they both admired. She was Stella and he was Stanley. She was Desdemona and he was Othello. They pounded these scripts into whatever shape their romance required, laughing all the while. Both found it surprising they'd never crossed paths before, a fact that made their love seem fated.

Initially, when Ixta and I spoke, she was reticent, loath to recall these early days with Nelson. I can understand, of course.

"What's the use?" she said. "It isn't easy, you know?"

I could tell by looking at her that she was telling the truth: it wasn't easy. But I insisted; and once she warmed to the task, the stories flowed. A couple of times she laughed so hard she even asked me to stop the recording. I didn't, only pretended to. "He was sweet," Ixta said. "And in the early days, he adored me. I'm not making this up—he told me all the time. I fell for him, completely."

"Did you discuss the possibility that he might leave?"

"Some, but only in the vaguest way. I knew all about the visa. About Francisco. He bragged to others that he was leaving soon, but I never took it very seriously. His papers came not long after we'd started seeing each other, and I didn't feel threatened. He got really excited, and I did too. We even talked about going together, to New York or Los Angeles, or somewhere. I was working with his mother all this time, you know, and she supported the idea. It was only after Sebastián died that things changed."

"Is that when you broke up?"

"No," Ixta said. "I'd met him maybe eight months before. And we stayed together for another two years, almost. But yeah, something shifted then. It was the end of our honeymoon. He loved his father. I did too. Sebastián was a wonderful man. Nelson didn't talk about leaving anymore. And neither did I."

She didn't want to say much about the breakup, so I asked instead about Diciembre. She chortled. "Nelson was obsessed. He loved them, their history, and his admiration for Henry Nuñez was really something. You've got to understand, this is not a universally recognized playwright or anything. Diciembre has some cachet at the Conservatory, but really, this was a private obsession. I read some of the old plays, you know. Nelson made me photocopies. He'd be so eager to hear my opinion, it was like he'd written them himself."

"And?" I said.

Ixta smiled politely. "I'll admit I never understood what the big deal was."

HENRY CAME to rehearsal one Thursday afternoon with a stack of his daughter's drawings, which he dropped in Nelson's lap, without explanation. He stood, arms akimbo, while Nelson flipped casually through the pictures, not sensing the urgency in his director's pose. They were drawings of boats and rainbows and horses.

"Thank you," Nelson said. "They're lovely." Only then did he notice Henry's expression.

Because of the slope of the floor, Henry wasn't much higher than eye level, and the stage behind him seemed immense. They were in the old Olympic, which in just a few weeks had come to feel like a home to them, its unique patterns of decay becoming familiar, even comforting. They were rehearsing every Monday and Wednesday night, Thursday afternoons, and all day Saturday. Sometimes other members of Diciembre came to watch, offer advice, but mostly Henry, Patalarga, and Nelson were alone. Once on tour, they would play in churches, garages, fields, plazas, fairgrounds, and workshops. One show would be performed beneath the blinking fluorescent lights of a nearly frozen municipal auditorium; another on the hosed-down killing floor of a slaughterhouse—but none in a proper theater, if a place like the fire-damaged Olympic could still be called as much. Henry and Patalarga were aware of this. Neither thought to tell Nelson; both assumed he just knew.

Now, it appeared the playwright had something on his mind.

"You want me," Henry said (*bellowed*, according to Patalarga), "to spend a month or two away from this delicate, budding artist, this daughter I adore, the only person I love in this world, so I can accompany you while you fuck up my play? Is that what you're saying?"

Nelson had not, to his knowledge, been saying that. He'd thought things had been going well. He stammered a defense, but Henry cut him off.

From across the theater, Patalarga watched. He told me later that he'd been expecting a scene like this for at least a few days before it happened. Nelson was not, in Patalarga's words, "fully submitting to the world of the idiot." There was only one way to satisfy Henry, and that was total immersion. Patalarga recalled an experimental piece from the early 1980s, a play about an imaginary slum built atop the remains of an indigenous graveyard. It was a dark, caustic three-act piece full of ghosts, and in the lead-up to opening night, Henry had a dozen doll-sized caskets built for his cast. He asked every actor to sleep with one of these tiny coffins beside him in bed, so they might better understand the emotion sustaining the work.

So, upon seeing Henry descend on Nelson this way, Patalarga chose to keep his distance "out of respect for the artistic process."

Nelson, after an initial moment of protest, fell silent, staring back at his tormentor, bewildered. He was not unaccustomed to this sort of treatment, in fact. His face went flat, expressionless, calm. It was a trick Nelson knew from childhood, from waging battles with his brother that he knew he couldn't win. It wasn't stoicism or deference or indifference; it was all those things.

Nelson deflected Henry's vitriol with a few phrases from his past. They came forth with surprising ease: "I'm sorry you feel that way." "What can I do to make you more comfortable?" "Is it something I've done?" "What would you like to get out of this conversation?"

It wasn't long before Henry's energy petered out. He gave up, slumping into a seat a few rows behind Nelson, spent. A few long minutes of silence passed, not a sound in the theater but those that emerged from the neighborhood outside: a revving motor, a distant horn, a few bars of music from a passing street vendor.

"You remind me of my ex-wife," Henry said finally. "I'll be needing a drink now."

"I'm sorry, but—"

"It's fine. I shouldn't have yelled. Come here."

Nelson stood, and walked a few rows back. What hadn't he done for the play? What wasn't he willing to do?

"I don't know what's going on with me," Henry said. He'd been having these swells of anger, righteousness, he explained, explosive moments that were catching him increasingly unawares.

"It's just part of the process," Nelson offered, unknowingly echoing Patalarga's interpretation.

Henry didn't buy it. "I haven't done this in more than ten years. I don't have a process."

Nelson shrugged, and handed over Ana's drawings. On top: a pastoral scene done in finger paint, a family of thumbprints adorned with dots for eyes and wide smiles, bounding about a prairie, or perhaps a city park. It was difficult to say. The sky was smeared across the top of the page in its traditional blue—here, in a city that suffers beneath thick gray clouds for ten months out of the year. Why do local children insist on coloring it this way? Is it simplicity? Wishful thinking? Nelson felt certain he'd done the same when he was Ana's age. Did the sky-blue sky reflect a lack of imagination, or an excess of the same?

Henry took the pictures without comment, and leaned down to put them in his shoulder bag. "Sit," he said to Nelson, gesturing to the seat beside him. His voice was calm now. "Look at that stage. Imagine this theater full of people. They don't know you or me or a thing about the play. Maybe they've never been to a play before. They aren't your friends. They've come to be entertained. Edified. Comforted. Distracted. Can you see it?"

"Yes."

"The lights dim. The curtain opens. Who comes out first?"

"Patalarga," Nelson said.

"The servant."

"Right."

"And what does he say?"

"He says, 'The time has come, like I told them it would.'"

"And what does he feel?"

"He feels uneasy. A little afraid. Angry. Oddly, a hint of pride."

"Good," Henry said. "And where are you?"

"Backstage."

Henry shook his head gravely. "There's no such thing as backstage. The play begins, and there's only the world it dramatizes. Now, where are you?"

"With my father, the president. In his chambers."

"Right. With me. Your father. And now—this is important—do you love me?"

Nelson considered this; or rather, Nelson, as Alejo, considered this.

"Yes," he said after a moment. "I do."

"Good. Remember that. In every scene—even when you hate me, you also love me. That's why it hurts. Got it?"

Nelson said that he did.

"Are you sure?"

"Yes."

"Good. Because it *does* hurt," Henry said. "Don't forget that. It's supposed to. Always."

IN THE DAYS THAT FOLLOWED, Henry recited his usual lines with a little more bite, berated Alejo with a little more vigor. It was hard not to take it personally, and even when the rehearsals ended, something of this bad feeling lingered. The president and Alejo were two members of a troubled family, with a complicated, tense history; Nelson and Henry were two actors who barely knew each other. Patalarga tried to run interference, but it wasn't easy. He suggested drinks at the Wembley one evening after rehearsal, but Nelson begged off. He proposed lunch the following day, but Henry arrived late. He organized a dinner of old Diciembre veterans, and the two actors spent the evening at opposite ends of the room, never interacting. And still: they were getting it, scene by scene; getting at the dark truth of it. *The Idiot President* could be an acidly funny farce about power, trickery, and violence, Patalarga told me. That much anyone knew. What he hadn't realized until now was that it was also a painful statement about family.

There was a scene toward the end of the first act, when Henry is having his boots laced up by the servant. Patalarga is on his knees before the president. It's an oddly intimate moment. "Rub my calves," Henry's character says, then confesses, "I'm sore from kicking my boy."

The startled servant says nothing—the president is famously cruel, and he assumes this statement to be true. With downcast eyes, he kneads the president's calves, while Henry exhales, relishing this impromptu massage. "In truth, I only dream of it," the president says, and then pulls his leg away and kicks the servant in the chest. "But oh, how I dream!"

In early rehearsals (and in the original 1986 performances at the Olympic) this moment happened with Alejo offstage; in later versions, Henry wanted Nelson's character there, hidden just a few steps behind the action, eavesdropping as his father daydreams about kicking him. This small change was, in part, a recognition of the realities of the tour that awaited: more likely than not, there would be no backstage (real or metaphorical) out in the hinterlands, when they were on the road. Still, it altered something, shifted the chemistry of the performance. They ran through it again and again one afternoon, and even set up mirrors so Henry could see Nelson's reaction. Three, four, five times, he kicked poor Patalarga, all the while locking eyes with Nelson.

"Remember, I'm not kicking him, I'm kicking you!" Henry shouted.

On the sixth run-through, he missed Patalarga's hands, and nearly took off the servant's head. Patalarga threw himself out of harm's way just in time. Everyone stopped. The theater was silent. Patalarga was splayed out on the stage, breathing hard.

"Okay," he said, "that's enough."

Henry had gone pale. He apologized and helped Patalarga to his feet, almost falling down himself in the process. "I didn't mean to, I . . ."

"It's all right," Patalarga said.

But Nelson couldn't help thinking: if he's kicking Alejo the whole time, why isn't he apologizing to me?

For a moment the three of them stood, observing their reflections in the mirror, not quite sure what had just happened. Henry looked as if he might be sick; Patalarga, like a man who'd been kicked in the chest five times; Nelson, like a heartbroken child.

"Are you all right?" Henry said toward the mirror.

It was unclear whom he was asking.

5

IN THE FINAL WEEKS before they left the city, Henry began to jot down a few ideas. Notes. Dictums. Data points. Pages of them, from a man who had all but abandoned writing since his unexpected release from Collectors fourteen years before. Later, when we spoke, he shared these folios with me, apologetic, even embarrassed, as if they proved something about the ill-fated tour, or his state of mind in the days prior. I was unconvinced, but I scanned the pages anyway, trying to make sense of them.

A sampling:

Bus was twelve minutes late today, read a line scrawled on a page dated March 16, 2001. *Reasons unknown and unknowable. Mystery. Could have driven.*

Two days later: *Woke to a serviceable erection at 7:00 a.m. Sat up in bed, turned on the light, to observe it. Watched it wilt, like time-lapse photography. My very own nature special. I should have been on television when I was young, before I was ugly. Slept awhile longer. Three eggs for breakfast. No coffee. Pants feeling tight in the thighs. A woman got in the cab today, black hair, asked if I would—*

The following week: *For seven months, I hardly talked about life outside. Except with Rogelio. Because he asked.*

March 27: *A play for Rogelio. Finally. A love story. A man learning to read in a rented jail cell. Being taught to read, in exchange for sex. A plainly capitalist transaction, between two men pretending to be in love. Perhaps they are. Awkward moments. Butter as lubricant, stolen from the commissary and warmed between their palms. Between their thumbs and two fingers. Strange that such a simple gesture could be so arousing. A woman got in my cab today, black hair, ruby lips. Asked if I would climb in the back and make love to her—*

Then pages of lists: *Dead things I've seen—telephones, light-bulbs, street corners, nightclubs. Also: pigs, painters, passengers, plays, presidents, prisoners . . .*

On and on like this.

Was Henry losing it?

I don't think so.

Or—perhaps.

Far worse things have been published as poetry and won awards; which is what I told him, in so many words, as I tried to hand the journal back. He wanted me to keep it. Correction: he *insisted* I keep it—as if the pages contained something toxic he wanted desperately to be rid of—and I obliged. The important thing for us to understand is this: Henry thought he was losing it, and it worried him. He entered the prison every night in his dreams, walked its dark hallways, inhaled its fetid air. He'd for-gotten so many details about his time inside that it terrified him: the color of Rogelio's eyes, for example. The number of the cell they shared on Block Seven. The meal they shared on the last night before his release.

But every afternoon, at every rehearsal, something struck him, some bit of the past emerging with surprising clarity. Henry began to remember, began to piece things together. This particular play, of the dozen or so he'd written, had special characteristics: it was the last one he'd finished, the one that had brought his career (such as it was) to a premature close. It had last been performed by men who'd died only a few months later, dead men who'd begun to appear in his dreams. Perhaps the script itself was cursed. These men, these ghosts, hovered about the stage at every rehearsal, sat in the ragged seats of the Olympic to critique every line of dialogue. They booed each poorly rehearsed scene, whispered their doubts in his ears. It was impossible not to feel unsteady when confronted with this text. After all, the man who wrote it had lived another life, and that life was gone. That's what Henry was dealing with. Nelson, unfortunately, and through no fault of his own, had to watch this up close. It wasn't pretty.

The kicking incident, for example, which Patalarga described so vividly—Henry recalled it too, answering all of my questions politely and without hesitation. He had experienced it this way: a feeling of looseness, a momentary disorientation. Anger. Impotence. Then, an image: in August 1986 he'd seen a man be kicked to death, or nearly to death, by a mob that formed unexpectedly at the door to Block Twelve. He and Rogelio had stood by, at first horrified, then simply frightened. Then, almost instantaneously, they'd accepted the logic of the attack: every victim was guilty of something. The chatter: What did he do? Who did he cross? The men watching felt safer. Less helpless. A crowd had formed around the victim, but no one moved. Henry took Rogelio's hand. Squeezed.

"Do you see what I mean?" Henry asked me.

I said that I did, but I could tell he didn't believe me.

Not every memory was poisonous. For example: one day, Henry gathered up his courage, and went to see Espejo, the boss, about doing *The Idiot President* in Block Seven; surely this was one of his fondest memories. Espejo was a small but well-built man whose lazy grin belied a long history of violence, a man who'd risen far enough from the streets to relax, and now controlled the block through sheer force of reputation. He was languorous and content, occasionally dispensing pointed but very persuasive doses of rage should any inmate question his authority. Mostly though, he protected them—there were less than two hundred men in their block, and after nightfall they were in constant danger of being overrun by one of the larger, more ferocious sections of the prison. Espejo directed a small army of warriors tasked with keeping those potential invaders at bay.

Henry was afraid of this man, but he had to remind himself: me and Espejo, we're Block Seven, we're on the same side.

Espejo's cell reminded him of a small but comfortable student apartment, with a squat refrigerator, a black-and-white television, and a coffeemaker plugged into a naked outlet. Espejo kept a photo of himself from his younger days framed above his bed, an image Henry had never been able to shake in all the years hence. He described it to me: in the picture, Espejo is shirtless, astride a white horse, riding the majestic animal up the steps of a swimming pool, toward the camera. He is handsome and powerful. A few delighted women stand behind him, long-legged, bronzed, and gleaming in the bright sun. Everything is colorful, saturated with tropical light. A child—Espejo's son, one might guess—sits at the edge of the diving board, watching the horse maneuver its way out of the water. On the boy's face is an expression of admiration and wonder, but it's more than that: he's concentrating; he's watching the scene, watching his father, trying to learn.

Henry would've liked to be left alone with the photograph, to study it, to ask how and when it had been taken and what had happened to each of the people in the background. To the boy most of all. He might have fled the country, or he might be dead, or he might be living in a cell much like this one in another of the city's prisons. There was no way of knowing without asking directly, and that was not an option. The photo, like the lives of the men with whom Henry now lived, was both real and startlingly unreal, like a framed still from Espejo's dreams. What did Espejo think about when he looked at it? Did it make him happy to recall better times, or did the memory of them simply hurt?

Rogelio had warned him not to stare, so he didn't.

"A play?" Espejo said when Henry told him his idea.

Henry nodded.

Espejo lay back on his bed, his shoeless feet stretched toward the playwright. His head and his toes shook left to right, in unison. "That's what we get for taking terrorists," Espejo said, laughing. "We don't do theater here."

"I'm not a terrorist," Henry said.

A long silence followed this clarification, Espejo's laughter replaced by a glare so intense and penetrating that Henry began to doubt himself—perhaps he *was* a terrorist after all. Perhaps he always had been. That's what the authorities were accusing him of being, and outside, in the real world, there were people arguing both sides of this very question. His freedom hung in the balance. His future. Henry had to look away, down at the floor of the cell, which Espejo had redone with blue and white linoleum squares, in honor of his favorite soccer club, Alianza. One of Espejo's deputies, a thick-chested brute named Aimar, coughed into his fist, and it was only this that seemed to break the tension.

"Did you write it?"

Henry nodded.

"So name a character after me," Espejo said.

Henry began to protest.

Espejo frowned. "You think I have no culture? You think I've never read a book?"

"No, I . . ." Henry stopped. It was useless to continue. Already he'd ruined himself.

They were quiet for a moment.

"Go on. If you can convince these savages," Espejo said finally, waving an uninterested hand in the direction of the yard, "I have no objection."

Henry thanked Espejo and left—quickly, before the boss could change his mind.

"I told Rogelio the news, and we celebrated," Henry said to me.

"How?"

Henry blushed. "We made love."

"Was that the first time?"

"Yes." His voice was very soft.

Then: "I don't remember."

Then: "No."

I told Henry we could stop for a moment, if he wanted. He sat with his head at an angle, eyes turned toward a corner of the room. He laughed. "It's not because we were in prison together, you know. You're making it sound cliché."

"I didn't say that. I'm not making it sound like anything. I'm not judging you."

"You were thinking it."

"I wasn't," I said.

He frowned. "Are you a cop? Is that what this is?"

I thought I'd lost him. I shook my head. "I'm not a cop," I said in a slow, very calm voice. But at the time, even I wasn't sure what I was doing.

"Nelson and I, we're almost like family," I said.

Henry's brow furrowed. "He never mentioned you."

Silence.

"The play," I said, after a moment. "Was it easy to get inmates to volunteer for the play?"

Henry sighed. That, it turned out, was easy, and he had a theory as to why:

Everyone wanted to be the president, because the president was the boss.

Everyone wanted to be the servant, because like them, the servant dreamed of murdering the boss.

Everyone wanted to be the son, because it was the son who got to do the killing. And it was this character, Alejo, whose name was changed. He became Espejo.

And indeed, the project sold itself. A week of talking to his peers, and then the delicate process of auditions. Henry had to write in extra parts to avoid disappointing some of the would-be actors. It was for his own safety—some of these men didn't take rejection very well. He added a chorus of citizens, to comment on the action. Ghosts of servants past to stalk across the stage in a fury, wearing costumes fashioned from old bed sheets. He even wrote a few lines for the president's wife, Nora, played with verve by Carmen, the block's most fashionable transvestite. Things were going well. Someone from Diciembre alerted the press (how had this happened? Neither Henry nor Patalarga could recall), and after he'd done an interview or two, there was no turning back. Espejo even joined the enthusiasm. It would be good for their image, he was heard to say.

Rogelio wanted to audition too, but there was a problem.

"I can't read," he confessed to Henry. He was ashamed. "How can I learn the script?"

At this point in our interview, Henry fell silent once more. He scratched the left side of his head with his right hand, such that his arm reached across his face, hiding his eyes. It was a deliberate and evasive gesture; I was reminded of children who close their eyes when they don't want anyone to see them. We sat in

Henry's apartment, where he'd lived since separating from Ana's mother more than four years before. There was a couch, two plastic lawn chairs that looked out of place indoors, and a simple wooden table. One might have thought he'd just moved in.

"Rogelio was my best friend, you know?"

"I know," I said.

"At a time when I needed a friend more than I ever had before. I loved him."

"I know."

"And even so—before we went on tour again, just now, I hadn't thought about him in years. I find this a little shameful, you know? Do you see how awful it is?"

I nodded for him to go on, but he didn't. "It's not your fault," I said. "You didn't destroy the prison. You didn't send the soldiers in."

"You're right," Henry said.

"You taught him to read."

"But I didn't save him."

"You couldn't have."

"Precisely."

We decided to break. It was time. I excused myself, wandered back to the bathroom at the end of the hallway and splashed cold water on my face. When I returned, Henry was standing on the narrow balcony of his apartment, wearing the same look of exhaustion, of worry. In the tiny park in front of his building, some children were drawing on the sidewalk.

"My daughter draws much better," he said.

When we went back inside, I asked him what he'd expected

from the tour, what his hopes were. He began to speak, then stopped, pausing to think. "If the text of a play constructs a world," Henry said finally, "then a tour is a journey into that world. That's what we were preparing for. That's what I wanted. To enter the world of the play, and escape my life. I wanted to leave the city and enter a universe where we were all someone different." He sighed. "I forbade Nelson to call home."

"Why?"

"I wanted him to help me build this illusion. I *needed* his help. This sounds grandiose, and dramatic, I know, but . . ."

I told him not to worry about how it sounded. "Did you have any misgivings about it?"

It was a poorly phrased question. What he'd been trying to tell me was this: his misgivings in those days were all encom-passing, generalized, profound. He could push them away for hours at a time, but with only great effort. And they returned. Always.

"To be quite honest, it wasn't the tour I was afraid of," Henry said. "It was everything."

AT MY REQUEST, Ana's mother took a look at the notebook, spending a few moments with the pages, smiling occasionally as her eye alighted on a particular phrase or observation. She read a couple lines aloud, letting out a short, bitter laugh now and then. When she was finished, she shook her head.

"He gave you these?" Henry's ex-wife asked, wide-eyed.

I told her he had.

"Henry's the moody type," she said, "nothing new. An artist. Always was. But he could enter these spirals of unpleasantness, just like what you describe. Only he wouldn't write it down, not like this. In eight years—was it that long? *Jesus*—in eight years, I never saw him write down anything that wasn't for the classes at that school where he taught. Teaches. Whatever. But he'd talk this way sometimes, stream of consciousness, chatter. At night mostly. Imagine living with this!"

She threw two hands in the air, and the notebook tumbled to the floor.

"I can't believe I'm going to tell you this," she said, "but listen. Toward the end, he was never home, God bless. He'd go to school, and then drive the cab till ten. He'd come home, climb into bed, and say: Baby, I fucked a passenger today, on the way to the airport. Wonderful, I'd say, half-asleep, but you still have to fuck me. I'm your wife. It was a game, see? And at first he would. Four times a week. Then three. Then once. But then, he wouldn't—sleep with me, I mean. Not at all. He'd sleep *beside* me, but I'd be awake, waiting. He'd snore, and I'd want to kill him. I'd put my hand on his cock. Nothing. Like touching a corpse. He would talk in his sleep, nonsense like this stuff here." She picked up the fallen notebook, shaking the pages at me. "And then one day, I realized that it wasn't just stories, it was true: he actually *was* fucking his passengers. I said, Henry, I'm leaving. Do you know how he responded? Did he tell you this?"

I shook my head.

"He said, 'Oh, no, the turtle's getting away! Hurry!' I thought he was drunk. On drugs. I slapped him. Do you hate me? I asked.

I was *hurt*, you understand. Angry. Do you hate me, I said. Is that it? Do you hate our life? Are you trying to break my heart?"

"How did he respond?"

"He collapsed, sobbing, and told me no. That he hated himself, that he had for years." She laughed drily. "That his unhappiness was a monument! Like a statue in the Old City. One of those nameless heroes covered in bird shit, riding a stone horse. I told him not to try his poetry now. That it was too late. He begged me to stay."

"But you didn't."

"Of course not. I left him, like any reasonable, self-respecting woman would've done. He'd slept with half the city, but it wasn't his fault because he was depressed? If I'd stayed a moment longer, I would've put a steak knife through his neck. Or through my own. So I took Ana, and we went to my mother's house."

"Did you ever meet Nelson?"

As it turns out she had, during the last week of rehearsals before they left the city. One afternoon she dropped their daughter off at the Olympic. ("What a dump, and how sad to see it that way! I don't know why Patalarga would've wasted a cent on that place.") She got to see some of the play. It was the last week of rehearsals.

What did she think?

"About the play, or about Nelson?"

"Both."

She frowned. Nelson admired Henry without reservation—that much was clear to her. She saw about half a rehearsal, enough to get a sense of the dynamic between them: Henry was hard on Nelson. Interrupted him, chastised him, explained a scene, a beat, once and again; and all the while, Nelson listened carefully to everything, suppressing the frustration he surely must have felt. And he was good. Intense. Very professional. You'd think they were preparing to tour the great halls of Europe, and not a bunch of frostbitten Andean villages.

"And the play?"

Ana's mother responded with a question: Did I watch much theater? I told her I did, my fair share.

"You know what? I'd remembered it being funny. Fifteen years ago, Henry had a sense of humor. I didn't remember it being so fucking dark. It was always there, in the script, I suppose, but he was emphasizing it now. What can I say? Life does that to a man. Patalarga was trying. He'd add a note of slapstick, but it just wasn't . . . I mean, it had its moments. I'll tell you this much, which I'm not sure Henry even knows. My daughter, Ana—she fell asleep. She's no critic, but there it is. She slept. Soundly."

When our interview was over, Henry's ex-wife excused herself for having spoken so crudely. "I don't hate him, I just wouldn't say Henry brought out the best in me. We're better off apart." She paused. "Or at least I am, which really is what matters. To me, I mean."

I told her that I appreciated her honesty.

She asked that her name not be printed. It's been years, but I'm honoring that request.

HENRY, PATALARGA, AND NELSON set out on April 16, 2001, on a night bus to the interior. That evening, in the bus station waiting room, the television news reported that a famous Andean folksinger had been killed by her manager. Groups of young men huddled together, sharing their titillating theories behind the murder, who had slept with whom, how the killer might have succumbed to the terrible logic of jealousy. Entire families sat glumly, staring in shock at the television, as if they'd lost a loved one—and they had, Nelson supposed.

The bus would leave in an hour. He drank a soda, ate plain crackers. It was practice for the austerity to come, for the rigors of life on the road, the cold, the rain. Patalarga and Henry had spent much of the last days painting vivid portraits of the misery that awaited, and each horrifying description seemed to fill them with glee. "City boy," they'd said to Nelson, "how will you ever survive life in the provinces?"

Now, at the station, the television spat out the latest news, confirmed and unconfirmed: the accused killer was on suicide watch. An accomplice was being sought. Tearful fans were already gathering in front of the deceased's home, laying flowers, holding candles, comforting one another. The singer had been dead for all of three hours.

"How do they know where she lives?" asked Henry. "Who told them?"

"Lived," said Patalarga.

Nelson had only a vague notion of who this dead singer was. In this bus station, on this night, among these fellow travelers, admitting such a thing would be like declaring oneself a foreigner. He'd always been taught it was two different countries: the city, and everything else. Some lamented the stark division, some celebrated it, but no one questioned it. Tonight, their bus would leave the city, and tomorrow when they woke, they'd be in the provinces. In truth, here at the bus station, where everyone was in mourning, it was as if they were already there.

"Did you say your good-byes?" Henry asked, interrupting his daydreams.

"I did."

Henry furrowed his brow, very serious. "Because we're entering the world of the play now, Alejo, its constructed universe. Give in to it."

"I'm giving in."

"Once we leave, none of this exists."

Nelson glanced about the crowded and dilapidated bus station. A few yards from them, a child slept on an uneven pile of luggage.

"It's so hard to say good-bye."

Henry threw a gentle arm around Nelson. "I know it is, Alejo. I know."

They were called to board just before midnight. The waiting room of the bus station came to life as everyone shook off their drowsiness and stepped out into the warm night. The bus idled loudly. The passengers lined up to force their overstuffed bags into the hold. There were smiles on most of the faces, Nelson noticed; no one was immune to the allure of travel. Even a night bus has some glamour, if only you let yourself see it.

Just before the bus pulled out, a thin boy in a baseball cap came aboard. He was chewing gum, and held a small video camera in his right hand. The boy moved slowly down the aisle, panning left to right and back again, stopping for a second or two on each passenger. Some smiled, some waved, some blew kisses. Henry flashed an enthusiastic two thumbs-up. When the camera came to Nelson, he stared dumbly into the lens, not quite understanding.

Henry whispered in his ear. "Smile. In case we plunge off a cliff and die, this is how your mother will remember you."

Nelson forced a smile.

When I went to the bus company to ask for this video, I was all but laughed at. "Are you serious?" the man asked.

I told him I was. I had the date, destination, and time of departure.

"If no one dies," he said, "we just record over it."

The ride out of the city was slow, but after an hour they came to the capital's eastern limits. Nelson didn't sleep but looked out the window instead, hoping to see something that might catch his eye. There was only darkness. A movie came on the bus's television—the kind his mother would have liked—but he tuned it out, and went over the script instead, replaying *The Idiot President* in his mind: its rhythms, its atmosphere, its famous gloom, which, contrary to what he'd been told, was in fact completely describable.

Henry hadn't known at the station how right he was, exactly how hard Nelson's good-byes had been. He'd arranged to see Ixta that afternoon, at a park in La Julieta. As they strolled, talking about nothing in particular, Nelson, with his heart thrumming in his chest, held a parallel conversation with himself: Should he, or shouldn't he? Was now the time to tell her? It was a warm day by the sea, and the vastness of the ocean was always remarkable to him. The boardwalk was full of joggers and skateboarders, and the sun shone through a scrim of early-autumn clouds hovering at the edge of the horizon. The longer they walked, the quieter they became, until Nelson couldn't bear his uneasiness. They'd come to another seaside park, this one with an unused lighthouse surrounded by a low wooden fence, so short you could step over it. Many had—they'd written their names, pairs of them, mostly, along the lighthouse's curving base of white brick.

"If they really wanted to protect it," Ixta said, "they'd make the fence higher."

Nelson considered the fence, as if it might yield a great secret.

"I love you," he said.

It just came out that way. He'd said it to the fence, to the lighthouse, to the wind. He'd done it, in other words, all wrong. He began to apologize, but it wasn't clear what for.

Ixta didn't respond. She told me later that she wasn't surprised, or overcome with emotion; she felt something different, something simpler. Relief. Weeks had become months, and Ixta had begun to fear she was inventing it all. She hadn't thought of herself as having an affair, but from the outside, that's exactly what it would have appeared to be. She'd fully understood this only a few days before. They'd entered the mirrored lobby of a cheap hotel on the side streets of the Metropole, and she'd happened to catch a glimpse of herself, arm in arm, with Nelson. Ixta never really thought much about their age difference, but suddenly, at that moment, it was noticeable—not her age; but rather, his youth. Nelson had the greedy, callow look of a boy about to get what he wants.

Why, she thought then, should I give it to him?

And: Don't I want things that he won't give me?

She was a woman sleeping with someone who was not her partner. It was an affair, and perhaps that's all it was. If he claimed to love her, did that make it different?

"Well?" Nelson asked. He still hadn't mustered the courage to look at her.

Ixta told me later: "It was like he felt the world owed him an award, just because he'd managed to say what was on his mind. It was about him, not me. I told him I didn't trust him anymore. That it had all dragged on for too long. That I was sorry."

"Is that all?"

"And I wished him a safe trip."

Ixta paused here, looked up, and bit her lip. Perhaps she expected me to interrupt, but I didn't.

"You know the truth? I almost felt bad. I felt regret—just for a moment. And I half expected that he'd call my name, but he didn't. He just let me walk away. I left him at the lighthouse, and I remember thinking, he'll probably write our names on the bricks, or something similarly helpless. He always liked those sorts of gestures. The useless kind."

She broke off, shut her eyes.

Both Patalarga and Henry report that Nelson seemed "not himself" on the evening of their departure. "Pensive" was the word Patalarga used; Henry went a bit further, calling him "dour." While they discussed with some curiosity the particulars of the singer and her murderer, Nelson offered no opinion on the matter. Once on the bus, they report, he pulled out his notebook and began to write.

Nelson could have chosen to share the story of his afternoon, or the content of his conversation with Ixta, but he didn't. In fact, he'd mentioned her only a couple of times, never by name, keeping her and a lot of things about himself private from his collaborators during those first weeks of the tour. He didn't tell them about Sebastián's passing, for example, or much more about Francisco beyond the vagaries he'd shared that first afternoon. He never showed them his plays, though he did admit, after some questioning, that he wrote.

That neither of the Diciembre veterans asked why he was upset should not, in my opinion, be interpreted as a lack of empathy on their part but rather as an indication of who exactly these three men were in relation to one another at the beginning of the tour. While Patalarga and Henry were old friends, they were also, in very important ways, strangers, two middle-aged men getting to know each other again after many years. They were working together for the first time since Henry had been imprisoned. And as for Nelson, the fact that they liked him, that they'd chosen him from among the dozens of actors who'd auditioned for the role of Alejo, does not imply any intimacy.

So, a snapshot of Diciembre as the tour begins: Nelson, troubled, fills the pages of his journal with words about Ixta and his heartbreak, before finally dozing off some three hours from the capital; Henry, beside him, attempting little or no conversation, dons a satin eye mask from the play's wardrobe, and promptly falls into a dream about the prison, about Rogelio; and Patalarga, who hasn't been to a movie theater in five or six years, sits across the aisle from his companions, engrossed by the action film blinking on the bus's tiny television.

IXTA WALKED HOME that afternoon a little dazed, trying to fix the details of her conversation with Nelson within the trajectory of their relationship. It had once seemed that the world would defer politely to their whims, but the disappointing last eight months had been a slow unraveling of all that optimism, a break and a period of mourning, a faltering attempt to recapture what had been lost. Doom. Starting over. Now this, whatever it was.

Mindo was not home, and Ixta was glad for this: a small

mercy that she celebrated with a cigarette (she almost never smoked anymore) and a few hours of television. She burrowed deep into the couch, clutching the cushions as if they were life vests. On the other side of the pulled curtains, day turned to dusk. Like Nelson at the bus station, Ixta took in the news of the dead singer, marveling at the scandal the press seemed determined to create. Unlike Nelson, she did know who the singer was. The newscasters played old videos, showed soft-focus stills of the singer's early days playing dusty fields at the edge of the city. Night fell, and the fans gathered in front of the murdered star's home; with candles and bloodshot eyes, they performed their sadness flamboyantly, pushing the very limits of realism. This is what Ixta thought to herself, and then: that phrase, it sounds like something Nelson would say. She put the television on mute, and watched for a minute, in silence, to verify that it was true. It was. Yes, she could hear his voice. Yes, it was still there: ironic, wry, curious. Ixta turned off the television, and sat very quietly, listening to the room hum, and waiting for Nelson's voice to fade from her consciousness.

One day, when they were just starting out, they'd blown off a class on the theory of representation and gone to eat at the Central Market. It was Ixta's idea, and Nelson wasn't opposed. The crowds got denser as they approached, and the lovers held hands casually, letting themselves be jostled by the passersby. The shoppers and pickpockets and stray dogs and maids and businessmen and lonely hearts. A teenage boy pushed through the masses, hoisting above him a wooden broomstick strung with cartoon piñatas. Ixta and Nelson followed him, past the vegetable stands, the dozens of varieties of potatoes, the fishmongers huddled over ice chests; past the boys tending to anxious lizards, those golden-eyed marvels destined to die behind glass for the amusement of the city's children. An old man sold shakes, made with frogs, boiled and skinned, blended with water and egg yolk. The savage little creatures crawled about in their aquariums, blissfully unaware of their fate. "For potency! For love!" the man shouted as Ixta and Nelson passed. He had the desperate voice of a faith healer, as if his primary concern were not commerce but their conjugal happiness.

They ate ceviche served in a paper bowl, while looking up at the market's old steel girders and the light leaking in through the high windows. There was something lovely about it, but they couldn't decide what exactly. When they finished, they headed straight east from the market, though it was the long way, into the sleepy, run-down neighborhoods on the edge of the Old City, until they were on a narrow side street, far enough from the tumult of the market to feel almost provincial. A woman in a bathrobe sat on her balcony, elbows on the railing, watching them pass.

And Ixta was watching Nelson. All day she'd felt it, a hazy sense of expectation, only she wasn't sure what she was waiting for. She slowed, and then stopped. She made Nelson stop too.

"Are you all right?" he asked.

He bit his lip, and she did too, unconsciously, so that for a moment they stood on the sidewalk, mirror images of each other.

I'd like to explain very carefully what happened next, as carefully as Ixta explained it to me: with his right hand, Nelson scratched his temple, and at that moment she felt a sudden itch on her temple as well. He covered his face, rubbing his eyes with the backs of his hands, and immediately Ixta's eyes too felt a desire to be massaged. He licked his lips, and hers felt dry. With every gesture he identified a need her own body was slow to register on its own. He blinked many times, and her eyes opened and closed of their own volition. He repeated his question—"Are you all right?"—but there was no point in answering it anymore.

I'm falling in love, she thought. That must be what's happening.

Years later, on the evening Nelson and Diciembre left the city, Ixta tried to get Nelson's voice out of her head. And failed. That night and the next, and for a week after, Ixta was not the same person everyone expected her to be. Or the person she herself wanted to be. It was odd, she said when we spoke. A sense of drifting. A fondness for quiet. The city seemed alien to her, and she found herself daydreaming about going on a trip herself. For the past few months she'd been looking for new work, but set that search aside for a moment. Though she was loath to admit it, Nelson's absence affected her, at least at first.

She even thought of writing him a letter, she told me, only there was nowhere to send it.

7

THE BUS ARRIVED in San Luis at dawn, stopping at the town's central plaza, where they were met by Patalarga's cousin Cayetano. It was far too cold out to be chatty, and while they waited for the bags to appear from the storage compartment beneath the bus, Nelson observed his new surroundings in silence. The light was gray and thin, mist still clinging to the hillsides, but there were small houses dotting the slopes and footpaths snaking between them. Those must be the suburbs, he thought. On the western side of the valley, the terraced hills were dark with recently tilled earth and he could make out a few human shapes—farmers—moving about in the half-light. It had rained overnight and the streets were rutted and pooled with water. At the far end of the plaza, a woman in traditional dress swept her front steps with a broom that seemed taller than she was. From a distance, it was impossible to tell if the broom was overlarge or if she was very small.

Cayetano announced that he was taking them to the market first. They needed to eat something; if not, the altitude would get to them. Everyone agreed. Cayetano wore a long, padded brown coat and reminded Nelson of a chess piece. A rook, perhaps.

They thought about waiting for a moto taxi, but decided against it: standing still in the cold wasn't such a good idea. "And anyway, it isn't far," Cayetano said. "It only seems that way."

The three actors ambled behind their host through the town's mostly empty streets, Nelson and Patalarga each carrying one strap of a green duffel bag the length of a corpse, or a small canoe. It swung between them as they walked. Inside were their supplies, their costumes, the president's long boots, his white gloves, the smock, the colorful pants, and the rubber sandals Patalarga would wear every evening (and many days) for the next two months. There was even a set of modified tent poles, and a blue tarp, which they could use as a canopy if they were called upon to perform in a light rain. Needless to say, the bag was heavy. Henry, who had fully assumed the role of president from the moment he boarded the bus, carried only his backpack, with a few books and pens, and walked a few steps ahead of the other two, gazing idly at the buildings. He wore the white eye mask raised to his hairline, like a headband. Now and then he made a comment—"What large windows!" or "Look at the workmanship on that wooden door!"—to which no one felt the need to respond.

Everything in San Luis was wet—the gravel streets, the walls of the houses, the hills, even the stray dogs. The puddles on the empty, shadowed streets seemed bottomless.

"It's been pouring every night," Cayetano said. The rainy season had started late that year, but now it had come with a vengeance.

"Oh, the rain!" said Henry.

They walked for much longer than seemed possible, until Nelson began to doubt—in his bones, in his gut—the very existence of a market. But it was there, in fact, at the edge of town: a squat concrete building painted blue, topped with a corrugated metal roof. The market was just opening, and it was a smaller but still inspired replica of that city market near where Ixta had realized she was in love: here, vendors unpacked boxes, sliced meat, unloaded vegetables from wooden crates; and Cayetano led the visitors through the corridors, until they stopped before a clean white-tiled counter stacked with elaborate pyramids of fruit. The woman working there greeted Patalarga with a shout, and came around the counter to welcome him properly. She wore her hair in a long braid and had a bright silver pendant around her neck. It was Cayetano's wife, Melissa. She embraced Patalarga, greeted Henry with similar enthusiasm, and offered Nelson a somewhat formal handshake. There was a baby in a basinet, a little girl named Yadira, asleep in the corner of the market stall. His other two children were at home, he said, preparing the house for their arrival.

While Melissa made juice, they discussed their plans. Henry noted that he hadn't seen any posters announcing the performance. Not on their walk, or at the market, which he found puzzling. A bus ride into the tour and already he'd acquired the arrogance of a president. Nelson was impressed.

Cayetano's lips stretched into a thin smile. He unzipped his heavy brown coat, and sighed. "The mayor, you see . . . He wanted to speak with you first, before we planned the performance. Just to be sure it was appropriate."

Henry scowled.

"Appropriate how?" Patalarga said, his voice rising. "No dancing girls? No blood?"

"So it hasn't been planned," Henry said.

Cayetano shook his head. "Not yet. Not exactly. But we'll talk to him. He's eager to talk. He loves to talk. This afternoon. Everything will be fine."

Melissa served them more of the local breakfast cocktail. Henry and Patalarga muttered between themselves.

"We'll talk to him now," Henry said. "The mayor—where can we find him?"

Cayetano looked down at his watch. "But it's only seven."

"The people's work begins early."

"Why don't you have rest first? Look at the boy."

"I'm fine," Nelson said.

"We'll take him to the house."

"I'm fine," Nelson insisted.

Patalarga nodded reluctantly. Henry, however, shook his head. He patted Nelson on the shoulder, as if to show he understood, then climbed upon the stool where he'd been sitting. No one had a chance to stop him. He began shouting for everyone's attention. He clapped his hands, asked for a moment. The market workers, along with the shoppers who'd wandered in, slowed now and looked up.

"Dear residents of San Luis! My two colleagues and I—stand up, Nelson! Stand up, Patalarga!"

He waited for them to climb upon their stools before continuing.

"Together," Henry announced, shouting, "we are Diciembre. You may have heard of us—we are a theater company! From the capital! We would be honored to perform for you this evening, at six p.m. in the plaza, weather permitting. Please come and bring your families! Thank you."

Then he sat down.

Nelson stayed up for just a moment longer, surveying the market. From this vantage point, he was able to register with great clarity the muted reaction to Henry's announcement. There was no romance associated with the name Diciembre— there would be elsewhere, in towns all across the mountain regions, but not here. Instead, there was a pause, a collective head-scratching, and then a quick return to the normal rhythms of the market. Vendors resumed their various tasks, the handful of early-morning customers went back to their shopping. Nelson quickly became invisible.

Eventually, Patalarga helped him down. He and Cayetano received the young actor into their arms, and Melissa gave him tea.

"Why does no one believe me?" said Nelson. "I'm fine!"

"Good," Henry said, without smiling. "We have a show tonight."

. . .

WHEN MAPPING OUT their itinerary, Henry and Patalarga had selected San Luis for three reasons. First, a matter of nostalgia: Diciembre had played a show there, nineteen years prior, on their very first tour into the interior. They had fond memories of the place: its placid river; the few cobblestone streets remaining in the center of town; and an old, pretty church with a leaky roof. Compared to the dreary mining camps they'd visit later, San Luis was positively picturesque, and therefore a good place to begin. Second: it was well located, just off the recently repaved central highway, a smooth six-hour ride from the capital. Third: the presence of Cayetano, who'd been loosely associated with Diciembre in the early days—though more as a drinking partner than as an actor. He wasn't just Patalarga's cousin, he was an old friend, with a rich understanding of Diciembre and its history. The years had been kind to him: he had a family now, had inherited his father's land, and money enough to become a prominent member of the community. The war had ended, and the new highway allowed his produce to arrive in the city overnight. Cayetano had risen to the position of deputy mayor of San Luis, something unthinkable to those who remembered the bearded, poorly dressed young poet known for staggering through the predawn streets of the capital back in the early eighties.

"But then, no one thought I'd be a science teacher," Henry said during our interview. "And no one thought you'd be . . ." He frowned and looked me over with his ungenerous eye. "Well, you aren't anything yet."

I let this go.

Whatever the case, they'd counted on Cayetano to make things run smoothly. They expected to be on the road for six weeks or more; it was important to get a good start. They left Nelson at the house to rest, and the elders of Diciembre went off to speak with Cayetano's boss and patron, the mayor.

The mayor opened by saying he wasn't "hostile to art, per se"; from there, things only got worse. He smiled often, but never warmly, tapping his long, slender fingers on his desk as he spoke. He described a number of killings that had taken place in the area since Diciembre's last visit in 1982, with a tone that implied the first event was somehow related to the others.

Patalarga later admitted that his mind wandered throughout the speech, that he found himself looking out the window, at the church with the leaky roof, and above, at the sky, only then beginning to clear. It was midmorning. His wife, Diana, was surely awake, but perhaps still in bed, enjoying the silence of an empty house. The Olympic was locked up and empty, costing him money every minute of every day. For no good reason, he remembered his childhood in the mountains, on the whole, happy memories, and his early schooling, during which he'd been subjected to long-winded harangues not unlike this one. He'd had a teacher who was a communist. Another who was a reactionary. Both were living abroad now, in Europe. In a week he'd see his mother, and as always, the thought filled him with ambivalence. He'd pressured Henry into this tour, presenting it as something his old friend had to do for himself, for his art; but as the mayor prattled, Patalarga realized that, in fact, *he* was the one who'd wanted it. Who'd wanted it badly. It was a way to be young again; to escape the city for a spell and relive times which, though difficult, constituted the central experiences of his otherwise uneventful life.

"The war years," he told me when we spoke. "It's not that I miss them, not at all. But I *remember* them. Every last detail. It worries me, but sometimes I feel like everything else is a blur. Does that make any sense?"

I shook my head. Honestly, I didn't understand.

"I was just a boy."

We were silent awhile.

In San Luis, the mayor's concern was the title of the piece.

"Idiot," he said. "If, at school, my son were to call another student an idiot, the teacher would send a letter home and the child would be punished. Would he not?"

Cayetano furrowed his brow. "Your son is twenty-two years old."

The mayor glared. "As usual, my esteemed Cayetano, you are missing my point." He turned to Henry. "Are you a father, Mr. Nuñez?"

"I am."

"And would you not punish your child if he—"

"She."

The mayor paused, as if having a daughter had never occurred to him. "If *she* said something like that to a classmate?"

Henry thought of Ana, who was too smart to toss around insults thoughtlessly. If his daughter were to call someone an idiot, it would mean they *were* an idiot.

He opted not to say this. "But Mr. Mayor, is a play subject to the same codes of behavior as a child?"

The mayor frowned, paused, and wrapped his long fingers around a glass of water. "I don't know the answer to that." If he was an imbecile, at least he was honest. He took a sip of water.

Henry felt he'd scored a point, and opted to forge ahead: after all, he was the president, and it was his role to defend his play, his partners, their art form. He intended to be respectful, to negotiate this fine balance between the ego of a small-town mayor and the needs of a theater collective like Diciembre. What, Henry argued, is a play without an audience? Isn't a script simply potential energy until that magical moment when it becomes something more? Isn't alchemy like that only possible when the words are made real, when the actors step out from behind the curtain (or the tarp, in this case) and *perform*? Henry could feel himself gaining momentum as he spoke. Every audience is different, and every audience is a gift which can never be overlooked or taken for granted; as for Diciembre, here they were—"Here we are!" Henry said, perhaps a bit too loudly—and they'd come to San Luis for an audience. To transform the *virtual* into the *actual*. They had hoped to use the recently remodeled school auditorium, but they would perform this piece one way or another; in the plaza, in the market, in the street beneath the pouring rain. They'd do it in Cayetano's home if they had to!

The mayor smiled.

"Perfect. Do it at Cayetano's house." He stood. "Gentlemen, have a wonderful day. I wish you much success."

. . .

TO PREPARE for the show, Patalarga, Cayetano, and Nelson
spent part of the afternoon carrying furniture outside, and covering it with Diciembre's tarp, in case of rain. They cleared as
much space as possible in the house, making room for an audience that would sit on the floor. While they worked, Cayetano
apologized for what had happened. Their play, he explained, had
fallen victim to a rivalry that had emerged in recent years between him and the mayor. A dispute about land. These things
are common in small towns. He began to go into the details, but
stopped himself.

"You know what? It's not interesting, even to me."

Meanwhile, Henry put on the presidential riding pants, the
ruffled shirt and long coat, the leather boots, the white gloves
and sash, and went down to the market once more.

"Everyone stared at me," he reported. "They stopped me, and
asked where I'd come from. It was wonderful."

This time, there were more people around, the market was
louder and more alive. Melissa borrowed a bullhorn from another vendor, and announced Henry to the crowd.

"Ladies and gentlemen: the president!"

With the people's attention, Henry once more clambered
atop a stool and spoke of Diciembre, the play, its surprising
change of venue. There was a buzz this time—who is that oddly
dressed man, and what exactly is he talking about?—and when
he finished, Henry bowed, taking care not to lose his balance,
and received the tour's very first round of applause.

According to Patalarga, Nelson was both nervous and determined not to appear so. He was not a complete novice; after all he'd performed in a few of the capital's more storied theaters. But this was undoubtedly different, Patalarga told me. "The intimacy of it, the nearness of these strangers, the way they look at you. It couldn't have been easy for him."

Did Nelson flub his first lines?

He did.

Did he miss his cue for the fight scene?

He did.

Did he see the faces of his audience, feel them close, smell their presence in the room, and long for the trappings of those theaters he knew back home?

He did.

But he pushed through all that, and by the time the mayor appeared, midway through the first act, Nelson had mostly recovered. Things were humming along. The mayor, full of bluster and pique, seemed unimpressed. He made his way to the corner opposite the door, and stood against the wall with his arms crossed, frowning.

Nelson had no idea who this man was, and later claimed it was mere coincidence that his line "But Father, you must be careful! Evil lurks everywhere!" was delivered with eyes locked on the latecomer.

Everyone noticed, and Cayetano laughed nervously; soon the entire room was laughing along with him. Everyone but the mayor.

"This is what Nelson had to learn," Patalarga told me. "That the play is different every time. That it doesn't matter if you mess up. There's no such thing as a mistake."

The mayor stormed out well before the climactic murder scene.

It was just as well. There was more humor at his expense once he'd gone. A gentle rain began moments later, just as Patalarga's character was stabbed. It tapped pleasantly on the roof. When the play was finished, the applause and the rain seemed to blend into one, each augmenting the other. There'd been no theater in town for as long as anyone could remember. No one wanted to leave. Nelson, immersed in the chatter, felt warm. Then a bottle appeared, and the volume was raised, and the dancing soon began. Nelson stood against the wall, shy, but Cayetano and Patalarga sent Melissa across the room to pull him onto the floor. He took his first tentative steps to the beat, and Henry yelled, "The city boy!" his voice somehow carrying over the music and the rain.

Everyone cheered, and this is when the tour finally seemed real to Nelson.

8

IN THE WEEKS THAT FOLLOWED, Diciembre played in small towns and villages up and down the region, subject to weather like nothing Nelson had ever experienced. Some mornings it was as if the sun never rose, the skies swirling with blue and purple clouds until late afternoon, when they finally broke into a downpour. Other days, it wasn't the rain but the winds one had to contend with: they blew fierce and merciless through the valley, leaving Nelson's cheeks red and his body chilled. Then, quite unexpectedly, the cloud cover would vanish, and the sun would appear. Everything glistened, even the mountains, and he'd think: this is the most beautiful landscape I've ever seen. It never lasted; after an hour the clouds would return. Nelson lost weight in those first days, and woke up many mornings with a terrible headache. For breakfast he drank coca tea, ate cold bread and cheese. For lunch: fried trout, some eight days in a row. Ten days. Fourteen. Occasionally, guinea pig, a welcome change, but which too often involved the unpleasant ritual of having to choose your lunch from among a pen of furry little animals.

("The fat one," said Henry, every time, without deigning to bend his head over the beasts.) They rode from one town to the next on a bus, if one was available; if not, and if there was no rain yet, the bed of a truck would do. They lay among piles of potatoes, gazing out across the valleys, the fields, the scattered, lonely houses, and the turbid sky that pressed down heavily on all of it. The higher they went, the more dangerous the roads became, at times barely wide enough for a horse cart; and Nelson would often peer over the edge of a crumbling mountain, and force himself to think of something other than death. His life back home came to mind, but Henry's instructions—to give in completely to the world of the play, to forget everything else—seemed particularly apt since his last, disappointing conversation with Ixta. He strained to put her out of his mind.

In spite of these physical and psychological hardships, the tour had its pleasures: they were greeted warmly in each town, with a certain ceremony and solicitousness Nelson found charming; almost every night the audiences gave them a standing ovation that made all their efforts seem worthwhile. Even if the community had never heard of Diciembre, they were often grateful for the visit. The village elder or mayor would insist on hosting them himself; and being welcomed into these humble homes was, for Nelson, an astonishing privilege. He'd try to catch Henry's eye or Patalarga's, just to make sure they felt it too: the significance of these people's unexpected, unearned trust. A party would be hastily organized, or spring up spontaneously after a performance. The villages might be just a handful of houses amid endless yellow-gray fields, but in many cases, these were the best audiences of all: no more than a dozen people altogether, with little education or experience with theater, a few farmers with ruddy faces, their long-suffering wives, and undernourished children, who'd approach Henry after the play, never looking directly at him, and say respectfully, "Thank you, Mr. President."

There was the show in Corongo, where Patalarga's elderly aunts and uncles lined up in the front row, his mother, beaming with pride, in the very center, an hour before the show was to begin. They sat quietly and very still, gazing upward as if posing for a photograph. When the performance began, their eyes narrowed in concentration, and when it was finished they stood to applaud. Afterward, they all ate potato and onion soup in the dining room of Patalarga's childhood home, pressed together at a long narrow wooden table that creaked one way and then another, depending on whose elbow happened to be raised. The room was dark and musty, and all the windows and doors had been thrown open to air it out, letting in the nighttime chill, which no one but Nelson seemed to mind. Everyone was happy, proud, but they were tight-lipped and circumspect, as if contentment were an emotion to be guarded like a secret. Unlike the rest of the family, Patalarga's mother was concerned. "I have a question," she said to her son, as the meal was ending. "Oh, and please don't take this the wrong way . . . but if you're the one with the money, why must you play the servant?"

To which Henry responded, "The role comes so naturally to him. It would be a crime to use his talents in any other way."

There was the night in the roadside community of Sihuas at

three thousand two hundred meters above sea level, where they were given a corner of a bar called El Astral to perform; they waited and waited for an audience—anyone would do—but no one arrived. It was after ten in the evening, and besides the mustachioed bartender, and the manager at the hostel, they hadn't seen another living soul anywhere in the vicinity. Henry and Patalarga each drank a beer in silence, unconcerned, or pretending to be, but Nelson was impatient. "They're not coming," he said, wishing only to rest. "No one's coming!" But the bartender pulled at the edges of his mustache. "Believe me, young fellow, you just wait. You'll do your show!"

A while later, he looked at his watch. "Go on. Go out there, you'll see."

Night had fallen; the sky was dark. Sihuas was set in a narrow slip of the valley, and Nelson saw nothing in the town's empty streets, but when he got to the corner and looked up, there they were: strings of tiny, bobbing lamplights, hundreds of them, rushing down the trails. They were gold miners, descending the mountains all at once. A half hour later, in a clamor of shouting and noise, they arrived, and instantly, El Astral was overrun. The men were small and lean, with reddish, windburned cheeks, inky black eyes, and a feverish desire to drink. Some were scarred, or missing fingers from dynamite accidents, but they didn't seem to care. They smelled of metal, and paid for their drinks with tiny bits of gold that glinted beneath the bar's neon lights. They sang songs, and packed the place so tightly that Nelson, Patalarga, and Henry found themselves pushed together into a tight huddle. Their stage had disappeared beneath the crush of men. A half hour later, a bus full of prostitutes appeared—how? where had it come from?—and suddenly El Astral smelled of sex, or the possibility of sex, this thick cloud of painted women pushing into the bar as if borne by a strong and lurid wind.

There was no chance of doing the show now.

"No wonder the hostel manager wanted us all in a single," Nelson said. He'd never been to a brothel before (though he'd imagined the setting enough to write a play about it), and now, quite improbably, the brothel had come to him. It was an impressive spectacle. Within the hour, there were couples having sex in the bathrooms, behind the remains of Diciembre's makeshift stage, on the steps of the bus that had carried the women there. Henry settled their bill, suddenly embarrassed, apologizing for being unable to pay in gold, but the bartender was nothing if not understanding.

"Next time," he said.

They walked the few blocks to the hostel together, the unlit streets of Sihuas alive with grunts and moans and women's laughter.

And there was the night in Belén when they met the town's much-aged former police chief, who, after a few drinks, agreed to share the story of how he'd briefly arrested some members of Diciembre nearly twenty years before. The old man had a chubby face and mottled skin, but his eyes shone at the memory: it was like he was watching a movie of the scene, admiring the version of himself played by a young and handsome actor. He'd made the papers in the capital, he recalled, something he'd never managed again. He told the story without reserve or shame, addressing Nelson directly, perhaps because he mistakenly believed that Henry and Patalarga were among the group that had been arrested. It was all right to laugh now, he said, but back then things were different. "We'd heard of the terrorists, but we had no idea what to look for. There were awful reports from the city, but no solid information. You probably don't believe me, but we were frightened."

Henry and Patalarga knew people in every town: old collaborators or antagonists from the early days of Diciembre, the men and women with whom they'd shared their youth. These acquaintances had lived most of their lives in the provinces, at a different rhythm. They told funny stories masquerading as tragedies, and sad stories purporting to be comedies; they drank heavily, and seemed not to notice those things most concerning to Nelson: the abject poverty of their surroundings, the terrible condition of the roads, the relentless rains and the bitter cold. He admired this too: their ability to preserve joy at any cost, the way prehistoric man might have preserved fire. Nelson had learned to chew coca leaves, had come to enjoy the numbness as it spread over his face, down his neck, and into his chest; a small pleasure that muted the harshness of the rainy season and smoothed over the effects of the altitude. And they were at the edge of a different region now: the lower valleys, where the forests began. If they went farther, another day or two or three, the cold would give way completely, and they'd be at the edge of the jungle, free to breathe again, almost normally. Now they sat around a rectangular wooden table in a cramped restaurant, listening to the old police chief tell this funny little war story about arresting actors. A fluorescent light buzzed; the television was on, but no one watched. Behind them stood a second line of men, anxious to listen in—if the table were the stage, they were the balcony, so to speak. Workers, all of them, men with rough hands jammed deep in their pockets, men who laughed when it was time to laugh, who fell silent when it was time for quiet. They were the chorus, carefully following the police chief's cues. If a glass of beer was offered, they accepted; if it wasn't, they didn't complain. They were indifferent to cold, didn't mind standing, and followed the conversation in the bar as closely as they'd followed the play itself.

The old man went on: "So then these kids, these ruffians, show up on the back of a pickup truck, wearing bandanas and smelling bad. They set up a tent in the plaza, without even asking. They play rock music from a boom box. You must think we're primitives here, but this is how it happened. My deputy— God bless him, he's abroad now—he says to me, *That's them!* That's who? I ask. *The terrorists!* But how do you know? I say, and this one, he was always reading the papers. He had an answer for everything: *Look how dirty they are!* What did we know? We'd never seen one. The ladies, they smoked cigarettes, they had patches on their jeans. The boys looked sickly, with stringy hair and thin mustaches. Look at them! Even now they look shifty! Was I wrong to worry? Tell me, son, was I wrong?"

The old man laughed with his entire body, the chorus too. Henry and Patalarga didn't, but no one seemed to notice.

"I'd arrest them now!" Nelson called out.

"But what would I charge them with?" the police chief said in an exaggerated whisper.

"I'm sure you could come up with something," Patalarga said.

"Anything will do," Henry added. "The courts aren't very picky, you know."

No one had anything to say to that. The police chief smiled politely, and the chorus held its breath for a moment. Nelson sensed the discomfort too, and when it had gone on just a second too long, he changed the subject, and brought up the rains; the police chief smiled, deferring to the chorus, who were the laborers, the ones who tilled the earth. They'd come into town for the show, but what they really knew was the land.

"How are things out there?" the old police chief asked. "What's happening over in the provinces?"

The provinces—this was another thing Nelson had come to understand. No matter where you went, no matter how far you traveled into the far-flung countryside, the provinces were always farther out. It was impossible to arrive there. Not here— *never here*—always just down the road.

One of the men said his fields might be washed away. Two straight weeks of rain this late in the season; it wasn't normal. The rivers are swollen, said another, the bridges could collapse. And then, a third man, with a broad face and black hair that fell limply just above his eyes, said, "Heard from my cousin that it's getting so bad in the lowlands that the planes can't even fly!"

At this, everyone fell silent.

"Planes?" Nelson asked.

He hadn't heard of any planes. He hadn't seen them, or even

imagined them. Though he'd never flown, air travel was his; it belonged to that other world, the one he'd left behind.

The former police chief's face was stern. He glared for a moment at the offending chorus member, who'd broken the rules by speaking out of turn and mentioning the lower valley's most important and fastest growing industry, the drug trade.

"Perhaps you could arrest him for *that*," said Henry, a comment that did nothing to lighten the suddenly oppressive mood.

After that night, and after Henry had explained, Nelson looked to the skies when they traveled. He noted it in his journal, welcoming this new way to pass the time, to distract himself from the precariousness of the roads or the raw winds. He never saw a plane. They spent four days in that area, descending toward the heat, before Henry decided they should turn back toward the highlands.

"I feel more comfortable when there's less oxygen," he said. "The play makes more sense that way. Don't you agree?"

And because he was the president, Diciembre returned to the highlands.

Then there was the night in San Felipe, when, after a particularly energetic performance, Nelson nearly fainted. Patalarga's murder took a lot out of him that evening, and he sat afterward, slumped in a chair, unable to catch his breath. Inhaling was like swallowing knives, and his head felt as if it might separate from his neck and float away. Eventually he recovered, and they were all invited to a party in a one-room adobe house on the outskirts of town. He was rushed inside, where the strangers paid special attention to feeding him and getting him drunk. Surprisingly, the liquor helped, and it felt nice to be doted on. When Nelson began to turn blue, the owner of the home, a gray-haired man named Aparicio, asked if he wanted a jacket. Nelson nodded enthusiastically, and his host rose and walked to the refrigerator, standing before its open door, as if contemplating a snack. Nelson thought, He's making fun of me. He watched Aparicio open the vegetable drawer and take out a pair of wool socks. He tossed them to Nelson, and when the door opened a bit more, Nelson saw the refrigerator was, in fact, being used as a wardrobe. The bottom shelves remained, but all the rest had been removed. There were mittens in the butter tray, sweaters and jackets hanging from a wooden bar nailed to the inside walls. Only then did he notice the few perishables sitting on the counter. In this cold, they were in no danger of spoiling.

The gathered men and women told sad stories about the war and laughed at their own suffering in ways Nelson found incomprehensible. Sometimes they would speak in Quechua, and then the laughter became much more intense, and also much sadder, or at least that's how it seemed to Nelson. Later, a woman arrived, Tania, and everyone stood. She had long black hair, which she wore in a single braid, and an orange and yellow shawl draped over her shoulders. She was beautiful, and very small, but somehow gave the impression of great strength. She circled the room shaking everyone's hand—except Henry's, who instead received a floating kiss in the air just beside his right ear.

"Are you still acting," Tania asked when she got to Nelson, "or are you actually that sick?"

He didn't know how to respond, so when someone shouted, "He's drunk!" Nelson felt relieved. The room roared with laughter, and then everyone sat.

The drinking began in earnest now, and a guitar soon appeared from a hidden corner of the room. It was passed from person to person, making a few laps around the circle before Tania finally kept it. Everyone cheered. She strummed a few chords, then cleared her throat, welcoming the visitors, thanking them all for listening. She sang in Quechua, picking a complex accompaniment, her agile fingers unrestrained by the cold. Nelson turned to Henry and asked him in a low voice what the song was about.

"About love," he whispered, without taking his eyes off her. It seems they had briefly been involved two decades before. Seeing her, he told me later, unnerved him, filling him at once with regret and optimism. He felt then that he'd entered a gray period of his life, from which there was no easy escape. One could not enter the world of a play. One could not escape one's life. Your bad choices clung to you. And even if such a thing were possible, it would require a strength of will he lacked, or a stroke of good fortune he didn't deserve.

As for Nelson, the night wore on and he found himself appreciating Tania's beauty with greater and greater clarity. Hours passed, and when he was finally succumbing to the cold and the liquor, Tania offered to lead him back to the hostel where they were staying. This was noted by the attendees with feigned alarm, but she ignored them. Outside in the frigid night, her eyes glowed like black stars. The town was small, and there was no possibility of getting lost. They trudged drunkenly through its streets, both wrapped in a blanket Aparicio had lent them.

"You sing beautifully," Nelson said. "What was it about?"

"Just old songs."

"Henry told me you were singing about love."

She had a beautiful laugh: clear and unpretentious, like moonlight. "He doesn't speak Quechua. Must have been a lucky guess."

When they got to the door of the hostel, she asked Nelson if he was happy. She was curious, she said, because his face was so hard to read.

"Hard to read—is that a compliment?" Nelson asked.

"If you want."

"Did you see the play?"

Tania nodded.

"And did you like it?"

"Yes," she said. "Very much."

"Then I'm happy."

He moved to kiss her, but she dodged him, surprisingly alert, as if she were an athlete specially trained in dodging kisses. She patted him on the head, and they stood there awkwardly for a moment, until she smiled.

"It's fine," Tania said. "You're sweet. You remind me of my son. Now, drink lots of water, and get as much rest as you can."

Then she walked back to the party. Nelson watched her go; and though he was hundreds of kilometers away from home—in a place as different from the boardwalk of La Julieta as it might be from the surface of a distant planet—he recalled Ixta, who had stopped believing in his love, and had walked away from him. Every day Nelson waged a pitched battle against the memory of their conversation at the lighthouse, a brutal war, in which he was both victor and vanquished. In his mind he tried to change the outcome of this moment, like a magician attempting to bend a spoon through sheer concentration. No matter what he tried, it never worked. He recalled his silence now, that he'd let her go, and felt ashamed.

"Tania!" he shouted.

She turned, but said nothing. She was waiting.

"I love you!"

She laughed elatedly, as if it was the most wonderful joke she'd ever heard.

"He was a handsome boy," Tania told me later. "If he were just a bit older, I would have taken him home with me."

It was more than a month and a half into the tour by then; six weeks separated from his life, from his friends, from his dreams. Nelson had turned twenty-three the first week of May, without sharing the news with anyone. He was on his own. Henry had asked them all not to call home, not to write letters, but to immerse themselves in the moment. Now it was worth asking: What good was that advice, really? What did it achieve if the present was not new or different at all, but fundamentally the same: the usual traumas, only now set on a cold mountaintop, on a pitch-black night? Inside the hostel, the owner gave Nelson a large rubber bladder, swollen with boiling water, and as he prepared for bed, alone now, he held it in his hands. It was like holding a human heart, his own perhaps. He felt what remained of his contentment evaporating. He tried to go over his day: what had happened, or what, to his chagrin, had not. The cold made coherent thought nearly impossible, so Nelson lay down with the bladder pressed against his belly, curling himself around it like a snail. His eyes began to close. Was it worth it, he wondered: the travel, and the cold, and the distance, which felt, at times, like that exile Henry had clamored for that first day in the cab? What did it all amount to if he'd already ruined his life by letting Ixta walk away? Was he ruining his life even now?

He willed himself to rise, went down once more, where he woke the owner of the hostel, apologizing. Would it be possible to make a phone call, he asked her, to the capital?

The woman stood in her nightgown, observing the young actor through narrow, half-closed eyes. "There's no telephone," she said, suddenly upset. "You and your people always want a telephone, but I keep telling you!"

ONE AFTERNOON, Henry brought up the story of his imprisonment. He was talking to Nelson ostensibly, but naturally he was also talking to himself. In 1986, he was thirty-one years old, and the night of his arrest, his first concern had been for the play itself. His work was all that mattered. He didn't notice the two men in dark suits hanging around after the show. They stood apart, talking to no one, leaning against the mildewed walls of the Olympic which, by hosting an experimental theater company like Diciembre, had officially entered a new, nearly terminal, stage in its long decline. ("We were there just before it went porno," Patalarga told me.) The theater had emptied, the audience dispersed, and the actors were alone. One of the two men in dark suits approached. "You're Henry Nuñez," he said, as Henry made his way from behind the stage. It wasn't a question. Henry wore a leather bag thrown over his shoulder, nothing inside but some smelly clothes and a few annotated scripts. He'd splashed water in his face, and argued with his cast of two, Patalarga and Diana, who weren't even dating then. ("You must understand, my dear Alejito, this was back when Patalarga was still a virgin. Don't laugh, he was barely twenty-five years old.") The performance had been disappointing, and he'd told them so, in an angry tirade adorned with profanities. The small crew had gone. Diana had cursed him, called him "insensitive and tyrannical" before she fled as well. The theater was empty by then, just Henry and Patalarga, who was, at that moment, still backstage.

"Do you remember?" Henry said to his old friend, and Patalarga nodded.

Henry's dissatisfaction turned to annoyance at the presence of these two strangers, who asked inane questions, when the entire theater universe of the capital *knew he was Henry Nuñez.* Who else, exactly, would he be?

When it became clear Henry wasn't going to respond, one of the men said, "You'll have to come with us." He spoke formally, very deliberately; Henry frowned, and the other man repeated the drab, rather passionless command, this time emphasizing the words "have to."

Patalarga emerged from behind the stage just then, quickly understood the situation (according to him), and tried to intercede; but by then a couple other men had materialized from the shadows of the Olympic; tough, unsmiling men, the sort who love settling arguments. They placed their giant hands on Henry. A few more words were spoken, some shouted, but in the end, this wasn't a negotiation. They were taking the playwright, and that was that. When Patalarga wouldn't shut up, they knocked him out and locked him in the ticket booth, where he would be found the following day by the custodian.

Henry was held without human contact in a mercifully clean, though still unpleasant, cell. It took him a few days to understand the severity of the situation. He was questioned about the people he knew, the plays he wrote, his travels around the country, and his motives; but it was all strangely lethargic, inefficient, as if the police were too bored by it all to decide his fate. He wasn't beaten or tortured; he surely would've confessed to anything at the mere threat of such treatment. On the third day, still thinking, breathing, and living in the mode of a playwright, he asked for a pen and some paper in order to jot down notes about his tedious imprisonment, things to remember should he ever need to write about his experiences. He was denied, but even then, in his naiveté, he still wasn't worried. Not truly concerned. Disappointed, yes, disturbed; but if he'd been asked, Henry would've said he expected to be released any day, at any moment. His captivity was so ridiculous to him, he could hardly conceive of it. He just couldn't understand why they were so upset—had they seen *The Idiot President*? It wasn't even any good!

Just when he was beginning to despair, he was allowed to receive a visitor. This must have been the fifth or sixth day. By then a story had been concocted: the authorities categorically denied Patalarga's version of the arrest, saying they found Henry hours later, drunk, wandering the streets of the Old City. They claimed to have held him for his own safety.

And why had they denied that Henry was in their custody for five days?

A bureaucratic mix-up. A record-keeping error.

And why were they still holding him?

It was under investigation. Henry was the prime suspect in the beating and false imprisonment of Patalarga. "Most likely a lover's quarrel," the police spokesman said, with a slyly raised eyebrow, "though I would prefer not to speculate."

The docile press, however, speculated.

Henry's older sister, Marta, appeared that fifth or sixth afternoon, representing the entire living world outside the small cell which held him—his family, his friends, Diciembre and its supporters. Everyone. It was a burden that showed clearly on her face. Her eyes were ringed with dark bluish circles, and her skin was sallow. She hadn't eaten, Marta reported; in fact, no one in the family had stopped to eat or rest for five days, and they were doing everything they could to get him out. He imagined them all—his large, bickering extended family—coming together to complete this task: it would be easier to put them on shifts and have them dig a tunnel beneath the jail. The image made him smile. Marta was happy to see Henry hadn't been abused, and they passed much of the hour talking about plans for after his release. She had two children, a daughter and a son, ages six and four, who'd both drawn him get-well cards, because they'd been told their uncle was at the hospital. Henry found this amusing; the fact that the cards had been confiscated at the door of the jail, he found maddening. Everyone assured the family not to worry, that they'd remember this little anecdote later, and laugh.

"Why wait?" Henry said.

"Don't be ridiculous," his sister answered, but already she was suppressing a grin.

He was referring to a game they'd developed as children: forced, spontaneous, and meaningless laughter. They'd used it to get out of chores, dismissed from church. With hard work and diligence, they'd developed and perfected this skill: rolling around, cackling, rubbing their bellies like lunatics, before doctor's appointments, or family trips, or on the morning of a school exam for which they had not prepared. Neither recalled the game's origins, but they'd been punished for it together on many occasions, always feigning innocence. We can't help it, they'd both say, laughing still, tears pressing from the corners of their eyes, until their protests landed them in weekly brother-sister sessions with a child psychologist. Even these many years later, both were proud that they'd never betrayed the other. In their prime, when they were as close as two human beings can be (Henry, age ten, Marta a couple of years older), the two of them could manufacture laughter instantly, hysterical fits that lasted for a quarter of an hour, or longer. Henry considered it his first accomplished dramatic work.

He insisted. "Why not?"

They'd been whispering until then, but now they took deep

breaths, like divers preparing for a descent. The cell, it turned out, had good acoustics. The laughter was tentative at first, building slowly, but soon it was ringing through the jail. Unstoppable, joyful, cathartic. At the end of the block, the guards who heard it had quite a different interpretation: it was demonic, even frightening. No one had ever laughed in this jail, not like this. They felt panic. One of them rushed to see what was happening, and was surprised to find brother and sister laughing heartily, holding hands, their cheeks glistening.

The hour had passed.

Leaving the jail that afternoon, Marta gave a brief statement to the press, which was shown on the television news that evening. Her brother was completely innocent, she said; he was an artist, the finest playwright of his generation, and the authorities had interrupted him and his actors in the legitimate pursuit of their art. Those responsible should be ashamed of what they'd done.

The following day the charges of assault and false imprisonment were dropped, and replaced by other, more serious accusations. Henry was now being held for incitement and apology for terrorism. A new investigation was under way. He was given the news that morning by the same guard who'd come upon him and Marta laughing, who thankfully refrained from making the obvious statement about who might be laughing now, a small mercy which Henry nonetheless appreciated.

He was driven from the jail in the back of a windowless military van, with nothing to look at but the unsmiling face of a soldier, a stern man of about forty, who did not speak. Henry closed his eyes, and tried to follow the van's twisting path through the city he'd called home since age fourteen. "We're going to Collectors, aren't we?" he asked the soldier, who answered with a nod.

On the morning of April 8, 1986, Henry entered the country's most infamous prison. He wouldn't leave until mid-November.

9

NELSON LIKED HEARING these stories; it was as if they filled in gaps in his knowledge he hadn't known were there. He asked again and again: why haven't you written about this?—but it was a question Henry never really answered convincingly. Every night in Collectors, friends paired off and walked circles around the prison yard, commiserating, confessing, doing all they could to imagine they were somewhere else. How do you set a play in a world that denies your characters any agency? Where do you begin? "Begin there!" Nelson would respond. "Or there! Or there!" ("Young writers believe everything constitutes a beginning," Henry told me later, in a stern, professorial voice.) Undeterred, Nelson even offered to help: he would transcribe the scenes, or they could talk them out together. He could sketch the arc of each moment, write character treatments—they could *collaborate*. ("I never liked that word, to be quite honest," Henry told me, noting its unfortunate political connotations.) Still, he pretended to be intrigued by the idea, that it was something worth considering, though he never committed to it. Perhaps, he told the eager young actor, when they returned.

Patalarga, who has the clearest memories of those days of the tour, says he sensed Nelson's admiration for Henry becoming more nuanced: no longer the blind respect of a young artist, or the ambitious striving of a protégé who wants recognition, it had become something more like the appreciation of a son who's come to understand his father as a man, with all the complexity that implies.

In other words: they were becoming friends.

Meanwhile, the rainy season was ending. By that point, they'd spent some eight weeks on the road; had gone from the coast to the highlands to the lowlands and back up again; passing through a succession of villages that seemed from a distance to bleed together in kaleidoscopic intensity. The country, which for Nelson had always been a mystery, was real to him now, a series of stark tableaux come to life: from mining settlements like Sihuas to lazy riverside towns in the lowlands to clusters of tiny houses spread atop a high mesa, homes to modest families of cattle grazers. This area fascinated Nelson most of all, these people who'd settled in ever-widening concentric circles around a massive slaughterhouse, smelling of offal and rot, a mean, dark place which was nonetheless the center of the region's economic, social, and cultural life, and which had even become, for one brief but magical evening, a theater.

They were mostly inured to the austere beauty of the land-scape by then; it was right in front of them, so commonplace and overwhelming they could no longer see it. In Nelson's journals his descriptions of the highland terrain are hampered by his own maddening ignorance, that of a lifelong city dweller who has no idea what he's looking at: mountains are described with simplistic variations of "large," "medium," or "small," as if he were ordering a soda from a fast-food restaurant. Trees and plants and birds, and even the color of the sky, are given much the same treatment. Greater attention is paid to the people: pages upon pages devoted to Cayetano, Tania, and others (descriptions which I've drawn from to prepare this manuscript), as well as a vast assortment of miners, laborers, farmers, money changers, and truck drivers whom they'd met along the way. They appear, unique and alive, often nameless, and then are gone.

On the morning of June 11, 2001, Diciembre arrived in the small city of San Jacinto, which felt, relative to all the previous stops on the tour, like a version of Paris or New York or London. It was the largest town on their itinerary, and they were due to perform a couple nights at a local English language institute named after Franklin D. Roosevelt. How Patalarga had programmed this particular show, no one knew; but once in San Jacinto, Henry and Nelson thanked him for it. Suddenly dropped into the town's delightful chaos, they became aware of the sensory deprivation they'd endured those long eight weeks. They walked casually through the city, taking in the movement with an appreciative mix of panic and wonder. San Jacinto's sixty thousand or so residents lived atop a flat, dry plain, trading anything and everything according to rules only they understood. One noisy street was overrun with musicians for hire. "All the hits!" shouted a saleswoman with manic streaks of red in her hair. "Pay for eleven hours, and the twelfth hour is free!" Another was filled with the cheerful, drunken employees of a trucking company, christening six new vehicles in the middle of an intersection, blocking traffic in all directions. The trucks shone brightly with wax, as if smiling in the sun, and were decorated with bunting fastened to the tops of the cabs. Men dashed about, tossing confetti in the air, spraying the chassis with champagne. It was like a wedding, only it wasn't clear who was marrying these giant, gleaming machines, or if they were marrying each other. Henry, Patalarga, and Nelson stayed to observe the confusing ceremony, and then, when the noise became too great, followed the railroad tracks away from the center, hoping for some quiet. For many blocks, they could hear the horn blasts, now fading, but still frantic and celebratory.

They came to a small plaza where dozens of men stood among large chalkboards placed in rows that zigzagged from one end of the space to the other. It wasn't at all clear what the men were after. A heavyset woman sat at one end of the chalkboards with a pen and clipboard in her lap; now and again, she would hand a piece of paper to an adolescent girl, who would then climb a small stepladder and begin copying the words out in colored chalk. The men would gather around, with severe expressions on their wind-bitten faces, scrutinizing her work. Henry, Patalarga, and Nelson watched from the edges of the crowd, waiting for the right moment to get a better look. For once Henry didn't pretend he knew everything, but took in the scene with the same puzzlement as the rest. He sent Nelson, finally, to investigate.

"You're an actor," Henry said, "you'll blend."

Nelson returned moments later. He had not blended, but been met instead with dozens of distrustful eyes.

They were job postings, he reported. Classified ads, performed live.

Henry rejoiced. "Theater for the people!" he said, as if the idea had been his all along.

That evening, they ate at a chicken restaurant near the center of town, its tables wrapped in thick plastic. They'd done well the previous night, recouping enough in donations to treat themselves to a real sit-down dinner. Lunch had passed without their even noticing it: confronted with the sights and sounds of San Jacinto, they'd simply forgotten to eat. Now a liter bottle of soda stood before them, but no one drank.

But Nelson had something on his mind; he had for days, since the night in San Felipe. He asked Henry about it now. He felt he was owed some clarification. "Have you been calling home?"

The playwright smiled, saying nothing at first, but finally, he nodded.

"I thought we weren't doing that," Nelson said.

Patalarga laughed.

"Why are you laughing?"

"Because I've been calling too."

The food came.

As it turned out, the only one of the three protecting the integrity of "the play's constructed universe" was Nelson. He lost his appetite. Henry and Patalarga found this very funny; Nelson, less so. They chided their friend playfully, trying to pull him from his bad mood, which they found entirely unreasonable. And perhaps they were right. How could he have been so literal? they asked, but he had no answers. The commitment Nelson had shown the project—something he'd been proud of only a moment before—was now a sign of gullibility.

Patalarga attempted to explain away Nelson's complaints: Henry had lied, yes, in the strictest sense, but this is what great directors do. They challenge their actors, prod them, force them against their will into a place of discomfort, in this way extracting some extra dose of magic for the performance. Isolated, mournful, longing for home—this was Nelson, the actor, at his best.

"Imagine a happy, well-balanced Alejo," said Patalarga. "That would never do. I should tell you one day how he treated my wife, when she had your role."

Henry agreed. "Diana still won't talk to me."

"This was what you wanted?" Nelson asked. "To make me unhappy?"

"Sure it was. We needed you to be. For the play." With that, he thrust a piece of chicken into his mouth.

"But—"

Henry's face was covered in grease, and he chewed for a long, luxurious minute. He loved these moments, loved Nelson's disappointment, in fact. Mentorship, such as he understood it, consisted primarily of didactic exercises like this one: transforming frustration into the building blocks of knowledge.

"Please, my dear Alejito: did you really expect me not to talk to my daughter?" Henry said finally. "Or for the servant not to call his wife?"

"I guess not."

"Who did you want to call?" Patalarga asked.

Nelson rolled his eyes. "*Now* you want to know?"

"We do," said Henry, softening. "We really do."

Henry, later: "I loved Nelson. Of course I wanted to know." After a pause: "I'm so sorry for what happened."

What did Nelson tell them?

Concretely: about Ixta. How she'd walked away, how he'd let her. How his world was poorer without her. Blank. What he told them that night at the Wembley wasn't true: he'd always wanted to leave, and he hated his brother for keeping him here. He even wanted to go now, and take Ixta with him. To start again. To try. This was what he'd realized on the tour. What he'd learned. He told them much more, Patalarga said to me later, many things which seemed to combine into a large, cosmic sort of complaint: a sadness pouring out of Nelson that began with losing Ixta, perhaps forever, but went much further. He was being condemned to a life he didn't want. It scared him.

"Naturally," Henry told me, "this was a feeling I knew firsthand."

"Did you offer to cut the tour short?" I asked.

The playwright shook his head. "That wouldn't have solved anything."

"So what did you do?"

"We told him to call her—what else? He loved her, and he knew he'd made a mistake. Talking to us about it wasn't going to help. We left the restaurant, and walked until we found a call center. It was across the street from a park, so we found a bench and said we'd wait for him there. When Nelson came out, he looked dazed."

I told Ixta about this later: I thought she might want to hear that description, might find it illuminating to know the impact their conversation had on Nelson. It was the complement to what she'd been feeling at the beginning of the tour. That everything he'd said on the phone to her that night was true: he did miss her fiercely. He had found time to think. He did have a plan now, however vague, and it did include them both. A future existed, and it could be theirs. He loved her.

She nodded as I spoke, betraying little curiosity at first, until a moment when I thought I saw a tear gathering in the corner of her eye. It didn't last long. She was nothing if not composed, and an instant later, she'd brushed the tear away with the back of her hand. She cleared her throat and cut me off.

"You don't have to tell me this. I know."

She remembered Nelson's phone call very well, in fact: though the connection from San Jacinto was snowy with static, his voice was clear enough. He was at a call center, he told her, and the town was coming to life for the evening. It was around nine, and the streets were thick with people. Lovers. Thieves. There were moto taxis whirring by, and packs of little boys huffing glue in the nighttime chill.

"It sounds lovely," Ixta said. "Did you call to tell me about San Jacinto?"

Silence for a moment. Then: "No."

"I should have stopped him," she told me. "I shouldn't have let him say anything. I already knew it didn't matter."

But she couldn't help it; she let him talk. It was painful to hear, Ixta admitted, and she was not unmoved.

When he'd finished, she told him her news.

"Do you think that had anything to do with what happened next?" I asked.

Ixta gave me a blank look. She was very careful with her words: "I think Mr. Nuñez and his associate are the ones who should answer that. I wasn't there."

I bent my head, pretending to look over my notes, but all the while, I could feel Ixta staring at me.

"You know," she added, "I don't see why any of this matters now."

"It still matters to me," I said, though if she'd asked me why I'm not sure how I would have responded.

Just then her baby called out from the other room. Ixta excused herself to attend to the child, and I sat in her living room, wondering if I should gather my things and go. I didn't. She came back a few minutes later with her little girl, wrapped in a pale yellow blanket.

"What's her name?"

"Nadia," Ixta said, and at the sound of her mother's voice, the infant's round green eyes popped open. "I'm here, baby," Ixta purred, and Nadia breathed again, sleepy. She spread her mouth into a cavernous yawn, as if trying to swallow the world, and then her eyes closed again; her face became small and peaceful.

"She's beautiful," I said.

Ixta nodded. "You can see for yourself she looks nothing like him."

10

NELSON'S MOTHER ALSO RECEIVED a phone call that night, but whether it was before or after the conversation with Ixta is not known. Mónica doesn't remember hearing anguish or heartbreak in his voice, but then again, she reminded me, her younger son was an actor, a boy who'd kept more than his share of secrets over the years. There's another possibility: that she was so surprised and happy to have Nelson on the line, she simply overlooked any hints about his emotional state. In any case, Mónica is certain he didn't mention Ixta—in fact, he hadn't mentioned her for many months. It was as if this girl disappeared from his life. Mónica had liked Ixta well enough, and even felt responsible, indirectly, for the pairing, but Nelson was young, and these things happen. The heart mends. Life is long. When I told Mónica that they were still seeing each other, more or less, up until the date of Nelson's departure, she was surprised.

"Oh dear," she said. "Really?"

That night, Nelson and his mother spoke in very broad terms about the tour, about how he was getting along with his fellow actors. Nelson claimed to have learned a lot about his craft, and assured her he was enjoying being away. (Perhaps he *had* called his mother first.) He said he'd been thinking about his future.

"What have you been thinking?" Mónica asked her son.

He sighed. "That I should go, finally."

Nelson's mother didn't need this to be explained. She knew what "go" meant, understood the implicit destination. Nor did she disagree, really. "The tour was giving him perspective," she told me, "and that was a good thing. Sebastián and I pushed him to leave for years, but after my husband died, all that was put on hold. I wondered if it was my fault, but Nelson never said anything. I should have kept pushing him, but the truth is, I was too tired. It was selfish, but I needed him."

"What did you tell him that night?" I asked.

"That I supported him, no matter what he wanted to do. You know, the original plan was New York or California, but even San Jacinto was a step. For years, he'd never left the city. After Sebastián passed, he stayed by my side. His friends went on vacation, they piled in cars and went on camping trips down the coast. And he hardly ever went with them. And yes, maybe he resented me for it. So now, in a way, I was happy to hear him say he wanted to leave. I'd been waiting for it."

About the tour, Nelson told his mother the play was "a hit"— though he qualified this by saying that the word meant something different out there in the provinces. He laughed then, and Mónica recalls how beautiful her son's laughter sounded to her. Nelson explained that successful shows might be performed before fifteen or twenty spectators, in ad hoc venues where the very concept of "a full house" didn't apply. How, for example, does one "sell out" a windswept field at the edge of town? If every known resident is there, huddled together for warmth in the limitless space? If the tickets themselves cost nothing, does it even matter? If a few of the audience members raise their hands to ask questions in the middle of a performance—is this a good thing? And if you pause in the middle of a scene to answer these questions (as Henry had one strange night, "a presidential press conference," he called it) is that really winning theater?

"Yes," Mónica recalls saying. She was enthusiastic: "It is!"

She was not an old woman, not yet, but the last two months hadn't been easy. She spent hours each day "tidying up"—this was the phrase she used, though it sounded more to me like a kind of archaeology, or an intensely personal subspecialty of that discipline: exploring one's own solitude, as if it were a dark cave. She might sit reading a paperback Sebastián had given her in 1981, the handwritten inscription no longer legible, the letters fuzzy and blurred, but special all the same. How and why had he given it to her? What had he been trying to tell her? Had he imagined that she'd be reading the inscription twenty years later, when he was dead and she was alone? A weekend afternoon might find her refolding a dresser drawer full of Francisco's old clothes, items she'd saved these many years for no reason she could recall, and then going to the old photo albums to verify that her elder son had actually worn them. It was as if she were fact-checking her own life. A full day could pass like this. She didn't enter Nelson's room, not yet, but felt certain that each night, as she slept, his things spread around the house of their own accord, to new and unexpected hiding places. Scripts appeared behind sofa cushions, a pair of laceless sneakers materialized in the pantry behind a bag of rice. Someone, she was sure, was moving the family pictures.

Now she stood in the kitchen, holding the receiver with both hands.

"How was your birthday?" Mónica asked.

"Great."

"When will you be back?"

From San Jacinto, Nelson rattled off the names of a few towns they hoped to visit in the coming weeks. It seems the word about Diciembre and its tour had spread, and many municipalities were interested in hosting them. The rains were ending, the festival season would soon be under way, and Henry had decided Diciembre would take advantage of these potentially large and boisterous audiences. Why wouldn't they? Was there any hurry to come home?

"Of course there isn't," Mónica said. "As long as you're happy, that's what matters."

"Are you doing all right, Mom?"

She told Nelson she was fine.

To me, she confessed: "I'd already had two months to begin imagining my life without him."

HENRY AND PATALARGA AGREE: When Nelson stepped out of the call center, he seemed a little stricken. They made room for him on the bench, but he opted to stand before them instead, hands buried in his pockets, chin to his chest.

"What happened?" Henry asked, but Nelson didn't answer, so they watched him, swaying left to right, looking down at his feet. A minute passed like this.

"Are you going to say anything?" Henry asked.

"Are you cold?" Patalarga said. "Should we go to the hotel?"

"She's pregnant," Nelson answered, still looking down. His voice was soft, almost inaudible over the humming noise of the park where they sat. He looked up then, and they saw his helpless eyes, the puffy skin beneath them. He pursed his lips: he had the bewildered expression of a student trying to solve a problem he doesn't quite understand.

"The baby isn't mine. That's what she told me. I asked her how she knew, and she said she just did. I asked her if she'd taken a test, and she said that was none of my business."

"Women know these things," Henry said.

"I'm sorry," Patalarga added.

"She's going to marry that other guy."

(Ixta is adamant that she never said this: "Nelson invented that. I'm sure he believed it, but Mindo and I never had plans to be married." She found the idea laughable.)

Henry stood and embraced his protégé.

"Did he cry?" I asked.

Henry frowned at the question in a way that suddenly embarrassed me. "No, I don't think so, though I'm not sure why it matters."

So either Nelson cried or he didn't. They spent the next few hours walking the streets of San Jacinto, rather directionless, trying to raise Nelson's spirits. It wasn't easy. Henry says he offered to cancel the next day's show, but Nelson wouldn't hear of it. The show must go on, et cetera, et cetera. Patalarga suggested they get drunk, an easy option, and cheap, considering the altitude; but Nelson shrugged off the idea. "He wasn't into it," Patalarga told me. "Everything we offered, he turned down. I think he just wanted us to keep him company."

"Did he say much?"

"He asked if anything like this had ever happened to either of us."

In response, Henry explained that heartbreak is like shattered glass: while it's impossible that two pieces could splinter in precisely the same pattern, in the end, it doesn't matter, because the effect is identical.

"I suppose so," said Nelson.

To further prove the point, Henry told of his infidelities, from which he claimed to have derived no pleasure, none whatsoever, and his subsequent divorce. He did not mention Rogelio, not yet—though his old lover would be making an appearance, indirectly, that very same night. One could call it serendipity or coincidence or luck (which comes in two, often linked, varieties); one could also just call it *life*.

Patalarga took up the argument, and told of his move at age seventeen from his hometown in the mountains to the city; and the girl he'd left behind.

"What was her name?" Nelson asked.

As it happens, I asked the same thing.

Her name was Mercedes—Mechis—and they were madly in love. She wanted to believe he'd come back for her, and Patalarga was afraid to let her think any different. So they conspired to never speak of it, both assuming the other believed this fiction. In fact, neither of them actually did. Once in the city, Patalarga changed his name, changed his life. They wrote letters for a time, but these fizzled out. He was embarrassed to tell her about his new friends. He never forgot her, but something shifted: he'd be riding the bus to the university, and realize, suddenly, that he hadn't thought of her in months. The longer this went on, the more ashamed he was. He didn't go home for three years, by which time he was a different person entirely. When they saw each other the first time, he expected she'd yell at him, curse him, beat him with small, closed fists and ask him why. He was prepared for this, but what actually happened was much worse.

"What happened?" asked Nelson.

Nothing. Mechis had married another man. She had a child, a little boy, who must have been eighteen months old, standing wobbly but on his own two feet, and clinging tightly to his father's pant leg. Mechis's husband was friendly, and shook Patalarga's hand with an appalling lack of jealousy. And Mechis? She was entirely indifferent to Patalarga, as if she didn't even recognize him.

"That night, I cried like a baby."

"That's awful."

"You know, it was probably just the altitude," Henry offered, which only managed to draw a weak smile out of Nelson.

Eventually, they ended up in the main plaza, the one section of San Jacinto that can conceivably be described as pleasant. There was a giant stone cathedral lit dramatically with flood-lights, and glowing like an apparition; at the other end, a recently built hotel fronted with greenish mirrored glass; hideous, but also startling, as if an alien spacecraft had landed in the center of town. Somehow the contrast was less troubling than intriguing. A troubadour sang before a sparse audience of foreigners and elderly, the colonial-era fountain bubbling behind him. There were no moto taxis, which gave the few blocks around this plaza a kind of solemnity banished from the rest of the bustling city. Henry, Patalarga, and Nelson strolled along the sidewalks, and happened by a shuttered tourist office. Its broad window featured a few posters of local attractions, and they paused before it, their attention drawn not by those images but by a very large and detailed regional map. The villages and towns were noted with black dots, the routes between them marked in red. As if by common agreement, the three actors stopped, all of them curious to find themselves on this map, trace their circuitous path through the mountains, the lowlands, and back. They placed their fingers to the window, laughing as the name of one village or another brought up some outlandish memory. Here we killed! Here we bombed! Here we triumphed over the elements! Henry would later tell me how happy it made him to see Nelson laughing along with them. They'd been through a lot together: eight weeks and a few days of movement, the only constant being the play they performed every evening. Different audiences in different towns, each with its own history and character, with its own unique interpretation of the play, and of the actors themselves. In one village, at the conclusion of the show, the local elder stood before the audience and, with great ceremony, gave them each a strip of long, rubbery material, as a gift. Something like leather, but different. To chew? To smoke? It turned out to be the desiccated tongue of a bull. No one knew what to do with it. Henry thanked the elder, the man's wrinkled face contorting into a pleasant smile, then a boy stood and tied the bands around each of Diciembre's wrists. Tightly.

Everyone clapped.

And the map seemed to contain it all. It was as if it had been made for them.

"Is this where you first saw the name of Rogelio's village?" I asked Henry during our first interview, many months later.

He nodded gravely. "It is."

"And what was your reaction?"

"It was just one of those things." He paused, and took a deep breath. "One of the many details I'd forgotten. Rogelio had told me where he was from—he'd told me everything—but if you'd asked me just a moment before what the name of that village was, I never would have remembered it."

"But when you saw it . . ."

"I knew."

"Did you tell Nelson and Patalarga right away?"

Henry did more than that: he placed his index finger on the dot next to this town's name, and upon realizing it wasn't far, a couple of hours at most from San Jacinto, he shuddered. He fell silent. He'd begun—dimly—to comprehend the possibility this town represented. A way to close off the past, to make peace with it.

Had he forgotten Nelson's heartbreak? Was he succumbing once again to his habitual selfishness?

"No," Henry told me. "I thought we'd all benefit."

He said the name to himself and felt its power, his finger pressed against the window, holding fast to the point floating on the map. To me, he explained: it might as well have been a flashing light, or a star.

"Gentlemen, there's been a change in plans," Henry said. "*This* is where we're going next."

PART
TWO

11

THERE WAS A MOMENT, sometime in the third hour of my
second interview with Mónica, when I found myself with one of
the family's photo albums spread across my lap. This shouldn't
have been unexpected, I suppose—in word and gesture I'd made
it clear this was precisely the sort of access I was hoping for—
and yet somehow it was. Already I knew more about Nelson
than I did about many of the people I'd grown up with, including dear friends, including even family members. I was coming
close to deciphering some of the mystery around our one brief
encounter, but there was something else too. It wasn't so much
what I'd learned, as how I'd learned it: Nelson's secrets revealed
to me by his confidantes, his lovers, his classmates, people who'd
seen fit to trust me, as if by sharing their various recollections,
we could together accomplish something on his behalf. Re-
create him. Reanimate him. Bring him back into the world.
Piece by piece, I was gathering a sense of the richness of his
inner life, and his imagination. I'd followed, at least partially,
the trajectory Diciembre had taken a half a year before. I'd been

to the same places, seen the same landscapes, talked to many of the same people. I'd tried to see things through Nelson's eyes, using his journals to guide me whenever possible. On good days, I felt I was succeeding.

Now it was January 2002. I sat on the sofa of Nelson's childhood home with his mother, listening to her stories of this shy, sensitive boy whom she'd raised into a man. She cried a little, apologized, then cried some more.

And I was turning the pages of this photo album, under Mónica's watchful eye, when I came across a picture of Nelson and Francisco, circa 1983, posing before the monkey pen at the zoo. Neither Mónica nor Sebastián are in the frame, the brothers stand alone in the foreground. Francisco looks bored, antsy, but Nelson is a guileless five-year-old, absolutely charmed by what he sees. His smile is goofy, his brown eyes wide. He has one arm around his brother's waist, and another pointing back over his shoulder, toward the animals.

"Look at him," Mónica said, and I squinted at this picture, at Nelson's smiling face. I compared this image with others I'd seen, with my own fragmented recollection of our one encounter, at the beginning of July the previous year; and suddenly, I had the strangest sensation, like double vision. For just an instant, I thought I saw myself standing just to the side of Francisco and Nelson, with another family—mine—and another set of siblings—my two sisters. An unlikely, but not impossible, coincidence. I stared at the image.

I also grew up in this city.

I was also once a brown-haired boy with thin legs and a bony chest.

I also went to the zoo. We all did.

It wasn't me hovering in the background of that old photograph, of course, but that's not the point. It could've been.

FOR A VARIETY OF REASONS I've decided not to include the name of this town. I'll call it T——. I was born there, after all, and though I left when I was only three, I suppose this fact gives me some right to call it whatever I please. My parents brought my sisters and me to the city when I was very young, and I'm grateful that they did. I have no memories of our life before the move, though we children were regularly subjected to my father's long monologues on the town and its lore, so it always hovered before us, an idyllic mountain dreamscape, its perfection taunting us from afar. My father only wanted us to feel connected to the place, a sentiment I understand and appreciate now that I'm older, but at the time, those notions felt imposed, like a state religion. In my memory, these speeches are always interrupted by a car alarm or a power outage or the neighbor's overloud television set. Once in a great while the three of us children were packed onto a bus and forced to visit. We dreaded these trips, or pretended to, in order to spite our parents. We stared at our books, and refused to be impressed by the scenery. When the war closed off travel to the provinces, part of me felt relief. By the time the shooting stopped, there was no reason to travel anymore: nearly everyone my parents knew and loved had left the old town, and come to the city to start over, just as we had.

But the T—— of my memory, or my parents' memory, is not the same place as the one Diciembre encountered on their visit. In order to prepare this manuscript, I conducted interviews with Patalarga and Henry in the capital, long conversations from which I've already quoted, dialogues that veered forward and back in time. T——, though they were only there very briefly, appeared too: in shadow, as a backdrop for a series of events unfolding in strict adherence to the highlands' acute surrealist mode (a mere two thousand nine hundred meters above sea level, in case you were wondering). Henry and Patalarga both report that they felt happy to be free of the itinerary, to improvise once more as they had on those first epic Diciembre tours, when they were younger. But according to both men, Nelson was the most enthusiastic of them all, the most eager to get moving again. There was no further mention of Nelson's heartbreak, Ixta's pregnancy, or whatever his plans might be as a result. From the moment Henry had pointed to the spot on the map, Nelson was sold. He was fleeing. He wanted to put distance between him and the news that had left him so shaken.

"Yes," Nelson said. "Let's get out of here."

Only Patalarga voiced any reservations, mentioning casually their performance scheduled for the following evening. Henry was unmoved. "We'll cancel it."

"Why can't we wait a day?"

Henry was far too anxious to explain. He pointed at Nelson

instead. "Look at the boy. He's a wreck. We have to keep moving. This is how life is."

"Don't do it for me," Nelson protested.

Patalarga stared at Nelson, as if this last line had been uttered in a foreign language.

"He's not doing it for you," Patalarga said. "He doesn't do things for you."

Nelson looked to Henry for confirmation, and the playwright shrugged.

There was no mention of Rogelio, or of the prison. No mention of the real reasons Henry felt so drawn to this place he'd never visited before. Up until that point, Patalarga, Henry's best friend and confidant for more than two decades, had never heard the name Rogelio in his life.

I wondered: Did either Patalarga or Nelson ask for any further explanation from Henry?

"No," the servant told me. "He was the president."

They left San Jacinto the next morning. "Fuck you, Roosevelt!" Henry is reported to have shouted from the bus window as it pulled out of the station, though Patalarga was surely more diplomatic when he called to cancel their performance at the English language academy.

Once in T——, what Diciembre noticed first about the town was what anyone would notice, what I noticed every time I visited: the abundance of empty, shuttered houses, roughly half on any given block. Every building, with the exception of the municipal offices, needed a new coat of paint. The town was surrounded on all sides by yellow-green hills that seemed almost lush for this altitude, hills which were themselves dwarfed by jagged snowcapped peaks, so appropriately cinematic that they appeared to have been painted along the horizon by a set designer. If the town itself was notable only for its charming abandonment, the valley where it was placed was one of the loveliest they'd ever seen. That contrast—the spareness of the town and the majesty of its surroundings—made T—— seem even smaller and more insignificant than it was. Something similar might be said of many mountain villages, I suppose, but the sense was somehow sharper here, that feeling of isolation, the illusion of being outside time.

Like many settlements one comes across in the highlands, T—— was a village without men. Nelson, age twenty-three, Patalarga, forty, Henry, forty-six—Diciembre had essentially no contemporaries. I feel the same absence whenever I visit. There were children; there were elderly; and there were a handful of adolescent boys, who were, in many ways, a species apart: restless, unpleasant, wearing expressions Henry recognized them from his past. "They were like inmates hatching escape plans," he told me. Rogelio had been one of them—that much was clear to Henry the moment he stepped off the bus from San Jacinto and saw the boys waiting in the plaza. They had a hunger in them, the same desire that had sent Rogelio to the city, pushing him along the accidental and luckless path that ended at Collectors prison, when he was only twenty-one.

Illiterate, hopeless, frightened. Far from home.

T——'s plaza was simple, relatively well tended, and picturesque: the two-story city hall stood on the east side, adorned with a fluttering flag; across from it was the stone cathedral, the oldest, and still the tallest, structure in the area, its empty niche filled once a year for the September festival of the town's patron saint. There were a few shops along the north end, businesses with spare, dusty shelves, whose doors opened and closed according to a schedule the actors of Diciembre never managed to comprehend. The hotel, called the Imperial, stood along the southern side of the plaza. It had three rooms, each with a couple of saggy twin beds. For Diciembre's stay, the owner brought in a third, crowding the room so completely that there was hardly any space to walk. The hotel also housed the town's only restaurant and its only bar, a pleasant balcony where I spent many evenings admiring the sleepy square. My favorite moment of each day came just after sunset, as daylight vanished behind the ridge to the west, and the plaza's four streetlamps came on. These tiny blooms of orange light warmed me somehow— they were so small, and the dark so immense. I liked to sit and watch them for long stretches, taking in the view of a plaza where nothing at all ever seemed to happen. I'll admit: the same oppressive calm I'd found maddening as a child had become almost charming.

But what does *nothing* look like?

A stooped elderly couple ambles by, casting soft shadows beneath these minuscule lights. They are trailed by their grandchildren, or a skinny dog; or perhaps they are alone, walking very close together to stay warm. The wind picks up, and later the moon begins to rise. Soon there will be stars dotting the sky. T—— is just like this, night after night—this quiet, this peaceful, this harmless. It was just like this when Nelson and Henry and Patalarga arrived. And it was probably just like this when Nelson was made to stay.

ROGELIO'S MOTHER lived four blocks from the plaza, on the west bank of the river that ran through town. Her home, I should mention, was across the street from the house where I was born. On those periodic trips back, I would sometimes see her, and she seemed ancient to me even then. About our house: it sat empty for more than two decades, until December 2000, when my parents finally tired of life in the capital. My sisters and I were grown, and my mother and father could be comfortable again in T——. Live quietly; cheaply, though with relatively few comforts. They sold the house in the city, and went home, to confront their nostalgia head-on. They were happy to be back, and encouraged us to visit often. My sisters had their families now, their partners and children a ready excuse. I was the youngest. Unattached. The pressure to go fell mostly on me.

"Come home," my father would say when we spoke, though I had never really thought of T—— as home.

Regarding Rogelio's mother, my old man confessed to me: "I couldn't believe she was still alive."

For Henry, the bus ride from San Jacinto was itself an act of bravery, a confrontation with a specific well of fear he'd avoided since the day he woke to the news that his old block in Collectors was burning down, with everyone inside. What is more frightening than our past? Than true love, snatched away? He wasn't fooled by the town's peaceful exterior. To him, T—— was vacant, a kind of still life, waiting to be animated by his presence. He'd hardly slept the night before, overwhelmed by the sense that a reckoning was imminent.

T—— was just as he imagined it would be, or like a museum of itself. Henry checked into the Imperial, and left immediately to look for his lover. He saw traces of Rogelio everywhere: a child has dragged a muddy set of fingers along the white stucco of an exterior wall; they extend nearly fifteen paces, in fading, vaguely parallel lines. Rogelio? Of course not, but still, the very idea filled Henry with expectation. He asked the occasional passerby for Rogelio's family home, and was met, more often than not, with blank stares. He couldn't remember Rogelio's surname; he wondered, in fact, whether he'd ever known it at all. Those he met were friendly enough, but most claimed ignorance, or gave him obscure directions that seemed designed to confuse. He entered a few of the open shops, and inquired there, with about as much luck. With every interaction, his anxiety rose, but he didn't give up. Finally, after a half hour of wandering, looking for a sign, he stopped an elderly woman in a purple shawl, hoping she might be Rogelio's mother. She seemed about the right age (though actually he had no idea), and in truth, that was the entirety of his logic. He all but babbled his story, or some version of it, to this startled stranger, who was surprisingly patient, nodding at Henry, as if urging him to go on. (Who this woman in the purple shawl might have been, I can't say with any certainty.) In any case, she wasn't kin to Rogelio, she said, but she knew him. And his family. And his mother, who—God bless!—was still alive.

"Oh yes, and her name is Anabel," the elderly woman added, voice trembling. She pointed a thin, bony finger in the direction of the river, and sent the grateful visitor on his way.

And so, by the early afternoon of his first day in T——, Henry had come to the place he never imagined he'd be: standing beneath the midday sun, on an empty, unpaved street, prepared to knock on the door of the house where his long-dead lover had been raised.

And though I was still in the city on that day, my life begins to intersect with Nelson's here, at this precise moment. My mother reports that she saw Henry just then. She remembers him for two reasons: one, because he was a stranger, and there are no strangers in T——; and two, because he looked nervous. ("What is there to be nervous about in a town like ours?") She happened to be walking out of our house at the precise moment of Henry's arrival, and this anxious stranger cleared his throat when he saw her.

"Is this Mrs. Anabel's house?" he asked.

"And you know," my mother admitted later, "I almost said it wasn't, just because I didn't like the looks of him."

But my mother is incapable of lying. Perhaps that's why she never got used to life in the city.

"Yes, dear, it certainly is," she said. Then she hurried off to the plaza, already blushing.

MEANWHILE, Patalarga and Nelson were engaged in a search of their own. They were looking for a place to perform. The kind but cautious man who ran the Imperial had demurred, though his underused balcony restaurant would have made a fine stage, indeed. He'd seemed so flummoxed by their inquiry that neither Patalarga nor Nelson pressed him. And anyway, there were other options, better ones: the municipal auditorium, though padlocked at the moment, wasn't booked until September. Surely the mayor would open it up for a night, if they asked. At this hour, they'd be likely to find him in his fields, on the north side, just past the school. And as long as they were headed that way, the school itself could work too. There was a nice courtyard, suitable for an afternoon show, before the sun went down; the manager of the Imperial even gave them the name of the principal, a nice man, he said, who would be happy to talk, though they should speak loudly, since his hearing was basically shot.

Nelson and Patalarga thanked him and walked north from the plaza in the direction of the school, over a decaying wooden structure which the locals called the New Bridge, and farther, out into the open valley.

When I spoke with Patalarga, I was curious how Nelson seemed to him; after all, he'd heard the news from Ixta only the night before.

"All right," Patalarga said. "In surprisingly good spirits, in fact. We really had no idea why we'd come to this town, and the newness of it gave him something to focus on."

But it wasn't new, exactly; in fact, in terms of Diciembre's tour, it represented a return to normal. They'd spent the last eight weeks in ramshackle towns just like T——; out-of-the-way places accustomed to long, uneventful days. The anomalous San

Jacinto interlude, with its crude nod to urbanism, couldn't have seemed farther away now. The streets of T—— were either hard-packed dirt or cracked cobblestone, but somehow the houses, even the empty ones, had a permanence to them that San Jacinto lacked. A city built almost from scratch in a decade is not likely to have much to recommend it (architecturally, culturally), whereas Rogelio's hometown, my hometown, even in its worn-down state, seemed destined to last.

Nelson was quiet as they walked, his eyes on the hills, on the sky, on this preposterously scenic valley. Streams of snowmelt bubbled down from the higher elevations, flowing into the creeks and then into the hand-carved canals that fed the surrounding fields. A boy in a red sweater hurried past, pulling a goat by a long rope; Patalarga and Nelson watched the child bound along the path toward the school.

"Charming," was how Patalarga described it. As striking as any place they'd been on the tour; tumbledown and imperfect, surely a difficult place to live, but lacking the malice of, say, a mining encampment. Or the primitiveness of a logging town. Or the squalor of a smuggling depot. And he was right: T—— was different. There was no economic activity to speak of besides farming and the twice-yearly festivals, which brought the town back to life, or to a kind of life. The rest of the year was quiet, and it was this calm that Patalarga and Nelson now breathed in as if it were mountain air itself. The long rainy season had finally ended, and there were no clouds marring the blue sky. In the midday sun, you could feel comfortable in short sleeves.

"It's beautiful," Nelson said.

They were the first words Patalarga had heard from him since they'd started their walk. Then he added: "I forgot to say congratulations, you know?"

"I'm sorry?"

Nelson shook his head. "When she told me she was pregnant, I didn't say congratulations." He slowed now, head bent toward the ground. "That's what you're supposed to say, right?"

They were almost at the school, and could hear a group of children getting ready for recess—the bubbling of their laughter, their impatience. Nelson stopped. "Maybe Ixta's pregnancy is good news."

"A baby is always good news," said Patalarga.

Nelson shook his head. "I mean good news for me."

His plans for life with Ixta—no matter how whimsical or undefined—might still be relevant. They could move in together, raise the child together. He told Patalarga that he'd woken that morning with the strangest feeling. He could see it now, the shape of another life. It could be his. She might still be his.

For Patalarga, it was a balancing act between offering hope and realism. "So what are you doing here?" he said. "Why don't you go back?"

"I will. Soon. I have to." Now he turned the question back on Patalarga: "What do *you* think I should do?"

Nelson's eyes blinked back the sun; he really wanted to know.

"What did you tell him?" I asked.

I met with Patalarga three times in the city. We ate meals together, and went over the history of Diciembre with old, yellowed programs in hand, laughing and marveling at the naive ambition of it all. We toured the shabby Olympic, imagining its past and future glory, drank beers at the Wembley as he recounted this story to me, and much more—details and anecdotes and confessions which haven't made their way into the manuscript. I don't think it's a stretch to say we established a kind of rapport. He's someone I could call up, even today, and expect a friendly conversation, perhaps even an invitation to drinks or dinner.

But of all the questions I asked, for some reason, this was the one that made him most uncomfortable.

His initial, unsatisfying answer was: "A lot of things. You have to remember I couldn't have known what would happen."

"Sure," I said, and let him sit with that.

He rubbed his chin.

"I told Nelson he had every option before him. I told him he could go home and fight for her. That he might win, or might lose, but that there was honor in both."

"And what did Nelson say?"

"That he wasn't a fighter, he never had been, and that scared him. And I said that was bullshit. Of course he was a fighter. He was more than that. He was a murderer, wasn't he? Didn't he kill me every night onstage?"

At this Nelson laughed; Patalarga too.

"That's right," Nelson said. "I'm a killer. Everyone be careful. Everyone watch out."

12

BEFORE THE MIGRATIONS BEGAN, back when the place was still lively, T—— was divided into four districts. The river cut the town into east and west, while the area north of the plaza was considered distinct in culture and class from the blocks south of it. Though T—— was small, the lines dividing the districts from one another were sharp and not to be contested.

Rogelio's family, like mine, was from the southwest, a detail meaningless to all but a handful of elderly still living, and maybe a few thousand former residents of the town. It meant something to my father, but in spite of his best efforts he was unable to pass this sentiment on to his children. This is what I learned about the southwest when I finally asked him: it was a district of large families and relatively modest homes. As a rule, the men did not own land to farm, but were sometimes hired to tend the fields of those who lived in the northwest, just seven or eight blocks away, but a world apart. The others were carpenters or stonemasons, later mechanics and drivers. The women of the district sewed curtains and hemmed clothes, earning small sums which they gave to their husbands for safekeeping. They were (the stereotype says) prone to gossip; specialists in spreading it; and, as a group, unashamed to be the protagonists of the local whispered hearsay. When their men went off in search of work, the women of the southwest district were rumored to receive male visitors late in the evening, after the children had been put to bed. If a marriage on the north side broke up, a woman from the southwest was assumed to be at fault. If something was stolen, the town's single, part-time policeman visited the southwest, gathering the boys en masse to lecture them about property rights.

As for T——'s children, they all went to the same school, and they might even be friends for a time, but by age nine or ten they'd fully internalized these petty district rivalries. Occasionally the boys fought, but it rarely got serious. As soon as the young men from the southwest understood their position, there were no more problems. They learned, as their fathers had before them, to bow their heads at the appropriate times.

Nowadays, the lines between the districts tend to blur, so that, at this late date, a quasi-outsider like me finds it almost impossible to tell the difference. Every part of T—— has been hollowed out, suffered almost equally from the neglect. At its height, the town was home to perhaps seven thousand residents— smaller, that is, than the total current population of Collectors— but when Diciembre arrived a little more than a thousand remained. My parents were the first new residents in more than three years, not counting the occasional highlander paid to look after a property during the rainy season. Rogelio's older brother, Jaime, had moved a few hours away to San Jacinto when Rogelio was just thirteen, and had eventually become quite wealthy, though he spent very little of that money in T——.

Rogelio's mother, known to all as Mrs. Anabel, had stayed, along with her daughter, Noelia, who took care of her. The afternoon Henry arrived, after he'd had his brief interaction with my mother and finally gathered the courage to knock on the door—it was Noelia who received him.

"He was polite," she told me later, "a bit odd, surely, but most of all polite. At least at first. He asked to speak to my mother, said he was a friend of Rogelio's, and of course I let him in. That's what we do here. I thought he might have some news."

Henry walked in, marveling at the disrepair. Even an act as simple as closing the door, he noticed, required a delicate maneuver: lifting as you pushed it shut, then wiggling the warped and swollen wood into place. When it would seem to go no farther, Noelia gently shouldered the door, once, twice, three times, and it was only then that she was able to pull the lock. Henry found it astonishing. One day, he thought, she'll find herself trapped inside.

The house was just a handful of rooms surrounding a hopelessly overgrown garden. Noelia led him to the living room and asked him to wait. There was a brief, confusing moment when Henry thought Noelia was Rogelio's mother, but she clarified with a laugh.

"Heavens no!" she said. "He's my little brother!"

Noelia explained that Mrs. Anabel was just getting up from her nap. "She sleeps quite a lot these days. She isn't well, you know."

"I didn't know. I'm sorry to hear that. If it's inconvenient, I can . . ."

Noelia smiled. "No, no. Stay. We don't get many visitors. I'll bring her out in a moment."

Henry thanked her, and was left alone. There were a few wooden chairs, a bench along one wall, and a long narrow dining table adorned with a festive tablecloth, covered in thick clear plastic, and stacked with old newspapers. In the far corner sat a chest topped with a few family photographs in dusty frames, and at the sight of them, Henry froze. He took a step toward the chest, stopped again, and took a step back.

When he described this moment during our interview, Henry felt it necessary to demonstrate his tentative dance for my benefit. He stood and stepped forward, back, forward, back. He wanted nothing more than to see the pictures, to examine them, one by one; to identify Rogelio as an infant, as a boy, as an adolescent, but he couldn't bring himself to do so. It had been more than a decade since he'd seen his old lover, and he had no real images with which to compare his memories. They'd never taken a picture together. Some of the wealthier inmates had their portraits painted, but neither Henry nor Rogelio had the money for that sort of thing. Meanwhile, this man had been coming to him in dreams since Diciembre left the city on tour. They rode together in Henry's taxi, sipped coffee down by the boardwalk. In one of these dreams, Rogelio appeared as a student at Henry's school, sitting uncomfortably at the tiny desk, frowning at an open book. As is often the case in dreams, it was the ordinariness of the images that made them so disconcerting, as if there were another life out there somewhere, one in which the two men lived side by side. This was what Henry was attempting to explain, and somehow, as he moved forward and back before me, I got a sense of his confusion. His uncertainty.

He couldn't stand to compare his memories or his dreams to the photos. What if he'd remembered incorrectly? What if his memory had tricked him?

So he sat on the bench instead, as far from the photographs as he could manage, facing in the opposite direction.

When Rogelio's mother finally came, or rather, when she was brought to him, he marveled at how small she was. He recalled that Rogelio had described her as a commanding presence, a woman with an exacting character and booming voice capable of frightening men; but time had faded all that, and what remained was something lighter, gentler. Her fair skin was nearly translucent and intricately wrinkled, like the texture of a piece of aluminum foil, crumpled, and then flattened again by hand. Her thin hair had gone completely white, and she was cloaked in what seemed like dozens of layers, a shawl atop a sweater atop a long-sleeve blouse atop another sweater. She wore knee-high wool socks pulled over a pair of sweatpants, and over that, a blue skirt that fell to the middle of her calves. She belonged to a culture and a generation that respected the cold above all else, a culture that did not trust warmth, but saw it as an occasional and temporary illusion. Cold is permanent, eternal, reliable. The day begins and ends with it.

I know this about her because my grandmother was the same way.

Mrs. Anabel greeted Henry formally, though in a feeble voice: "So you've seen my little Rogelio?"

Henry nodded.

"That's nice."

Noelia smiled. "Let's sit in the sun, shall we, Mama?"

The two women turned and went out into the bright afternoon. Noelia steered her mother through the garden with subtle, almost imperceptible movements. They covered the short distance slowly, pausing for a moment to admire one of the cats hiding in the brush. "Kitty, kitty, kitty," Mrs. Anabel said, and laughed girlishly to herself. Henry watched the two of them from the doorway, admiring their progress, until they were both seated in a pair of low wooden chairs set near an outdoor woodstove. He was so impressed by the delicacy of the maneuver—how carefully Noelia helped her mother into the seat—that he forgot to offer a hand. And they were so used to being ignored, so accustomed to doing it all themselves, that they hardly noticed his oversight. Belatedly, he stepped out to join them, and took the seat facing Mrs. Anabel, their knees almost touching. Noelia sat to his right, the unlit stove serving as the fourth side of their square.

At this point, everything was fine.

They sat in the sun, the three of them enjoying this last instant of calm. Then Noelia asked how he knew Rogelio, and Henry smiled.

It's true he was prepared to unburden himself.

"We met at Collectors," he said.

"What's that?" Noelia asked.

He let out a long sigh. "The prison. We shared a cell there, just before he died."

Then there was silence, long enough for Henry to realize something was terribly wrong. He saw it in their faces, in the way the women stared at him. Mrs. Anabel's eyes got very small, and he watched the color drain from the old woman's cheeks.

"I'm sorry," he said, because he didn't know what else to say.

Mrs. Anabel turned to her daughter. "Did he say *died*?"

There was terror in her voice.

"No, Mama."

"What does he mean?" She was speaking in a whisper now. Henry glanced toward the door, just a scamper across the courtyard. Five running steps, seven at most.

"There must be some mistake," Noelia said.

The early-afternoon sun was blinding.

"Rogelio is not in prison," said Noelia. "Rogelio is not dead."

"He isn't."

"He lives in California. He has for years."

There was something very hopeful in her tone.

"I know," Henry said, because he wanted more than anything to believe it. Maybe he'd gotten it all wrong. Maybe Rogelio *was* alive.

"Rogelio is a mechanic, like my brother Jaime. He lives outside Los Angeles."

"Los Angeles," Henry repeated.

Noelia paused. "Are we talking about the same person?"

Henry didn't—couldn't—answer.

"My Rogelio," said Mrs. Anabel, her voice cracking. "My baby." With every sentence she uttered, she seemed to be getting smaller and smaller, curving her back and sinking lower in her seat, as if attempting to disappear.

Suddenly Noelia got up and walked off.

For a moment, Henry was left alone with Mrs. Anabel. Her friendliness had all but vanished, and she seemed to cringe in his presence, as if she were afraid he might attack her. He closed his eyes against the bright sun, and tried to remember everything Rogelio had ever told him about this woman. His mother.

He came up blank.

Instead, he said this: "Everything's going to be fine."

She raised her eyes to look at him, but didn't respond.

Just then Noelia returned with a photo, one of the framed images that he'd been too frightened to look at before. She thrust it at Henry.

"Is this him?"

He bent his head toward the photo, using his sleeve to wipe the glass clean. He sat back with a start. It was the face of a young man, a boy. A miracle of a human being. The image was faded and old, but those were the same dashing brown eyes, the same narrow face and high forehead. The same Rogelio. He rubbed the glass some more, and smiled. He had to withstand the urge to jam the frame into the pocket of his coat and flee with it.

Mrs. Anabel and Noelia were waiting.

"No, this isn't him," Henry said. "I'm afraid I've made a mistake."

Noelia let out a breath.

"See, Mama? He doesn't know anything. He doesn't know what he's talking about."

"I've upset you both. I shouldn't have come."

"Call Jaime," said Mrs. Anabel. "I don't trust this one."

Noelia stood. "Don't worry, Mama. He's going now. Say good-bye."

Henry met Noelia's stare, and felt ashamed. He handed the photo to Mrs. Anabel, who accepted it without comment. There were tears welling in her eyes. With one hand she took hold of her daughter's arm, and was gently tugging at her sleeve, like a child demanding attention.

"Where is Rogelio?" she said. "I want to see Rogelio!"

"He's coming, Mama."

"Is he dead?"

"Of course he's not dead!"

Henry stood. There was nothing left to be done. He bent forward in a formal and exaggerated bow, drawing his hands behind his back so that Noelia and Mrs. Anabel wouldn't see them shaking.

"I beg your pardon," Henry said. "I'm very sorry to have disturbed you both. I'll see myself out."

. . .

HENRY HURRIED BACK to the hotel in a state of alarm. "I wanted to leave town right away," he told me later, but that was impossible. The bus that had brought them to T—— that morning had already returned to San Jacinto, and there would be no way out until the next morning. T—— felt menacing to him now; a place where people died and were never mourned. He'd thought a great deal about Rogelio in the previous weeks, thoughts which had only intensified since coming upon that map in the window in San Jacinto. He'd imagined many different versions of this encounter, wondering all the while if attempting to make this kind of peace with his former life was a sign of maturity or selfishness. I believe him when he says none of what came after was what he intended. It simply hadn't occurred to him that Rogelio's family would not know that their son was dead.

Henry went directly to the Imperial, where he convinced the owner to open the second floor veranda, and bring him a drink. There was only beer, but that was fine. It would do. Henry sat at a table overlooking the plaza, while the owner kept his distance, huddling in a far corner and listening to his transistor radio with the volume down low.

When Patalarga and Nelson appeared an hour later, Henry was halfway through his third beer. He wasn't exactly happy to see them, and would've preferred to be alone for a while longer. Still, he stood to greet his friends, and when he did, his glass tipped over. No one moved to catch it. The three of them watched it roll slowly and stop at the edge, while the beer spread over the surface of the table and then tumbled over in a long thin line.

"Graceful," said Patalarga.

Henry righted the glass, shook his fingers dry, and called for a towel.

"Leave it," the owner shouted from across the bar.

Henry wiped his hands on his jeans. It was midafternoon; the sun was high. The entire valley was bathed in light, and the streets of T—— looked like an unused stage set. It all gave him a headache.

"Well, what is it?" Henry said.

Nelson was fully recovered, or seemed so. He beamed with satisfaction. "We have a show tonight. The mayor is going to open up the auditorium for us."

"Tonight?"

Patalarga frowned. "Yes, tonight. This is good news, Henry."

"It was," he answered. "Two hours ago it was great news. But I'm not sure it's so good now."

Nelson and Patalarga waited for an explanation, but Henry had no idea where to begin. If he were just quiet long enough, he thought, maybe they could avoid the show altogether. His friends stared.

Finally he relented. "I went to see the family of an old friend of mine who died in Collectors."

"Okay," said Patalarga.

"That's why we're here. Why we came. But my friend's family, his mother, his sister—they had no idea he was dead. I upset them. They accused me of lying. They threw me out."

"They threw you out?" Nelson asked.

"Sort of."

The three friends were quiet for a moment.

Nelson seemed unconvinced. "And?"

It seemed so simple to Henry, so obvious.

"And I feel bad."

Nelson laughed in spite of himself, and turned to Patalarga. "He feels bad?"

Patalarga didn't answer, just shook his head and turned away.

"I don't expect you to understand," Henry said.

Nelson glared. "Why's that exactly? What don't I understand?"

"That I can't do the show."

"You're canceling?"

"Henry, you can't cancel," Patalarga said.

Henry crossed his arms over his chest. "I am. I just did."

What happened next surprised them all: Nelson pushed Henry with two hands, sending the playwright tumbling backward. One of the chairs tipped over with a crash, and the empty beer glass toppled over once more, this time landing on the floor.

Nelson stood over Henry, his face red with fury. Perhaps he was a fighter, after all.

Patalarga forced his way between them, as best he could, trying to calm Nelson down. It wasn't easy. "What's wrong with you? Why did you bring us here?" Nelson shouted. "What do you want from us?"

"I'd never seen him like that," Patalarga told me later.

He managed to push Nelson back, enough for Henry to get to

his feet. The playwright stood, straightened his shirt, and raised a hand to the startled owner. Then he faced Nelson, glaring. He took a deep breath. There was some swagger to him.

"Patalarga," he said. "Did I deserve that?"

"Honestly?"

Henry nodded.

"Yes."

Henry looked puzzled for a moment, then deflated. That flash of vigor vanished as quickly as it had come; he considered his friends, the empty veranda, the plaza before them, and felt small.

"You're wondering why," Nelson said, still scowling. "I'll tell you. You're being selfish. For a change."

Henry slumped into a chair. "Is it true?" he asked Patalarga, with searching eyes.

Patalarga nodded.

Henry rubbed his eyes. "Okay," he said. "You win. We'll do it."

AT ROGELIO'S CHILDHOOD HOME, the situation was deteriorating, and Noelia had begun to worry. This was the story these two women had been told, the story they knew: their beloved Rogelio had gone first to the city for work, then immigrated to the United States in 1984 at age twenty-one. Jaime told them all this, in broad strokes, with just enough detail to seem true. Rogelio had braved border crossings and skirted civil wars in Central America, negotiated Mexico by bus, and passed into the

United States through a tunnel in Nogales. Eventually he made it to the city of Los Angeles. As far as they knew, that's where he remained; and he hadn't returned to visit only because he had no papers. Jaime claimed to speak to him roughly once a year, and they believed him. Noelia had never doubted it; and as for Mrs. Anabel, she held on to the idea with fierce resolve. Every year for her younger son's birthday, she'd baked him a cake.

If Mrs. Anabel's gullibility on this count seems far-fetched, remember this was T——: the rows of padlocked houses are all the context one needs. In another place it might strain credulity, but here nothing could be more normal than Rogelio disappearing for seventeen years, and still being thought of as *alive*. My father still speaks warmly of people he hasn't seen or heard from in forty-five years, and by the tone of his voice you might expect them to appear tomorrow and renew their unbreakable friendship. Time means something very different in a place like T——. As does distance. As does memory. Almost every family had a son who'd gone off into the world. Some sent money; some vanished without a trace. Until proof to the contrary was offered, they were all to be thought of as living. It was the town's unspoken credo.

The truth about Rogelio's fate, the story Henry shared, had upset this balance. Mrs. Anabel was the most affected, naturally; even on a good day, dementia made her subject to mood swings she was unable to control. But that afternoon, the very thought of Rogelio dead threw her into a panic, and not long after Henry had gone, she was weeping with rage and helplessness.

"She kept calling for Rogelio, for her baby," Noelia told me later. "I didn't know what to do. If he was dead, why had no one told her? Shouldn't a mother always know these things? Why had no one told *me*?"

A few minutes before three, she managed to give her mother a sedative and coax her back to bed. This was not easy. She deflected all questions about Rogelio until the old woman was asleep, then Noelia pried open the door to the street and hurried into town. If Henry, Patalarga, and Nelson had not been caught up in their own discussion, they might have seen her rushing across the plaza, one hand clutching the hem of her skirt so as not to drag its edge across the cobblestones.

It was a little after three in the afternoon when she finally got her brother Jaime on the line. She tried to explain it as best she could, but she herself didn't quite understand what had happened, why this stranger had appeared out of nowhere, talking about their Rogelio. Jaime didn't seem to get it either, or pretended not to, and finally Noelia lost her patience. She changed tacks, stopped trying to explain.

"Why didn't you tell me?"

The sound of her own voice startled her. Her hands were shaking. She hadn't shouted in years.

On the other end of the line, there was silence. Then: "About what?"

"About Rogelio," she said.

She could hear Jaime's long sigh. "Does Mama know?"

"She's in terrible shape."

"I'm on my way," he said. A moment later he'd hung up.

Jaime got in his car and arrived by early evening, just as the yellow lights in the plaza were flickering to life, and just as Diciembre was preparing to go onstage before a few dozen audience members in the municipal auditorium. Nelson had won the argument, perhaps the first time in the history of Diciembre that Henry had lost one.

It was June 12, 2001. As it turned out, this would be the troupe's last show together. Though they didn't know it yet, Diciembre's first tour in fifteen years was over.

13

THE PREPARATIONS for Diciembre's performance in T——
began around five, when the mayor's deputy, a cheerful high
school student in his last year, unlocked the municipal auditorium. The deputy's name was Eric. He was young and fresh-
faced, and he'd be leaving T—— within a few months.

"This is it!" he said brightly.

"This is it," repeated Nelson, whistling a long, fading note to
himself. He dropped his end of the heavy duffel bag, and considered the space before him.

The auditorium was one of the town's newer buildings, a
charmless and impractical metal box that stayed cold in the
rainy season and hot in the dry. It had been underutilized for
years, suffering from a neglect that reminded Diciembre of their
spiritual home, the Olympic. Eric left them just inside the door,
and slid along the wall to the raised stage. There, he disappeared
behind a curtain and began to turn on the lights, first one row,
then another, then a few at once, and so on. Henry, Patalarga,
and Nelson stood with arms crossed, watching the fluorescent

tubes above hum on and now off, in various combinations. None cast a particularly pleasing light on the dank space, but the young man finally settled on the arrangement that was the least offensive.

"How's this?" he called out from behind the curtain.

Henry held his hands out in front of him, fingers spread. His white presidential gloves were a grayish yellow.

"It's terrific," said Patalarga.

They carried their things backstage, and began to unpack and then change, each man floating to different corners of the dressing area, hardly speaking. Henry was brooding; Nelson seemed distracted; Patalarga fretted about his costume. Somehow his clothes didn't feel right, he said to no one in particular. Had they shrunk, or had he put on weight? There was no mirror, so they had to rely on each other, which might have worked if they'd been in a different collective mood. But they weren't. The three of them dressed sloppily, and scarcely spoke. At six-thirty, Henry convened a brief meeting to go over some rough spots in the play, but this was entirely unnecessary, of course. What rough spots was he referring to exactly? What surprises could the performance hold at this point? Still, Nelson and Patalarga listened to Henry's rambling instructions out of respect and a sense of duty. He might have gone on longer, but soon the people began shuffling in, and the three men fell into a reverent silence. It's a sound every actor loves, and, in a sense, lives for: the murmur of a crowd, the patter of feet, hum of strange voices. You perk up in excitement, anticipation. You begin to imagine who your audience will be, what they will look like. Before you ever cast eyes on them, they are real people. Before you ever see them, you are connected.

Around seven-fifteen, Eric appeared again. He poked his head behind the curtain and announced it was about time to begin.

"How many are out there?" asked Henry.

"Thirty or so," the young man said. "Thirty-five, I'd guess."

Henry shook his head. "Don't guess. Go back and count them."

Eric bowed his head, and returned a few moments later with downcast eyes. "Twenty-five. I'm sorry. But there may be more coming."

Patalarga grinned, and thanked the boy. Eric's disappointment was touching. He'd played for audiences far smaller. "We'll begin in a minute."

Eric nodded, and just as he was turning to go, Henry stopped him.

"Just one more question," the playwright said. "Do you know everyone in this town?"

"Just about."

"Good. So, is Noelia out there? Or her mother, Mrs. Anabel? Do you know who I'm talking about?"

The young man looked confused. "Yes. Why?"

"They're old friends," said Nelson. Until that moment, you wouldn't have guessed he was listening at all. He and Henry locked eyes.

Eric nodded, as if he understood. "Well, Mrs. Anabel doesn't really leave the house much."

"So she's not here?"

"I haven't seen her. Not Noelia either."

Henry thanked him, and the deputy disappeared on the other side of the curtain.

"Are you expecting them?" Patalarga asked. "Do you want them to come?"

"I don't know." Henry looked genuinely puzzled. "I really don't know."

A few moments later, the curtains parted, and the show began.

THE DRIVE from San Jacinto to T—— is roughly four hours. You can shave a little off that, but not much. The road is narrow and the consequences of misjudging a turn in the high mountains are fatal. Still, Jaime made good time. Of the protagonists in these events, he's one of the few that has refused to speak to me, but I can imagine what he was thinking as he drove along those narrow, twisting roads. He was thinking of his brother, Rogelio, and the facts of his death. Whether Rogelio was angry when he died, or scared. Whether Rogelio blamed him, or felt abandoned. He was thinking how often he'd made this trip, and how it never changed. The scale of the mountains. The smallness of everything else. He'd known about Rogelio's death all along, and kept his younger brother's imprisonment a secret, just as he kept the nature of his business a secret. This was easier than you might expect. In T——, the riot and subsequent massacre at Collectors had never made much of an impact.

Jaime arrived around the time Diciembre was coming out onstage. At this point, the story of that night moves along parallel tracks: Patalarga appears beneath the pallid yellow lights, before a small but expectant crowd. He opens with a monologue about loneliness, delivered on this particular night with greater feeling than ever. The mayor's young deputy stands at the auditorium's back wall, wearing a dark suit and watching the proceedings with relish. He reports that the crowd was entranced. ("We'd never had a theater company in town before," he told me later.) At the same time, Jaime rushes to the home where he was raised, embraces his sister, and hurries behind her to their mother's room. Brother and sister stand in the doorway and watch their mother sleep, listening for her shallow breaths. Without exchanging a word, they marvel at her fragility, the way one might contemplate a newborn. Jaime steps forward, to her bedside, and places a palm on his mother's forehead. He strokes her hair.

"She was very upset?" he asks Noelia.

His sister answers with a nod.

By the time Henry steps out onto the stage, looking slightly less presidential than usual—by then, Jaime and his sister, Noelia, are sitting in the living room, going over the details of a very well-kept family secret. Not much is said about Rogelio's unfortunate arrest. Collectors is described in shorthand—hell, Jaime says. And everything after that can be reduced to a single sentence. Their little brother was dead. He'd been dead so long now it felt almost dishonest to mourn him.

All afternoon, since Henry's visit, Noelia had known it was

true. She'd known it as she put her frantic mother to bed, as she raced across the plaza, as she waited for her brother to arrive. A stranger does not appear and announce a death by mistake. Very few people are cruel in this way, and Henry had not struck her as cruel. He'd looked at the photo of Rogelio and claimed not to know him—and it was this act of mercy which made her like him, in spite of everything. It was also the moment that had confirmed his story.

For an actor, this man was not a good liar.

"Why didn't you tell me?" she asked her brother, the one she still had left.

But Jaime didn't answer. He wanted to know one thing. "Who told you? Who was this person?"

"He said his name was Henry," Noelia answered.

"And where is he?"

"At the auditorium. They told me in town he was in a play tonight."

"A play?" Jaime frowned. There was a moment of silence, and then: "I'm going to kill him. I'm going to kill that faggot motherfucker."

Noelia looked up. There was hatred in his eyes. She understood then that her brother knew this stranger, this Henry. And it frightened her. She began to cry. Her brother watched her without speaking. He didn't reach out to her, and Noelia attempted to cry quietly, so as not to disturb him.

They spent many minutes like this, but by a quarter to eight, Jaime was unclenching his jaw, drawing his creaky wooden chair closer to his sister, and telling her he was sorry. These were not words he said every day. She bowed her head, wiped her tears, and accepted his apology.

"What will we tell mother?" she said.

"Nothing," Jaime answered. "We won't be telling her a goddamn thing."

They left shortly after, closing the door carefully so as not to wake Mrs. Anabel. It was a cold night, and the quarter moon was just beginning to rise above the edge of the mountains. By the time they passed through the doors of the municipal auditorium, Diciembre had come to my favorite scene in *The Idiot President*. In it, the president is having his correspondence read aloud. The letters come from the country's citizens, and they all begin with a long list of fairly standard honorifics: Your Highness, Your Honor, Your Benevolence. The president listens (or pretends to listen) to the appeals—pleas for work, for relief, for mercy, for land, for refuge—but he is unmoved. His posture is regal, his bearing severe. "Statuesque," says the note in the script. Alejo, Nelson's character, the idiot son, and Patalarga's, the servant, take turns reading one letter each, while the president files his nails and brushes his hair. Over the course of the scene, a kind of competition arises between the son and the servant. Who can read better? Who can make this routine act more pleasing and more interesting to the president? Henry's character, naturally, doesn't notice at all, or pretends not to notice, but we do: the idiot son and the servant shoot each other angry, jealous looks and begin to read over each other, interrupting. The lists of honorifics preceding each letter becomes longer, and more ridiculous, until it's clear that Alejo and the servant are simply making them up. Their voices grow louder, and the increasingly bizarre titles are delivered rapid-fire—

"*To our dear leader, personification of the nation's purest desires!*

To the bright sun of liberty, most high and most alarming!

To the most chaste and supreme one, munificent, magnificent, and beneficent!"

—words tumbling out and overlapping, until it's just a jumble, no longer discernible words but only noise.

"They watched the whole scene without sitting," Eric told me. "I noticed them because Henry had asked me about Noelia."

What were they thinking?

Or more specifically, what was Jaime thinking?

Though he'd lived in San Jacinto for more than two decades, Rogelio's older brother was a well-known figure in town. He'd done well for himself, made money—and nothing earned the people's respect like money. That night of the play in T——, he stood beside his sister with his arms crossed, squinting at the stage, staring intently at Henry. He hadn't seen the playwright in fifteen years, but he knew it was him. He had no trouble recognizing that face, those gestures, that posture.

According to Henry, they'd met only once, in Collectors, a scene I imagine Jaime was playing over in his mind. A winter's day in 1986, in the yard of Block Seven. Jaime had come from San Jacinto to see his brother. He spent a few hours with Rogelio, strolling up and down the yard. Seen from a distance, they were like fish caught in a current, Rogelio and Jaime and all the others. Henry had been watching them all afternoon. Then visitors' hours were almost over, and as the two brothers were saying their good-byes, Henry couldn't resist any longer. "I'm not sure why or how," he told me later, "it just came out." Perhaps he was hurt that he hadn't been introduced, though he found that hard to admit. He barreled toward them now, furious, protective, jealous, catching both brothers by surprise.

This is what he said to Jaime that afternoon in 1986, in a voice far too loud for Collectors:

"You need to take better care of your brother."

Jaime frowned. "I'm sorry?"

"You owe him that. I know what you do."

"Who's this?" Jaime asked his brother.

"No one," said Rogelio.

There was no time for that betrayal to sting. Henry had already gone too far. "It doesn't matter who I am. I know who you are. You're the reason he's in here."

Jaime glared at this stranger. To his brother, he said, "Get this idiot away from me."

"That's enough, Henry."

It was more than enough, but he couldn't stop. He was shouting now: "You have the money. I know what you do!"

Jaime shook his head, then he threw a punch at Henry, landing it on his jaw. Henry staggered and fell. Jaime threw an arm around Rogelio, and together they walked to the gate of Block Seven. Jaime never visited Collectors again. Rogelio didn't speak to Henry for three days.

Now, onstage at T——'s municipal auditorium, the president accepted tribute from his son and his servant. As the scene devolved into noise, Jaime and Noelia found a place to sit.

"Who is he?" Noelia whispered to her older brother, but Jaime didn't respond.

For Noelia, the next forty minutes were something of a revelation. She'd never seen a play before, except the ones the schoolchildren put on every spring to commemorate the founding of the town. This particular play wasn't necessarily easy to follow, and as the scenes barreled toward their conclusion, she began to wonder about the young lead. He was handsome, she thought, and it occurred to her he was the same age as Rogelio had been the last time she saw him. That was all. It was an idle thought. They didn't look alike; it's just that Nelson was an odd sight in a place like T——. He was a young man in his twenties with a drifting gaze and bad posture. He looked lost, and perhaps this is why she thought of her missing, suddenly dead, brother.

Perhaps it was something else; when pressed, Noelia admitted she didn't really know. "There was something about him," she said, and that was all she could manage.

Meanwhile Jaime sat by her side, stone-faced. The actors floated back and forth across the stage, recited their lines, made their jokes, and the audience laughed, or shouted with joy, or fell into a meditative hush. Jaime was unmoved. The play's climax, when Nelson's character chats up the servant, tricks him, and then kills him—this was particularly powerful that evening, and the audience responded with gasps that could be heard all over that chilly auditorium. According to Eric, there were even some tears. When asked if it was Diciembre's best performance of the tour, Patalarga was unequivocal. "Of course," he told me. "Nelson's anger that night was real. And Henry's despair was too."

Noelia agreed: "It gave me chills."

The play ended ten minutes before nine in the evening, to sustained applause.

There was no one to close the curtain, so the three actors spent a moment onstage, smiling and waving at the audience. Then the clapping died down, and most of those in attendance headed toward the exit. But not everyone. Not Jaime. He stood, lingered in place for a moment, rocking side to side almost imperceptibly and never taking his eyes off the stage.

"Are you all right?" Noelia asked.

Her brother nodded.

"Should we go, then?"

"Not yet."

"Please," said Noelia. "Don't hurt anyone."

Jaime turned to her then. There was a look in his eyes that she couldn't place, almost like pity.

Then he walked straight forward, pushing through the metal folding chairs that stood between him and the performers. I imagine something akin to a parting of the waters, the chairs clanging this way and that, Jaime cutting a rough path through them with long, heavy steps. Eric, still lingering along the wall, thought the gesture was rude, but chose not to say anything. It was Jaime, after all. You didn't say anything to Jaime.

Nelson, Patalarga, and Henry had begun to gather their props: the scattered letters; the presidential scarf used to mimic a hanging in the third scene and then tossed off to the side at the beginning of the second act; the flimsy but surprisingly realistic plastic knife used in the murder scene. The houselights had come on, but they were weak, and none of the actors noticed Jaime until he was standing before the stage. He called Henry by name. Noelia hadn't moved from her seat. She saw the whole thing.

"He said something to the president, the one who'd come to see us."

Henry knelt down until they were almost at eye level with each other. They exchanged a few words.

"I saw my brother nodding. Then I saw the president's expression drop. He was facing me, you see. He went pale. My brother grabbed him by the collar, pulled him from the stage, and tossed him to the floor." She paused and took a deep breath. "At that point everything got very confusing."

From the corner of his eye, Patalarga saw Henry tip off the stage. "My first thought was that he'd fallen, that it was an accident." He hadn't really paid much attention to the man Henry was talking to, but then he heard a shout.

Jaime had Henry on his back (once more, all these years later), but this time, he got six or seven good kicks in before anyone could respond. "I jumped off the stage and tried to grab the guy, but he shook me off," Patalarga told me later. "It was the second time in five hours that I'd had to defend Henry." For his trouble, he caught an elbow to the face.

Patalarga lunged at Jaime again, and by this time Nelson and Eric had rushed over too; together they were able to pull him away. Jaime was shouting, struggling against them, but no one seems to recall what he was yelling.

They all remember Henry though, the shock of him: the president lay on the floor, writhing and covering his face with his bloodied white gloves. His lip was busted, his nose broken. There was blood on his chin, and though he didn't know it yet, two of his ribs were cracked. He lay on his back, taking shallow breaths; after a moment, he opened his eyes. The lights above blurred in and out of focus.

And all the while, Noelia sat frozen in her seat. It was extraordinary, the weight she felt, the absolute impossibility of moving. She held her hands tightly in her lap, and gave in to it. Everyone else had gone. This was all part of the play, an extra scene performed just for her, as if to reveal some special secret. This was why they all fear my brother, Noelia remembers thinking. This is why they're scared of him. Maybe those stories she'd heard were true, after all.

Nelson, Patalarga, and Eric held Jaime, while Henry got to his feet, holding the edge of the stage to steady himself. The prop knife was there, just an arm's length away, and he grabbed it. With that, Henry turned to face his attacker once more, brandishing it with surprising conviction.

"Come on!" Henry shouted. He was manic, dancing back and forth, and carving the air with his plastic knife. His voice echoed through the nearly empty auditorium. "Come on, you asshole!"

For all Henry's fury, there was no threat in the spectacle. Jaime eased, and his captors instinctively relaxed with him. They still held him, but without the same force or fear or urgency. Patalarga was afraid his old friend might faint before them.

"Okay," Jaime said. "Enough. If I wanted to kill this piece of shit, I would've done it already."

He shook himself free. Eric, Nelson, and Patalarga backed off.

At that, Henry stopped. Out of breath, he dropped both arms to his side, still gripping the knife in his left hand. He and Jaime locked eyes.

"Tell me you remember me now," Jaime said. "Go ahead. Think real hard."

Henry nodded. "You're Rogelio's brother."

"Good," said Jaime.

Henry bowed his head. He dropped the plastic knife, and with his sleeve wiped a thin line of blood from his chin. "I'm sorry for your loss."

Jaime raised an eyebrow. "Are you?"

Noelia was still pegged to her seat, watching it all. Henry called out in her direction: "I'm sorry! I'm very sorry!"

It was at this point that she finally snapped to. It was not a play after all; it was real, and once again that strange man was talking to her. His voice, shouted across the auditorium, was ghostly. She stood, and as she rearranged her shawl, noted that they were all looking at her: these men, her brother, the actors, the mayor's deputy. She took a deep breath and walked down the path Jaime had made only a few moments before, through the carelessly strewn metal chairs, to the foot of the stage, where the lights shone brightest. As she got closer, it was as if the air changed. There was heat pulsing off these men, the lingering remains of the fight. She saw Henry up close and gasped. His right eye had begun to swell, and his shirt was ripped at the collar. He leaned against the stage, as if he might tumble over at any moment.

She turned to her brother.

"Shame on you!"

Jaime shrugged and looked down at his hands, his knuckles, the way one might admire a well-built tool or a machine.

There was quiet.

MUCH LATER I asked Henry about that night. This was back in the city, months after the events recounted here had run their course. I was trying to piece it all together based on versions provided by Patalarga, Noelia, and to a lesser extent, Eric. As for Henry, his recollections were cloudy. He talked at great length about his recovery, the slow easing of pain over the weeks that followed that night; but the play, the fight, its immediate aftermath, that, he said, was all a blur.

Instead he talked about fight scenes in general. The fake kind. He talked about how they are staged; and he seemed more comfortable speaking this way, in the abstract. Like any scene involving large numbers of cast members, Henry told me, fight scenes are complicated and unwieldy. A good one must mimic chaos without being chaotic, must be confusing without being confused. The crowd must delight in the tension, while the actors themselves are perfectly relaxed. Henry ran his fingers through his hair, and leaned forward, briefly animated, evidently pleased with this series of contradictory phrases. Did I get it? Did I understand?

And I began to wonder if he saw it all as a performance. If that night, when the play ended and the attack began; when his past, as represented by Jaime, stood before him, and his friends demanded answers; at that point, was he conscious of himself as a performer?

"I don't know," he said. "Jaime kicked the shit out of me. I fell to the ground. I grabbed a plastic knife. I wanted to defend myself. I wanted someone to save me. Is this performing?"

"I'm asking you."

Henry rubbed his face. He stood from his seat, and raised his shirt with his left hand. "There were bruises here," he said, pointing to his stomach and chest. "And here. And here. These two ribs"—he pinched one and then the other—"these two were broken."

"I know. That's not my question. I didn't say you were faking it."

He frowned. "So what are you asking, then?"

"When it was over, were you aware that a delicate negotiation had begun? Were you careful as you were playing it?"

"Of course I was careful. I was scared this man might kill me."

That night, Jaime wore a grimace, aloof and distant. He wasn't handsome, Patalarga told me later, but he had "an interesting face." His too-small mouth stayed closed, lips pressed together with the hint of a smile. People were afraid of him and he enjoyed that. His sleek black hair had gone wild in the skirmish, but he didn't mind.

"I guess we were expecting him to say something," Patalarga said, "but he didn't."

Instead, it was Noelia who spoke, addressing her brother: "Do they know too?" she asked, her voice desperate. "Do they know Rogelio is dead? Does everyone know but me?"

Patalarga responded. "Madam, I can assure you we don't know anything."

She looked at them all skeptically. Her brother and Henry nodded.

"Just to be clear, Rogelio is . . . ?" asked Nelson.

"My little brother," Noelia said.

"My cell mate," said Henry. "My friend."

The six of them made a wary circle, with Jaime pushing in close so they could feel the threat of him. Eric fidgeted. Nelson picked the plastic knife off the floor, and wiped its flimsy blade against his leg. It was Eric who told me this detail: he found it was almost tender, the way the actor cared for this prop, the way he wiped the blade as if it were real. During the performance, when Alejo murders the servant, Eric had been impressed. He remembers thinking: He looks like he could use it, and for next few minutes, Eric said, while they all spoke, Nelson held the knife at the ready, as if he might.

"How's your mother now?" Henry asked.

"She was in a fit all afternoon," Noelia answered. "I had to give her a sedative, the poor thing."

"She's ill?" asked Patalarga.

"She was fine until he came," Jaime said.

Noelia interrupted. "No. No no no no no. That isn't true, Jaime. It just isn't." Her shoulders were shaking now. "Mama's been faltering. She doesn't remember. She talks to our father all the time and he's been dead for years. She doesn't know the difference. But when you said Rogelio was dead . . . Well, you know what happened."

"I'm sorry," Henry said, not for the last time.

Noelia wiped a tear from her eye, and sighed. Henry would have offered her the presidential handkerchief, only it was dotted with blood. They were silent, out of respect for a woman's tears.

"How did my brother die?" she asked finally.

Henry offered a weak smile, and would've answered, but Jaime spoke instead. "There was trouble, that's all."

His face was blank, impassive, and Noelia didn't press him any further. She looked up, trying to catch his attention, but he had his eyes locked on Henry.

"What do you want from me?" Henry asked. "Why are you looking at me like that?"

The conversation was Jaime's once more. He pressed his hands together, palms flat.

"Why were you in that prison, Henry? Will you tell my sister that? I'd like her to know the kind of person you are."

Henry shrugged. "I was accused of terrorism."

"Falsely," added Patalarga.

Jaime smiled. "So this terrorist comes to my house, to my family, and tells my mother awful things. Things I never wanted her to hear. She's sick. She isn't well."

"I'm sorry."

"I know you are. Here's what I want. I want you to tell my mother you were wrong. That you made a mistake. That this was all a misunderstanding." His eyes narrowed, and there was anger in his voice. "I want you to say you're very sorry, and I want you to convince that poor woman that this was all your fault, and leave her mind at peace. I want her to have no doubt that her youngest child is alive."

"I told her that already," Henry said.

"It didn't work."

Patalarga shook his head. "Look at him. Do you really think that going back to her, looking like that, is going to help anything?"

"Put some makeup on him. She won't even notice."

"Jaime, be reasonable," said Noelia.

"I am reasonable. He comes. He apologizes. He goes."

"I'm apologizing now."

Jaime shook his head. "You apologize to her. Is this too much to ask?"

Henry dropped his head into his chest. "No," he said.

14

THAT NIGHT IN T——, after Jaime and Noelia had gone; after the props had been put away, and the auditorium padlocked; after Eric had said good night; Diciembre trudged back to the Imperial. Everything in town was shuttered, and no one was out. When they got to the hotel, it was as if the man at the front desk had already heard what had happened. He handed them the key with a sad shake of the head.

The three friends went up to their room. The mood was funereal. Without much talk, they prepared for the long trip back to the coast. Henry began by removing the red presidential sash, the presidential eye mask, the white presidential gloves, which were no longer white. These items were all folded and packed away. The presidential dress shirt too, its ruffles now spotted with drops of blood. Patalarga followed: he pulled off the smock he'd worn almost every night for the previous months, untied the colorful pants cinched at the waist with rope, and removed his rubber sandals. Then, Nelson: the riding boots and pants, a wig he wore briefly in the third act. From his bag, he pulled a set of hand cymbals, played by the servant in one key scene, a flourish offered whenever the president wanted one of his own witty statements celebrated. "You sure you don't want to keep those out for later?" Patalarga said, but no one was in the mood for jokes. The fake knife was put away as well, wrapped in an old pair of socks, as if its plastic blade needed protecting. It was a simple production, really; everything was packed away in a matter of minutes.

Then Henry found his way back to the window.

"Let's go out," he said after staring at the plaza for a while. "Can we go out?" and to his surprise, his friends were not opposed. It was early yet, and none were ready to sleep. They seemed to know instinctively that if they stayed indoors, the gloom might overcome them; so they headed out, into the night and toward the school, the same direction that Patalarga and Nelson had gone only a few hours before.

When they were nearing the edge of the town, crossing one of the bridges toward the fields, Henry began to talk. It might have been less an apology, and more a listing of regrets—but it was something, and this was important. It was a start. Nelson and Patalarga listened. We never should have revived his moribund play, Henry said. Another one, perhaps, but why *this* play, which carried with it so many ghosts? This play, which had caused nothing but trouble since it had been written? He went on: we never should have gone on tour, never should have left the city, where we were safe, or interrupted our lives with these quixotic aspirations toward theater, toward art. He spoke with great feeling, but there was a fallacy at the center of his logic.

The idea to revive the play had not been his but Patalarga's. The idea to take Diciembre out on tour once more—he'd had to be convinced, after all, and the one who'd done that convincing was Patalarga.

"I told them it was my fault," said Patalarga. "I wanted to take that burden off Henry. He was eating himself alive."

Of their walk that night, Patalarga remembers most clearly the sky, indigo graced with stars. Clouds had followed them everywhere throughout their travels; they'd suffered cold rain and hail, but now, here was their reward.

"You should've told us about Rogelio," Patalarga said.

He wanted this to come out differently than it did: he hadn't intended it to be a complaint but an affirmation of solidarity. He didn't feel betrayed, or even disappointed; only confused. For years, Henry had insisted on believing that he was alone. He'd refused help, refused counsel. His marriage had fallen apart. His life had stalled. It was painful to watch.

"What I mean is, you could have. We would've listened."

Henry nodded. "Thank you," he said, but he was very far away.

The cold was tolerable; you could even say it was invigorating. They'd come to the school, just five classrooms and an office arranged around a barren courtyard, beyond which lay the vast planted fields of T——. There was a low concrete retaining wall at the edge of a rusting playground, and here, Nelson and Henry sat. Patalarga had his back to them, his eyes trained on the town they'd left behind. Without realizing it, and without much effort, they'd risen in elevation, just enough to sense the faintest glow of light from the plaza. This place is so very small, Patalarga thought. It could be erased in a moment, and it would be as if none of this had ever happened. Not the play. Not this evening. Not Rogelio, or any of us. It would all be a rumor from a far-off place, something folded into the long history of that which has been forgotten. Somehow, Patalarga found this thought comforting.

He turned to share this mundane insight with his friends, and noticed, to his surprise, that they were holding hands. He couldn't tell if it had just happened, or if they'd walked a long way like this without his noticing. Nor could he say who had reached out for whom, who'd offered comfort and who'd accepted it; but in a sense, it didn't matter.

Patalarga turned away. He sat on the wall, and kept his eyes trained skyward. When he looked again, his friends had let go.

But for a light breeze, the valley was almost silent.

"Do you want to know?" Henry said.

"Know what?" Nelson asked.

"What he was like. Who he was." Henry sighed. "I'll tell you. If you want to know, I'll tell you."

ROGELIO WAS THE YOUNGEST OF THREE, the skinniest, the least talkative. As a boy he slept with Jaime in the same room, and his earliest, most profoundly comforting memories were of those late nights, before bed: the chatter between them, the camaraderie. Then Jaime left for San Jacinto, and shortly afterward, when Rogelio was eight, his father died. In the months afterward, Rogelio began to skip school and spend hours walking in the hills above town. He liked to be alone. He gathered bits of wood, and used his father's tools to carve tiny animals, birds, lizards, that sort of thing, which he kept in a box under his bed. They weren't particularly lifelike, but were surprisingly evocative, and at age twelve, he presented one to a girl he liked, as a gift. Her name was Alma. With trembling hands and a look of horror on her face, she accepted it, and for the next week she avoided his gaze. The other children whispered about him whenever he came near. There was no need to hear the exact words, for their meaning was clear enough. Alma's family came from the northwest district. The following year, at age thirteen, Rogelio quit school officially, and his mother and older brother agreed there was no practical reason for him to stay in T—— any longer; so he left for San Jacinto, to join Jaime.

Rogelio was small for his age, but tough, good with his hands and his fists. Unlike his older brother, he didn't have a temper, but instead possessed an equanimity the entire family found almost disconcerting. He'd been shunned all his life, or that's how he felt, and he'd grown accustomed to it. He loved his brother, looked up to him, and never worried whether Jaime loved him in return. He was trusting. He could follow instructions, had decent mechanical intuition, but he could not read. Jaime even tried to teach him, but soon gave up: the boy kept getting his letters backward. A decade later in Collectors, Henry would be the first person to tell him there was a condition called dyslexia.

"How about that?" Rogelio had said, but his face registered nothing—not regret or shame or even curiosity—as if he were unwilling to contemplate the ways his life might have been different if he'd had this information sooner.

For those first couple of years in San Jacinto, he worked on the broken-down trucks his brother bought on the cheap, and together they would cajole these heaps of rusting metal back to life. Each machine was different, requiring a complex and patient kind of surgery. Parts were swapped out, rescued, jerry-rigged. It was as much invention as it was repair. When a truck was reborn, they sold it, and reinvested the profits, which weren't much at first, but the brothers were very careful with their money, and not ostentatious. Henry recalled a photograph he saw, one of the few that remained from that era, which Rogelio had tacked onto the wall by his bed: in it, Rogelio is lithe, wiry, sitting on a gigantic truck tire with his shirt off. He wears the blank expression of a child who asks no questions and makes no demands of the world. I never saw this photo—it was buried beneath the rubble of the prison—but I can imagine it: not a happy boy, but given his situation, perhaps a wise one.

Eventually Jaime bought his kid brother a motorbike, the kind outfitted with a flatbed of wooden planks in front. This machine became Rogelio's source of income for the next few years; he drove it across town, from one market to another, carrying cans of paint, lashed-together bundles of metal pipes, chickens headed for slaughter, crammed in pens stacked so high he had to lean to one side in order to steer. San Jacinto was growing steadily, but not yet at the torrid pace that would later come to define it; Rogelio knew every corner of the city then, and years later, in Collectors, he'd drawn a map of it on the walls of the cell he shared with Henry. He used white chalk to trace the streets, the railroad tracks, and even labeled the old apartment he'd shared with his brother.

Henry asked him why he'd gone to the trouble.

"Because one day I'll go back there," Rogelio said.

("See," Henry added, when he told me this. He had a wry, almost pained smile. "I guess our love story would've ended anyway.")

In 1980, the year Rogelio turned seventeen, his brother took him to a brothel near the center of town. It was the first of its kind, and had been built for the hoped-for wave of young, fearless men with money. There were rumors, even then, of gold in the hills, and the brothel's fantastical anteroom paid tribute to those still-unconfirmed stories. The walls were painted gold, as was the bar, as were the wooden tables and chairs. In fact, that night even the three prostitutes on display for Rogelio's choosing had followed the color scheme: one in a gold miniskirt, another in gold lace panties and bra, and a third in a gold negligee. Three little made-up trophies, all smiling coquettishly, hands on their hips. Jaime encouraged Rogelio to choose, but he couldn't. Or wouldn't. The moment stretched on and on, far past what was comfortable, until the girls' put-on smiles began to fade. And still the boy stood there, immobilized, amazed.

"Oh, fuck it," Jaime said finally. He pulled a wad of bills from his pocket, and paid for all three.

It seems that Jaime had begun to sell more than just refurbished vehicles.

"He told you this?" Nelson asked Henry that night they sat by the school in T——, and the playwright shrugged.

"There was nothing to do inside but talk."

When Rogelio was eighteen, he traded in his motorized cart for a small loading van, and shortly after, he traded that in for a truck he bought himself, and brought back to life with his own hands. The first time the reconstructed engine turned over was one of the proudest moments of Rogelio's life. Each new vehicle expanded his world. Now he was a driver; he ferried a dozen laborers down to the lowlands, men who stood for hours without complaint as the truck bounced along the rutted and bumpy roads. Once there, Rogelio discovered a prickly kind of heat he'd never felt before. He began volunteering to drive that route whenever it was available. The following year, his brother sent him in the other direction, over the range to the west; and on that trip, Rogelio first saw the ocean. It was 1982; he was almost twenty years old. He remembered sitting along the edge of the boardwalk in La Julieta, along the bluffs overlooking the sea; not far, incidentally, from the spot where Nelson would let Ixta walk away and out of his life nineteen years later. The fancy people of the city strolled by, confident-looking men in blazers and women in bright dresses, boys he took to be his age, but who appeared to possess a variety of secrets that Rogelio could only guess at. None so much as glanced in his direction. He wondered if he looked out of place, if they could tell he was a stranger here, or if they could even see him at all. But when he considered the ocean, Rogelio realized how insignificant these concerns were. He was happy, he told Henry, and later, in Collectors, he liked to re-member the hours he'd spent there, staring at the sea.

For the next few years, he drove the route to the coast, to the lowlands, and back again, carrying vegetables to the city, raw materials to the mountains, laborers to the jungle. He was a quiet young man, still a boy in some ways, but Jaime trusted him. He was dependable. He began to ferry other packages as well, small, tightly bundled bricks, which he kept under the seat or in a compartment hidden above the wheel well. One or two at first, then dozens. These were delivered separately, to other con-tacts. Rogelio never opened them to see what was inside (though he knew); he never touched the money (though he assumed the quantities in play were not insubstantial). He had no qualms about this work. He trusted his brother. He never considered the consequences, not because he was reckless, but because what he was doing was normal. Everyone was doing it. He was only dimly aware that it was not allowed.

Nelson found this hard to believe, as did I. In fact, Henry had too: How could Rogelio not have known?

Well, he knew; but he didn't *know*.

On the last of these trips, Rogelio's truck was searched at a checkpoint along the Central Highway, sixty-five kilometers east of the capital. The war was on, and the soldiers were search-ing for weapons and explosives, randomly stopping trucks from the mountains to have a look. Rogelio was very unlucky. Perhaps if he'd been more astute, he could have arranged to pay off the police, but he didn't. Instead he waited by the side of the road while the men in uniform went through his vehicle with great care. Young Rogelio had time to consider what was happening, how his life was changing course before his very eyes. Not everyone has this privilege; most of us lose sight of the moment when our destiny shifts. He told Henry he felt a strange sort of calm. He might have run into the hills, but the soldiers would've shot him without thinking twice. So instead he admired his truck, which he'd had painted by hand, emerald and blue, with the phrase "My Beautiful T——" splashed across the top of the front windshield, in cursive lettering. At least that's what they told him it said. He recalled thinking, What will happen to this truck? Will it be waiting for me when I get out? In any case, he had time enough to decide to keep his mouth shut. He'd never spent more than a few days at a time in the city, and besides the ocean, he had no real affection for the place. Now he'd be staying. The soldiers found the package, just as he'd expected they would, and to protect his brother, Rogelio said nothing about its origins. He played dumb, which wasn't difficult. Everyone—from the soldiers who did the search to the policemen who came to arrest him, to his ferocious interrogators, to the lawyers charged with defending him—saw Rogelio as he assumed they would: a clueless, ignorant young man from the provinces. All these years, and nothing had changed: he was invisible, just as he'd always been.

It was true that Rogelio couldn't read or write, but that said more about his schooling than it did about him. His attorney assured him that his ignorance would work to his benefit at trial. "And don't go learning," he told Rogelio, without clarifying if this cynical piece of advice was meant seriously or as a joke. In any case, it didn't matter, since Rogelio would die before having an audience with a judge.

When Henry arrived in Collectors, Rogelio had been waiting more than eighteen months for the hearing in his case. Waiting, that is, for an opportunity to affirm that he was a victim, that he knew nothing about the laws of the country, that he'd never been educated, and could not, therefore, be held accountable. He'd laugh as he said these things to his new cell mate. They were neither exactly true nor exactly false, but when he rehearsed his testimony aloud in their cell, Henry was more than convinced. He was seduced.

That would come later, and almost by accident; at first, they were friends. But even before that, they were strangers. Henry's family had tried to arrange a private cell, but none were available. He knew he should be grateful for what he had—many others were in far worse condition—but under the circumstances, he found it difficult to muster much gratitude. For the first few days, he hardly stirred. He didn't register Rogelio's face or his smile, and he knew nothing of his new home, beyond what he'd managed to glean on that initial terrifying walk. Henry was given the top bunk, and for three days he slept long hours, or pretended to sleep, facing the wall. Thinking. Remembering. Trying to disappear. He didn't eat, but he felt no hunger. The night of his arrest had been cataloged, divided into an infinite series of microevents: he remembered each flubbed line of the performance, the expressions on the faces of the audience members who'd expected and hoped for better, every heated

word that had been exchanged immediately after the show between him, Diana, and Patalarga. Could any of those details
shift slightly, just enough to alter the outcome? Was there a light
revision one could make to that evening's script so that it would
not end with him—he was Henry Nuñez, for God's sake!—here,
in Collectors?

Those three days, Rogelio, with whom he'd hardly spoken,
came and went, seemingly uninterested and unconcerned by
Henry's well-being. But by the fourth day, Rogelio had had
enough. He tapped Henry on the back.

"You're allowed to get up, you know."

These were his first words, and Henry could hear the smile
with which his cell mate had said them. As a director, he'd often
found himself exasperated with the performance of an anemic
actor who refused to bring his character to life. He'd say, "I want
you to recite this line with a fucking smile! I want to be able to
close my eyes and hear you smiling!"

Now Henry turned.

"You're alive," Rogelio said.

"I guess."

"You can get up. You can walk around. You can talk to people. This isn't solitary confinement. People live here, you know.
If you're going to stay, you're going to have to realize that."

That afternoon Henry took his first real walk through the
block. He met a few people who would later become friends, or
something like friends; and he saw much to remind him of the
danger he was in. There were men covered in scars and blurry

tattoos, men whose faces seemed congenitally unable to smile, men who locked eyes with him, and spat on the ground. When he shuddered, they laughed.

Rogelio wasn't talkative, but he was helpful, and explained many things that day. According to him, Henry was lucky—it was clear he wouldn't have to work ("You're rich, aren't you?" Rogelio asked), but almost everyone else inside did. Rogelio did plumbing, repaired broken plastic chairs (he shared a workshop on the roof with a few other men), and made pipes out of bent metal scraps, which he sold to the junkies. The junkies were everywhere, a miserable lineup of half-dead who roamed the prison, offering sex or blood or labor for their fix. Rogelio wasn't proud of this work, but without it, he wouldn't survive. His brother sent money only occasionally, enough to cover the cost of the cell and little else. Otherwise he was on his own. His mother hadn't even come to visit, he said, and though his voice was firm as he spoke, Henry could tell this weighed on him.

Neither Henry nor Rogelio owned the cell where they slept. It belonged to the boss, Espejo, who made extra money on visiting days by renting it out so that men could be alone with their wives. Those days will be difficult, Rogelio warned. They'd have to be out of doors all day, and in the evening, the room smells different, and feels different. You know someone has made love there, and the loneliness is infinite.

Henry nodded, though he couldn't understand; would not understand, in fact, until he had to live through it himself. There was a lot to learn. There were inmates to steer clear of, and others whom it was dangerous to ignore. There were moments of the day when it was safe to be out; others when it was best to stay inside. The distinction didn't depend on the time, but on the mood, which Henry would have to learn to read, if he hoped to survive.

"How do you read it?" Henry asked.

Rogelio had a difficult time explaining. It involved listening for the collective murmur of the yard, watching the way certain key men—the barometers of violence in Block Seven—carried themselves on any given day. Small things: Did they have their arms at their sides or crossed in front of them? How widely did their mouths open when they talked? Could you see their teeth? Were their eyes moving quickly, side to side? Or slowly, as if taking in every last detail?

To Henry, it sounded impossible.

Rogelio shrugged. "Remember that most of us here are scared just like you. When I first came, I didn't have a cell. If there was trouble, I had nowhere to go."

They were sitting in a corner of the yard, beneath a dull gray winter sky. The light was thin, and there were no shadows. Henry had been inside a month now, and still didn't understand quite how it had happened. Nowhere to go—he understood these words in a way he never could've before. He wrote letters to his sister every day, but they were cheerful, utterly false dispatches that didn't account for the gloom he felt, or the fear. His letters were performances, stylized and essentially false outtakes of prison life. Inside he was despairing: This is what it means to be *trapped*. To be frightened, and to be unable to share that fear with a single soul.

"You'll get it," said Rogelio. "It just takes time."

The frenetic daily exchange of goods and services went on about them. Two men waited to have their hair cut, sharing the same day-old newspaper to pass the time. A pair of pants, a couple of sweaters, and T-shirts stolen from some other section of the prison were on sale, the items hanging on a line strung between the posts of one of the soccer goals. Three junkies slept sitting up, with their backs against the wall, shirtless in the cold. Henry saw these men, and felt even colder.

"Where did you sleep back then?" he asked. "Before you had a cell."

"Beneath the stairs," Rogelio said, laughing at the memory. "But look at me now!"

Henry did look.

His new friend had a bright smile, and very large brown eyes. His skin was the color of coffee with milk, and he was muscular without being imposing. His clothes were mostly prison scavenged, items left by departing men, appropriated by Espejo or some other strongman, and then sold. Nothing fit him well, but he seemed unbothered by it. He kept his black hair very short, and wore a knit cap most of the time, pulled down low, to stay warm. These dark winter days, he even slept with it on. His nose was narrow, and turned slightly to the left; and he had a habit of talking low, with a hand over his mouth, as if sharing secrets, no matter how mundane an observation he might be making. His eyes sparkled when he had something important to say.

As if we were accomplices, Henry thought.

Visiting days weren't so bad at first. His family and friends took turns coming to see him, the ones who could tolerate the filth, the overcrowding, the looks from the junkies. They left depleted and afraid; and most didn't come back. Patalarga did. He visited twice during the first month, and twice the next month, one of only a handful of Diciembre sympathizers who risked it. The others sent messages of support, empty-sounding phrases that Patalarga dutifully relayed, but which made Henry feel even more alone. The idea of the prison performance of *The Idiot President* was likely hatched on one of these visits, though neither could recall exactly when.

Patalarga had no memory of ever meeting Rogelio. His enduring image of these moments in Collectors involves Henry looking down at his feet, nodding, but not listening. "I wanted him to know we were with him, that we hadn't forgotten him. But I don't think he understood what was going on. What we were doing for him." In truth, only one thing stood out. The smell of the place, Patalarga told me; *that* was what he remembered. "You could close your eyes and not see, cover your ears and not hear; but that smell, it was always there."

Henry agreed: Collectors was fetid and unsanitary, and when you ceased to recognize the odor, it was because you were losing part of yourself to your environment. "Three weeks inside," he told me, "and I didn't even notice it."

But the hours immediately after the visitors had gone were the most difficult of the week. The prison never felt lonelier. It required a great collective energy to welcome so many outsiders, to put the best face on what was clearly a terrible situation. Collectors was falling apart, anyone could see that. The damp winters had eaten away at the bricks, and the walls were covered with mold. Every day new men were brought in. They were unchained and set free inside, made to fight for a place to sleep in the already overcrowded hell of Collectors. The terrorists just over the high fence from Block Seven sang without pause, and many men complained that their families were afraid to come. Family day, when women were allowed in, came on alternate Wednesdays, and these were brutal. By the end of the afternoon, everyone was worn out from smiling, from reassuring their wives and children and mothers that they were all right. (Fathers, as a rule, did not visit; most of Henry's fellow inmates did not have fathers.) It wasn't uncommon for there to be fights on those evenings. So long as no one was killed, it was fine, just something to relieve the tension.

Nine weeks in, and Henry felt almost abandoned. Only Patalarga came. On family day, he was alone, as alone as Rogelio. Espejo rented out their cell, and in the evening, as each man lay on his bunk, Henry could still feel the warmth of those phantom bodies. Their perfumed scent. It was the only time the smell of the prison dissipated, though, in some ways, this other scent was worse. It reminded you of everything you were missing. Henry had been unable to convince any of the women he used to see to come visit him, and he didn't blame them. He'd had nothing special with any of them, though at times his despair was so great that he could concentrate on any one of their faces and convince himself he'd been in love. As for Rogelio, he was far from home, and hadn't had a visitor, male or female, in months.

Jaime had come once, and would come once more before Rogelio died.

There wasn't much to say now, so the two men let themselves dream.

"Did you see her?" asked Henry one evening after the visitors had all gone, and because Rogelio hadn't, he began to describe the woman who'd made love on the low bunk that very day. She'd come to see an inmate named Jarol, a thief with a sharp sense of humor and arms like tense coils of rope. Henry talked about the woman's ample curves, how delicious she looked in her dress—not tight, but tight enough. She had long black hair, doe eyes, and fingernails painted pink. She was perfect, he said, because she was: not because of her body or her lips, but because of the way she smiled at her husband, with the hungry look of a woman who wants something and is not ashamed. A man could live on a look like that.

Henry said, "She didn't care who saw."

He could hear Rogelio breathing. They were quiet for a moment.

"What would you have done to her?" Rogelio asked. His voice was very low, tentative.

This was how it began, Henry told me: speculating aloud about how he might spend a few minutes alone with a woman in this degrading, stifling space. He had no difficulty imagining the scene, and he could think of no good reason not to share it. How different was it? Just because there was another man in the room with him—why should it be different?

He would have torn off that dress, Henry said, and bent her against the wall, with her palms flat against that stupid map of San Jacinto. He would have pressed his hard cock against her pussy, teased her until she begged him to come in. From the bottom bunk, Rogelio laughed. He would have made her howl, Henry said, made her scream. Cupped her breasts in his hands and squeezed. Is *this* why you came, woman? Tell me it is! Already Henry was disappearing into his own words. He had his eyes closed. The walls had begun to vibrate.

"What else?" said Rogelio, his voice stronger now. "Go on. What else would you do?"

When they finished, each on his own bunk that first time, both men laughed. They hadn't touched, or even made eye contact, but somehow what they'd done was more intimate than that. For one moment, the pleasure of each had belonged to the other, and now everything looked different as a result. Something dark and joyless had been banished.

Years later in T——, Henry told the story, and even allowed himself a smile.

15

HENRY, PATALARGA, AND NELSON arrived at the door of Mrs. Anabel's house the next morning, at precisely nine. They hadn't slept well, and it showed. Henry's right eye had swollen nearly shut, his ribs still hurt, and he described his walk along the cobblestone streets of T—— as a kind of teetering shuffle. "I was stumbling like an old man," he said, and admitted that he might have toppled over but for Nelson, who steadied him all the way. The beating felt more severe that morning, and it wasn't just Henry who noticed it. Nelson and Patalarga felt it too, an achy kind of hangover, as if they'd all been attacked.

Noelia met the three men at the door, and observed them warily. She hadn't expected them all to come, she said.

"Is there a problem?" Patalarga asked.

She crossed her arms. "I just don't see why you all need to be here. She's very old, you know."

Nelson was the one who answered, steady, firm, and respectful. He held his hands clasped behind his back, and leaned forward slightly, as if sharing a secret.

"Madam, after last night, we really can't let our friend go in there alone. I do hope you understand."

She considered them for a moment. Nelson, especially. She liked him, she told me later, from the first. From the moment she'd seen him onstage the night before.

"My mother is waiting," Noelia said finally, and led them out into the courtyard, where Jaime sat with Mrs. Anabel, talking in whispers. Both looked up when the members of Diciembre stepped out of the dark passage and into the light. Nelson was the first to emerge. The morning sun shone directly into his eyes.

"Good morning," he said.

"Rogelio!" said Mrs. Anabel. Her face lit up. "We were just talking about you, son. Come, come, boy! Have a seat."

IF I WERE a different sort of writer, I might have discussed Mrs. Anabel's dementia with an expert or two, tried to make some medical sense of what was happening to her mind. But I didn't, in part because I suspect no psychiatrist could convincingly explain the abrupt twists and turns in her cognitive understanding. There was no logic. What I know about her unpredictable reactions I've learned from Noelia, who'd lived with her mother and her moods for years, attempting to decipher a pattern. By the time of these events, she'd given up.

Noelia reports that her mother woke that morning refreshed, that she greeted Jaime as if it were no surprise at all to find him there, and asked him about his schoolwork. He told her he was out of school now, had been for many years, and was living in San Jacinto. To which Mrs. Anabel responded, "I was just telling your father I never liked that town."

She hadn't been to the provincial capital in nearly twenty years.

Jaime sighed.

"Did you marry yet?"

"Yes, Mama. You've met my wife."

"Is she pretty?"

"Yes, Mama."

Mrs. Anabel frowned. "I remember her now. The pretty one."

Noelia watched this exchange as she prepared breakfast. The morning chill hadn't yet receded, and Jaime and her mother sat with heavy blankets draped over their laps. "I enjoyed that moment, in fact. It was good that Jaime see exactly the state our mother was in. He needed to know."

After breakfast, they settled in the courtyard. Mrs. Anabel held a cup of tea in her hands, and said she'd dreamed of Rogelio the night before. Jaime and Noelia braced themselves, but to their relief, Mrs. Anabel confessed she couldn't remember any of the details.

"It was very confusing, like all dreams. Sometimes I'm very confused."

Still, all things considered, Mrs. Anabel seemed at peace, so much so that Jaime considered calling off Henry's visit. He probably would have, but then his mother's mood shifted once more. She had something to say, Mrs. Anabel told her children. It had been nagging her all morning. That man from yesterday might be on to something. She'd been unable to shake the feeling that it might be true: that her younger son might be dead.

Jaime began to argue, but Noelia shushed him.

"It just can't be," Mrs. Anabel said. "Have you talked to him? When was that? Are you sure? We'll have to tell your father, but I'm afraid it will kill him."

This is the world Nelson walked into.

"I was just a step behind him when the old woman called him Rogelio," Patalarga told me later. "And I saw him freeze. Just for a moment. We froze too, in the dark still, in the hallway that led into the courtyard. I guess they do these kinds of improvisation exercises all the time at the Conservatory, and maybe that explains why he responded the way he did. I don't think you could even call it *a decision*, because it wasn't. He just reacted. He went with it."

The sun in Nelson's eyes was like stage lights, I imagine.

"Yes, Mama," he said. "I'm here."

And then something else happened, which tilted the scene once more. At the sound of Nelson's voice, Mrs. Anabel's certainty began to fade, as if she were suddenly frightened by what she had conjured. Henry and Patalarga had stepped into the daylight, and perhaps this too gave her doubts. She squinted at this young man before her, the one she'd just called Rogelio, and couldn't recognize him. "Is that you?" she said, and no one uttered another word until Nelson spoke again.

"Mama, it's me," he said—he purred—repeating the words once and again, such that their sound and meaning began to

soothe Mrs. Anabel. *Mama, it's me.* Nelson stood in the courtyard, chest out, face full of love.

Jaime, Noelia told me later, wore a look of utter bewilderment.

"I'd never seen anything like it," Patalarga said, with pride
evident in his voice.

I can picture it: down to the unsteady posture of Mrs. Anabel, suddenly frightened, suddenly curious. Heartbroken, but in
some very deep place inside her, lonely enough to want to believe. It's the drama of any family separated by space and time. I
can see the way she stood with the help of her son, Jaime; the
way she shuffled her feet toward Nelson, then paused, then shuffled some more. *Mama, it's me.* According to Noelia, "It was like
trying to coax a kitten from under the bed. He was very patient."
When Mrs. Anabel finally approached, Nelson held her very
tightly against his chest. She was so very small, it was like holding a child.

They must have stood there for three or four minutes, while
the rest of them watched, awed by this scene they could hardly
explain. "No one spoke," Henry told me. "We couldn't. Something special was happening, and we all knew that, even Jaime."

When the old woman had gathered herself, the questioning
began. These questions were random, and for the moment, contained no skepticism at all. The skepticism would return later,
flaring up unexpectedly, once or twice a day—but not just yet. It
was as if a circuit had been suddenly connected.

Did you go to school today, boy?

Is your brother treating you nicely?

Will you be going out to the fields with your father this afternoon?

Are there big buildings where you live?

How old are you now?

Fortunately, there was no wrong answer to this final query, since Mrs. Anabel drew from all the periods of her life in conversation with her son, the stranger. He was a boy, an adolescent, a young man—all at once. Through it all, Nelson remained composed, good-humored, and generous. According to Noelia, "He performed marvelously. You almost wanted to applaud."

Mama, it's me.

Of course, one applauds at the end of a performance, not at the beginning.

EVENTUALLY IT WAS TIME for Mrs. Anabel's nap. It had been a satisfying performance; everyone could agree on that, and Mrs. Anabel's joy at being reunited with Rogelio was undeniable. She'd given out a round of hugs before heading to bed, even to Henry, whose earlier visit she seemed to have either forgotten or forgiven altogether. Before Noelia took her to her bedroom, the elderly woman made Rogelio promise that he'd stay for dinner, and Nelson answered with a bright, noncommittal smile. Mrs. Anabel squeezed his hand, and said Noelia was preparing something special. "Your favorite."

A few minutes later, Noelia returned from her mother's room to announce that the old woman was asleep. Henry, Patalarga, and Nelson stood to go. The daily bus back to San Jacinto left at two, and they were still in time to make it. The previous night's tension seemed to have dissipated, and if the mood was not exactly friendly, there was something new: a sense of shared accomplishment. Even Jaime seemed pleased. They'd managed it, the five of them together, and now a previously troubled elderly woman was sleeping peacefully.

"I'm glad we could help," Henry said. He turned to Nelson. "You were wonderful."

"Thank you," Nelson said.

Noelia nodded her agreement. "I almost wish you could stay!"

Everyone laughed but Jaime, who raised a hand, teasing the air rather vaguely. He had a pensive look. "Would you?"

Nelson grinned. Patalarga too.

"It's not a bad idea," Jaime said.

Henry objected: "It's a terrible idea."

"I'm not talking to you," Jaime said. Then to Nelson: "Is it something you'd consider?"

"Jaime."

He frowned. "Sister, let the boy talk."

Nelson cast anxious glances at Henry and Patalarga. "No. I wouldn't consider it."

"That's a shame. My mother likes you. You could do an old woman a lot of good."

"I'm sorry. I can't."

"I think you can." He paused. "And I think you could, if you wanted. I can pay you. I can make it worth your while. Why don't you give her a week. Think of it as a performance. You'll do quite nicely. What's the problem?"

Henry saw in Jaime's smile the seriousness of the proposal. This wasn't a suggestion at all, but a command.

"You're serious?" Nelson asked.

"He is," Henry mumbled.

"You can't be."

"I am," Jaime said.

Noelia couldn't believe her offhand comment had led to this. Her brother's idea was appalling—but it was also marvelous. To have company. To have a guest. Jaime visited only rarely, and never brought his wife or his children. The idea of being accompanied, she admitted to me later, sounded intoxicating. She couldn't hide her enthusiasm, nor did she try.

"We'll set you up in his old room," she said to Nelson. "I'll clear it out, and you'll be very comfortable there."

"I didn't say I was staying."

Henry rubbed his eyes. "You're staying," he said, defeated. He'd intended to communicate the futility of arguing, but it sounded instead as if he were turning on his friend.

"Henry!" Patalarga said.

Henry turned to Jaime. "We'll wait for him. Stay in town, but out of sight. She won't even know we're here."

Jaime shook his head. "I don't want you in my town. I want you as far away from my mother as can be."

"We're not leaving our friend here," Patalarga said.

"Your friend will be fine. You'll take good care of him, won't you, Noelia?"

She smiled innocently. "Of course."

Jaime clapped his hands together. "See?"

"I'm not staying here. Don't be ridiculous."

"You are," Jaime said. "Let's not argue about this. I don't enjoy arguing."

It was an awful feeling, Patalarga told me later: "I looked at Nelson and then back at this violent man, and knew there was nothing we could do. Henry looked as if he might cry. It didn't sink in right away, but then we knew. It was Nelson who put an end to it."

He held up his hands in surrender, the way you might if you were being robbed at knifepoint.

"Okay," he said. "I'll do it."

THAT AFTERNOON, the three friends walked to the plaza, and said their good-byes in the shadow of the bus to San Jacinto. Jaime had come to watch, to verify that it all went according to plan, but he kept his distance, out of respect for the moment. Henry, Patalarga, and Nelson embraced, and Nelson asked his friends not to speak with his mother. "Better she doesn't worry," Nelson said, and they all agreed this was for the best. "I'll be home soon."

Henry and Patalarga nodded.

Then they boarded, and the bus pulled out, and just like that, Nelson was alone in T——. *Now the tour has really surprised me,* he wrote in his journal that night. *It's become my very own one-man show.*

As for Henry and Patalarga, they rode out of T—— in silence. The views along the route were spectacular: sheer mountain faces, the sky almost unnervingly blue. There were wildflowers growing at the roadside, pushing out from the dry rock in exquisite and surprising shades. Halfway to San Jacinto there was a river to cross, and when they turned the last switchback before the bridge, they came to a stopped line of trucks. Their engines were off, and many of the drivers were out of their vehicles, standing along the edge of the road in groups of three or four, caps pulled low over their eyes, smoking.

They could go no farther. The bus stopped too, and all the passengers got out.

It seemed a small van had collided with a truck full of mangoes just sixty meters beyond the bridge. "If you walk up to the edge, you can see it," one of the men said with a shrug, and Henry and Patalarga, along with a few others, moved in that direction.

The scene was grisly. The remains of the van were strewn down the side of the gulch, metal twisted and bent like a crushed toy. Pieces of the windshield glinted in the sun, and one of the tires had come to rest at the water's edge. It was impossible, at that distance, to make out any human remains, but the rumor circulating among those gathered at the lip of the drop-off was that there were no survivors. Some of the kids were crying; their mothers tried to comfort them. "Don't look," Henry heard a woman say to her boy, as the child peeked anxiously through his fingers. The only witness to the crash was the driver of the mango truck, who was still in shock. Someone said a medical team from San Jacinto was on its way.

Henry walked back toward the bus. Accidents like this happen all the time, but somehow in all his travels he'd been spared seeing one up close. He felt sore all over, in his jaw, in his back, in his hips. It wasn't overwhelming pain, just enough to make him feel old.

A few moments later, Patalarga returned. "Three hours, at least," he said. "Get comfortable." They stood by the roadside, looking out over the valley. "Are you all right?"

Henry answered with a nod.

"Our friendship began to unravel then," Patalarga told me later, "just when it should have been strengthened. I tried to talk to him, but he was hard to reach. I thanked him for last night, for telling us everything. I got no response. I told him not to worry about Nelson, that he'd be fine, and he just shrugged."

Henry doesn't exactly dispute this. "The wreck put me in a mood. The wreck and everything else. I couldn't help it, but I felt like he was judging me."

"But Patalarga was your best friend," I said.

"That's true," Henry told me, "and it also isn't true. You get to an age when that phrase isn't quite what it used to be. There is no best friend role waiting to be filled. You're alone. You have a life behind you, a series of disappointments, and perhaps a few things scattered ahead that might give you pleasure. I wasn't happy. What else can I tell you? I felt like a failure. I lost everything in Collectors. And in T——, I'd felt for a moment like I might be able to get it back. I wasn't worried for Nelson, but there was no escaping the reality of it: we were going home without him."

This was our third interview. He was thin and unshaven,

with a grayish pallor, and had deteriorated even in these few short weeks since we'd first spoken. He'd just told me a version of what he told Nelson and Patalarga the night before their departure—the story of Rogelio. It was summer on the coast, and the windows of his half-furnished apartment had been thrown open, the curtains pulled. The room was filled with light, but Henry slumped in his chair as if he'd just woken from a nervous sleep. A fan whirred in the corner. I had the sense we were acting out the very scene he was describing: metaphorically, there we were, he and I, standing by the side of the road high in the mountains, observing the wreckage. Only in this case the wreckage was him.

It was almost dusk when the traffic on the road to San Jacinto finally began to move again. All the cars and trucks and buses and vans followed in a long, slow procession, rolling along as a block, never more than a few car lengths between them, as if by riding together, they could steel themselves against the impact of the accident they'd just seen. They arrived in San Jacinto that evening, in time to catch a night bus to the coast. Everyone was tired; nerves were raw. Henry and Patalarga bought their tickets, and waited.

Even at that late hour, the station was manic. There were children everywhere, Patalarga remembers, not children who were traveling, but children working the station: selling cigarettes or shoe shines or simply begging. Below the constant noise, if you concentrated, you could hear the dull buzz of the fluorescent lights. Everyone looked like wax dummies. I can't wait to leave this place, Henry thought. We can't possibly leave soon enough.

At nearly one in the morning, the bus was ready to board. Before it pulled out, the passengers were videotaped, this time by a girl of fifteen wearing a tank top and a pair of unnaturally tight jeans. She had black hair, a moon face, and was shy. Perhaps half the people on board had heard the news of the deadly crash at the bridge, and as a result the taping was more somber than usual. No one waved, no one smiled; they peered into the camera's glass eye without blinking, as if searching for a loved one on the other side.

Henry didn't even face the girl, but turned instead toward the window.

"Hey," she said, "over here," but the playwright didn't respond.

Patalarga shrugged an apology on behalf of his friend. "I'd never seen Henry like that," he told me later.

After a few seconds the girl moved on, muttering complaints under her breath.

They hadn't been on the road long before Henry turned to Patalarga. He wore an expression of worry, or even heartbreak.

"I guess that's it," Henry said to his friend, his voice low.

Patalarga had been on the verge of sleep. "Yeah?"

"The tour's over."

The two friends didn't speak again until morning.

PART
THREE

16

NELSON WAS GIVEN what was simultaneously the largest and smallest room in Rogelio's family home: the largest in terms of sheer physical space; the smallest because it had become, in recent years, a de facto storage locker. The rusty bunk bed where Jaime and Rogelio once slept now served as the essential infrastructure holding, but not containing, the family's history in objects: bundled, precariously balanced, stacked from floor to ceiling, the remains of twenty-five years, thirty years, five decades of life in T——. In this house. Nelson spotted an old sewing machine, a teetering heap of newspapers from the seventies, a dead man's mothballed clothes. There was an overstuffed cardboard box sitting on the lower bunk, with a dented teakettle and a few cracked wooden kitchen spoons peering out from the top. There were mismatched shoes beneath the bed; a couple of soccer balls, deflated and ripped open; bent wire hangers linked together like a makeshift cage; a box of marbles; and a child's tricycle that appeared to have been taken apart violently. Nelson even saw a few of the old sculptures Rogelio had made out of wood.

Together, it was something to behold. Had it stood in a museum or an art gallery, the critics would have been unanimous in their praise.

Noelia must have noticed Nelson's expression, or the sharp breath he drew at the sight of it all.

"We don't throw anything away," she said. "We just don't. I'm not saying this is a good or a bad thing."

Nor could Nelson decide.

Rather than attempt to make space on the lower bunk, Noelia had Jaime and Nelson bring in a cot, along with three heavy blankets that smelled powerfully, but not unpleasantly, of woodsmoke. She was eager to get her guest settled in. "Go ahead, give it a try," she said, standing in the doorway, and watched as Nelson lowered himself carefully onto the cot. The fabric sank beneath his weight, like a hammock, but it held.

"Not bad," he said.

"Lie down."

Nelson flipped his legs onto the cot. His toes hung just off the edge. "It's fine," he said.

"I'm sorry, but it's the best we can do for now."

"It's fine," Nelson repeated. "Really."

It was early evening, and Mrs. Anabel was resting. It had been a big day for her. The temperature was dropping, so Jaime, Noelia, and Nelson moved to the main visiting room, that dark and dusty place where Henry had first been received. The family photos were right where he'd said they'd be. Nelson glanced back at his hosts, as if for permission.

"Go ahead," Jaime said.

Nelson nodded, and searched the menagerie of black-and-white images, the faces blurred, but recognizable. Young Jaime, young Noelia, and the youngest, Rogelio, he assumed. He examined that face most carefully of all, looking for some resemblance that might explain his own presence in this strange home, in this strange town. They looked nothing alike, which was both a relief and a disappointment. It felt unsettling to be suddenly so connected to a dead man. There were a few scenes from the plaza, from the days when T—— had been alive. There was one photo of the family stepping out of the cathedral, dressed in their finest, Mrs. Anabel's stern late husband with an arm around his wife, and a date scrawled in the corner of the image: May 1970. Nelson studied the old man's face, an opaque, unreadable mask; it was the face of a man accustomed to suffering. Husband and wife both wore this expression, in fact; but the children clustered about them—two smiling, irrepressible boys, plus one prim and beautiful little girl—did not.

"What a lovely family," Nelson said.

Noelia smiled. "Yes, we were. My mother thinks we still are."

"We made a good team," Noelia told me later. In spite of how it ended, she had fond memories of Nelson's time in T——. "I told him everything I knew. Not just that night, but every day I added something, every day I remembered. He helped me, just by being there."

Noelia began that evening by explaining Mrs. Anabel's peculiar sense of time, the seven or eight key events which her mind played in a continuous and maddening loop, and the connective tissue between them. For example, it might be necessary to understand how the death of Rogelio's father related to the 1968 earthquake. Noelia explained to Nelson (and later to me) that something in the chemistry of the soil changed after the quake, and the small plot he'd saved up years to purchase became suddenly infertile. The old man all but gave up hope after that. Though he didn't die until a few years later, as far as Rogelio's mother was concerned, he'd *started* to die at the moment of the earthquake.

"You would've been five in 1968," Noelia told Nelson, like a schoolgirl slipping answers to her favorite classmate. "And almost eight when my father finally passed."

She kept on, and Nelson took notes. Jaime was mostly quiet, nodding now and again, or correcting Noelia's dates. Together, brother and sister conjured this memory: they'd last been together, all three of them, at a party in San Jacinto in the early 1980s. Neither could remember what they were celebrating, or why Noelia had been visiting the provincial capital. They remembered this: the sun setting, the three of them and perhaps a half dozen friends in a circle of plastic chairs on the unpaved street in front of Jaime's house. It had rained the night before, and the chairs sunk and waddled in the soft earth. Music played from a handheld radio, they swapped stories, pulled bottles of beer from a bucket full of ice. Friends came by all through the night, and Rogelio was quiet—"He was always quiet," Noelia said—until a certain song came on the radio, something bouncy and pop. Then, to everyone's surprise, he stood up and started dancing.

"Everyone stopped to watch," Noelia said, shaking her head at the image. "He was so shy back then."

"It was a real sight," Jaime said, and laughed to himself. It was the first time Nelson had seen him laugh.

They're not talking to me now, Nelson thought. It's like I'm not even here. He kept his eyes wide open, his ears perked, and did what he could to inhale this memory, to make it his, as if the truth of this emotional detail could make any difference at all to Mrs. Anabel.

"I was watching you today," said Jaime finally.

"You were very nice," added Noelia.

"That's true. You did fine."

"But?" Nelson said.

Jaime pressed his hands together, and held them against his chest. "But Rogelio had no schooling. He didn't read plays or write books. He couldn't read at all."

"He was in Henry's play, wasn't he? In Collectors?"

"Just something to keep in mind." He pointed at Nelson's notebook. "Don't let my mother see you writing, that's all."

"You have to remember who our brother was," Noelia added.

Jaime frowned, and ran a hand through his hair. "And who my mother thinks he was."

"Okay," Nelson said. "I'll try."

When they'd finished for the night, Nelson went back to his room and sat on the cot with his back to the window. He'd heard many stories, some true, some invented; his journal was filled with notes, and his head was spinning. He stared at the clutter on the bunk bed, as if examining the gears of an inscrutable machine. It was impossible not to appreciate its size, the stunning illogic of its composition, and the history embedded within. He felt duty-bound to understand it, or attempt to. All this junk was something more: it was a family's history, and wasn't he, at least temporarily, part of this family?

If Nelson had known more about T——, known more about the region and the relentless out-migration that had changed it, he'd have known that all the houses in town had rooms like this. That some houses, in fact, were nothing but large, sprawling versions of this room, no living space left, no people, only assorted objects gathering dust behind padlocked doors. He might have appreciated that Mrs. Anabel and Noelia had managed to contain the past, more or less; that by holding it within the four walls of the boys' old room, they were living, to a greater degree than many of their neighbors, in the present. It would have impressed him, certainly, but for an entirely different set of reasons. For now, he couldn't escape the sense that this lawless room was simply the physical representation of Mrs. Anabel's mind, that if only he could place these many items in some kind of order, he might discover the secrets of her dementia. He might resolve it. And find a place for Rogelio within it.

NELSON WOKE THE NEXT MORNING to find the family in the kitchen, chatting over a simple breakfast. He crossed the courtyard, wearing his best smile, and joined them. There was no mistaking Mrs. Anabel's happiness; it was evident in the way she greeted him—brightly—and in every gesture thereafter. He drank tea, ate a hard-boiled egg and not-quite-fresh bread with cheese, and sat by the window, letting the sun hit his face. Mrs. Anabel kept her eyes on him, which might have been unnerving in another context, but which here seemed exactly right, and even expected. He performed for her.

"How did you sleep?" the old woman asked, and though his back hurt and his neck was sore, he didn't hesitate: "The best I've slept in years, Mama. It's so nice to be home."

Her contentment was palpable, and it meant something to Nelson. *When she took my hand, it made sense somehow,* he wrote later. *At least as much sense as the tour did.*

That morning, his first full day alone in T——, would be the template for each of the mornings to come. The work of impersonating Rogelio, of convincing an elderly and senile woman of this identity—it was a task to be accomplished at the local rhythm, that is, slowly, carefully, making no hasty or unnecessary gestures. The breakfast table was cleared, and he helped Mrs. Anabel to her spot in the courtyard, where she sat with her back against one of the adobe walls. She asked him—Rogelio, that is—to sit with her, and he did, very close, in fact, side by side on the sunken top of an old leather chest, the outsides of their thighs touching. Their conversation could barely be called that: they enjoyed long silent spells, interrupted by Mrs. Anabel's occasional questions, queries which did not require specific answers. Here and there, she made the odd statement about which there could be little or no disagreement: "The sky is good" or "The wind is nice." She'd smile afterward, nodding at her own insight with an air of satisfaction. Nelson smiled back, and gently squeezed her hand to show her he was listening.

She asked Nelson about his life, and he improvised based on the general script he'd heard the night before: his Rogelio was a version of the lie Jaime had invented. He lived on the outskirts of Los Angeles, in a working-class neighborhood of small, tidy houses. There was an industrial area nearby, where giant factories ran all day and all night, frantic and bustling, belching thick smoke into otherwise blue California skies. In his description, the factory was good work, and everyone was happy to be there. Satisfied to be *making something*. It was the sort of cliché of which Henry might have disapproved, but still, Nelson owned it, holding his hands out, palms flat, when he said this.

"But your hands are so soft," Mrs. Anabel said, not skeptical so much as delighted by her son's lovely hands.

"I wear gloves. We're required to wear gloves."

Nelson had never been inside a factory. Still, Mrs. Anabel accepted his answer with a contented smile.

"What do you make?"

"Movie sets," he said, because it was the first thing that popped into his mind.

She seemed to take this answer in stride.

Nelson's Rogelio, like his brother Jaime, was a mechanic; unlike Jaime, he'd never married. He lived a quiet life, though he spoke with great conviction about his desire for a family. Soon, he told Mrs. Anabel, but insisted it would all come in due time. "I'm still too young for that," he said that morning, a statement which worked on a variety of levels. At the sound of those words, time collapsed for Mrs. Anabel. If Rogelio was still young, then she must still be young too!

"Oh yes, you're very young," she said, and her eyes glistened with a pleasing confusion.

Then it was time for her nap, and Nelson was left alone with Jaime in the courtyard. A cat meowed from somewhere inside the weeds. Nelson had done good work that morning; he was sure of it, but his employer (for that is what Jaime was) kept his distance, observing him from the kitchen doorway.

Finally, Nelson said, "Were you watching? How did I do?"

"Not bad."

"Did I get anything wrong?"

Jaime shook his head. "Not really." He stepped out of the doorway, and into the courtyard. "A matter of degree, I guess. I see you and I don't see Rogelio. But that's not your fault. You're not doing anything wrong, it isn't that. My mother sees what she wants to see. And she likes you. I don't know how you people do it."

Nelson shrugged.

"How it is you pretend, I mean. Come with me. Let's take a walk."

It would become habit to break up the tedium of the morning with a stroll just before lunch. This was the dry season in the mountains, when every day is a replica of the day before. Above, a smattering of white, cottony clouds. They walked the few blocks to the plaza in silence, passing only a few people along the way: a girl skipping in the direction of the school, and an elderly gentleman with his hat pulled low against the sun.

The narrow side streets of T—— were shadowy and cool, but the plaza was blanketed in boiling sun. And it was empty, but for a few people milling around the bus that would leave in a few hours. The owner of the bodega sat on the steps outside his store, reading a newspaper. He waved to Jaime, and they walked over to greet him.

"Mr. Segura," Jaime said, "you remember my brother, Rogelio, don't you?"

Nelson narrowed his eyes. He was being tested.

"Of course," said Segura, and he nodded deferentially.

Nelson stretched out his hand. "So nice to see you again. It's great to be home."

Jaime bought a couple of sodas, then told Nelson to wait outside while he made a phone call. Segura motioned for Nelson to join him. "It came today," he said, waving his newspaper in the air proudly. "The bus driver gave it to me. Look."

The front page carried the story of the accident between the mango truck and passenger van. Twelve people had died. There were photos.

Nelson had gone many weeks without much interest or curiosity in something as abstract as "the news." It was a concept that had no relevance on tour but which suddenly seemed necessary. Not because of these deaths, but because of everything else. Another world existed, and he felt suddenly reminded of it. Now that leaving T—— was temporarily out of the question, Nelson felt a very keen desire to know what was happening. It was something he hadn't realized until he saw the newspaper.

Nelson opened the front page. He looked for news from the

city, politics, sports. National news was relegated to an inner section, a few poorly written items that read like dispatches from a distant planet. A senator had proposed a law against drunk driving. (Bar owners were opposed.) A police dog had been wounded in a fire, and would have to be put down. (Animal rights groups were opposed.) A building in the colonial center had partially collapsed, and would have to be demolished. (Preservation groups were opposed.) Nelson scanned the paper, then the empty plaza, and failed to see any connection at all.

Just then Jaime stepped out. He saw Nelson and frowned. "Let's go."

"Just a second."

"We're leaving," Jaime said. "Segura, I understand my sister owes you some money."

The man nodded.

Jaime reached into his pocket and pulled out a few bills, which the storeowner accepted with his head bowed. Then Jaime turned, and began to walk off. Nelson closed the paper, and hurried after him. He saw then—and it was strange that he hadn't realized it earlier—how physically impressive Jaime was. It was somehow more apparent at this distance: he wasn't tall, he was wide. His shoulders were broad and strong, and now that Nelson saw his shape, Jaime's swift attack on Henry was even more surprising.

"I'm coming," Nelson called out.

"Rogelio doesn't read," Jaime said when Nelson had caught up. "Not the newspaper, not anything. I told you that."

Nelson apologized.

They walked on, across the plaza, toward the northeast district, over a footbridge, and then up the steep hill that rose to the east of town. A few blocks on and the houses petered out, giving way to terraced fields and irrigation ditches carved expertly into the earth. By whom? Nelson wondered. Where were the people? He wanted to ask, but was afraid to.

"Do you know San Jacinto?" Jaime asked when they were above the town. He didn't wait for an answer. Below them, lay T——, its red-roofed and white-walled houses, its narrow, picturesque streets. "San Jacinto is a terrible place. Nothing like this. Hideous. But it's where the work is." He cleared his throat. "What did you earn on this little tour you did?"

"You mean money?"

He always meant money.

One page of Nelson's journal was dedicated to a rough accounting of what he'd made and spent on the tour. The figures were a jumble, but the basic arithmetic was clear enough: he'd broken even. Nelson knew that, and he'd had no opinion on this information until that very moment. One didn't join Diciembre for the wages, after all. But now, the idea of breaking even seemed suddenly disappointing. He glanced at Jaime and saw opportunity. He made up a number, *an outrageous, ambitious number,* he wrote that evening, to which Jaime laughed.

"That's it?" he said.

Nelson blushed.

"I'll give you twice that. Now start thinking like Rogelio."

"What does that mean?"

"It means don't say silly things like 'It's great to be home.' If it was great, you would've come home ten years ago."

"Okay," Nelson said.

Jaime sighed. "You know what I think, when I see this?"

"No."

"I think, How lovely. Thank God I don't live here. Now, do you have your wallet? Good. Take it out. Give me your ID card."

Through it all, Nelson was still thinking of money, the possibility it implied. He could pay a few months' rent. Or take Ixta on a trip. Buy his mother something nice. Not all of those things could be done, but some of them could. In particular, this phrase stood out: "twice that." He did as he was told. Jaime squinted at the picture on the ID card, smiling. He held it up and compared it to the young man standing before him. Then he put it in his pocket.

"I'll be back in a week," he said to Nelson. "In the meantime, be nice to your blameless mother."

17

IT'S DIFFICULT TO WRITE about these days in T——, about this lull in the action (for that is precisely what it is) without succumbing to the pace. Such is the languorous nature of small-town life. I know it well enough. Thought slows, the need for conversation vanishes. You are prone to introspection, never a productive habit, and one which city life, for example, quite rightly suppresses in the name of efficiency. On the third day of any visit to T——, I give in to a specific kind of melancholy that is part depression, part boredom. The normal stimuli one associates with human activity begins to seem aberrant, even unnecessary. Throughout my childhood and early adolescence, arriving in T—— was like stepping outside time, just as it might have been, I suppose, for Nelson, had he not had the length of the tour itself to adjust, at least in part, to the rhythms of provincial life. Perhaps this is why the appearance of a newspaper was so striking to him that first morning. It reminded him just how far away he was.

For the most part he spent his days listening to Mrs. Anabel;

keeping her company. At night, he and Noelia swapped stories, and with her, he could be Nelson again, something they both seemed to welcome. "He was very funny," she told me later, "and I hadn't had anyone to talk to in so long. He told me about his mother, about his brother. He told me about Ixta, and even said he was going to be a father."

"When was that?" I asked.

She thought for a moment. "It must have been at the end of the first week. We were expecting my brother back any day, and Nelson had even packed his things. He was glad to be going home, he said, so he could see her." She paused here, offering a bemused smile. "But then Jaime didn't come, so he unpacked his things and stayed."

Nelson was getting anxious.

On the ninth day, they got a note delivered by the man who drove the bus to San Jacinto. It was from Jaime:

Something's come up, it said. *I'll be there in a week to settle up.*

"See?" said Noelia. "He hasn't forgotten about you!"

At least the work was manageable. They'd settled into routines, and the old woman seemed quite happy about that. She peppered him with questions, but they were mostly variations on the ones she'd had at the beginning, and Nelson felt enough confidence to shift his answers—just slightly—to suit his mood. One day, to his surprise, he didn't make movie sets when Mrs. Anabel asked; instead, he fixed boats in the harbor. He wasn't sure why he said it. The old woman clapped with delight. "Where did you learn boats?" she asked, as if boats were a language one studied in school.

"In the city, Mama. When Jaime sent me to the city."

She nodded very seriously. "And when was that?"

"Oh, you know how Jaime is. Always bossing me around. Sending me here, sending me there."

"That Jaime!"

To keep things interesting, Nelson invented an accent, a variation on the sort of voice he imagined might result from two decades living in California, among Mexicans and Salvadorans and Guatemalans. It didn't take. He shed it, almost without thinking, a few days later, and she didn't seem to mind. What was the point of this invented vernacular anyway? Had she even noticed this dash of authenticity?

I'm not going to try so hard anymore, he wrote that evening. *If all goes well, I'll be home in a week.*

WHILE NELSON WAS in this state of suspended animation, playing Rogelio for his very small audience, his life was going on without him. And by life, I'm referring to *his real life,* his life in the city. This is not urban chauvinism or elitism or discrimination against the provinces; only fact: Nelson's rural exile did nothing for the problems waiting for him back in the capital.

Ixta was never far from his mind. If Nelson was able to expel his private troubles from his thoughts during his first days alone in T——, once the routines of his new life were settled, he could no longer manage it. By the end of the first week and the beginning of the second, his journal entries are less and less about the details of his days with Mrs. Anabel, and more meditations, or even speculations, on parenthood. Try as he might, he simply could not accept Ixta's assertion that the child was not his. He drew a chart tracking the instances when he and Ixta had made love since their reconciliation the previous winter: where they'd been, how long it had lasted, and how careful they'd remembered to be. He scoured his memory for details, filling pages with clinical accounts of the final weeks of their affair that read more like legal briefs than erotica. He argues for paternity and presents the evidence. He notes clues and small gestures that might give him some hope, for if one reads the journals, this much is clear: hope was what he needed and wanted most. Accepting he was not the child's father would have meant relinquishing his claim on Ixta. It would've meant letting her go for good.

Meanwhile, in the city, Ixta's belly kept growing each day, and with it, she confessed to me, her anxiety. Nelson's late morning walks took him, more often than not, to Mr. Segura's store, where he ignored Jaime's admonition and read the newspaper whenever it was available; and where, on no fewer than seven occasions, he managed to reach Ixta by phone. These mostly unwelcome incidents served only to deepen her unease. She knew what she knew about her baby, and still he tried to convince her that it was his. It had to be. "That was all he wanted to talk about," Ixta said when we spoke. "He was obsessed. It wasn't that the child *couldn't* have been his. But she wasn't. That's all."

She occasionally succeeded in steering the conversation elsewhere; the truth was she enjoyed talking to him, and didn't have the heart to hang up.

"I should have, I know, but I just couldn't."

As uncomfortable as those conversations could be, Ixta needed to hear Nelson's voice; apart from being her lover, he had also been her friend. She was tormented by the usual set of questions: whether she was too young or too selfish to handle the responsibility of motherhood; whether she'd be a good parent, or even an adequate one; whether the maternal bond would be felt right away. Though it seems cruel to mention them now, given the events to come, Ixta had even begun to have doubts about Mindo, her partner, the father of her child, a man I never had the opportunity to meet. But this was all in the future: while Nelson was in T——, Ixta's misgivings were only just taking shape. She'd begun to find Mindo rather unresponsive, insensitive to the idiosyncrasies of her pregnancy (which were not idiosyncratic but absolutely normal), and, in a broad sense, "unimpressive." This last, unkind word was the very one she used, albeit reluctantly and only because I pressed her.

"I don't like to talk about him, not anymore," she said, but then she went on: it was all part of a slow realization she'd had over the course of her second trimester, when her ankles began to swell and the night sweats interrupted her sleep. "A man should cause an impression," she said. "He should leave you with something to think about. Without that, there's no magic."

"Was there magic with Nelson?" I asked. "Was he impressive?"

I knew the answer. It took her a moment.

"Once you knew him, he was. Very much so. And I knew him well."

The changes in her body were some compensation for her

melancholy: it was an aspect of the pregnancy she found dramatic and wondrous, confirmation that there was, undoubtedly, some sort of miracle taking place, even if that miracle sometimes made her recoil with fear. But there was a problem: while she'd never felt more beautiful in her life, this man of hers wouldn't lay a finger on her. Her breasts had grown, her hips—she finally had the curves she'd always wanted—and Mindo scarcely seemed to notice. She found this simply unforgivable. He came home late, something he'd always done; smelling like the Argentine steak house where he worked long hours, just as he always had; only now she found it all intolerable. The odor of grilled beef was repellant. One evening in May, when she was four months pregnant, she asked him to shower before getting in bed. He agreed, with a frown. The next night, she asked him to do the same, and to her great surprise, she woke up the following morning at dawn, alone. It was a chilly early-winter day: she padded out into the living room in her socks, and found her unimpressive, unwashed man on the couch. He was asleep with his mouth open, still in his work clothes, still smelling of steak, his feet hanging off the edge.

How else was she to interpret this except as an insult?

Perhaps, I suggested, he was simply frightened. First-time fathers often are.

"Maybe you're right," she said. "It doesn't really matter anymore."

I didn't argue this point. "Did you think much about Nelson in those days?"

She nodded. "Sure. Whenever he called, I thought about

him. I was angry, I was hurt, but I thought about him. Sometimes fondly. Sometimes not. I missed him. I felt very alone."

"And when he called—did you feel less alone then?"

"No," she said. Her eyes closed very briefly, just an instant. "I
resented the phone calls, but I looked forward to them too. The
connection from that shit town of his, wherever he was, it was
terrible. I couldn't understand what he was doing." She sighed.
"Sometimes I wanted to talk to him, to tell him things, but he
wouldn't listen. He would never listen. That was always his
problem."

MINDO, the putative father of Ixta's child, Nelson's rival, was
an artist, a painter—and not a bad one, by all accounts. He was
thirty-one years old that year, and worked as a waiter.

It's true he was not cut out for fatherhood. When I suggested
to Ixta that he might have been afraid, I was merely repeating
what many of his friends told me. To a person, they hated Ixta,
and a few even blamed themselves for not helping Mindo escape
her clutches sooner. I understood their anger, but their vision of
Ixta was at odds with everything I knew about her. Still, I listened mostly, didn't interrupt as they spoke.

Mindo came from a working-class district of the capital
known as the Thousands, and that's where his artistic education
began. He began painting murals when he was very young, only
twelve, memorials to friends who'd passed away. Given the circumstances of the neighborhood (known colloquially as Gaza),
this was steady work. Mindo was featured in *Crónica*, one of the

city's main newspapers, when he was only sixteen, a back-page feature under the headline "Teenage Artist Paints War Memorial." In the photo he stands before one of his murals, a painted wall along Cahuide, one of the main arteries of his district. He has a heavy build, and looks much older than his age. He has stubble on his chin, and dark, piercing eyes. Like Nelson, Mindo has curly hair, but beyond that there is no similarity.

Ixta and Mindo met in August 2000, when he opened a show at one of the newer galleries in the Old City. He was no longer painting murals but very detailed, stylized portraits of his old neighborhood friends, some of whom had been dead now for fifteen years. Mindo painted them as adults, as if they'd survived their troubled teenage years and skated past the dangers that had prematurely ended their lives: the drugs, the street battles, the allure of crime. It was speculative biography, in images. Some gained weight. Some lost their hair. Some wore suits and ties, or aprons, or soccer uniforms. Some went shirtless, showing off intricate tattoos. Some held diplomas and smiled proudly. It was simple, affecting work; in Mindo's paintings, all these tough young men had lived, and by living had earned the right to be ordinary. Beneath each image was a brief text noting the age at which they'd died and the circumstances of their passing.

The opening was very well received, most of all by Ixta, who spent the evening drinking glass after glass of wine and trying to get the artist to smile. It wasn't easy, she told me: the ghosts of Mindo's violent adolescence were on every wall in the gallery. But she persisted. And we know that in mid-September, Ixta gathered her things and moved in with him. We know Nelson was shaken by the news, and that many of Mindo's friends expressed their concern. Who is this woman? What do you know about her?

It was never a good match. Mindo was handsome and charming and troubled. He'd never been in a serious relationship before. It couldn't have worked out, though it seems petty to assign blame for this now. Ixta, for her part, accepts much of the responsibility herself, while noting the ways in which he let her down after she got pregnant. Mindo was jealous and frightened by the responsibility that fatherhood entailed. We know he suspected that Nelson was still part of Ixta's life. Though Mindo never had proof of the affair, he certainly had his doubts, and it seems he was relieved when Nelson joined Diciembre on tour.

"Maybe he'll stay gone," he commented bitterly to a friend. That was in mid-June, when Nelson was newly arrived in T——, and things with Ixta were beginning to unravel.

"Perhaps," his friend said.

They even toasted to the idea.

Everyone agrees he didn't deserve what happened to him when Nelson came back.

MEANWHILE, Mónica would have loved to have been in touch with her son, to have received those phone calls from T——, but she didn't. She knew nothing of what was happening because her son didn't call her even once. In fact, besides Ixta (who claimed to be uninterested), no one knew much about Nelson's whereabouts, because neither Henry nor Patalarga shared the story. They expected him home in ten days at most, so there was really no point.

Faced with this silence, Mónica daydreamed of her son on ad hoc, rural stages, images which inspired a mix of pride and anguish. In her mind, it was all a continuation of the tour he'd described from San Jacinto, a tour she felt might never end. And in a sense, it never did. Mónica didn't compare Nelson's adventures to Francisco's, at least not consciously, though she found herself approaching both absences the same way. She'd acquired, over the years, a certain skill for projecting herself into the lives of her children, a talent all mothers have—it's what allows them to intuit a child's hunger, his frustration, his fear—but Mónica had honed it, by necessity. With Francisco, she'd managed to create memories where there were none, build an elaborate, and mostly factual, time line of his travels. She'd formulated opinions about all the major events of her son's life, and of the friends he'd acquired and discarded along the way. She kept a catalog of certain details, and, having committed these facts to memory, felt reassured about herself as a mother: she knew, for example, where her elder son had spent each of his birthdays since he'd left her side in 1992, even though she hadn't been present at a single one of these celebrations. It didn't matter. She'd *imagined* herself there. In her mind, she'd eaten cake and helped blow out the candles (whether there had been cake or candles being entirely beside the point). The fact that she and Francisco were still close was something she felt proud of, an achievement not to be minimized. This isn't as obvious or as simple as it might seem; every bond, even that of a mother and child, is breakable.

If Mónica and Ixta had been in touch during those final weeks of Nelson's absence, they might have had a lot to talk about.

So now, with only the clue of Nelson's last phone call from San Jacinto to guide her, Mónica began to consider the scope of Diciembre's travels, and do what she'd always done, perhaps what she did best: fill in details where there were few to be had. Her younger son, her Nelson; he'd been gone about two months by then, longer than he'd ever been apart from her. Too long—though she felt guilty for begrudging him this adventure he'd surely earned. There was, it seemed, nowhere in the country that he couldn't have seen on this journey. Were there any villages left to explore? Any hamlets? Any rural roads he hadn't yet taken? And if there weren't, why didn't he come home already? It was June, the dry season, a healthy time to be in the mountains. On the coast, the cold had begun in earnest. The heavy sea air clung to the shoreline, enveloped the city. She prayed that her son was enjoying himself, that he'd learned what he needed to learn on this trip, grown in the ways that he'd expected, and in others that would surprise him. She hoped most of all that he would come home soon, though she wrestled with this notion, and wondered if it was selfishness, if a better mother wouldn't prefer that her son wander and live every adventure he desired. Mónica imagined young village girls falling in love with her son; she found it easiest of all to picture this, since she was in love with him too: with his bright brown eyes and crooked smile, with his curls and the way the edges of his mouth dropped into a frown when he was deep in thought. He looked like a young

Sebastián; everyone remarked on the resemblance. She hoped he was careful, at least, if there happened to be an affair in the offing, and that no hearts were broken unnecessarily along the way—especially not Nelson's. In truth, his was the only heart she cared about. Never mind the girls.

In the city, her days went on without him; not in a blur, but yes, actually, in something of a blur. There was little to distinguish one from the next. Mónica hoped for news, but didn't expect any. She fell asleep every night, certain that there was no greater torture than an empty house, than *this* empty house. When she told me this, she gestured with a delicately waving hand, palm up, pointing to the lifeless rooms that surrounded her. I asked if all her careful imagining had been useful at all; if, in all that conjuring, she'd managed to have a sense of what Nelson was going through. Not the details—she couldn't have had an idea of the details—but a sense.

She thought about it. I think she wanted to say that she had, but found it dishonest, given what came after. That mother's intuition—she was forced to admit that perhaps it had failed her.

"Maybe I didn't want to think of him in any real trouble."

"It wasn't trouble," I said. "Not exactly."

She shook her head. "But it was close enough."

CERTAINLY THERE WAS NO ONE who missed Nelson more intensely than Mónica. Other people in his circle admitted that his absence in those months was noted, but not often. He was missed—but only in the most abstract sort of way. It was as if in the process of becoming Rogelio, he'd completed some mystical erasure: Nelson almost ceased to exist, temporarily, though it would eventually be seen as a prelude to a more serious kind of erasure. Again and again, I heard versions of the same sentiment: Nelson was well liked, but hard to know. The role they'd all wanted, to form part of Diciembre's historic reunion tour, had gone to him, their talented, arrogant friend; and now he was off in the provinces, becoming a new, if not improved, version of himself. There was a hint of jealousy to all this, but little curiosity about the specifics of the tour; and in truth, what curiosity there might have been was soon eclipsed by the news of Ixta's pregnancy. The world over, people are the same. They love to gossip. They love scandal. People asked the usual questions: If Nelson knew, if he was heartbroken, if he was the father, the jilted ex-boyfriend, or both. If he had regrets. If it was true love, or just sex. Any hint of squalor made ears perk up—it was what they lived for. Old girlfriends offered theories and shared indiscreet stories. Those who'd been friends of the erstwhile couple chose sides; and most, it should be said, chose the proud but ultimately likable Ixta over the absent Nelson. No one knew for certain that Ixta and Nelson had been sleeping together until just before he left—their discretion had been absolute—but taken as a group, the students and alumni of the Conservatory were a rather promiscuous bunch, so many suspected it. The conversation among this particular generation of Conservatory alumni played out along the sordid lines of a television talk show, the kind where couples proudly displayed their dysfunction in front of enthusiastic audiences who pretended to disapprove. More than a few of Nelson and Ixta's friends had played roles on those shows, as drug dealers or teenage mothers, as no-good boyfriends or lying girlfriends, so they understood the tropes well. Betrayal and infidelity had been normalized long ago. They were actors, after all.

One friend of Nelson's that I spoke to, Elías, was almost sheepish about the way they'd all forgotten their old classmate. We met in a creole restaurant not far from the Conservatory, on a warm afternoon in late January 2002. The tile floors were sticky and we tried three different tables before we found one that didn't wobble. Nelson's friend smoked one filterless cigarette after another, a compulsion which seemed to bring him no pleasure at all, but which I finally understood when I noticed that he was studying himself in the mirrored walls of the restaurant, as if critiquing his performance. He caught me watching him—our eyes locked momentarily in the mirror—and blushed.

"I've been thinking of quitting," he said, raising the cigarette above his head.

I nodded, not out of solidarity or comprehension, but out of sheer politeness. Pity. It was clear he was a terrible actor, or perhaps he was simply suffering a bout of low confidence. In any case, he didn't want to say anything bad about Nelson, so he shared a few memories instead, funny anecdotes about their time studying together, the mediocre scripts they'd endured, the dreams they'd had, which neither, he guessed, would ever achieve. Elías was working at his father's advertising agency now, making photocopies, fetching coffee, receiving far-too-generous pay for such simple and mindless work. He resented this bit of good fortune; told me it was, in fact, debilitating to his art (he blew a plume of smoke in the direction of the mirror as if to underline the point) and that he was all but torturing his old man, doing everything he could to get fired.

"If it's so bad," I asked, "why don't you just quit?"

The would-be actor stared at me. His expression told me I hadn't understood a single thing he'd said. He began to answer, but instead picked a bit of tobacco off his tongue. It was a practiced gesture of disdain, which he pulled off fairly well. Then he asked me how I knew Nelson.

"I'm a friend of the family," I said, which was, by that point, true.

"Sure," he said.

I brought us back to the subject: Elías carefully blamed the generalized indifference toward Nelson's disappearance on the actor himself. You reap what you sow, after all.

"He'd always cultivated this air of superiority, this sense of not belonging, of standing apart."

"I've heard that," I said. "But you were still friends?"

Elías said they were, in a manner of speaking. "But the longer he was gone, the farther away he began to feel. No one said anything at first. But it wasn't as if he called us. It wasn't as if he made any effort to reach out to us, to stay connected. He disappeared. Just like he'd always said he would. He'd always pretended not to be one of us. I guess we began to assume it was true."

18

BACK IN T—, in his free moments, Nelson was asking himself similar questions. And there were many free moments, plenty of time for a young man of Nelson's character to ask himself all sorts of uncomfortable things. About his past, his mistakes—many of which he cherished—and his future, which he found unsettling. With each passing day, he was more anxious to leave. He said as much to Ixta by phone.

"I knew he meant it," she told me later. "I could hear in his voice that he was serious."

"When are you coming home, then?" she asked him.

"Soon," Nelson said.

A week passed after Jaime's message, and still they heard nothing. On the seventeenth day, Nelson demanded Noelia call. "Your brother promised me money," he explained. "It isn't a lot, but it's a lot to me." She said she understood, but Nelson wasn't finished. Then there was the matter of the ID card; it was technically illegal to travel without one. Any police checkpoint could spell trouble. "Did you know that? Did you know I could be arrested on the road? While they confirm my identity, I'll be en-listed in the army, clearing land mines on the northern border!"

Noelia had not known that. He was exaggerating, she was sure of it. Still, she'd never really traveled, except to San Jacinto. And she hadn't even been there in a few years.

"I tried to tell Nelson there was nothing I could do. I assured him Jaime hadn't forgotten, and that he hadn't lied."

"So where is he?" Nelson asked. "Where is this powerful brother of yours?"

"Jaime's always busy," she said carefully. "That's all it is. He'll be here soon. I bet we'll hear from him tomorrow."

But when they didn't, Nelson insisted they go to Mr. Segura's bodega to make the call. The bus from San Jacinto had come and gone; no news from Jaime. Noelia relented. Mrs. Anabel saw them getting ready to leave, and began to panic.

"Where are you going?"

She hadn't been alone since Nelson had arrived, a fact nei-ther he nor Noelia realized until that moment.

"Just to the plaza, Mama," said Noelia.

Mrs. Anabel opened her eyes wide. "Without me?"

I almost snapped at her, Nelson wrote in his journal that night, without guilt, only wonder. He saw it as further proof that it was past time to leave this place, to abandon the performance before he made some mistake.

"No, Mama, of course not. We're all going together."

And they did: across town to Segura's shop. It took them more than twenty minutes to make the six-minute walk. Segura was just closing up, but he seemed happy to have company. Noelia went in to call and Nelson waited outside with Mrs. Anabel. He and Segura lowered her delicately onto the steps so she could sit.

"It's like I'm a queen," she said.

Nelson had never been with Mrs. Anabel outside the house. Her eyes darted about the plaza, marveling at everything she saw. The heat of the day had passed, and a few locals were out for a stroll. Mrs. Anabel seemed happy to watch them go by. The shawl around her shoulders slipped, and Nelson helped her rearrange it.

"This is my boy," Mrs. Anabel said.

"And a very nice boy, indeed, madam," Segura answered. "Are you enjoying your stay?"

"Quite a bit," Nelson said.

"And how much longer will you visit us?"

Mrs. Anabel looked on. They'd never discussed it.

"A while longer yet."

"Wonderful," said Segura.

A moment later Noelia came out of the bodega, apologizing. There'd been no answer on Jaime's phone.

"What are you sorry about?" Mrs. Anabel asked. She smiled gamely at Segura. "These children are always so polite."

Nelson sighed. "We need to talk to Jaime, Mama. That's all."

The old woman nodded as if she understood. "That sounds nice."

"We'll try again tomorrow," said Noelia.

. . .

NELSON DID GO BACK the next day, in fact, only this time he went alone. Segura was friendly, as usual. "Calling your brother?" he asked, but Nelson shook his head.

"Calling the city," he said, and Segura nodded.

He was calling Ixta. There was very little in Nelson's journals about the content of those conversations, but he scrupulously noted the length of each call: five minutes, eight and a half, three, seventeen. He made no mention of the long silences she reported to me, just these numbers, now rising, now falling. Perhaps the simple fact that she wasn't hanging up on him was what mattered; perhaps what he feared most was that one day she might.

Segura had a weather-bitten face and a heavy brow. His hair was mostly gone, so he wore a red cap on his head to protect it from the sun. That day, he dialed the number, then drifted outside to wait. It was his habit, a way of showing respect for his client's privacy. The call was four minutes long, and when it was over Segura came in to write the amount in his red notebook. Nelson stood at the counter, tapping his fingers and forcing a smile.

"You wanted to talk to your brother, didn't you?" Segura said, and without waiting for an answer, he reached below the counter. "Take a look at this." It was a drying, crinkled newspaper from the previous week. "Go ahead, you can take it. If I had to guess, I'd say your brother is busy these days."

Nelson thanked the shopkeeper and left.

Months later, I found this paper folded into Nelson's journals. By then it was yellowed and fading, but entirely legible, a copy of San Jacinto's local tabloid, dated June 21, 2001. On the cover was a photo of a truck surrounded by policemen. The headline read BUSTED, and the accompanying text recounted the seizure of eighteen kilos of processed cocaine at a checkpoint just fourteen miles outside San Jacinto, on the road to the coast. It was the largest seizure in the area in more than three years. There was another fact, mentioned only in passing, but which Nelson, or perhaps Segura, had underlined: the seized truck was registered to Jaime's company, but had been reported stolen three months prior. Police were investigating. The driver, a young man surnamed Rabassa, was being held in the local jail. The paper said his transfer to another facility was imminent.

THAT NIGHT, Nelson dreamed of the play. In the dream, he and Henry and Patalarga switched roles at random and constantly, even within a scene. It was dizzying and frenetic, but they couldn't stop. The feeling was terrifying: to be onstage and not be in control. Nelson tried to apologize to the audience, but he couldn't; nor was it necessary. Far from being put off by these sudden and confusing shifts, the crowd seemed to be loving them. Peals of laughter rose from the dark theater. Bursts of applause. Each time the actors changed characters, the spectators roared wildly, as if the members of Diciembre were acrobats on a wire, improbably cheating death. Henry, Patalarga, and Nelson barreled along. Nelson might begin a line as the president, and finish it as the servant, then shift immediately to Alejo, all without the consent or agency of the actor himself. In the midst of all this chaos, Nelson realized the stage was familiar to him: it was the Olympic, only now the theater was filled with miners and farmers and half-starved children with wind-burned cheeks, the people he'd been performing for up in the mountains. His head hurt. It was like running on a speeding treadmill, and he couldn't keep up. He didn't want to. Meanwhile, Henry had given in to it: the playwright flashed a manic, energized smile, nodding toward the audience with each new round of applause. At a certain point, Nelson realized they were saying "Olé!" as if it were a bullfight; as is often the case in dreams, the metaphor seemed right for an instant, and then fell apart. Who exactly was the bull? Who was the matador?

In the audience, Nelson caught sight of Ixta. (*How?* he wrote in his journal. *Wasn't the theater dark? It was, and yet, I could* see *her.*) And just like that, he was free of the play. Volume dropped off. Henry and Patalarga went on without him, while Nelson tiptoed to the edge of the stage, and peered out into the dark (which was not so dark, in fact). It was her. It had to be. He could see her clearly: Ixta's hands rested gently on her very pregnant belly, her black hair pulled back in a ponytail. She was frowning. She was the only person in the theater who appeared not to be enjoying the play at all.

She and Nelson himself, that is. Ixta didn't call his name or wave or offer any gesture to acknowledge him. She just sat and watched.

Nelson woke with the disturbing sense that many years now

separated him from the heady days of his past. From the tour, his life before, and the optimism he'd once had. It was still early, an hour before dawn, the time of day when one's doubts are most devastating; they hang heavy on your bones. The room was very cold: if there'd been light enough, Nelson might have been able to see his breath. He didn't understand why he felt the way he did, but there was no denying it. That morning, he was afraid of becoming old, and it was a very specific kind of old age he feared, one which has nothing to do with the number of years since your birth. He feared the premature old age of missed opportunities. He turned on the bedside lamp, but the bulb flashed and burned out all at once. In that brief instant of light, Nelson was able to make out the contours of the messy sculpture with which he shared this icy space. A monster, he thought, and forced his eyes closed. He felt very alone.

He forced himself to sleep again, and this time he did not dream.

Morning came, as it always did, and Nelson readied himself for the day's performance. He wrote down the dream in his journal and gathered his thoughts. This was what he must have expected of the hours to come: a few quiet moments sitting in the sun with Mrs. Anabel; a sputtering conversation, reminiscent in rhythm and tone of the squeaky up and down of an old children's teeter-totter. A day like all the others, spinning in place. At some point, he would go for a walk, moving through the streets like a ghost. No one would speak to him unless he spoke first. No one would approach him, or ask where he was from. He'd been introducing himself as Rogelio, and no one in

T—— questioned him. Some people shrugged, as if they knew already; others nodded without skepticism. A few even smiled. Not complicit, knowing smiles, but ordinary, guileless expressions of approval, of satisfaction: Of course you're Rogelio, they seemed to be saying. Who else would you be?

When Nelson emerged from his room, Mrs. Anabel was up already, sitting in her usual place in the courtyard. One of the cats, the gray and black tabby, had curled up at her feet in a patch of sunlight. At the sight of Nelson, the cat yawned and stretched, then retreated into the tall weeds. Mrs. Anabel, on the other hand, smiled at him, a hopeful, contented smile, just as she had each of the previous twenty days. But this morning was different. Nelson didn't smile back, not right away.

"What's wrong?" Mrs. Anabel asked when he sat.

"Nothing, Mama," he responded.

Noelia watched from the kitchen window as she cleaned up after breakfast. She saw Nelson sit by Mrs. Anabel's side and rub the back of his neck. He sat for a long time without talking. She was in and out of the kitchen that first hour, her usual flurry of morning activity; scrubbing, cleaning. As soon as she was finished, she started right in on lunch. Nelson hadn't mentioned leaving again, not for two days, and she had come to hope he might stay, just awhile longer. She'd miss him when he was gone. At around ten-thirty, she went to the market for some vegetables, leaving her mother and Nelson alone. "They had their heads bowed and were whispering. I even saw my mother smiling, heard her laugh, and I thought everything was fine."

But when she returned an hour later, things were not fine.

Mrs. Anabel's face was full of worry and her eyes rimmed with red. Nelson wasn't there.

"Is everything all right?" Noelia asked. "Where's Rogelio?"

"He's packing," Mrs. Anabel said, despairing.

"He's what?"

"He said he's leaving. He said he has to go." The old woman shook her head, then shuffled her feet, as if to stand. "I'd like to talk to your father. Is he out in the fields?"

When she recounted the events of that day, Noelia paused here. There were, she said, some things I should know about her mother. Mrs. Anabel's deterioration had come slowly, over the course of many years, a process so subtle that at times you wondered if it was happening at all. And even now, when that deterioration was an indisputable fact, her mind was always shifting: there were days when the old woman seemed completely lost, unable or unwilling to connect; and then, just when you'd begun to lose all hope, she'd recover. Like a fog lifting. There might be a spell of three days or more when she was something like her old self. Nelson's stay in T—— had coincided with a relatively consistent period. While Mrs. Anabel was not exactly sharp, she was not lost in the muddle, something Noelia attributed to Nelson's steadying presence. This was the context, part of what made Mrs. Anabel's remark about her husband all the more disconcerting. She had scarcely mentioned him in the previous days, and when she had, he'd always been dead.

Noelia took a deep breath. "No, Mama. Papa's not in the fields."

"And Jaime?"

"He's in San Jacinto."

"Then why won't he pick up his phone?" The old woman frowned. "Who's going to give this boy the money he needs?"

Mrs. Anabel slowly got to her feet.

"Where are you going, Mama?"

"I must have something in there somewhere," Mrs. Anabel said. She was standing now, gesturing toward the room where she slept. "Something I can give him."

"Sit down, Mama," Noelia barked. "I said *sit*."

Mrs. Anabel gazed at her with big eyes.

"Sit! Now wait here." Noelia called out for Nelson. She was angry. She wanted an explanation. She deserved one.

"Who is Nelson?" her mother asked.

"I knew immediately I'd made a mistake," Noelia told me later. She turned back to her mother, attempted a smile, but it was too late.

"Who's Nelson?" the old woman said again. "Why did you call Rogelio that?"

Noelia knelt before her mother. Mrs. Anabel was breathing heavily, looking pale and worried. Her voice trembled. "You said Nelson."

"I know, Mama. I made a mistake."

"Who is that?"

"It's no one. Now calm down. Everything is going to be all right." Noelia held her mother's hands. "Do you understand?"

"Yes," Mrs. Anabel whispered.

Noelia put a hand to her mother's cheek, and held it there for a moment, until Mrs. Anabel had closed her eyes. "Stay," she said, then got to her feet and went into the room where Nelson had been sleeping these last three weeks. She didn't knock, just pushed the door open, and found him sitting on the cot with his back against the wall. He had his legs stretched out, resting on top of his already packed bag.

"What's going on?" Noelia said.

Nelson didn't answer. He offered her a space on the cot, but she shook her head and stood with her arms crossed, unsmiling, unmoved.

"You know what's going on. I want to go home. That's all. I told her I was leaving." His voice was full of exhaustion. "I told her I had to go see Jaime. She asked me what it was about, and I said money."

"Why would you confuse her like that!"

Nelson turned very serious. "I never broke character."

"Are you sure?"

"I'm not the one who just called me Nelson."

"He was right," Noelia told me later. "And I'm not angry with him. Not really. I was then, but I'm not now. It's just that I'd hoped things would work out differently."

"Different how?" I asked her.

She thought for a moment. "I wanted things to go smoothly. I wanted it all to glide to the end. Most of all, I didn't want my mother getting upset."

Just then, they heard a voice—Mrs. Anabel—calling out for Noelia.

"Yes, Mama?"

Then to Nelson: "You can't just leave like that. You have to give her warning. You have to prepare her. It isn't fair."

Again, Mrs. Anabel called for her.

"I'm coming, Mama."

Nelson stood. "Of course it's fair."

Just then there was a shout.

Nelson and Noelia ran to the courtyard. Mrs. Anabel hadn't gotten very far from her seat, only a few steps, in fact. She lay on the ground, face pressed against the stone path. She wasn't moving.

"Mama!" Noelia shouted.

Nelson reacted quicker; he ran to her side, saw that she was breathing. He helped her turn over. She looked ashen. There was a cut just below her hairline, and a knot forming on her forehead. A tiny rivulet of blood ran down her temple. "Why did you leave me all alone?" she said.

Nelson held her gently. "We didn't. We were here all the time."

Mrs. Anabel shook her head. "I don't know you."

Noelia had stood back, but she hurried over now.

"Rogelio," she said. "Go across the street and get Mrs. Hilda. She's a nurse."

Noelia held her mother. Nelson hesitated for an instant.

"Go now," Noelia said.

He did as he was told.

I was the one who answered the door.

19

I HAD ARRIVED on the bus from San Jacinto that morning. So
began my direct involvement in all this. I had no firm plans for
my visit: stay a few weeks, perhaps, not longer, spend time with
my parents, help my old man repair the roof of their house. I'd
brought along a couple of books to read, the long ones I never
seemed to find time for in the city, and was determined to enjoy
myself. As far as the roof, I was frankly enthusiastic about the
task, a fact that surprised even me. The prospect of working
with my hands, as my father had done for his entire life, as his
father had done before him, seemed appealing. In the days before I left for my hometown, I must have been feeling something
akin to what Nelson had, just before embarking on the tour: the
heady anticipation of change, the desire to shake up my life, if
only slightly, only temporarily. I'd been laid off and I was bored.
My friends bored me, my routines. The block I lived on, with its
drab storefronts and constant noise. The implacably gray city
sky bored me infinitely, and every morning when I stepped out
into the streets, I imagined squatting on the roof of my parents'

home in T—— after a few hours of work (the details of which I had a hard time conjuring), looking out over the valley, the hills, the cartoonishly blue sky, and feeling good about myself. Proud. I hadn't felt that way in many months.

That day when Nelson arrived, part of me couldn't believe I was in T—— again. I hadn't been back in five or six years. Everything was the same, and yet not at all as I remembered, as if every item from my childhood home had been replaced by a smaller, and less impressive, version of itself. My old hiding place, for instance, the tree in the courtyard—from that spot, I'd spent many hours spying on my parents. I saw them argue on occasion, but on one family visit back to T—— I also saw them kiss. I must have been eight or nine years old, and no gesture could've been more shocking. All displays of affection were scrupulously hidden from us, the children, and to see them touching so unself-consciously had dazzled me. My recollections of that moment are vivid, even filmic, but the tree, I realized now, couldn't possibly have kept me hidden; it was thin and weak, with narrow knotty branches and a few scraggly leaves, suitable for hiding a cat but not a boy, and I was forced to consider the real possibility that my parents had kissed in the full knowledge that I was watching them.

This is what I was thinking when Nelson arrived. There was a knock, and my mother called from the kitchen that I should answer it. I went to the door. He was slight, with wavy dark brown hair, a little overgrown, and narrowed eyes that betrayed real worry. He was young, about my age, which might not have been important in any other context, but certainly was in a

270

place like T——. It's likely that on the day we met, Nelson and I were the only two men in our twenties in the entire town. Eric, the mayor's deputy, was our closest contemporary, and he was still in high school. So we stared, neither quite believing in the presence of the other. If there was no complicity, there was, at the very least, curiosity.

But all he said was, "There's trouble next door." Then he asked for my mother. Noelia needed her, he said. Without quite understanding, I called for her. Though I offered, he wouldn't come in; because I had nothing to say, I told him my name. The stranger nodded and introduced himself as Rogelio.

It was habit, I suppose. I don't recall if we shook hands.

"Mrs. Anabel fell and hit her head," he said to my mother when she came to the door, and a few moments later we'd crossed the street, the three of us, and were standing in the courtyard. This is what I remember: Mrs. Anabel sat on the ground, in the sun, looking very small, very frail. She had let herself sink into Noelia's arms, and at first, didn't appear to be in any pain, but such a flurry of words poured out of her—names, half sentences, questions—that it was clear she was not well. Noelia was trying to calm her down, and had cleaned her up as best she could with her shirtsleeve, which was stained pink with blood. There was an alarming bump on the old woman's forehead, and she kept touching it gingerly, before pulling her hand away.

"Don't touch it," Noelia said again and again. "Leave it alone. You're going to be fine."

I wasn't so sure.

My mother rushed over, and Noelia's expression was of relief.

I watched my mother in action. She asked Mrs. Anabel to explain what had happened. Then to follow her finger with her eyes. "Can you get up?" my mother asked. "Can you move your toes?"

Mrs. Anabel never answered any of the questions directly. She followed my mother's finger as it drifted left, and then she stayed there, holding her gaze on the empty space in front of her.

I heard my mother sigh.

Together, my mother and Noelia helped the fragile old woman to her feet. I offered to help, but my mother waved me away. They held her steady. They brushed her off. Mrs. Anabel had a cut on her elbow too, and she held it up for inspection. I watched my mother brush the dirt from the wound, and pick out a few tiny pebbles that had stuck to the broken skin.

Then they all but carried her to her bedroom.

Mrs. Anabel wasn't dying, or at least it didn't seem that way to me—but she was on the border of something. That sounds inexact, I know, and perhaps it does lack a certain medical precision, but what I mean is that even then, in the first moments after her fall, Mrs. Anabel appeared to be drifting between two states of consciousness. Her voice would accelerate and then fall off, then pick up again; and neither my mother nor Noelia, and least of all Mrs. Anabel herself, could control it. I watched her move across the courtyard, held up by Noelia and my mother, and it seemed almost as if she were floating, her feet barely touching the ground. She kept up a steady stream of words, calling for friends and relatives, calling for Rogelio, for Jaime, for her husband, quite clearly beginning to panic.

We made eye contact as she passed me. "Where is everyone?" she asked, but I didn't respond.

Noelia and my mother took the old woman inside, and Nelson and I pressed in too. After a few moments, my mother announced that she was afraid Mrs. Anabel might have suffered a concussion. We'd have to observe her carefully over the next few hours. The danger was swelling, and since no one had seen her fall, we had no way of knowing how bad it really was.

I didn't want to be there. I didn't want to hear any of this. Watching her loosed something within me; like I was a young boy, suddenly aware of nakedness, unprepared for it, and ashamed. I shouldn't be here, I thought, and somehow this emotion felt selfless at the time, though I see now that it was just the opposite. I wasn't respecting Mrs. Anabel's privacy; I was protecting myself from something I feared instinctively. This too was clear: the young man standing beside me felt much the same way. Outside, the earth glowed beneath a miraculous Andean sky, but from the corner of her room, the shrinking Mrs. Anabel exuded only darkness. It was like standing at the mouth of a deep cave and being chilled by its cool breath.

My mother and Mrs. Anabel whispered together for a moment, the old woman shaking her head again and again. Then, in a surprisingly loud voice, she asked for Rogelio. I turned to Nelson (though that was not yet his name to me), who stood with downcast eyes, his fidgeting hands momentarily still, jammed in the pockets of his jeans. He rocked back and forth on his feet, very slowly, and then, without a word, turned and left the room. Even now, this gesture seems very cruel, and I looked to Mrs. Anabel, then to my mother, then to Noelia, who shrugged. There was nothing for me to do there, so I followed him.

I found Nelson pacing the yard, looking alternately at his feet and then up at the sky. I sat by the wall, relieved to be out of doors, and watched this fitful stranger, whose theatrical display of anxiety relieved me of the necessity of displaying my own. There was something very genuine to it, and at the same time, exaggerated. I asked him what had happened, and Nelson frowned.

"My name isn't Rogelio," he said.

"So what is it?"

"Nelson," he answered, then apologized for having misled me.

I told him it didn't matter.

"You live here?" he asked. "I haven't seen you."

"I'm visiting. My mom lives across the street. But you knew that."

"That's my room," he said, gesturing with a half-raised arm toward the bedroom where he slept. "I've been here three weeks. Almost." He shook his head then, as if the very thought of these past three weeks made him tense.

"You're from the city?" I asked, though I could tell the answer just by looking at him.

"Yeah."

And then, for some reason, I asked him how he liked our town.

He smiled wanly, then shrugged. "It's very pretty," he said, which I would've expected him to say. Then he went on: "What I can't figure out is what people do for fun here."

It was an odd remark. As odd and misplaced as my question, perhaps. The wounded Mrs. Anabel was raving just a few steps from us, and suddenly Nelson wore an amused look, as if the idea of fun had only just now occurred to him, as if *that* were his complaint—the lack of fun—and not the terrible scene unfolding in the other room.

"That's what you can't figure out?"

He laughed nervously. For this, I liked him. "Among other things."

"What are you doing here?"

Nelson shrugged. "You know what? I can't remember."

"She's your grandmother?" I asked.

I honestly had no idea what their connection might have been. He shook his head, but didn't explain.

My sense of him, in those first moments we spent together, was of someone who'd lost his way. He was tentative, unsure of himself. He showed not the slightest interest in my presence. I could've been anyone. The sun was in my eyes, and when I looked at Nelson now, it was almost as if he were being swallowed by the light.

"Do your people know you're here?" I asked.

"Ixta does," he said.

"Who?"

"My girl."

The name stood out. I'd never met anyone by that name. Never even heard that name before, in fact.

It was then that Noelia ducked her head out of the room where Mrs. Anabel was languishing. She wore a look of worry.

"Go to the store," she said. "Ask Segura for hydrogen peroxide and aspirin and bandages."

Nelson nodded, but made no move toward the door.

"And try Jaime. Segura has the number." Noelia frowned at me, at my unnecessary presence. We hadn't even exchanged a greeting. "You go with him." We were two young men being shooed away from a crisis. Sent on an errand, like children. I was happy to be dismissed.

Except for the walk to my parents' house that morning, this outing with Nelson was my first in many years through the streets of T——. I was always misremembering the place. The stunted tree in the courtyard was just one symptom of a broader condition. In my mind, the shuttered church had always been open; the dusty, neglected plaza had always been neat and tidy. It was a town where people did not die so much as disappear very slowly, like a photograph fading over time. And here I was again.

The bus I'd come in on that morning was still parked in the plaza, preparing to make its return trip to San Jacinto. A few locals hovered around its open door. They loaded the bags, re-arranged them, made space, and jammed in some more. Buses like this one were never full. They left half-empty, and picked up passengers along the way, as many as could fit. Nelson glanced in the direction of the bus. I must have said something about T—— not being as I remembered it. I'd been having versions of this very ordinary realization all morning.

"What was it like?" Nelson asked, with something like genuine curiosity.

"Bigger," I said, though that word was not exactly correct. I thought back to my childhood, in the shadow of these mountains, beneath this sky, and it was the only word that came to mind.

"Everyone's childhood seems bigger from a distance," Nelson said.

Segura greeted us both warmly, even me, though he probably hadn't seen me in years. Nelson was all business: peroxide, aspirin, and bandages. Segura shook his head sadly. "Bandages, I have," he said. "And the aspirin. How many do you need?"

Nelson held up an open hand, and Segura uncapped a dusty bottle, and carefully tipped five pills into a small envelope. "Anything else?"

"I have to make a call."

Segura took the phone out from under the counter. Nelson wrote a number down in the storeowner's red notebook, while the old man spent a long moment and considerable energies untangling the cord. When this task was complete, he bent over the machine and lifted the handset, pressing it carefully to his ear.

"Good connection today."

Nelson nodded. "Clear weather, I suppose."

"God bless," answered Segura. He squinted at the paper, then at the keypad, before pecking deliberately at the numbers, as if selecting which were his favorites.

And meanwhile, I had time to look around: time enough to see the dust motes floating in a bar of sunlight, to test my weight on different sections of the warped and creaky wooden floor, to notice the empty store shelves, featuring one of each item—

a single bar of soap, a single box of pasta, a single bottle of Coca-Cola—as if these artifacts were not to be sold but maintained as visual reminders of a lost way of life.

"It's ringing!" announced the old shopkeeper in a bright voice that seemed out of place in his dreary store.

I stepped outside and sat on the curb, closing my eyes against the early-afternoon sun. I could hear Nelson talking from inside the store, just the rising and falling murmur of his voice, and I made no effort to parse the words themselves. In any case, I didn't understand much of what was happening, and felt only dimly that it had any connection to me at all. There was a frail and wounded old woman, a neighbor of my parents, that much I knew; and this stranger, whose foreignness in T—— made him recognizable. Beyond that, there was nothing, just the ordinary confusion a young man feels when confronted with the place of his birth. My parents were nearing old age, and if they'd come home to be comfortable, part of me knew that they'd also come home to die. Not now, not soon, perhaps, but eventually. Mrs. Anabel's sallow skin and bloodshot eyes had made that clear to me. The way my mother had rushed to her side only confirmed it. I would have preferred not to think about all this, and so when I felt a pat on the head, I welcomed the interruption. It was Segura, who smiled at me and, not without some effort, lowered himself down to the curb, placing a hand on my shoulder to steady himself through the process. When he was seated and comfortable, he spread his short legs out in front of him, pointing his toes at the sky, and let out a long, satisfied breath. Then he lifted the brim of his cap and let the sun hit his face.

"I like to give my customers some privacy," he said with a wink.

I nodded, not because I agreed, or thought it was funny or even understood, really; I nodded because I'd been trained my entire life to agree with my elders. If I sometimes forgot this when I was in the city, it came back to me instantly in T——.

The shopkeeper didn't wait for my answer. "You're the Solis boy, aren't you?"

"Yes," I said.

"Here to help your old man with the roof, I guess?"

I nodded, not at all surprised that he knew my business.

"You're a good boy." He paused. "Rogelio, he's your friend in there?"

And again, out of a sense of respect, I agreed. "My neighbor," I said, noting briefly that the stranger's name had shifted yet again.

"He's always in here, always calling. His brother is going to have a big bill to pay when he comes home."

Then Segura clapped his hands together at the prospect, a gesture that was not so much greedy as anxious. That money, that windfall, I quickly realized, had already been spent. Lest I misunderstand, the old man began to explain all the ways business had slowed since I'd last come to visit. I listened respectfully, and when the moment was right, told him that Anabel wasn't well. The bandages, the aspirin—they were for her.

"She hasn't been well for many years."

"This is different. She fell."

Segura shook his head. "At her age that can be very bad."

Just then Nelson stepped out of the shop. He stood in the doorway, squinting against the sun. The shopkeeper and I turned to face him.

"I couldn't get through," he announced.

Segura eyed him quizzically. "That's odd."

"Happens."

"Would you like me to dial again?"

Nelson shook his head.

"Just the bandages and the aspirin, then?"

"Sure," Nelson said. "Write it down."

The movement around the bus had all but subsided now, the last few passengers making their way aboard. A light breeze scattered a few leaves across the plaza, and the driver honked his horn twice to announce his imminent departure. It rang across the town like a shot. A few heads ducked out of windows; a sleeping dog sat up with a start, and stared in the direction of the bus.

Nelson did as well. His back and shoulders were straight, and from where I sat, he appeared almost statuesque. The bus clicked into gear, and slowly rounded the plaza in our direction. Without a word, Nelson stepped into the street, and blocked its path. It all happened very slowly. There was something robotic in his movements, as if he were being pulled by some force he could not resist. He held an open palm before him, and the bus slowed to a stop. The door opened. Nelson looked in my direction one last time, then stepped aboard.

PART

FOUR

20

A WEEK LATER, on a frigid mid-July afternoon in the city, there was a knocking at the gates of the Olympic. The bell hadn't worked in nearly a month, and Patalarga was accustomed to long stretches without interruption; so for many minutes, he went on about his business, scarcely noticing the sound at all.

What was *his business*?

Since returning from the tour, it was no longer clear. The scale of the task before him, the restoration of the Olympic, seemed crushing; nor was the theater all that needed restoring. He'd always been prone to bouts of sadness, but the sharpness of this feeling was entirely new.

When Patalarga finally went to the gate, he found Nelson, shivering. Winter had arrived on the coast with its usual cruelty; the colorless sky, the damp sea air, and it was all reflected in the tightly pressed eyes of the people on the sidewalk, who walked past the two reunited friends as if pushing against an impossible weight. Whatever a welcome feels like, the city streets offered up just the opposite; and Nelson seemed in every way unprepared to be home again. Physically, he was a wreck. He wore the same clothes he'd been wearing the moment he stepped on the bus in T——. And this too was clear: spiritually, he was elsewhere. You could see it in his eyes.

"He looked as if he hadn't slept in a month," Patalarga said. "As if he hadn't slept since we'd left him."

Or perhaps: as if he'd walked from the bus station, halfway across the city. Or even more exactly: as if he'd traveled for a week with only the little money he'd had in his pocket that afternoon in T——; as if he'd survived days and covered many hundreds of kilometers by haggling or begging for rides in small towns across the provinces, journeying in silence, suffering cold and dizziness at high altitudes; as if, in that spell, he'd become accustomed to both external silence and interior turmoil. Fear. As if he'd tired of explaining himself to strangers, and started doing all that he could in those days to become invisible. As if all his money had been spent halfway through the voyage, and since then he'd eaten only what he was proffered by one kind family or another that happened to take pity on him: a can of cashews and a cup of juice one day, half a mango and a Coca-Cola the next. Evidence of those meals could be found on his T-shirt, which he hadn't had a chance to wash. He wore no jacket, and hadn't shaved. His hair was overgrown, and more unruly than normal. And even so, there was something manic in his exhaustion, something Patalarga recognized immediately: Nelson wasn't happy, or free from worry, or even optimistic—but he seemed liberated.

"I asked him how he'd gotten here, and he laughed."

"The long way," he said.

Once inside the theater, Patalarga dealt with Nelson's most immediate necessities. He lent him a clean shirt and a sweater, made him something to eat, and set a pot of water to boil. A few minutes later the two of them were sitting in the orchestra, drinking tea, and considering the empty stage where they'd first met, not many months before.

While Nelson ate, Patalarga did most of the talking. He didn't mind. He'd felt very alone since the tour's abrupt end, and the transition home had been more difficult than he'd expected. Turns out he liked being on the road. Turns out his wife Diana didn't mind spending long days without him. Turns out she'd decided, while he was gone, that she wanted children, after all. This last point was at the center of every disagreement now: if they bickered about the dishes or the laundry or the bills or the car or his family or her job or which movie to see or what to make for dinner, Patalarga understood that they were in fact arguing about this other, more vexing issue. It was exhausting. Her life had become disappointing to her, and by extension, Patalarga had as well. "If you die, I'll have nothing," she'd said to him one evening, and he'd made the mistake of responding, "You'll have the Olympic." That night, by mutual agreement, he'd left the house and been sleeping at the theater ever since. Six nights now. Patalarga felt ashamed. He missed her. It was only his pride that kept him from going home, something he understood quite clearly. But a man is helpless before his own pride.

"Didn't you tell me a child is always good news?" Nelson asked.

"In the abstract."

"You don't want one?"

"Where would we put it?" Patalarga said with a shrug.

Nelson ate his simple snack (a couple of rolls, each adorned with a bit of avocado and a slice of cheese); he sipped his tea and listened to his friend without judgment. Or without the appearance of judgment, which is just as important. Patalarga kept talking, and sometimes Nelson would close his eyes as if in deep concentration. Mostly he was quiet. Thinking. Processing. According to Patalarga, he looked "like a man floating inside a dream."

When Nelson had put away the last bite, he stood, left his empty plate balancing on the armrest, and walked toward the stage. Halfway down the aisle, he stopped, with his hands on his hips, gaze shifting stage left, stage right, then back again. This is the image Patalarga remembers most vividly from that day: Nelson, arms akimbo, his thin silhouette framed by the curtains of the dilapidated theater.

"I asked him what was on my mind, the only question I could think of," Patalarga told me later.

Which was this: "Are you in trouble?"

Nelson's voice carried well. "Yes. I believe I am."

Patalarga joined his friend. They made their way down to the front of the theater, where Nelson climbed to the stage and sat, just as Henry had on that day of the first rehearsal: in precisely the same spot, in fact, with his feet dangling off the edge just as Henry's had. Nelson, unlike Henry, let them swing, almost playfully, banging the hollow wooden stage a couple of times with the backs of his heels. The sound boomed in the empty theater like a giant bass drum.

"So what happened?" Patalarga asked.

Nelson shook his head. "That's the thing. I don't really know. The old woman had a fall. That last day, just before I left, she fell and hit her head."

"And?"

Nelson shrugged. "It didn't seem so serious at first. But then it did. She was sort of coming apart."

"And you left?"

"Yes," he said, color rushing to his cheeks. "That was a week ago."

Now he was in a rush. Every day counted. Ixta was moving on. A week in T—— hadn't seemed bad, twelve days was doable, but the longer it stretched on, the worse it got. He began to describe the endless hours in T——, its dreary routines. There was something essentially sad about the place, he said. The challenge was not the acting; it was staying focused. Fighting boredom. Beating back the melancholy, which was almost chemical. It was floating in the air. In the morning, you could smell it.

"That's woodsmoke," said Patalarga.

Nelson shook his head. "It was a prison."

"Ask Henry what he thinks about that. What about Jaime?"

"He promised to come back, with my money, but he never did." Nelson sighed. "How long was I supposed to wait?"

"And what did you think when he told you all this?" I asked Patalarga.

This was months later, during our final interview. We sat in the Olympic, which, even in its ruinous condition, maintained a stately beauty; we exchanged stories about Nelson, a young man with whom I'd spent no more than an hour but who had almost come to feel like a version of myself. By that point, no one thought our relationship strange anymore. Not even me.

"I understood why he'd left, but I imagined my own mother, falling like that. He shouldn't have left like that, and I told him so. He should've waited to see if she was all right."

That's what we all felt in T——. As it happened, I was the one who had to explain what he'd done. First, Noelia and my mother; then everyone wanted to know: What did he say before he boarded the bus? How did he seem? Was he upset, hopeful, angry? After Mrs. Anabel died, the stories began: That he stole from the old woman. That he killed her. That Noelia had fallen in love with him. In the weeks after Nelson's disappearance, I— of all people!—was asked to confirm or deny these theories. How many times did I say I barely knew him? That I'd just met him? Even Jaime, when he finally arrived in town, dragged me in to bark a few questions at me.

None of that mattered to Nelson. "I came for Ixta," he explained to Patalarga that first night in the Olympic. Needless to say, this answer wouldn't have satisfied anyone back in T——.

"So what are you going to do?" Patalarga asked.

He didn't have a plan, only an urgent feeling in his chest that he could hardly bear. He'd spent days moving away from the town, retracing Diciembre's haphazard route toward the coast, and his goal the entire time had been to release himself of this pressure in his heart. "I need to see her," he told Patalarga.

"What if she doesn't want to see you?" Patalarga asked. He was thinking of his own wife, darkly.

Nelson frowned. "But she does."

Of Nelson's week on the road, we do know this: a few days into his journey, he managed to speak with Ixta from a small town called La Merced. It's even possible (though unconfirmed) that he spent the very last of his money paying for this frustrating, three-minute conversation. She doesn't recall much about it ("At this point, does it really matter?" she said when I asked her about it), except that Nelson reiterated those things he'd said to her from Segura's store on his last day in T——. That he was coming to see her. That she should wait for him. Again, that hopeful, anxious tone of voice. Pleading, you could call it. And if Ixta gave him the impression that she wanted to see him, "Well, I didn't mean to," she told me. "I shouldn't have. But he was very persistent. And yes, it was flattering. I was lonely, you understand."

"Just knock on her door," Patalarga said. "Just like that?"

Nelson nodded.

Patalarga didn't disagree; what's more, he thought it was likely the only way to resolve things. But having heard the story of Nelson's departure, he had another, slightly different, concern:

"What if the old woman didn't make it? How do you think Jaime's going to react?"

Nelson was silent.

"He'll send someone after you, won't he?"

"He has my address. He took my ID. That's why I'd rather stay here. If that's okay."

That first night they slept on the stage of the Olympic, and so high did the ceiling seem to them, it was as if they were camping beneath a dark and infinite sky. They were safe here, they reasoned. They batted around a few ill-considered but pleasing metaphors: the theater was an old galleon adrift on the seas, or a cave hidden deep inside the earth, or a bunker housing two old, grizzled warriors, the last of a once great army, now contemplating certain defeat. They laughed a good deal. They solved the conundrum of Patalarga's faltering marriage. They remembered Henry in tones usually reserved for a man who'd passed. Nelson couldn't believe that his two friends weren't talking. He'd thought of them as an indivisible unit.

Patalarga had too. "He'll come around," he said, without really believing it, and Nelson nodded politely.

They talked for hours. Nelson described the terrible morning of Mrs. Anabel's fall, which, he argued, was the logical end to his time in T——. He didn't feel guilty, just relieved to be gone.

"Another week there and I might have tripped the old lady myself."

They both laughed, then fell silent for a spell, until Nelson said, "I never should have gone on tour, you know?"

"That's what Henry said on the bus ride back."

"If I'd never left the city, I'd be with Ixta now."

"I told him that you could never know these things." Patalarga sighed. "People believe what they want to believe."

This is a fact.

When Patalarga woke up the next day, Nelson was already gone.

. . .

THAT MORNING, in the quiet, empty theater, Patalarga made yet another attempt to reach out to Henry. He told himself then (as he had on every occasion) that he was doing it for his old friend, persisting out of a sense of loyalty, but he later admitted that his motives were more selfish than that. Patalarga wasn't doing well either. He was only forty, estranged from his wife, sleeping on the stage of an abandoned theater. The starkness of his own situation made it clear that he couldn't afford to give up on friends like Henry.

Their handful of conversations in the few weeks since the end of the tour had been short and unsatisfying. This occasion would be no different. The phone rang for what seemed like an endless stretch, and Patalarga simply let it. A minute, and then another. He had no real expectations. When Henry finally answered, his "Hello" was forced, just above a whisper; then he apologized, cleared his throat, and tried again. Better this time. Patalarga laughed to himself. Henry was acting. He wouldn't answer questions, only complete the declarative sentences that Patalarga began for him:

"And you're doing . . . ?"

"Well."

"Staying busy with . . . ?"

"Work."

"Feeling more or less . . . ?"

"At peace."

They spoke in this manner for no longer than three minutes,

during which time Patalarga informed Henry of the news that pertained to them both, that Nelson had come home.

"And this news strikes you as . . . ?"

"Good," said Henry.

Patalarga sighed. "We're at the Olympic if you want to come see us."

Henry said neither yes nor no; and the conversation, as Patalarga recalls, didn't end so much as slip away: a tiny balloon on a string, sliding through the fingers of a child. In his mind's eye, Patalarga watched it float up to the sky and vanish. "At a certain point, I realized I wasn't talking to anyone. I sort of laughed to myself and hung up."

And afterward, he sat in the dark theater for a moment, trying to will himself to call his wife, to apologize.

AS FOR NELSON, he'd woken before dawn, showered, shaved, and left the Olympic full of hope. He'd slept very little, but once on the streets, felt nothing but energy. The morning traffic was just humming to life, the city's stubborn refusal to capitulate in the face of another dismal winter's day. And Nelson—he too would not give up. He too would fight. That pressure in his chest, what he'd been feeling for a week or more, was still there; he'd come to think of it as part of him. He walked in the direction of Ixta's office, and at around seven, not yet halfway there, stepped into a crowded café. He wasn't hungry; he only wanted to see up close the men and women who had gathered there. They were, to a person, loud, brash, and rude; and it was precisely their rudeness that reminded him of what he'd missed about the city. He loved them, loved the sound of their laughter, the way they heckled one another. They told vulgar jokes while sipping espresso, shook folded newspapers furiously to underline the validity of their complaints. They cursed politicians, mocked celebrities, grumbled about their families. The place was so busy that no one approached to take Nelson's order, and so he stood in one corner, content to watch the proceedings in silence. When it became too much, he closed his eyes and just smelled the place: the sharp scent of coffee and steamed milk, fresh bread and sausage. He opened his eyes once more and noted the length of the long wooden bar; the shine of the polished metal banister that led to the upstairs dining room; and the oil paintings on the walls, heroic canvasses composed by artists who'd been dead since his father was just a boy in short pants.

We know Nelson stopped here because it so happened that an uncle of his, Ramiro, married to Mónica's sister Astrid for two decades, spotted him. He'd been a regular at this particular restaurant since 1984, and by now his morning coffee was the very highlight of his day. He hadn't seen his nephew in over a year, and the young man was so changed that Ramiro didn't even recognize him at first. As soon as he did, he made his way over, moved in part by curiosity, in part by familial obligation (Ramiro was nothing if not correct), and gave Nelson an enthusiastic hug. Their brief conversation went as follows:

UNCLE RAMIRO: Nephew!

NELSON: . . .

UNCLE RAMIRO: What are you doing here? When did you
  get back?

NELSON: . . .

UNCLE RAMIRO: How was the tour?

NELSON: . . .

And so on, for an interminable few minutes. Nelson answered all questions with a blank stare, except one. Ramiro
asked, "Where are you going?"

"I'm going to be a father," Nelson said.

Ramiro smiled generously, with a hint of condescension, as if
such a thing were inconceivable.

"That's wonderful."

The conversation was over; Nelson's steadfast gaze made him
nervous.

An hour later, Ramiro was on the phone, reporting to his
wife that Nelson must be on drugs. He omitted any mention of
his nephew's impending paternity, which he'd simply chosen not
to believe. Astrid dutifully passed along Ramiro's message of
concern to her sister, who took the news relatively well. She knew
her son wasn't on drugs, but couldn't help being concerned
nonetheless. Why hadn't he called to tell her he was home? By
midmorning, Mónica had all but given up on the workday. She
told her colleagues she didn't feel well, which was true, and went
straight home to wait for her son.

She crossed the city in a cab, thinking of Nelson.

She paid the driver with two bills from her purse, and forgot
the change, thinking of Nelson.

She unlocked the door to her empty house, thinking of Nelson.

BY THE TIME Mónica heard from her sister, her son was standing in front of Ixta, in the reception area of a documentary film-maker's small but not unpleasant offices, a converted guesthouse attached to his palatial home in the Monument District. Though Ixta doesn't specifically remember telling Nelson about her job, she assumes she must have. There's no other way he could've found the office, which was hidden on a side street she herself had never heard of until she started working there. This was a new job, just as everything about her life in those days was new: her body, her home, her sense of the future. When I asked Ixta to describe the work, she screwed her face up into a frown.

"It was paid idleness," she said. "That's all."

She worked for a man whose vanity and self-image demanded the employment of a secretary. In absolute terms, there was very little to do: the occasional ringing phone to answer, now and then an appointment to jot down. Her employer, the filmmaker, had won an international award eight or nine years prior for a documentary denouncing the coerced sterilization program the government had run during the war. It was, like many award-winning documentaries, rewarded for its grim and outrageous subject matter, and not for the film itself, which was mediocre. The director could not understand why his career had stalled ever since. His reputation, such as it was, depended on that award, which was fast losing its luster; and as a result, everything this man did (and by extension, everything Ixta did) was designed to stave off his impending and inevitable professional oblivion. There was a problem: No one cared about human rights anymore, not at home or abroad. They cared about growth—hoped for and celebrated in all the newspapers, invoked by zealous bureaucrats in every self-serving television interview. On this matter, the filmmaker was agnostic—he came from money, and couldn't see the urgency. Like many of his ilk, he sometimes confused poverty (which must be eradicated!) with folklore (which must be preserved!), but it was a genuine confusion, without a hint of ill intention, which only made it more infuriating. He kept a shaggy beard in honor of his lost, rebellious youth, and employed a booming voice whenever he suspected someone might be listening. In the 1980s, he'd moved in the same circles as Henry and Patalarga, though he'd never been close to them, and, when pressed, admitted to me that he'd deliberately stayed away after Henry's "unfortunate arrest." He wore colorful woven bracelets around his unnaturally thin wrists, and had, quite predictably, fallen in love with Ixta. She'd come well recommended by a professor at the Conservatory, and now the filmmaker hovered around her desk for hours at a time, making conversation, telling bad jokes, and ensuring that neither of them could have accomplished anything, had there, in fact, been anything to accomplish. She found him charming, even handsome from certain angles, at certain times of the day; and his awkward, boastful flirting was a welcome distraction from her troubles at home, with Mindo, which had unfortunately continued to fester.

On some days, she even permitted herself to complain about the father of her child, whom the filmmaker would never meet.

As it happened, Nelson's arrival in the city coincided with a terrible realization for Ixta: that she and Mindo were not meant to be together. She'd known it since the previous spring, but now things were approaching a boiling point. Or not—the metaphor was perfectly imprecise: it was the lack of heat she feared, the lack of heat that made her tremble. She imagined the barren months to come, then the years, the decades, and felt something approximating terror. She and Mindo didn't fight; that would have required some essential spark they'd already lost. They floated in parallel spaces, all their conversations reduced to the necessary minimum, stripped of whimsy or invention or humor. They talked about the baby as if preparing for an exam, and though they paid the rent together, that did not make their apartment a home. She bored him; and the feeling was mutual. He'd gone too long without touching her, and she could think of nothing worse. Sometimes in the shower she found herself weeping. At moments like these, Ixta placed a hand on her beautiful, swollen belly to remind herself she was not alone in this world. Not entirely, at least.

That morning when Nelson appeared at the office door, this is where Ixta's left hand went instinctively. And that's where she kept it, for a long moment, taking in the sight of her former lover, her former partner, her friend. He'd told her by phone to wait for her, and now, days later, he was here. His very presence took her breath away. He looked young, younger than she remembered him, and this fascinated her: Who lives through a tour like that and comes out looking younger? He'd shaved that morning in the backstage bathroom of the Olympic, and had that fresh, scoured look of a recent graduate prepping for a job interview (though Nelson had never gone on one of those). He offered her a tentative smile. She nodded back. There was nothing she wanted to say, she told me later. She didn't stand to greet him. She waited for him to make the first move.

Meanwhile, her employer was in the kitchenette, preparing coffee, carrying on his part of a one-sided conversation with Ixta. (No one remembers the topic.) Twice Nelson began to say something to the woman he loved, only to be interrupted by this oblivious voice from the other room. When it happened a third time, both he and Ixta laughed. His laughter was tinged with nervousness; hers was involuntary, and it was the sound of this combined laughter that made the filmmaker step out into the hallway to see that his lovely, pregnant, and much desired assistant was not alone.

"I assumed at first that he was the father of the child," the filmmaker told me later. "The painter. From the pictures I'd seen, they looked similar, I suppose. The same kind of person. I was nice enough. Polite, at least. Did she say anything? He seemed callow, insubstantial, but that's probably not very charitable. It's a pity what happened. I haven't spoken to her since that day, you know? She never even came to pick up her last check."

Nelson introduced himself ("My friend," Ixta added solemnly), hands were shaken, and the first awkward moments the two former lovers spent together were in the company of this filmmaker, who attempted to mask his jealousy with a too-strong dose of bonhomie.

"Congratulations," he said.

"He's not the father," Ixta clarified.

"Thank you," Nelson added.

The filmmaker blushed. Then he clapped Nelson on the back, asked a few impertinent, vaguely sexual questions, filling the room with his grand and exaggerated laughter. Then he disappeared to his office, where he shut the door softly, and fired off a few strongly worded memos to colleagues. He'd have Ixta type them up later, and hoped she'd read in his tone the depth of feeling he had for her.

(She would not.)

The filmmaker's conversation with Nelson took five minutes, not more, and through it all, Ixta had sat, as still as she could manage, breathing slowly, talking very little, with her left hand resting on her belly. She didn't hear much of what was said, willfully blurring the words because she knew they had almost nothing to do with her. She wished for silence. Now that she and Nelson were alone, she began to pay attention again. The light in the room was dim, almost cloudy, and Ixta felt for a moment she had to strain to see him, though he was only a few steps away.

"Are you all right?" he asked.

"I didn't think I'd see you," she said, which was a lie. In fact, in her bones, she'd been expecting him, only she didn't know how she would feel when he arrived.

Nelson proposed they go out somewhere, just as she had assumed he would. Ixta began to protest that she couldn't, that she had to work, but then she stopped herself. "I realized that would have been cruel. And it wouldn't have been true. I wanted to see him. I wanted to talk to him. He was right there, right in front of me."

She stood for the first time, and noticed Nelson's eyes opening wide to take in the sight of her. Nelson, admiring her figure. Nelson, accepting and appreciating the possibility she represented. She loved being pregnant for moments like these. Pregnancy is always mythic; it can be medicalized and quantified, carved into trimesters or weeks, but nothing can subvert its essential mystery. Ixta had a strange kind of power over men; and though their desire manifested in different ways now, it was still desire. For a moment, she let herself revel in it.

"You look very beautiful," Nelson managed, which was the only sensible thing he could've said.

Ixta nodded regally.

"Are you sure you can walk?"

"Of course I can walk," she said quickly, and Nelson blushed.

The truth was, she'd been waiting for some last, desperate gesture on Nelson's part ever since the day of his phone call from the road. "I've always had a sense for these kinds of things," she told me. Life's big events, those moments of real, even unbearable emotion—if you were paying attention, they tended to announce themselves, as the ocean swells in anticipation of a wave. Ixta's childhood and adolescence were littered with these instances of premonition: the tearful day her father left the family for good, the day of her first period, the day her cousin Rigoberto was killed in a car accident.

And when Nelson ended their relationship, in July of the previous year; she'd felt it acutely then. Ixta could have mouthed his words as he uttered them. What he said that day was somehow not surprising to her; in fact, it was the utter predictability of his words she found shocking. She watched him break her heart, marveling at how thoroughly he believed in phrases she knew to be untrue. No, Ixta thought to herself: No, she was not keeping him from his dreams. She was not shutting him out of the world. She was doing none of those things. If they were happening, he was doing them to himself.

But Ixta didn't argue with Nelson that day. His complaints were banal and selfish, and she anticipated all of them. He would regret it—she'd known this even then, had known it in her gut—but she felt no pride or comfort in this knowledge. It would not heal her.

Now they went for a slow walk, heading west into the dull residential sections of the district, where all the houses appeared to be identical, distinguished only by the varying colors of their exterior walls. There are few monuments in the Monument District, and almost nothing to see. An earlier, now ousted and forgotten, government had intended to make the area its showplace, but those plans never came to pass. History intervened. The war happened. The district was colonized, not by museums or libraries or statues as its name implied but by private citizens, a guarded, rather anonymous group of upper middle class who lived quietly and traveled exclusively by car. Ixta and Nelson were the only people on the street. They walked side by side ("but not together," she pointed out), struggling to have a conversation.

Nelson was careful, asking as politely and obliquely as he could about the state of her pregnancy. His voice was low, and at times Ixta had to strain to hear him.

She remembers being disappointed: This was what he'd come for? To mumble at her?

They walked for ten minutes, coming to a small, greenish park with a few concrete benches, and it was here that they decided to sit. The blank gray clouds showed no signs of relenting; not today, perhaps not ever. Nelson would've preferred a café or a restaurant, a place where he could have performed any number of chivalric gestures (pulling Ixta's chair out for her, taking her coat), but it seems they'd walked in the wrong direction, away from everything, and into a warren of residential streets from which there was no visible escape. Perhaps she'd planned it that way. Perhaps she wanted no gestures. I've seen the park myself, and it's true: in winter, it's desolate and empty and feels not like the city but like an outpost of it. Nelson quietly despaired.

In the half hour that followed, he and Ixta touched on the following subjects: Ixta's mother's health; the latest film offerings; a near stampede at a local soccer stadium the previous Sunday, which Ixta's younger brother had narrowly survived; the untimely death of a much-loved professor they both knew from the Conservatory; an article which had critiqued—quite harshly—a mutual friend's latest gallery show, and the content of the paintings themselves (which Nelson hadn't seen) but which Ixta described "as if a mad Botero had decided to reinterpret the oeuvre of Georgia O'Keeffe."

She played that line as if it were hers, and both of them laughed.

In fact, that observation came from the critique, which, coincidentally, I had written, just before leaving the city for T——.

While Nelson was waiting for his courage to appear, Ixta observed the man she'd once imagined to be hers, and felt many things—heartache, nostalgia, even pity, but not romantic love; and the desolate streets of the Monument District provided an appropriate backdrop to these realizations. He kept up a nervous, steady stream of questions—about her work, her friends, her family—but for many minutes made no declarative statements and offered no confessions. Then she placed a hand on his shoulder—"To see if he were real," she explained to me—and Nelson tensed like a child about to receive an injection.

"I'm sorry," he said then. It was as if he'd been jolted to life. "I've been thinking I should tell you that."

He paused, and turned sideways on the bench in order to face her. Ixta kept looking straight ahead.

"That's what you've been thinking? That you're sorry?"

He nodded, a gesture she didn't see but sensed, the tiniest vibration in the winter air. She'd locked her eyes on the edge of the park, on a wall painted with a once colorful mural, now faded and scissored with cracks. It helped her remain steady, she confessed later, and in the anxious few moments that followed, she studied the turns and pivots of those cracks, as if attempting to memorize them.

It felt almost cruel to ask, "What is it you're sorry for?"

"I should have treated you better."

Ixta nodded. "Yes, I think we can agree on that."

"That's the first thing I wanted to say. There's more." He took a deep breath, and continued, his voice markedly different now. Strong, clear. "I thought about you every day in T——. Do you understand? I thought about you and me and the baby. I want to be someone you could love again. I'm sorry. I've wasted so much time. Do you hear me?"

She heard him.

"Look at me," Nelson said, and she turned to face him. He reached out his hands. "I'm serious."

"I know you are," she answered.

Years before, a few weeks after they'd first met, Nelson and Ixta had gone south for a few days and camped along the beach. They were part of a large, boisterous group, and brought more alcohol than food. They'd made a bonfire and drank vast quantities. Nelson and Ixta spent the first night in a single sleeping bag that quickly became coated with a fine layer of sand. They hardly slept, but pressed against each other, the coarse sand between them, so that they emerged the next morning red-skinned and bleary-eyed. The day that followed and the next night and the day after—they all blurred, and when the sun rose behind them on the third morning, they watched in wonder as the surface of the ocean slowly distinguished itself from the horizon, like one of those old instant photos developing before their eyes. First, a thin, almost imperceptible line, a dark wall splitting in two; then the texture of the waves appeared, or was hinted at; and then, almost miraculously, there were gulls, floating lazily against a still-dark, purple sky. Finally—and this was most surprising of all, because their infatuation with each other had led them to believe they were alone in the world—they could make out the fishing trawlers bobbing in the distance, like the toys of a child. Nelson hadn't said it at the time, because then as now he was afraid, but that morning, as dawn became day at the beach, he'd realized that he loved her.

He told her now. And when she didn't answer, he asked:

"Do you remember that beach? Do you remember what it was called?"

Ixta said she didn't know.

"I felt like he was talking about someone else," she told me. "About things that had never happened to me."

Nelson didn't give up. He described a life, their life. He reminded her how much they'd laughed. "A lifetime of that!" he said, and she almost smiled.

It didn't matter where, as long as they were together.

"I'll do anything to make you believe in me again."

To which she responded simply, "I don't love you anymore."

She was crying because it was mostly true.

"You don't stop loving someone like Nelson," she told me later. "You just give up."

Ixta turned now to face him, just in time to see Nelson's eyes press closed. Neither one of them said anything for a half minute or more.

"I'm sorry," Ixta added.

"That's all right." There was something dogged and resolute in Nelson's voice. He'd steadied himself. You could say he was acting. "There's time."

Ixta shook her head warily. "There is?"

Jaime had already sent someone after him. Ixta's heart had already closed to him. Even that morning, on that park bench in the Monument District, Nelson's bleak future was tumbling toward him.

Still:

"There is," he assured her.

He walked her back to her office, heart pounding in his chest, looking any and everywhere for a flower to pick for her along the way. There was nothing. He left her with a chaste kiss on the cheek, a whispered good-bye, and headed toward the Olympic, following a version of the route he'd taken that morning. Ixta sat glumly at her desk and did the crossword. Hours passed and the phone didn't ring. The filmmaker saw her this way, in such a state, and felt pity for her. He decided not to tell her that Mindo had phoned and, seeing her troubled countenance, profoundly regretted what he'd done.

"If I could take it back, I would," he said to me later. He'd told Mindo that Ixta had gone out for a walk with a young man named Nelson.

"Nelson?" Mindo said. "Are you fucking kidding me?"

Then the painter hung up.

"Yes," the filmmaker told me, "yes, he sounded very angry."

As for Nelson, he was in no rush. Midday streets are very different from early-morning streets—different in character, different in sound. There are more people, but they're less harried somehow; they're the late risers, the men and women escaping from work, not racing toward it. Nelson didn't want to think much about what had just happened, what it meant. He paused to read the alarming newspaper headlines at a kiosk on the corner of San José and University, front pages announcing disturbances in mining camps, power outages in the suburbs, and the details of an astonishing daylight bank robbery, among other noteworthy events. Nothing could be as alarming as what Ixta had just told him. His head hurt from the effort of not thinking about it. He waited at bus stops, but let the buses pass; he walked some more, and stood before a half-finished building on Angamos and considered its emerging shape, watching the workers move about the steel beams like dancers, never pausing, and never, ever looking down.

For this, Nelson admired them. Later that afternoon, he'd tell Patalarga about these agile, fearless men, and wonder aloud how they managed it.

In the likeliest scenario, Nelson was, by this point, already being followed.

MÓNICA SPENT THE DAY at home in a state of high anxiety. She waited for her son to appear, and considered the possibility that he might not. She spent an hour dusting every surface of Nelson's room, hoping that this task might take her mind off things, but when she'd finished, she stood in the doorway, observing her work, unsatisfied. It was awful, Mónica decided, perverse, to have made this space so clean and antiseptic; it no longer looked like her son's room but more like a stage set. What she wanted was for the bed to be unmade, for Nelson's things to be scattered about in no particular order. She wanted his chest of drawers open; and his books facedown on the floor, their covers open and spines cracked. She wanted his unfolded clothes draped over the chair in the corner, and a half-empty glass of water leaving a ring on the wooden nightstand. She wanted signs of life.

Suddenly exhausted, she lay down on Nelson's bed.

She woke a few hours later when the phone rang. It was Francisco calling from California, asking about his brother. It seems Astrid had written him an e-mail, detailing (and quite possibly exaggerating) Ramiro's brief encounter with Nelson. Naturally, Francisco was concerned. He wanted to know what his mother thought. Mónica, still shaking off sleep, heard the worry in her elder son's voice, surveyed her youngest son's empty, lifeless room, and felt she had nothing to say. She didn't know what she thought.

This much was true: Nelson was surely home again. In this city, somewhere. Ramiro was an honest man, known to fib about his weight and his income, or perhaps embellish the modest achievements of his children, but in something like this, he would not bend the truth. Nelson was here, in the capital. Surely.

Mónica could think of no good reason why he hadn't called, and speculating about this matter was, for someone like her, a dangerous game. Members of her generation needed little help conjuring awful scenarios to explain otherwise ordinary situations. It was a skill they'd perfected over the course of a lifetime: reading the newspapers; serving as unwilling participant-observers in a stupid war; voting in one meaningless election after another; watching the currency collapse, stabilize, and collapse again; seeing their contemporaries succumb to stress-induced heart attacks and cancer and depression. It's a wonder any of them have teeth left. Or hair. Or legs to hold them up. Mónica's imagination had gone dark, and she could think of only one word: trouble.

"Be calm," Francisco counseled her from afar. He knew his mother.

"I'm trying," Mónica whispered into the phone.

The tour she'd imagined didn't end this way, with her son hiding out in the city, unable or unwilling to come home again. She began to consider the possibility that he'd never left, that it had all been a ruse, that he was living another life, in another district, and had invented the tour as a cover for his planned reinvention.

"Did he say anything to you?" she asked Francisco.

There was silence on the other end.

"When?"

"I don't know. Whenever you talked to him."

There was a long silence.

"We haven't spoken in months," Francisco said finally. "You know that."

Sometimes, when she was at her most pessimistic, she wondered if her two boys would ever have reason to speak to each other, after she was gone and buried.

"I'm sorry. What should I do?"

"Find the actors," Francisco said. "What else?"

. . .

THAT'S WHAT MINDO was doing. That afternoon he made appearances at many of the usual places young actors congregate in this city. The bars, the plazas, the playhouses. Mindo paid a visit to the Conservatory, and asked for Nelson there, but no one had seen or heard of him since he'd gone away. The general consensus was, *That was ages ago.* They were immediatists, like all actors. They barely remembered their classmate, their friend. Everyone seemed surprised by the news that Nelson had returned, and Mindo's frustration only grew.

We can suppose he was driven by jealousy, and suppose too that his own jealousy caught him unawares. He found the emotion unsettling, just as he'd found it unsettling to wake each of the previous five mornings on the couch in the living room of the apartment which had been, until not so long ago, his and his alone. From what I've been able to piece together, Ixta's reading of the state of the relationship was essentially accurate: she and Mindo were two perfectly nice but thoroughly incompatible young people who'd managed, quite by accident, to bind themselves to each other. The unbinding would have happened one way or another, given time; and even under the best of circumstances, the child they'd made together, Nadia, would have been raised at a certain distance from her father. Many people in their respective circles understood this fact intuitively, and, in all likelihood, had things gone differently, Mindo and Ixta would have both found a way to live with this natural and necessary estrangement, as adults often do.

But that afternoon, after learning that Ixta had been with Nelson, Mindo was furious. He'd never liked the man he'd replaced, never liked the suggestion of him. He didn't like the look in Ixta's eyes when Nelson was mentioned, or the way she avoided saying his name when recounting anecdotes that self-evidently starred her former lover. She'd replace "Nelson" with anodyne phrases like "an old friend" or "someone I used to know," a tic she'd never noticed until Mindo pointed it out to her. If Mindo had any suspicions about Ixta's liaisons with Nelson, he didn't bring them up with her. It may have been a matter of pride, or perhaps he preferred not to know. It doesn't matter: now Mindo only wanted to find his rival.

Instead of Nelson, however, Mindo found Elías, who happened to be at the Conservatory that day, visiting old friends. Mindo knew he and Nelson were close. After the standard and truthful denials ("No, I haven't seen him. No, I didn't know he was back"), Elías, a little disconcerted by Mindo's aggressive posture, suggested he check the old theater, the one at the edge of the Old City.

"Which one?"

Elías was being deliberately vague.

"The Olympic," he said finally.

He felt as if he'd given up a secret, he told me months later, though in truth, he was only guessing, only thinking aloud.

"The porn spot?" Mindo said, then thanked him gruffly, and left.

"I don't think we'd ever really talked before," Elías told me. "I knew who he was, but not much more than that. And of course I never spoke to him again."

"Did you ask why he was looking for Nelson? Did you wonder?"

Elías folded his hands together primly. "I wondered, yes. But I didn't ask. He sounded like he was in a rush. He looked upset, and the truth is . . ." He paused here, as if ashamed to admit this: "I prefer not to speak to people when they're like that."

Mindo made his first appearance at the Olympic about a half hour before Nelson arrived there himself. There was knocking, pounding, fruitless bell ringing, shouting. Eventually, Patalarga heard the commotion, and went to the gate.

"I thought he was someone Jaime had sent," Patalarga told me. "I just assumed that. I mean, who else would it have been?"

There were many plausible tactics available to him. Patalarga chose obfuscation. "Nelson's not here," he told the stranger.

"When will he be back?"

"Back?" He was careful to keep the gate closed, and not show his face. "Is he in the city?"

Mindo left without saying another word.

According to Patalarga, that afternoon Nelson was quiet, pensive, and answered every question in a way that seemed deliberately vague. He didn't say, for example, why he'd left so early, where he'd been, or whom he'd seen; and soon enough Patalarga decided to let it go. The two of them ate an austere lunch, in the best tradition of their tour, and over this meal, Patalarga told Nelson the news: someone had come to the theater looking for him.

"Who?" Nelson asked.

Patalarga didn't know. He told him about his brief inter-

action with the stranger, and they could come to only one conclusion: This man must be from T—— or San Jacinto.

"Does anyone know you're here?"

By that time, Mindo was drinking at a bar near the Conservatory, executing fine illustrations of clenched fists in his sketch
pad. He would stay in the bar until well past nightfall, after it
had swelled with a cast of regulars whom he mostly ignored
(while ignoring Ixta's increasingly urgent phone calls as well)
before heading back to the theater just past midnight. He paid
his bill but left no gratuity. His sketch pad would be found early
that morning, tossed on the sidewalk a few blocks from the
Olympic, next to his lifeless body.

21

MRS. ANABEL HAD DIED earlier that week, leaving the town in a state of shock. The funeral was held a few days before Nelson arrived in the city, a beautiful, lugubrious affair, full of black-clad mourners, their faces twisted with sadness. Seeing them was more moving than the ceremony itself, than the death of this woman I barely knew: more than half of the town's remaining residents gathered in the plaza, the stooped men and wrinkled women of my parents' generation, the survivors. The principal brought the entire school too, fifty or sixty excitable children with no apparent understanding of what had happened or why they were there. They teased each other, giggling at all the wrong moments. It was refreshing. My father wore his dark suit, my mother her black shawl. A brass band struck up a warbling melody, and then the funeral party marched toward the cemetery, so slowly even Mrs. Anabel could've kept up. The people of T—— never gathered this way anymore, except to say good-bye to one of their own; the event became something like a reunion. Jaime gave his eulogy at the grave site. "Everything

I've accomplished is because of her," he said, and the town nodded respectfully because they knew what that meant. He'd accomplished a lot; he was rich, wasn't he?

Then the casket was lowered, and we all went home.

I spent the days after with my old man, pulling the rotted
clay tiles off the roof. Oddly, the town had felt most alive at the
funeral, but now it was as if we were the only people left in all of
T——. Our work was done mostly in silence—this had always
been my father's way—but occasionally he'd pause and ask me to
tell him again what I was doing back in the city, and what I
hoped to do in the future. I liked these moments. It wasn't a
conversation I minded. I didn't feel put upon, or pressured; I
heard no disappointment in his voice, only a genuine curiosity
about my life and my plans. The fact that I had no good answers
felt less like a stressor and more like an opportunity. Each day, I
offered a new hypothetical—going back to school, working in
television, starting a restaurant—all fanciful, but not impossible,
as if I were performing a kind of optimism I didn't really have.
My father seemed to appreciate it.

One morning, a few days after the funeral, we heard my
mother calling up to us from the courtyard. She was with Noelia, and they stood side by side, necks craned in our direction,
each with a curved hand shielding their eyes from the sun. Both
wore long burgundy skirts and white blouses, with dark shawls
draped over their shoulders, and for a moment, I thought they
looked almost like sisters.

"Come down," my mother said. "Noelia wants to speak
with you."

It was a bright, silent day, and the air was still. I love the way the human voice sounds on days like this—clear, warm, like it could carry all the way across a valley. I looked down at my mother, not realizing at first that she meant me, not my father. My old man shrugged, and pulled the brim of his cap down over his eyes. With that, I'd been dismissed.

I climbed down. Noelia smiled politely, not saying much. She kept her eyes narrowed against the sun, and she looked well, all things considered. The loss of her mother, the chaotic days after—she looked recovered, I thought, or perhaps I was only comparing her to my idea of what this kind of suffering should look like, how it would show on her face, in her eyes, in the tilt of her shoulders.

"I have something to show you," she said.

My mother nodded.

Noelia went on. "Something I want you to see."

We crossed the street, to her sunlit courtyard, overgrown and wild. The cats slept in the tall grass, and we ignored them, just as they ignored us. Jaime had gone back to San Jacinto, and for the first time in Noelia's life, the house was all hers. She didn't like the idea. Not one bit.

"I'm sorry," I said.

She pursed her lips. "You don't remember me, do you?"

Like most grown-ups in my hometown, Noelia was familiar, in a very broad sense; she had a look of stoicism that I associated with every adult from T——. I remembered her, even if I knew almost nothing about her beyond the fact that she lived across the street from the house where I was born.

I lied: "Of course I do."

"It's fine. Really."

"I do."

"I was there when you were born. I've known you since you were a flea." She smiled now. "And look at you! You're all grown."

Noelia asked me to wait while she went to the room where her mother had died. I sat in the courtyard with my back against one of the walls, resting in the shade. It was another perfect day. She came back with the journals. They were handed over with some ceremony, these three ordinary notebooks tied together with a piece of string, covering most of the previous six months. They had no decoration, no stickers or markings on the outside, nothing, in fact, to identify them, beyond the normal wear. Now Noelia untied the string for me, flipped through them idly. The last of them, the most recent, was on top, a quarter of it still empty.

"They're Rogelio's."

"Nelson's?" I asked.

"If you prefer."

"What should I do with them?"

"You should take them when you go home, to the city. You can give them back to him."

It must have been clear by my expression that I was less than eager to take this on.

"But mostly, I think I should get them out of this house." She leaned in: "My brother wants to find Nelson. He sent someone to the capital to look for him."

"To look for him? Why?"

She offered me a careful smile. "You don't know?"

I assured her I didn't.

"My brother is very proud. He feels disrespected." Noelia sighed. "It's best for everyone if we forget all this. My brother especially. So take them. Don't make too much of it. Just take them."

She nodded, and I found myself nodding too. I could have said no, I suppose, but no good reason to refuse came to mind; Noelia stood before me, with her simple, pleading smile; I froze. She wanted me to have them.

I took the notebooks, reading relief on her face as she handed them over. I carried them back across the street, where I wrapped them in an old paper bag, and left them untouched at the foot of my bed. My father and I returned to our work, to our panoramic views of T——, the empty town below us, and our steady, plodding conversation about my future.

Eventually I went back to the city, and in truth, I almost left the journals behind. I happened to see them as I was packing, thought back to my conversation with Noelia, and decided to take them along.

Still I didn't read them. This is the truth: I had no interest. Not for many months, not until I heard what had happened.

HENRY APPEARED at the Olympic just before six in the evening. In truth, he hadn't intended to come at all, but driving his cab after school he'd chanced to drop off a fare not far from the theater. As he made note of this coincidence, a parking spot opened up before him. He shuddered, then eased the car to the curb, shut off the engine, and sat for a moment. He listened to the news on the radio, waiting for a signal.

See him: his severe expression, his keen sense of victimization. He likely sat for a quarter of an hour, listening for something only he would recognize, wearing what his ex-wife described to me as "his pre-crucifixion face": furrowed brow, unfocused eyes gazing at the middle distance, pursed lips, and his chin pulled back toward his chest, like a turtle trying but unable to get back in its shell. "A fake stoicism," she called it, for Henry, in her view, was anything but stoic. "He could play stoic," she clarified, but that was different. Still, she knew this pose well, for it was this face, she admitted, that had seduced her "back when we were young and beautiful." She laughed then, not to dismiss what she'd just said, or make light of it, but as if to perform it: in laughter, Henry's ex-wife was transformed before my eyes and became, in spite of the years, young and indeed very beautiful.

Eventually Henry tired of waiting, got out of the car, and walked toward the theater. He used his keys on the gate, surprised that they still worked, and found his two friends on their knees in the lobby of the Olympic, with hammers in their hands, talking wildly about a man who'd come to the city to murder Nelson. They were pulling up rotten wooden floorboards, a repair Patalarga had been talking about for months.

"It was startling to say the least," Henry told me later.

The supposed murderer, the one Nelson and Patalarga had conjured out of an initial bout of genuine concern, had been replaced by another, less frightening villain, a blend of various comic-book bad guys and assorted ruffians they'd met on tour. Men with potbellies and bad teeth, men who swore in ornate neologisms and kept shiny rings on every finger. Nelson and Patalarga felt better in the company of these invented scoundrels, who needless to say had nothing in common with Mindo.

Nelson and Patalarga were laughing, working at a furious pace, and obviously enjoying themselves. Months later, when I first visited the Olympic, I'd come across this very same pile, those slats of rotting wood that Nelson and Patalarga pulled up that day. They were lying in the middle of the space, like kindling for a bonfire. Patalarga and I strolled past them, without comment.

"I had a hard time joining in," Henry said to me. He asked them to back up and explain, and they did, partially. He gathered the basics: Something had gone very wrong back in T——, and Nelson was in danger. Rogelio's mother might have died, and though it wasn't Nelson's fault, it was possible that Jaime was holding him responsible. He'd escaped.

Henry frowned. "And the girl?"

Nelson shrugged. It was the part of the story he didn't want to tell. So he didn't.

"When did you come home?" Henry asked instead.

"Yesterday."

Henry nodded. "You don't look well."

"Neither do you."

It was true. He'd seemed healthier, more alive on the tour; now Henry's age showed. These late middle years offended his vanity. He was looking forward to being old, when he would no longer be tormented by memories of youth.

"I suppose you're right," he said.

Patalarga offered Henry a hammer, but the playwright demurred. He did so wordlessly, gripping his right shoulder with his left hand and grimacing, as if he were nursing some terrible injury. Patalarga set the hammer down, and the two old friends looked at each other warily. Besides the odd conversation here and there, they hadn't spoken since Jaime shipped them back to the city. Each of them considered the other to be somehow at fault for this.

Henry sighed. "So this bad guy, this villain. Are we afraid of him?"

He asked in a tone very specific to the world they inhabited: it was the way an actor inquired about his character.

Patalarga nodded. "We are."

"No," Nelson said, suddenly buoyant. "We aren't."

Patalarga laughed, but qualified his friend's denial. "We aren't terrified. We're concerned."

"Nelson smiled in a way that put me at ease," Henry told me. "And understand that I had no context for any of this. If he was calm, why shouldn't I be?"

If it wasn't quite old times, it was a passable facsimile. They abandoned the work and moved into the theater itself, spreading out on the stage where Nelson and Patalarga had slept the night before. They laughed a little, and filled each other in on recent developments. Henry was appalled to learn that Patalarga was having trouble with Diana, and urged him to reconcile. There was a surprising insistence to his tone.

"Immediately," he said. "Right away."

Nelson agreed, and Patalarga could hardly argue. They were right, but this sort of thing was easy to say, and not so easy to do. He played along, even stood up and took out his phone. "You know what?" he said. "You're right, and I'm going to call her." His friends applauded.

He went backstage ("for some privacy"), and there, among the variegated junk that crowded the hallways and dressing rooms, he once more lost his nerve. He held the phone in his hands, could hear Diana's sweet voice in his head, but the in-between steps seemed impossible.

"I wanted to call," he told me later. "I just couldn't."

So he waited a moment beneath the single fluorescent light that illuminated the hallway, breathing the stale air. Fifty years of theater. Longer. When enough time had passed, he returned to his friends, to the stage, and announced: "She still loves me!"

He had a bottle of rum handy, and brought it out now. "To celebrate," he said. It was all made up ("And they knew it, I assume"), but he did feel like celebrating. "It made me happy to see Nelson and Henry again, to be together, even if it was just one night." They drank and laughed some more, and at a certain point, they reenacted a scene from the play, rewriting it on the fly to suit their mood and their circumstances. Patalarga's servant had been kicked out of the house by his wife; Nelson's Alejo had murdered an old woman in the provinces; Henry's idiot president was losing his mind to loneliness. This improvised scene was so satisfying and felt so real that it was a surprise to look out on the empty theater and realize they were alone.

Only they weren't.

It was past midnight then, and Mindo was at the gate, calling Nelson's name.

THROUGHOUT THAT AFTERNOON and into the evening, Mónica looked for her son without success. She didn't know where to begin, and the process made her aware of just how little she knew about his life, or at least about his life now. Nelson's friends, the ones she remembered, were from middle and high school. They appeared in her mind's eye, effortlessly, a row of adolescent boys standing on a sidewalk in their gray and white school uniforms, performing a world-weariness they could scarcely have understood. She smiled at the memory, could see their dark eyes, their slumped shoulders, their vanity beginning to manifest itself in surprising ways (the carefully maintained shadow of a mustache, or the sneakers whose wear and tear was as curated as any gallery exhibit). Fifteen, sixteen, almost men but not quite—this was not the age she most loved, but it was the one she recalled most clearly, in part because she'd had Sebastián by her side to help record it. Those were the years they talked most of all; the happiest years of their marriage: they were alone in the house with a somber teenage madman whom they loved, two hostages who admired and feared for their captor. They discussed Nelson's moods the way farmers analyze the weather, looking for some logic in it, some reason. They worried over his choice of friends, worried most of all because it was something they could not control: Santiago, Marco, Diego, Sandro, Fausto, Luis. She remembered their faces, but not their surnames. They were good kids, but not good enough, boys with easily identifiable weaknesses, talents they hadn't yet discovered; and more worrying than their lack of maturity was their lack of curiosity. On this count, Mónica and Sebastián saw a clear difference between their son and the others. The boys came to the house, and spent hours in a locked bedroom. She could not, at the time, conceive of what made these children laugh. The years passed, she and Sebastián watched them grow; and then Nelson entered the Conservatory, and these boys simply faded from view, to be replaced by others. These others—now that she needed them, Mónica realized she had only the vaguest idea who they were. She looked among her papers and found programs to various plays Nelson had been in. She scanned the names of the cast members, and not one of them jogged anything in her memory. She searched for Ixta's number, and couldn't find it. She even called the Conservatory, and spoke to a secretary, but found it impossible to explain what she wanted: for this woman, this stranger, to tell her who her son's friends were.

After dinner, Mónica decided to go see her sister, who lived only ten blocks away. She went by car for it was dark out, and one never knew. She found the family—Astrid, Ramiro, and their two teenage daughters, Ashley and Miriam—gathered in front of the television, as if for warmth, a portrait of togetherness that made Mónica long for another kind of life. Perhaps if I'd had girls, she thought idly. For her extended family, she offered a broad smile, and they made room for her on the couch. Not long after, Mónica was breathing at their rhythm, laughing when they laughed. Soon, she'd almost forgotten why she'd come at all, and looked down to discover, with some surprise, that her shoes had slipped off her feet. She wiggled her toes in her socks, a childish gesture that made her smile. She was comfortable, and hadn't even noticed.

When the program ended, the adults left the television to the girls. Ramiro disappeared into the garden for a cigarette, while Astrid and Mónica prepared the hot water, set the table, brought out fruit and cheese and olives and bread. Mónica liked the routine, and looked forward to not eating alone. A year after Sebastián died, Astrid had suggested that she move in, but at the time Mónica had been offended by the proposal, so offended it had never been mentioned again. And still, ever since, the house looked very different to Mónica. Whenever she visited, she imagined herself living there, growing old there, and to her surprise, the notion didn't bother her as much as it had then. Years later, it had begun to make sense, more so now that Nelson was gone.

When we spoke in early 2002, she was still mulling it over. "I believe less and less in autonomy," she told me. "I don't know what it means anymore, at my age. I can only tell you it seems less desirable each day."

Ramiro returned, tea was served, and he recounted for his sister-in-law all the relevant details from that morning's conversation with Nelson, including his odd comment about becoming a father. Astrid and Ramiro found it troubling; Mónica did not, and she couldn't say why. She puzzled over it. Part of her hoped it was true. It would be nice to have a grandchild, even if she had to travel to the provinces to visit.

Mónica's questions were basic: Was her son skinny? Did he look healthy? How was he dressed? Did he appear unhappy?

With each query, Ramiro became more and more uncomfortable. He had excuses, and he employed them: he'd been rushed, he'd been caught off guard and hadn't paid attention to the details. Mónica continued to press him, and finally, Ramiro raised his hands in exasperation.

"Do you want to know the truth?" he asked Mónica.

She stared at him intently. It was a ridiculous thing to ask.

"I've never understood your son." Ramiro paused, and took a sip from his teacup. "I've always found him to be . . . inscrutable."

Mónica slumped back in her seat. As if on cue, her nieces laughed along with the television, along with each other; two lovely, well-adjusted girls whom this mediocre man had no trouble understanding. She glared at her sister's husband. He responded with an insipid smile.

"Well," she said, and for a long moment this was all she could manage. "That's not very helpful."

Astrid reached a hand across the table. "What he means is—"

"Your boy is complicated, that's all," Ramiro said. "And no, he did not seem well. He hasn't seemed well to me in years. Not since . . ."

He paused here, and now they all fell silent, for he had gone too far. Sebastián's absence shifted the air in the room.

"I'm sorry," Ramiro said, but it was too late. Mónica had already closed her eyes, which had begun to tear. She went home soon after, and hardly slept all night, wondering if what her brother-in-law had said was true.

THE FACTORS THAT LED Mindo to the theater that night are plain enough—jealousy, a general frustration with his circumstances, compounded by an afternoon and evening of heavy drinking. What's just as clear is that they needn't have. Any number of small shifts might have led him away from danger, instead of toward it. He might have answered one of Ixta's half dozen calls to his cell phone, for example, rushed home, and made peace with her. He might have run into a friend, who would've helped steer him back to his apartment. He was, according to the accounts of the waiters who served him, so staggeringly drunk that it's a small miracle he was even able to find the Olympic in the dim labyrinthine streets of the Old City. But he did find it. And when he arrived, he fulfilled the role the script required of him: he pounded his fist on the gate, he shouted for the man he now realized was his rival.

"We heard him yelling, and we were scared," Patalarga later admitted. "Concerned. It was a howl, almost like something from a horror film."

They froze, fell silent, and let the sound of that distant, haunting voice float through the theater.

They put down their props, and sat on the stage. Perhaps, the three of them thought, he would simply tire and leave, but many minutes passed, and the voice showed no signs of flagging.

"Open the door!" Mindo called, the vowels stretched long. "Open up!"

Henry described it to me as eerie: the lonely, pained, sing-song voice of a jealous man, now weary, now menacing, filling the old theater like a dirge. "It was nice, in a way," he said. "I think that's what I remember most about it. How disconcertingly beautiful it sounded."

Meanwhile, Nelson wore a look of deep concentration. Finally he said, "I know that voice."

"We assumed," Patalarga told me, "that he meant that he knew the voice from back in the mountains. I asked him who it was, and he shook his head."

"I've heard it before, that's all."

Then Nelson stood.

"Where are you going?" Patalarga asked.

"To see who it is."

Patalarga was horrified, but it was exactly as Ixta said: Nelson never listened. He strode through the theater, through the lobby, and out to the gate, his two concerned, disbelieving friends trailing behind him. He was still safe, on his own side of the metal barrier that separated the Olympic from the street, when he called out, "Who is it?"

"I know that voice," Nelson said again, in a whisper this time.

Much later, Ixta would run down for me the very limited contact the two men in her life had chanced to have. There was the time Mindo picked up her cell phone when she was in the shower. They spoke for a few minutes, Nelson pretending to be a cousin who was in town visiting from the United States.

"A bad lie," Ixta told me darkly. "A very bad and unnecessary lie. Ninety-nine out of one hundred people would have simply hung up. But he was an actor, and he told me it would've been unsporting."

Unsporting or not, it would have been wiser. The only stroke of good fortune was that Nelson had called from a pay phone. For a few days afterward, Mindo asked again and again about this phantom cousin.

When will we meet him?

What does he do?

How exactly is he related?

Mindo asked with such persistence that Ixta was inevitably drawn into the lie.

"And in spite of what you might think," she said to me, "I hated doing that to Mindo."

They each knew about the other, perhaps more than they would've cared to know. Nelson had asked around about Mindo, taking some care to steer clear of him. On several occasions, Mindo quizzed Ixta about Nelson, all the while feigning a lack of interest.

The two men had acquaintances, but not friends, in common, so perhaps it was inevitable that they'd cross paths eventually. One afternoon, in November of the previous year, not long after Nelson and Ixta's affair got under way, Nelson ran into the couple at a bar in La Julieta. If it was awkward, it was also mercifully brief—a grimaced exchange of pleasantries, a handshake, and little else. Ixta watched, her heart racing, as her two lovers shared a few words. She laughed now and again to paper over prickly silences, and breathed a heavy sigh when Nelson excused himself. Later that evening, when she and Mindo were alone, he confessed that he'd recognized Nelson immediately, not because they'd ever met before, but because he'd opened Ixta's old photo albums one day while she was at work, just to have a look.

"Why would you do that?" she asked.

"They were poking out of a box. I got curious. And also, because I barely know you."

His tone, Ixta reported to me, was neither accusatory nor grim, only resigned. Then he smiled, as if he were afraid he'd said something wrong. He hadn't. They'd rushed into it. Ixta was, by then, moved in; and yet their life was under construction. In some ways, it never really got much farther.

That night at the Olympic, the three members of Diciembre stood on the safe side of the metal barrier, listening. The closer you got to the sound of Mindo's voice, the less frightening it was. Still, both Henry and Patalarga were surprised when Nelson announced that he was letting the man in.

"What if he has a weapon?" Patalarga remembers asking.

"He doesn't," Nelson answered. His eyes were bright, as if he'd just solved a puzzle. "It's Ixta's boyfriend."

And he opened the gate. Just like that.

Months later, when Patalarga described this moment to me, he was still shaking his head. There was very little time to prepare. "I imagined a raging jealous lunatic. I imagined an animal."

Instead they got Mindo. Asked to describe him, both Henry and Patalarga began with the same word: "drunk." The toxicology report concurs. This should not necessarily imply that Mindo was a drinker; in fact, by all accounts he drank only occasionally. But given the circumstances, one understands why he was in that state. "It must have been a terrible shock," Ixta told me. "He must have thought something was happening between me and Nelson."

I pressed her on this—I mean, something *was* happening, something *had been* happening, right?

She blushed. "You know what I mean. I'd turned him down."

"And you meant it?"

She frowned.

"What are you doing?" she asked. "What do you want?"

What Ixta did confirm was that Mindo had a remarkable tolerance, and could keep himself upright long past the point when lesser men would have succumbed. One imagines an alternative version of this evening, in which Mindo passes out at the bar, his drawings of clenched fists scattered beside him, and is woken a few hours before dawn, heartsick, disappointed, but alive. He would have no such luck. As it happened, Mindo appeared before the suddenly open gate of the Olympic with drunkenness painted on him like a carnival mask. He hadn't shaved that morning, and his features had a blurred, unsettled quality. His eyes sagged, his lips drooped. His olive green jacket appeared ready to slip off his shoulder at any moment. He glanced left and right, and then down at his feet, as if to confirm that he was actually standing there, at the rusted gate of the Olympic.

Night had brought with it a blanket of wet, heavy fog, and the streetlights above flowered in hazy yellow bursts.

"You're Mindo," Nelson said.

They didn't shake hands, but there was no violence. The threat evaporated the moment they saw each other.

Patalarga still didn't know what to make of this. He hadn't dismissed the idea of a deranged killer coming from T—— to snuff out Nelson. He desperately wanted them all to move inside the theater, "where we'd be safer, and dry," he said, but Mindo was nailed to the ground. He wouldn't budge.

"I had the sense that anything could happen," Patalarga told me later.

Not anything. This:

"Come with me," Mindo says to Nelson. He slurs his words, but there's no menace in them, just the quiet authority of a jilted man. "We have to talk."

"We do," Nelson says, nodding gravely, like a child who knows he's done wrong. Mindo never crosses the threshold, and Nelson simply floats out of the gate, as if being pulled by something irresistible, something magnetic.

That's all.

Ixta's lovers walk off into the dark, lightly drizzling night; Henry and Patalarga stand side by side, like worried parents, watching them go. A half block on, and they've disappeared into the murk. Only one of them comes back.

22

IXTA SPENT that evening at the apartment, reading old magazines and waiting for Mindo. He had the night off from the restaurant, and she assumed he was at his studio, painting, though
it was just as likely he was doing the same as she was—sitting
around, reading idly, staving off boredom by daydreaming of a
more creative life. If they'd been in a better place, they might
have done that sort of thing together. They might have even enjoyed it. She considered surprising him with a visit, but it was
cold out, and besides, he might not welcome the interruption.

She didn't mind calling though: Ixta tried Mindo's cell phone
several times, beginning just after seven, calling every hour or
so until around eleven-thirty. She left no messages, and at about
midnight she went to sleep. "I wasn't worried," she told me later.
"I was annoyed. We usually talked at some point in the day. This
was it, you understand? I was bored. I was thinking to myself:
what an asshole. I was thinking: this is my life now. I stay at
home with the baby, he comes home when he pleases. He makes
art. My breasts swell, my nipples turn black. It felt very dark, you

see? I wasn't even thinking about Nelson. He didn't cross my mind. I'm telling you, just like I told the police."

This is what we know: the two young men left the theater headed in the direction of the plaza. A fine drizzle hung in the air, and the sidewalks were slippery. Mindo was very drunk, and they walked carefully so as not to fall, one empty city block and then another, shuffling as best they could through the curtain of fog. For a long time, they didn't speak.

"Do you love her?" Mindo finally asked. They were five or six blocks from the theater by then.

"Yes," Nelson said. And then: "But she doesn't love me back."

Mindo nodded. "So at least we have that in common."

We know they made it to the plaza, that they walked diagonally across it and sought refuge at the Wembley. This was Nelson's suggestion. It was a slow night, and one of the white-haired bartenders sat behind the counter, doing a crossword puzzle. He remembers when they came in, about a quarter to one in the morning. For every crossword, he wrote down his start and end times, so he was able to provide the police with a fairly accurate estimate. He told them he knew Nelson, recognized him: he'd served drinks to Sebastián back when Nelson was still a boy, and he'd seen him a few times after rehearsals. The other one, Mindo, he'd never seen before.

"The tall one was drunk, which was none of my business. I shook hands with the kid. I hadn't seen him in a few months."

They chatted for a few moments, and then Nelson ordered a liter of beer and two glasses. Mindo watched the exchange, unimpressed.

"My old man used to bring me here," Nelson said when they'd sat.

"Your dad," Mindo mused. "Did he mess with other men's women too?"

They locked eyes. The evening could still go any which way, and Nelson knew it. He hadn't decided what would happen. What he wanted to happen. He took a deep breath.

"My old man was a prince."

Mindo sucked his teeth. "Skips a generation."

"I guess it must," Nelson said.

Just then the old bartender appeared, all smiles. He had the beer and a couple of glasses. Patalarga had lent Nelson some cash, and he paid right away. Mindo didn't protest, only watched suspiciously, examining the transaction as if attempting to decipher a magic trick.

"Are you all right?" Nelson asked.

"Of course I'm all right."

"Because you don't look all right."

The bartender, when we spoke, offered much the same assessment. He stood over them for a moment, observing. "The taller one, he looked like hell."

"I'm fine," said Mindo. He looked up at the bartender. "And you, old man, why are you still here?"

The bartender frowned and went back to his crossword puzzle.

"What were you doing with Ixta?" Mindo asked once the beer had been poured.

Nelson considered his rival. In this bar, beneath this

warm light, any hint of menace was gone. He was hurt; that was all.

"Just talking," Nelson said.

"Yeah? What about?"

"Not much." Nelson turned away. The content of that morning's conversation was so disappointing he could scarcely bring himself to think of it. "I was surprised at how little we had to say."

"Not what you'd planned."

Nelson shook his head. "It wasn't what I'd *hoped*." He paused, and looked up at Mindo. It was merciless to push forward, with more courage than he'd had that morning with Ixta, when he'd most needed it.

"I wanted to talk about us. Me and her."

He enunciated these last three words carefully, clearly.

Mindo laughed. "You don't have an *us* to talk about. There is no *us*."

"There was once. There might be."

For a few moments they didn't say much, each drank their beer, never breaking eye contact. Mindo processed the brazenness of it, shaking his head. He set his beer down.

"But we're the ones having a baby! You get that, right? She and I. Me and her."

Nelson shook his head. "How do you know it's yours?"

With that, the bar's quiet evening was shattered.

When questioned (by me, by police) the Wembley's old bartender recalled this moment very clearly. Mindo stood abruptly, lunging at Nelson and tipping the table over. Beer was spilled, one of the glasses shattered, and in an instant a few of the tables nearby were at the ready; the men, who a moment before had been drinking peacefully, were standing now, alert and prepared to intervene or defend themselves. When they saw it was just these two, everyone stepped back, giving Nelson and Mindo the room they required. They tussled for a while, neither very skilled but neither relenting, until they were on the ground, the both of them. It fell to the old bartender to break things up. Men like him are devoted to their service. Perhaps this was for the best; regarding barroom scuffles, he might have been the most experienced server in the city.

"Boys! Please!" he shouted, because they were all boys to him. "Stop!"

Nelson and Mindo stopped. Boys always did.

"Get off the floor!"

They stood.

He had them now. He told me later that he was sure of it. If they couldn't be civilized, he said, they'd have to leave. Did they really want to leave?

In case they didn't believe him, the bartender added, "Look at it out there!"

The drizzle was heavy now; they could see it swirling in the light just outside the window. He went on: "Outside, it's cold; outside, it's wet. Inside, it's warm, and inside there's beer. But inside, there is no fighting. Do you understand?"

He'd given this speech before.

Nelson and Mindo both nodded gravely; then they shook themselves off, gathered their things, and went outside.

. . .

NELSON ARRIVED at the Olympic past two, opening the gate with the key Patalarga had given him. He was soaked and out of breath. Henry and Patalarga had all but finished the bottle of rum, and were lying about the stage, now covered with cushions and blankets, like a pasha's den.

"You're back!" Henry said.

"You're alive!" Patalarga shouted.

He was only joking, but then Nelson stepped into the light. He was bruised and scraped. He peeled off his wet coat, ripped at the sleeve. He slumped onto the stage, gesturing for the rum, and Henry quickly poured him a glass.

"What happened?"

Nelson downed a shot.

The story he told his friends that night is the same as the one he'd later tell police.

He and Mindo stepped out of the Wembley. There was no plan. "We just knew, I guess, that we weren't done fighting." They stood for a while beneath the streetlamp just outside the door of the bar, breathing the damp air. From inside the bar, faces pressed up against the window, as if expecting a show.

Mindo swayed. "You're fucking her?"

Nelson didn't respond. He didn't have to.

"I knew it." Then: "I'm going to kill you."

According to the old bartender, everyone heard it. "The drunk boy looked very upset."

Nelson wasn't rattled. He held his hands out, palms up.

"No you're not."

There was no aggression in his voice, no defiance. It was just a statement of fact. He went on: "I shouldn't have said what I said. I'm sorry." Nelson gestured toward the Wembley. "They're all watching. Are you really going to kill me in front of all these people?"

Mindo cupped a hand over his eyes and turned toward the windows of the bar.

"Fine," he said.

They walked toward the plaza, and at this point there are no other witnesses besides Nelson. The plaza was empty except for a few stray taxis, and the occasional drunk stumbling out of one of the underground bars. The night was cold and uninviting, and they walked as fast as they could manage on the slippery streets. A few blocks on, Mindo started to talk. According to Nelson: "He was upset, but he seemed fatalistic about it all. I wasn't his rival. He said he knew that. Only Ixta had answers. She'd loved him once, and now she didn't. I didn't know what to tell him."

"It's the baby I worry about," Mindo said.

Nelson knew the streets of the Old City. He knew, for example, that at certain hours of night, on the narrower streets, you don't use the sidewalks. This is common sense. You walk straight down the very center of the road, eyes sharp, scanning for the thief that might pounce from the shadow of a recessed doorway. He and every student at the Conservatory had been robbed at least once. For most, once was all it took; then you learned. Nelson didn't have to think about it. This was instinct.

They were walking down the center of a narrow street called Garza when their conversation was interrupted by the light tap of a horn. They moved to the sidewalk, still talking, and barely registered the station wagon that rolled by. It pulled over just ahead of them, and two young men got out. A moment later, it took off, disappearing into the fog. Still Nelson and Mindo thought nothing of it. Just ahead, the two men dawdled, and, according to Nelson, "When we passed them, one of them pushed me hard against the wall." That's how it began.

Both assailants were young, both snarling, and it wasn't a holdup—it was an attack. A beat down. Everything happened very fast: Mindo and Nelson and these two violent strangers. No conversation. No demands. No negotiation. Nelson never saw their faces. It was fight or flight.

At the first opportunity, he flew.

"What about Mindo?" Patalarga asked, just as the police would later. "Why didn't you help Mindo?"

"I don't know."

Nelson ran as fast as he could. "I should've gone toward the plaza, but at the time I wasn't thinking. I just wanted to get away."

One of the attackers was chasing, but Nelson didn't look back. He ran for three blocks, turned one corner and then another, sprinting until his lungs burned. When he finally stopped he was six or seven blocks from the scene of the attack, standing at the edge of a park he'd never seen before, in a tumbledown section of the Old City known as El Anclado. He saw no one in the deserted streets: not his attackers, not Mindo, not a single person he could ask for help.

"So what did you do?" Patalarga asked.

"I sat for a moment to catch my breath. I figured out where I was, roughly, and then I headed back."

His destination was the Olympic, where he would be safe, but first he wanted to see about Mindo. He walked quickly, almost frantically. The fog was heavier than before, heavier than he'd ever seen it. When he got to the corner of Garza and Franklin, he peered down the street, to the spot where they'd been jumped.

He saw nothing, and breathed a sigh of relief.

"I was frightened," he said to Patalarga and Henry. "I didn't go any closer. I just assumed Mindo had done what I did. I assumed he'd gotten away."

In fact, he hadn't. Mindo had crawled into one of the recessed doorways, where he was almost completely hidden. That's where a passerby found him the next morning, with five knife wounds to his stomach and chest.

23

THE FOLLOWING MORNING Henry offered to give Nelson a ride to the Monument District. It was understood that Nelson had to see Ixta, to make sure Mindo was all right, and to apologize for any trouble he might have caused between them. Traffic was unusually light, and though the two friends didn't talk much, both found it comforting not to ride alone. Neither had slept more than a few hours. They listened to the news on the radio and, in particular, to the tenor of the announcers, which fluctuated unexpectedly between horror and amusement. It was frankly confusing, and perhaps this was the point: bad news was almost indistinguishable from good, or perhaps there was simply no such thing as good news anymore.

"You don't drive like I thought you would," Nelson said when they were near their destination. "I somehow expected you'd be more erratic."

To Henry, this sounded about right. He did almost everything erratically, but behind the wheel, he'd always been possessed with a certain calm. The congested streets of the capital disturbed most drivers, but not him. He had a surprisingly high tolerance for traffic jams. When he was in Collectors, he told Nelson now, he sometimes sat in bed, looking up at the ceiling, and imagined himself behind the wheel of a car, any car, on any city street. He and Rogelio shared this love, in fact: the tranquillity that came only from being alone, at the wheel, that sense of autonomy. He'd first conceived of *The Idiot President* while driving a tan 1976 Opel hatchback to visit a friend who lived outside the city. In an alternate life, if he'd been a criminal, Henry mused, he would have made a decent wheelman.

"Do you drive?" he asked Nelson now.

The young actor shook his head. He'd never learned. Henry smiled and offered to teach him. After all, Nelson would need to know, if he were to go through with his plans to travel to the United States.

At the mention of this, Nelson frowned.

"I was trying to be positive," Henry told me.

Nelson confessed that he was spooked by what had happened the night before. Hopefully that had been the worst of it. Nelson held his hands up, as if to offer proof of his nerves. "Look," he said, "they're shaking!"

They were in the Monument District now, with its quiet, smoothly paved streets, its sleek houses shielded by high walls. Nelson turned his attention to the roads, pointing out a few turns ahead. "It's a tricky part of town."

"This," Henry told me when we spoke, "was when I began to notice the station wagon behind us."

"Did you mention it to the police?" I asked him.

He shrugged. "I told the police everything. And they believed nothing. Then again, let's say a car was following us. What does that prove?"

It was a light blue station wagon, and it had been behind them for a long while now. Henry recalls thinking how strange it was, that he was likely imagining it—a low-speed chase along an otherwise deserted street. They took a turn, and the station wagon followed, just a few car lengths behind.

"Did you see the driver?" I asked.

He didn't. He couldn't.

In any case, Henry didn't mention his suspicion to Nelson, who had enough on his mind; later he saw this as a mistake. Instead he slowed the car to a stop, and kept his eyes on the rearview mirror. The blue station wagon slowed too, and then, almost reluctantly, drove on, past them and off into the neighborhood beyond. Henry and Nelson heard a hot blast of *cumbia* as the car rolled by.

"Why'd you stop?" Nelson asked.

"That car needed to pass."

They drove a little farther on, and pulled up in front of the filmmaker's house. Nelson got out to ring the bell, just as he had the previous morning, and Henry watched. "I saw him rocking back and forth on his feet, looking nervous and pale. Then the door opened. He leaned in, talking to someone I couldn't see."

That someone was the filmmaker, who, by his own admission, "was not having a good morning." Ixta hadn't come to work, nor had she called. She wasn't answering her phone, and he was annoyed. When he opened the door, he was expecting to find her, not Nelson.

"I shooed him away," the filmmaker told me. "I didn't want him around. He looked terrible. And I didn't like the way he looked at me. She didn't come in today, that's all I told him. He tried to peer past me, as if he thought I might be lying, and at that point . . . well, I just shut the door in his face."

Nelson rang the doorbell again, and the scene was repeated, with a little more vehemence. Again the door was shut. This time Nelson ambled back to the car, a little dazed, and told Henry what had happened.

"So what do we do?" Henry asked. He glanced at his watch involuntarily as he asked. It was already past ten. On this particular day, he had his first class in an hour. He needed to get moving. What Henry meant by his question was: Where can I leave you?

"I'll walk from here," Nelson said.

"You're sure?"

"I'm sure."

Nelson didn't say where he intended to walk. Back to the theater, Henry assumed, though Nelson went to Ixta's instead. The two friends embraced.

"The next time I saw him," Henry told me, "was that night on the television news."

IXTA HAD BEEN WOKEN at around five in the morning by a ringing doorbell. It was a policeman. He took a look at her belly, blanched, and asked her to sit. She was still rubbing sleep from her eyes. They sat. The policeman's voice trembled as he spoke.

"What is it?" she asked.

"I'm sorry," the officer said, then asked if she knew a man named Mindo.

But for a few stray details, her memory of the morning ends there. Mindo, dead. She was already beginning to lose herself to the hysterics that would take over for the next six hours.

The officer meted out in small doses what information he had: the exact location where Mindo's body was found (four and a half blocks to the west of the Olympic, slumped in a recessed doorway on Garza); the cause of death (bleeding from multiple knife wounds). No wallet, telephone, or identification had been found, so they were treating this death as a robbery and homicide. They'd found her name beneath a drawing Mindo had made in his notebook.

"Did Mindo have any enemies?" the policeman asked. He'd already pulled out a small reporter's notebook.

"I just remember that nothing he was saying made any sense," Ixta told me.

"Enemies?" she asked. "Enemies?"

She cursed the policeman and called him a coward, while he tried in vain to calm her down. A neighbor heard the commotion and knocked on the door to find out what was going on. At one point, Ixta passed out. Her mother was summoned. Her brother. A medic. And just like that, the small apartment she'd shared with Mindo was full: more family; cousins; friends of hers; friends of Mindo; and eventually, another policeman, a woman this time. Their shoes piled at the door; a dozen mourners and cops standing around in their socks.

It should be noted that a similar scene was unfolding on the other side of the city, where Mindo's parents sat before a somber officer, having their lives politely shattered. Mindo's father, who was almost seventy, didn't speak for three days afterward. He never recovered from the shock.

One friend of the family put it to me this way: "If their son had died violently at age eighteen, *that* they might have understood. But to die now? When he'd already escaped?"

Mindo had painted three quarters of the neighborhood's death murals, which you can still see along the streets that surround his childhood home in the Thousands—bright, colorful, expansive portraits of young men laughing at death. Ignorant of death.

Now he has his own.

According to the reports, Nelson left Ixta's work in the Monument District, and crossed his city one last time on foot. He went north on the boulevard known colloquially as Huanca (though on most maps it appears under a different name), turned right just past the cathedral, zigzagged through the neighborhoods on the south side of Marina, crossed that broad avenue, then went east, along Brazil, where the cheap, poorly built highrises were just beginning to go up. He didn't talk to anyone, or stop anywhere. Some press reports would imply that he was hoping to escape, but wanted to try once more to convince Ixta to come with him. We know this isn't true. If he were fleeing, would he have walked right into an apartment filled with police?

He arrived just before eleven in the morning and stepped into a horror show. Ixta was in a terrible state, and Nelson's arrival didn't make things any better. By then Mindo's sister had arrived, an emissary from that other world of pain. There was no solidarity. She yelled at Ixta, cursed her, and once she figured out who Nelson was, spat her vitriol at him as well. When Ixta admitted she'd seen Nelson the day before, Mindo's sister all but demanded they both be arrested. There was even a moment when it appeared this might happen, but in the end no officer wanted to arrest the pregnant woman.

That left Nelson, and nothing could've been more convenient. In a city with hundreds of unsolved and frankly unsolvable crimes, the police could hardly believe their luck: a suspect had strolled right in. He looked guilty; his motive was clear.

"Do you know a man named Mindo?" they asked him.

"Sure I do," Nelson said. "I was with him last night."

They had their killer.

There would be no mention of the events of T——; none of Rogelio nor Jaime; no attention paid to the possible motives of a provincial thug avenging the death of his mother. All the dots were lying out in the open, waiting to be connected. For the police, and then the prosecutors, and then the judge, it was simply irresistible.

"Call my mother," Nelson shouted to Ixta as he was taken away. "Please call my mother."

"I did that, at least," Ixta told me. "I don't know how, but I did it."

Mónica confirmed this. "A call no mother should ever receive," she said when I asked. Her eyes were closed tightly. "I didn't see him for another three days."

And when she did, it was in Collectors.

24

THE NEWS NEVER MADE IT to our town, though I suspect Jaime must have heard. I imagine it concerned him; I don't believe he intended for anyone to die, and, if he did, that person was certainly not Mindo. But these things happen, and Jaime was well acquainted with unexpected outcomes. His work had taught him about the occasional necessity of violence and the randomness of the law. When he learned of Nelson's arrest and the accusation against him, one imagines he might even have smiled. Setting aside for a moment Mindo's unfortunate demise, from the point of view of Mrs. Anabel's grieving son, justice had been done.

I left T—— in late August, but heard nothing of Nelson's predicament until a few months later. I wouldn't say that I'd forgotten him, only that my life went on. I was lucky enough to find work at a magazine that had launched while I was away, a publication that quite miraculously still survives, and where I work even now. There were four of us on staff then (today we are twelve), and at the beginning we did everything: the writing and editing, the layout and design. We were the accountants, which explains why bankruptcy loomed each month; and we were the custodial staff, which explains why the office was in a state of constant disarray. The owners, the impatient but enthusiastic Jara brothers, would come by the office once a month; we'd all pile into their battered old van, and deliver the magazines ourselves. We ended these days at our favorite bar, just a few blocks from the office. I liked the Jaras, liked my coworkers, and this was something I'd never experienced before. We were paid laughable wages, but in exchange were allowed to write whatever we wanted, more or less. Every month we got letters from readers, which we passed around the office like love notes.

On one of these nights after having delivered an issue, the managing editor, Lizzy, brought up the many local scandals I'd missed on "my Andean sabbatical." That was what she called my time in T——, a phrase made charming by the playful manner in which she offered it to the group. It had become a running joke: when I interviewed for the job I'd only been back in the city a few days, and must have seemed a little out of sorts. Still, I was hired, and often entertained my new friends with the folkloric details of provincial life; they, in turn, pretended to be amazed. I let this playacting go on, because it was obvious to me that we all came from similar backgrounds, that we all had similarly tense relationships with our families, with our cultural inheritance.

"That hometown of yours," Lizzy or one of the others might say. "What year is it out there?"

Everyone would laugh, including me. Time, we all knew, was a very relative concept.

That evening—it was late October 2001—among the scandals mentioned was the story of a young theater actor who'd murdered his rival in a fit of jealous rage. "The sort of thing that never happens where you're from," Lizzy said, waving an open hand to signify the provinces. She went on, others joined in, and together my new friends told the story. They cycled through what details they could remember: the disputed paternity, the actor and painter dueling on a late-night street in the Old City. Some particulars had vanished: my friends had a hard time remembering the name of the theater where the killer had been hiding out, or the plays he'd been in before his arrest. But the pregnant girl, the woman at the center of all this; they remembered her. She was an actress, like her lover; very striking, though she never smiled in photos. She'd appeared in the papers under a number of unflattering captions: "The Ice Woman Cometh" or "Blood Wedding."

And they recalled her name. It was unforgettable, a name rarely heard in these parts.

"Ixta," they said as one.

Ixta, I repeated to myself.

Our bar—we considered it ours—was and remains one of the places I feel most at home in the world. There are no surprises and not a thing is out of place. But when I heard the name Ixta, I felt a kind of vertigo. This comfortable setting looked suddenly strange to me. My friends too. What they were saying struck me as so dismaying, so arbitrary, that I wondered for a moment if they were having fun at my expense.

Finally I asked, "Was the actor named Nelson?"

"That's it," Lizzy said, grinning. "Nelson!"

That is what sent me on this path. I told them about T——, about my interaction with the murderer, and they didn't believe me. I insisted, and that evening we decided I should write it all down. I even had his journals! We thought it would become a piece for the magazine, maybe even a cover story. It would've been my first.

I went back and looked at the press from the days immediately after Mindo's death, and saw that it was all true: Nelson's name and photo had been splashed across the front pages of all the local papers. It was unsettling to see him, this man I'd met so briefly, back in July. I spent many days gathering clippings, making lists of places to visit, people I might want to see. The Olympic appeared in a few television reports I managed to find, described as if it were some sort of criminal hangout; this, I later learned, is what finally drove Patalarga to reunite with his wife, moving home in the dead of night, in the hopes of avoiding any further attentions from the media. In the papers I saw many of the people who would later become my informants. Some, like Mónica or Ixta, did all they could to avoid the cameras; others, like Elías and a few of Nelson's other friends, took the opposite approach, speaking all too freely, as if they were auditioning for a role.

I FINALLY READ Nelson's journals, the ones Noelia had given me, and after a good deal of encouragement from my colleagues at the magazine, decided to visit Mónica. At the time I had no real sense of Nelson's guilt or innocence. Just curiosity. It wasn't difficult to find her, and one evening in November, I knocked on her door. Until that point, I'd been another kind of journalist; she appeared behind her gate, watching me, and I became someone else. She was a slight, tired-looking woman with short hair and a pair of reading glasses twirling in one hand. I was so nervous I could barely explain who I was, or what I wanted.

"I know Nelson," I blathered finally, and this seemed to get her attention. At the sound of her son's name, she narrowed her eyes at me, and opened the gate.

We sat in the living room, and while I told her my story, Mónica focused her attention on an origami swan she was making from the tea bag wrapper. When she was done, she placed it on the coffee table with the others, a flock of six or seven, all of them looking in different directions.

"So you met my son in T——," she said. "Is that all?"

Then I showed her the notebooks, and she almost broke down. She held them for a moment, flipping through the pages quickly, inhaling the scent. After a moment, she shook her head and set them beside her on the sofa.

"What do they say?"

I considered lying, just telling her I hadn't read them. She gave me a searching look, and I realized the only option was to tell the truth. Of course I'd read them; that's why I was there.

"They're about the tour," I said. "Up until the morning he left to come home."

She nodded gravely. "Should I read them?"

"Yes," I said. "They might help."

By the time I left it was nearly ten o'clock. I gave her the journals (which had always belonged to her, which had never been mine) and promised to visit again.

November passed, the New Year came, and I went to see Mónica again. This time we spoke for many hours. I recorded that conversation. She'd read my magazine. "It isn't bad," she said. I told her I was going to write about Nelson's case, and she gave me her blessing. We looked through the old photo albums, and when I left that day, she lent me some of his journals. We made a list of the people I should talk to; old classmates mostly, a few kids from the neighborhood, but also a couple of names from the Conservatory, classmates who'd come to visit her since the news had broken.

"But I don't really know who his friends were," she confessed with a sigh.

"At a certain age, that's normal."

She smiled. "Is it? I'm not so sure." She gave me Francisco's number in California, and I promised to call him. "And have you spoken with the actors? The gentlemen from Diciembre?"

I'd already planned a visit to the Olympic, and chatted briefly by phone with Henry.

"Good," Mónica said. "But you should start with Ixta."

I had tried her twice already and been rejected—but after seeing Mónica, I insisted. The third time I rang her door, Ixta let me in, scowling.

"Again?" she asked. "For the love of God, what's wrong with you?"

. . .

IN APRIL 2002, while the court proceedings were being held up, I went back to T——, following the path that Diciembre had taken the previous year. I spoke with as many people as I could, taking notes, making recordings, and helping them make sense of their memories. I spoke with Cayetano and Melissa, with Tania, and attempted to find the bar in Sihuas where they'd seen all the gold miners, but the authorities had shut it down. I spoke with people who'd seen Diciembre's performances, and heard a few phrases again and again: "He was such a nice boy!" and "What a show!" In my hometown I managed, with some coaxing, to draw a few people out of their reticence. Nothing having to do with Jaime was ever openly discussed. Whenever anyone asked, I said I was writing a piece for a magazine, and they'd look at me suspiciously. A newspaper, that they would've accepted; even a book would've made sense. But a magazine?

Who did I think I was?

I went to see Jaime in San Jacinto, intending to pose all the questions I could safely ask. I would not say, for example, "Why did you let your brother take the fall for your drug shipment?" or "Did you send someone to kill Nelson?" or "Who was driving that station wagon the night Mindo was killed?" I had a list of other questions, more innocent-sounding ones, but in the end, it didn't matter, because he refused to see me at all.

In August 2002, Nelson's trial got under way, and I attended as many days as I could. I often saw Henry or Patalarga there, sitting in the back, whispering among themselves, and during breaks we'd discuss the proceedings like fans at a sporting event. Our team was losing; that much was clear. I was there when the judge refused to allow the notebooks to be entered into evidence, and decreed that no theory relating Mindo's death to events in T— was admissible. "Hearsay," he called it, and Nelson was sunk. I was in the courtroom the day Mindo's sister called Ixta "a dirty slut" from the witness stand; Mónica sat in the third row with her sister, Astrid, weeping. She appeared in a few of the papers the next morning, under headlines about "a mother's sadness."

One day, at the courthouse, Nelson's uncle Ramiro turned around in his seat, and eyed me, frowning. Then his expression softened.

"It's like you're always here," he said, in a tone of amazement. "Don't you have something else to do?"

I sometimes wondered the same thing. My colleagues at the magazine, the ones who'd encouraged me at first—they wondered too. "Where's your article?" Lizzy asked me from time to time, and I'd put her off. Eventually she stopped asking.

I was at Nelson's sentencing in February 2003, a full two years after the auditions that had changed his life. Mindo's father had passed away by then, but his mother was there, stoic, and unblinking. She barely reacted at all when the judge announced a sentence of fifteen years. The term felt like an eternity to all of us who sided with Nelson, who believed he was incapable of murder, but I could tell that to Mindo's mother it felt like an insult.

Only fifteen years.

In the gallery's front row Mónica collapsed into her sister's arms, and Nelson was taken away again, back to Collectors, with a look on his face of utter bewilderment. He'd lost weight and had an unhealthy pallor. I don't think he ever understood that this was actually happening, that this was his life now.

IN THE MONTHS that followed, he wrote letters to his mother, which she showed me, very beautiful letters that described his friends, his surroundings, and detailed his concerns. He'd been placed among inmates from the northern districts, as far from the Thousands as possible, for his own safety. There was a very real possibility that someone from Mindo's old neighborhood might seek to avenge the painter's death. He described the power structure of the prison, the fearsome men who ran it, who hailed from districts of the city Nelson had never set foot in, but which he now knew intimately. He knew the way these men spoke, what worried them, what motivated them. They were men who demanded respect, and who were prepared to go to war over any perceived insult, no matter how slight. Nelson described the cramped quarters, his melancholy cell mate (whom he called "roommate," because it sounded "less institutional"); and how quickly a placid day inside could shift and become spectacularly violent. He told his mother about the roving bands of homeless inmates who camped in the rocky field outside his block, and he expressed wonder at their plight. What surprised him the most was that everyone else accepted the situation of these people as normal. There was nowhere to house them, no one wanted them, and so there they were: three hundred shirtless, shoeless men, hungry, drug-addled, dying slowly en masse. The year before Nelson's arrival, one young addict had climbed up the radio tower (which hadn't worked in two decades) and hung himself with a gray scarf. When they brought his body down, they left the scarf, and it had stayed there, the prison's new and unofficial flag. Nelson never knew the man, but could understand him, he said in a letter, not to his mother but to Patalarga—he kept the worst details from her, so as not to add to her worry. He talked about the view from the roof of his block, the open sky, the hillsides dotted every day with new homes. He watched the women carrying water up the hill in plastic buckets, watched them pause to wipe the sweat from their brows. They were very poor, but he envied them.

"By the time I come out, the hillside will be covered," he wrote to his mother, "and I won't have anywhere to live." Sometimes, he confessed to Patalarga, he lost track of who he was. "I stopped playing Rogelio a long time ago, and yet here I am."

This was the point that most troubled Henry. Some six months after the verdict, he called and asked if I could come see him. Like all former inmates accused of terrorism, he was barred from visiting, and was anxious to know how Nelson was holding up. He and Patalarga had had another falling out since the end of the trial; so that left me.

I felt almost sheepish admitting that I hadn't gone to Collectors yet.

"But you've talked to him."

I shook my head.

Henry couldn't hide his disappointment. "I *can't* go. What's your excuse?"

I didn't have one; or rather, I didn't have a good one. I wasn't family. Strictly speaking, I wasn't even a friend.

He smiled slyly. "Are you scared? Is that it? Do you think something unspeakable will happen to you?"

I'd never been teased by Henry Nuñez before.

"Yes," I said. "I'm terrified."

Henry slumped back in his chair. "Well, you're no fun."

His apartment was messier than usual, with piles of books on the floor and dirty dishes in the sink. A white dress shirt was draped over one of the plastic chairs in the corner, drying stiffly.

"So what happened here?" I asked.

Ana wasn't allowed to visit, he explained, so there was no need to keep up appearances. "Not that I would've fooled you anyway." It seems that on Ana's last overnight, there'd been a gas leak somewhere in the building. Everyone on the block had been evacuated, and many had slept in the park, including Henry and his daughter. It was a warm night, a neighborly night tinged with the mood of a carnival. But his ex-wife was furious.

"Sleeping outdoors. Must've reminded you of the tour."

Henry shook his head. "It was nice, but no. There's nothing like being on tour."

We talked for a while about his plans, went over a few questions I had about the history of Diciembre, and when I was about to leave, I asked why he'd called me. It was odd, given that for each of our previous interviews, I'd had to work to track him down.

Henry looked up, nodding, as if trying to remember. Then: "I'm ready to write that script. The one we were going to do together."

I gave him a puzzled look. "We?"

"Nelson and I. Our prison story."

"Your prison story."

He was energized, almost manic. "A love story. Rogelio's story. We were going to write it together. A play. We can take it on tour. He said he wanted to help. Now we can. Now I'm ready. Will you ask him?"

"Is this what you and Patalarga fought about?"

Henry frowned and rubbed his neck. "Just ask him," he said. "Will you ask him?"

IT WAS JANUARY 2004 before I could get the proper permissions to visit Nelson myself. I remember we'd just hit ten thousand subscribers at the magazine, and were celebrating at the offices with an impromptu party. In the middle of it, my letter arrived.

You are granted permission to enter Collectors Prison on this day, at this hour.

I was given an appointment at the ministry building in the Old City to have my fingerprints taken. The celebration became more serious, more sincere. It was as if I'd won an award.

"Maybe we'll finally see that article," Lizzy said.

I'd been petitioning for something more than an ordinary visit: I wanted the okay to bring in a microphone and a tape recorder; and given the conditions inside, the authorities were skittish about these kinds of requests. No one wanted a journalist to embarrass them. I think back now and wonder why I insisted, and can only conclude it was a stalling tactic. These things take time, and I knew that. Perhaps I could've pushed harder against the sluggish prison bureaucracy, but I didn't. I was busy, it was true, but I'll admit that part of me was hesitant to compare my invented version of Nelson with the man himself.

Mónica went to see her son every couple of weeks, a ritual she both looked forward to and dreaded; and she often called me the next day to read me Nelson's most recent letter over the phone. I'd hear the shuffle of papers through the receiver, she'd clear her throat; I'd make myself comfortable and listen. I liked hearing his words in her voice. When she finished, I'd thank her. I knew these letters were edited, because I'd read the ones he gave Patalarga.

"When are you going to see my boy?" Mónica would ask. "He says he has something to tell you."

"Soon," I'd respond.

I finally went to Collectors in March. Nelson was almost twenty-six years old now, and coming up on the third anniversary of his incarceration; an unimaginable length of time, but only a fraction of what he'd been condemned to serve. That was the thought I couldn't shake as I presented my papers to an unsmiling guard, as I handed my bag over to be searched by another. *Fifteen years.* My tape recorder was removed from its case, examined by a guard who looked at it curiously, as if

considering some obscure tool from another age. *Twelve to go.*
He searched for and eventually found the serial number, which
he then compared with the one on the document I'd presented.
The numbers matched, and he let out a little sigh of disappointment. Then he checked my microphone, my headphones and
cables, and once everything was confirmed to be in order, my
arm was stamped, and I was on my way. All of this was accomplished without exchanging a single sentence.

I was patted down at the next gate, and then sent through
with a grunt. I stepped out of the primary holding area and into
the bright, beating sun. I covered my eyes. Standing between
the two gates, neither inside the prison, nor out of it, but in a
neutral zone, I stared through the heavy chain-link fence at the
inmates of Collectors: young men milling about, looking bored.
I would've liked to observe them for just a moment, but the next
guard hurried me along, and quite suddenly I was inside. The
gate closed behind me: just closed, it didn't slam or make any
noise at all. It's subtle, in fact, the difference between inside and
outside.

I looked all around, trying not to seem overwhelmed. There
were so many men, but no Nelson.

Then a voice: "It's really something, isn't it?"

He'd pushed through the gathered, idle men, and come up
from behind. There was a playfulness to his expression that told
me this had been deliberate.

We shook hands. He looked different; better in fact. He'd cut
his hair, and this alone changed the tenor of his features. No
boyishness left; no whimsy. His face had lost its youthfulness,

and it had been replaced by something else, something tougher and more determined. He wore jeans and a clean, light blue T-shirt. Last time I'd seen him at the courthouse, he'd been thin and callow and frightened; there was none of that now. He'd put on weight, had a certain heft to his shoulders.

Nelson was observing me too. "I don't remember you. I've been wondering if I would, but I don't. Nothing."

"That's okay."

"I just thought you should know." He pressed his lips tight. "My mother says you were at the trial. I didn't notice you."

"You had other things on your mind."

He smiled cautiously. "She thinks we'll be friends or something."

A couple skinny, shirtless men hovered just behind Nelson, eyeing me.

"Seems like you have friends."

"A man needs them. Is this your first time?"

"It is."

"So take a look."

This is what I saw. There were men: ordinary men as you might find on any street, in any neighborhood, tall men, short men, skinny men, fat men, black men, brown men, white men (though only a few of those), tired men, frantic men, old men. They looked like people I'd known, people I'd seen before, only harder, perhaps. But that was only part of the story: together, they were outnumbered by another group, the broken men, and these were legion. They were shirtless and desperate and wilting in the late-summer heat. This was their home, the front of the prison, the public spaces that no one owned. These fallen ones were sinewy and gaunt, covered in scars and the blurry tattooed names of lovers they'd forgotten and who'd forgotten them, men with sunken cheeks, men with dirty hands. They watched me with great intensity, or perhaps I only felt like they were watching; perhaps they were so high they didn't even notice who I was. An outsider.

"What are you looking for?" Nelson asked.

"Guards," I said.

Nelson's laugh was odd in that it did not contain within it an invitation to laugh along. It was dry, cutting.

We went left up the path that rounded the prison's edge, past the entrances to the odd-numbered blocks. The shirtless pair followed us at a distance. We reached the top of the hill and stopped, facing an alley that led to the even-numbered blocks.

"They call it Main Street," Nelson said.

It was the width of a bus, and served as both thoroughfare and market: mismatched pairs of plastic sandals, shaving mirrors and old batteries, plastic combs and razors were for sale, displayed on square patches of plastic lying on the ground. Every few steps there was a man slumped against the wall, smoking crack from a tiny metal pipe. Or maybe it only seemed this way; maybe I was so taken aback by the sight of the first addict that in my mind this one helpless man was multiplied, until I saw him everywhere, like a bright light present even with your eyes closed. In any case, I can describe him, and the men just like him, very easily: he had a narrow face dotted with uneven stubble, a receding hairline. He held up the pipe, and when he did, I noticed his thin, almost delicate wrists, his long fingers. He sat on his haunches with his knees bent, and I saw the stained black bottoms of his feet. He flicked the lighter, and curled his toes in anticipation of the high.

Nelson and I both watched him as he struggled with the lighter. He flicked it, a soft breeze blew down Main Street, and the flame went out. He tried again, and then again. Beneath it all, there was an eagerness that was almost childlike. It was impossible not to root for him.

We walked halfway down to Nelson's block, Number Ten, and I watched through the rusty bars, trying to be invisible, while Nelson explained who I was, and why I was there. He was negotiating with an inmate, so I could pass.

Our two escorts kept their watch.

"Who are they?" I asked.

"They're protecting you," Nelson said.

Then we were let inside. All of us.

Men shouted from the third floor to the ground floor, from the second floor to the roof, voices straining to be heard above blasting stereos, above blaring televisions, above a dozen other voices. Noise everywhere. Nelson led me through the tier; following him was like trying to walk in a straight line through a windstorm. I wanted to see everything, remember every detail. I knew, even then, that this was my one chance, that I wouldn't be coming back. I saw a blackened tube of a fluorescent light dangling by its cord, swaying dangerously above me. I watched how Nelson moved through the space, the way he held himself. He didn't talk to anyone, and no one spoke to him. I remember thinking, it's as if he's not even here.

He told me he'd arranged for a quiet cell, so we could talk. "Terrific," I said. It was on the second floor. His two friends waited outside while Nelson and I went in, and I quickly discovered it wasn't actually quiet at all, only quiet in comparison to the cells on the other side of the block, overlooking the yard. I wanted good sound on this interview, but I hadn't anticipated how difficult that would be in a place like Collectors.

"Is this okay?" he asked.

I nodded. "It'll do."

"I can't understand why you're here," he said as I set up my recorder and microphone. I was checking the levels, and his words came blasting through my headphones. I looked up, startled.

"I'll explain. Just give me a second."

He waited. He sat in one of those white plastic lawn chairs, the same kind Henry kept in his dour bachelor's apartment. Nelson leaned back now. With a nod he gestured toward the block, toward the men roving and shouting just outside the cell door.

"Pick any of them," he said. "Stick a microphone in their face, and they'll tell you a story. They're dying to be heard."

"You aren't?"

He shook his head.

"What do you want?"

"I've been trying for months to get Ixta to visit me. I want her to bring Nadia. That's what I want most of all. Why won't she come?"

"I don't know," I said.

"I know you don't. Have you seen the baby?"

I nodded. We lived in the same neighborhood now; it felt cruel to say I saw her all the time. "She's beautiful."

"I imagine."

"And what does she tell you?" I asked.

"Reasonable things. That she wants to move on with her life. That she's got to look forward and not back." He frowned. "She doesn't think I killed Mindo, does she?"

"No one thinks you killed Mindo."

"The judge does."

He gave me a sharp, almost defiant smile, as if he were happy to have proven me wrong.

"Will you tell me what happened?" I asked.

He didn't answer right away, but something in the way he looked at me made me think: *Finally, an opening.* I was sure of it. He rubbed the top of his head with his palm, bit his thumbnail, and narrowed his eyes. "Everyone in here is innocent, you know? Ask around, they'll all tell you the same thing."

I leaned toward him. "Sure. That's what they say. But you really are."

"So what?"

I stopped. I wasn't getting anywhere. Maybe it was time to admit that. "Would it be better if I put this away?" I asked, gesturing at my tape recorder.

Nelson nodded, and I pressed Stop. I peeled off the head-phones and the world dropped to its regular volume again.

He smiled. "This is better, isn't it?"

"Sure," I said.

"We can just talk now."

I nodded.

"Can I hold it?"

I gave him the tape recorder, then the microphone. I handed over the headphones too. He left it all in his lap.

"What if I did kill Mindo? Have you thought about that?"

There was something very cold in his voice.

"You didn't."

"What if I did? What if I were that kind of person?"

Nelson had been inside for thirty-odd months, studying this very sort of performed aggression. And he was good. He let the questions hang there. I knew it couldn't be true, but then he shifted his gaze, and part of me wondered why I thought that, why I was so sure. I felt a chill.

"All right," I said. "Let's suppose."

"So what do you think I would do to someone who was out-side while I was in here, and had decided he had the right to tell my story? If I were the person capable of killing a man on a dark street?"

I didn't know what to say.

"Just think," Nelson said.

I smiled, but now he didn't smile back, and for a few long moments nothing was said. He'd made his point, and while I mulled it over, he busied himself examining my tape recorder and the microphone. He pressed Record, and pointed the mic in different directions. He snapped his fingers at the working end of the mic, and watched the needle jump.

"It's not recording yet," I said. "It's on pause. If you want to . . ." I said, and reached for the machine. There was a button he hadn't pressed. That was all I wanted to show him.

But he pulled the recorder away from me. It was a quick gesture, very slight. "I'll hold it," he said.

"I just . . ."

"You're fine."

I could feel myself turning red. I understood what was happening.

"You're robbing me?"

Nelson gave me a disappointed look. "Is that what you think?"

"Well, I . . ."

"Let's just be clear about who's been robbing whom."

When I didn't respond, he stood. He took my tape recorder and the microphone and placed them on the table behind him. I could have tried to grab them, I suppose, but Nelson set his body between me and my equipment, as if daring me to take them back. And I thought about it, I did. We were the same size, neither of us particularly imposing, but my last fight had been in middle school. And now I was in Collectors, which was, for better or worse, his home. His two friends, the ones who were protecting me, stood just outside the cell. As if to underline the point, Nelson pushed the door open, and all the noise from the block came rushing in.

"Do you understand?" he asked.

"I do," I said. "Thank you for your time."

I stepped out, and he closed the door behind me.

The two shirtless men had gone, and I found myself in the middle of the block, buried in sound. I had nowhere to go. I was in no hurry. I stood there for a moment, trying to pick out a voice, any voice, from the din.

ACKNOWLEDGMENTS

I would like to thank the Lannan Foundation, the Headlands Center for the Arts, and the Guggenheim Foundation for their support. Mark Lafferty, Lila Byock, Joe Loya, and Adam Mansbach all stepped up at various points in the process to give me insight and encouragement on a manuscript that seemed, frankly, impossible to resolve. I am forever grateful.

This novel, like almost everything I write, is the product of a meandering, limitless conversation with my friend Vinnie Wilhelm. Thanks, brother.

Collectors is an invented place, but I owe a debt of gratitude to Carlos Álvarez Osorio, who first took me inside Lima's prisons in 2007, and who has, on each subsequent visit, helped me understand what I was seeing. The men I met inside Lurigancho and Castro Castro trusted me with their stories, and for that I will always be grateful. My editors at *Harper's*, Claire Gutierrez and Chris Cox, were very supportive of the research that became first a piece of nonfiction, and eventually part of this novel.

I'd like to thank Gustavo Lora and the Collazos family, who

helped me discover T——. Walter Ventosilla's play *El Mandatario Idiota* served as an early inspiration, and with his permission, I have adapted it here. Both Walter and Gustavo were members of Setiembre, the theater troupe on which Diciembre is based, and I have borrowed liberally from stories they shared with me.

My agent, Eric Simonoff, was helpful every step of the way. My editor, Megan Lynch, offered great advice, patience, and generosity, and helped make this book better in innumerable ways. Thank you.

Most of all, I'd like to thank my family—my parents, my sisters, their partners, their children, and especially my wife, Carolina, who made me laugh when I wanted to give up, gave me love when I needed it, and space when I was scared to ask for it.

Gracias, mi amor.

where she went

GAYLE FORMAN

DEFINITIONS

WHERE SHE WENT
A DEFINITIONS BOOK 978 1 849 41428 9

First published in the United States by Dutton Books,
a member of Penguin Group (USA) Inc.

First published in Great Britain by Doubleday,
an imprint of Random House Children's Publishers UK
A Random House Company

Doubleday edition published 2011
Definitions edition published 2012

20

Penguin Random House is committed to a sustainable future for
our business, our readers and our planet. This book is made from
Forest Stewardship Council® certified paper.

MIX
Paper from
responsible sources
FSC® C018179

Printed and bound in Great Britain by Clays Ltd, St Ives plc

Definitions are published by Random House Children's Publishers UK
61–63 Uxbridge Road, London W5 5SA

www.randomhousechildrens.co.uk
www.totallyrandombooks.co.uk
www.randomhouse.co.uk

Addresses for companies within The Random House Group Limited can be found at:
www.randomhouse.co.uk/offices.htm

THE RANDOM HOUSE GROUP Limited Reg. No. 954009

A CIP catalogue record for this book is available from the British Library.

It well may be that in a difficult hour,
Pinned down by pain and moaning for release,
Or nagged by want past resolution's power,
I might be driven to sell your love for peace,
Or trade the memory of this night for food.
It well may be. I do not think I would.

Excerpt from "Love is not all:
it is not meat nor drink."
BY EDNA ST. VINCENT MILLAY

Every morning I wake up and I tell myself this: *It's just one day, one twenty-four-hour period to get yourself through.* I don't know when exactly I started giving myself this daily pep talk—or why. It sounds like a twelve-step mantra and I'm not in Anything Anonymous, though to read some of the crap they write about me, you'd think I should be. I have the kind of life a lot of people would probably sell a kidney to just experience a bit of. But still, I find the need to remind myself of the temporariness of a day, to reassure myself that I got through yesterday, I'll get through today.

This morning, after my daily prodding, I glance at the minimalist digital clock on the hotel nightstand. It reads 11:47, positively crack-of-dawn for me. But the front desk has already rang with two wake-up calls, followed by a polite-but-firm buzz from our manager, Aldous. Today might be just one day, but it's packed.

I'm due at the studio to lay down a few final guitar tracks for some Internet-only version of the first single of our just-released album. Such a gimmick. Same song, new guitar track, some vocal effects, pay an extra buck for it. "These days, you've gotta milk a dollar out of every dime," the suits at the label are so fond of reminding us.

After the studio, I have a lunch interview with some reporter from *Shuffle*. Those two events are kinda like the bookends of what my life has become: making the music, which I like, and talking about making the music, which I loathe. But they're flip sides of the same coin. When Aldous calls a second time I finally kick off the duvet and grab the prescription bottle from the side table. It's some anti-anxiety thing I'm supposed to take when I'm feeling jittery.

Jittery is how I normally feel. Jittery I've gotten used to. But ever since we kicked off our tour with three shows at Madison Square Garden, I've been feeling something else. Like I'm about to be sucked into something powerful and painful. Vortexy.

Is that even a word? I ask myself.

You're talking to yourself, so who the hell cares? I reply, popping a couple of pills. I pull on some boxers, and go to the door of my room, where a pot of coffee is already waiting. It's been left there by a hotel employee, undoubtedly under strict instructions to stay out of my way.

I finish my coffee, get dressed, and make my way down the service elevator and out the side entrance—the guest-relations manager has kindly provided me with special access keys so I can avoid the scenester parade in the lobby. Out on the sidewalk, I'm greeted by a blast of steaming New York air. It's kind of oppressive, but I like that the air is wet. It reminds me of Oregon, where the rain falls endlessly, and even on the hottest of summer days, blooming white cumulus clouds float above, their shadows reminding you that summer's heat is fleeting, and the rain's never far off.

In Los Angeles, where I live now, it hardly ever rains. And the heat, it's never-ending. But it's a dry heat. People there use this aridness as a blanket excuse for all of the hot, smoggy city's excesses. "It may be a hundred and seven degrees today," they'll brag, "but at least it's a dry heat."

But New York is a wet heat; by the time I reach the studio ten blocks away on a desolate stretch in the West

Fifties, my hair, which I keep hidden under a cap, is damp. I pull a cigarette from my pocket and my hand shakes as I light up. I've had a slight tremor for the last year or so. After extensive medical checks, the doctors declared it nothing more than nerves and advised me to try yoga.

When I get to the studio, Aldous is waiting outside under the awning. He looks at me, at my cigarette, back at my face. I can tell by the way that he's eyeballing me, he's trying to decide whether he needs to be Good Cop or Bad Cop. I must look like shit because he opts for Good Cop.

"Good morning, Sunshine," he says jovially.

"Yeah? What's ever good about morning?" I try to make it sound like a joke.

"Technically, it's afternoon now. We're running late."

I stub out my cigarette. Aldous puts a giant paw on my shoulder, incongruously gentle. "We just want one guitar track on 'Sugar,' just to give it that little something extra so fans buy it all over again." He laughs, shakes his head at what the business has become. "Then you have lunch with *Shuffle,* and we have a photo shoot for that Fashion Rocks thing for the *Times* with the rest of the band around five, and then a quick drinks thing with some money guys at the label, and then I'm off to the airport. Tomorrow, you have a quick little meeting with publicity and merchandising. Just smile and don't say a lot. After that you're on your lonesome until London."

On my lonesome? As opposed to being in the warm bosom of family when we're all together? I say. Only I say it to myself. More and more lately it seems as though the majority of my conversations are with myself. Given half the stuff I think, that's probably a good thing.

But this time I really will be by myself. Aldous and the rest of the band are flying to England tonight. I was supposed to be on the same flight as them until I realized that today was Friday the thirteenth, and I was like no fucking way! I'm dreading this tour enough as is, so I'm not jinxing it further by leaving on the official day of bad luck. So I'd had Aldous book me a day later. We're shooting a video in London and then doing a bunch of press before we start the European leg of our tour, so it's not like I'm missing a show, just a preliminary meeting with our video director. I don't need to hear about his artistic vision. When we start shooting, I'll do what he tells me.

I follow Aldous into the studio and enter a soundproof booth where it's just me and a row of guitars. On the other side of the glass sit our producer, Stim, and the sound engineers. Aldous joins them. "Okay, Adam," says Stim, "one more track on the bridge and the chorus. Just to make that hook that much more sticky. We'll play with the vocals in the mixing."

"Hooky. Sticky. Got it." I put on my headphones and pick up my guitar to tune up and warm up. I try not to notice that in spite of what Aldous said a few minutes ago, it feels like I'm *already* all on my lonesome. Me alone in a soundproof booth. *Don't overthink it*, I tell myself. *This is how you record in a technologically advanced studio.* The only problem is, I felt the same way a few nights ago at the Garden. Up onstage, in front of eighteen thousand fans, alongside the people who, once upon a time, were part of my family, I felt as alone as I do in this booth.

Still, it could be worse. I start to play and my fingers nimble up and I get off the stool and bang and crank against my guitar, pummel it until it screeches and screams just the way I want it to. Or almost the way I want it to. There's probably a hundred grand's worth of guitars in this room, but none of them sound as good as my old Les Paul Junior—the guitar I'd had for ages, the one I'd recorded our first albums on, the one that, in a fit of stupidity or hubris or whatever, I'd allowed to be auctioned off for charity. The shiny, expensive replacements have never sounded or felt quite right. Still, when I crank it up loud, I do manage to lose myself for a second or two.

But it's over all too soon, and then Stim and the engineers are shaking my hand and wishing me luck on tour, and Aldous is shepherding me out the door and into a town car and we're whizzing down Ninth Avenue to SoHo, to a hotel whose restaurant the publicists from our record label have decided is a good spot for our interview. What, do they think I'm less likely to rant or say something alienating if I'm in an expensive public place? I remember back in the very early days, when the interviewers wrote 'zines or blogs and were fans and mostly wanted to rock-talk—to discuss the *music*—and they wanted to speak to all of us together. More often than not, it just turned into a normal conversation with everyone shouting their opinions over one another. Back then I never worried about guarding my words. But now the reporters interrogate me and the band separately, as though they're cops and they have me and my accomplices in adjacent cells and are trying to get us to implicate one another.

I need a cigarette before we go in, so Aldous and I stand outside the hotel in the blinding midday sun as a crowd of people gathers and checks me out while pretending not to. That's the difference between New York and the rest of the world. People are just as celebrity-crazed as anywhere, but New Yorkers—or at least the ones who consider themselves sophisticates and loiter along the kind of SoHo block I'm standing on now—put on this pretense that they don't care, even as they stare out from their three-hundred-dollar shades. Then they act all disdainful when out-of-towners break the code by rushing up and asking for an autograph as a pair of girls in U Michigan sweatshirts have just done, much to the annoyance of the nearby trio of snobs, who watch the girls and roll their eyes and give me a look of sympathy. As if the *girls* are the problem.

"We need to get you a better disguise, Wilde Man," Aldous says, after the girls, giggling with excitement, flutter away. He's the only one who's allowed to call me that anymore. Before it used to be a general nickname, a takeoff on my last name, Wilde. But once I sort of trashed a hotel room and after that "Wilde Man" became an unshakable tabloid moniker.

Then, as if on cue, a photographer shows up. You can't stand in front of a high-end hotel for more than three minutes before that happens. "Adam! Bryn inside?" A photo of me and Bryn is worth about quadruple one of me alone. But after the first flash goes off, Aldous shoves one hand in front of the guy's lens, and another in front of my face.

As he ushers me inside, he preps me. "The reporter is named Vanessa LeGrande. She's not one of those grizzled types you hate. She's young. Not younger than you, but early twenties, I think. Used to write for a blog before she got tapped by *Shuffle*."

"Which blog?" I interrupt. Aldous rarely gives me detailed rundowns on reporters unless there's a reason.

"Not sure. Maybe Gabber."

"Oh, Al, that's a piece-of-crap gossip site."

"*Shuffle* isn't a gossip site. And this is the cover exclusive."

"Fine. Whatever," I say, pushing through the restaurant doors. Inside it's all low steel-and-glass tables and leather banquettes, like a million other places I've been to. These restaurants think so highly of themselves, but really they're just overpriced, overstylized versions of McDonald's.

"There she is, corner table, the blonde with the streaks," Aldous says. "She's a sweet little number. Not that you have a shortage of sweet little numbers. Shit, don't tell Bryn I said that. Okay, forget it. I'll be up here at the bar."

Aldous staying for the interview? That's a publicist's job, except that I refused to be chaperoned by publicists. I must really seem off-kilter. "You babysitting?" I ask.

"Nope. Just thought you could use some backup."

Vanessa LeGrande is cute. Or maybe *hot* is a more accurate term. It doesn't matter. I can tell by the way she licks her lips and tosses her hair back that she knows it, and that pretty much ruins the effect. A tattoo of a snake runs up her wrist, and I'd bet our platinum album that she has a tramp stamp. Sure enough, when she reaches into her bag for her digital recorder, peeping up from the top of her low-slung jeans is a small inked arrow pointing south. *Classy.*

"Hey, Adam," Vanessa says, looking at me conspiratorially, like we're old buddies. "Can I just say I'm a huge fan? *Collateral Damage* got me through a devastating breakup senior year of college. So, thank you." She smiles at me.

"Uh, you're welcome."

"And now I'd like to return the favor by writing the best damn profile of Shooting Star ever to hit the page. So how about we get down to brass tacks and blow this thing right out of the water?"

Get down to brass tacks? Do people even understand half the crap that comes spilling out of their mouths? Vanessa may be attempting to be brassy or sassy or trying to win me over with candor or show me how real she is, but whatever it is she's selling, I'm not buying. "Sure," is all I say.

A waiter comes to take our order. Vanessa orders a salad; I order a beer. Vanessa flips through a Moleskine notebook. "I know we're supposed to be talking about *BloodSuckerSunshine* . . ." she begins.

Immediately, I frown. That's *exactly* what we're supposed to be talking about. That's why I'm here. Not to be friends. Not to swap secrets, but because it's part of my job to promote Shooting Star's albums.

Vanessa turns on her siren. "I've been listening to it for weeks, and I'm a fickle, hard-to-please girl." She laughs. In the distance, I hear Aldous clear his throat. I look at him. He's wearing a giant fake smile and giving me a thumbs-up. He looks ludicrous. I turn to Vanessa and force myself to smile back. "But now that your second major-label album is out and your harder sound is, I think we can all agree, established, I'm wanting to write a definitive survey. To chart your evolution from emo-core band to the scions of agita-rock."

Scions of agita-rock? This self-important wankjob deconstructionist crap was something that really threw me in the beginning. As far as I was concerned, I wrote songs: chords and beats and lyrics, verses and bridges and hooks. But then, as we got bigger, people began to dissect the songs, like a frog from biology class until there was nothing left but guts—tiny parts, so much less than the sum.

I roll my eyes slightly, but Vanessa's focused on her notes. "I was listening to some bootlegs of your really early stuff. It's so poppy, almost sweet comparatively. And I've been reading everything ever written about you guys, every blog post, every 'zine article. And almost everyone refers to this so-called Shooting Star "black hole," but no one really ever penetrates it. You have your little indie release; it does well; you were poised for the big leagues, but then this lag. Rumors were that you'd broken up. And then comes *Collateral Damage*. And pow." Vanessa mimes an explosion coming out of her closed fists.

It's a dramatic gesture, but not entirely off base. *Collateral Damage* came out two years ago, and within a month of its release, the single "Animate" had broken onto the national charts and gone viral. We used to joke you couldn't listen to the radio for longer than an hour without hearing it. Then "Bridge" catapulted onto the charts, and soon after the entire album was climbing to the number-one album slot on iTunes, which in turn made every Walmart in the country stock it, and soon it was bumping Lady Gaga off the number-one spot on the *Billboard* charts. For a while it seemed like the album was loaded onto the iPod of every person between the ages of twelve and twenty-four. Within a matter of months, our half-forgotten Oregon band was on the cover of *Time* magazine being touted as "The Millennials' Nirvana."

But none of this is news. It had all been documented, over and over again, ad nauseam, including in *Shuffle*. I'm not sure where Vanessa is going with it.

"You know, everyone seems to attribute the harder sound to the fact that Gus Allen produced *Collateral Damage*."

"Right," I say. "Gus likes to rock."

Vanessa takes a sip of water. I can hear her tongue ring click. "But Gus didn't write those lyrics, which are the foundation for all that oomph. You did. All that raw power and emotion. It's like *Collateral Damage* is the angriest album of the decade."

"And to think, we were going for the happiest."

Vanessa looks up at me, narrows her eyes. "I meant it as a compliment. It was very cathartic for a lot of people, myself included. And that's my point. Everyone knows something went down during your 'black hole.' It's going to come out eventually, so why not control the message? Who does the 'collateral damage' refer to?" she asks, making air quotes. "What happened with you guys? With you?"

Our waiter delivers Vanessa's salad. I order a second beer and don't answer her question. I don't say anything, just keep my eyes cast downward. Because Vanessa's right about one thing. We *do* control the message. In the early days, we got asked this question all the time, but we just kept the answers vague: took a while to find our sound, to write our songs. But now the band's big enough that our publicists issue a list of no-go topics to reporters: Liz and Sarah's relationship, mine and Bryn's, Mike's former drug problems—and the Shooting Star's "black hole." But Vanessa apparently didn't get the memo. I glance over at Aldous for some help, but he's in deep conversation with the bartender. So much for backup.

"The title refers to war," I say. "We've explained that before."

"Right," she says, rolling her eyes. "Because your lyrics are *so* political."

Vanessa stares at me with those big baby blues. This is a reporter's technique: create an awkward silence and wait for your subject to fill it in with babble. It won't work with me, though. I can outstare anyone.

Vanessa's eyes suddenly go cold and hard. She abruptly puts her breezy, flirty personality on the back burner and stares at me with hard ambition. She looks hungry, but it's an improvement because at least she's being herself. "What happened, Adam? I know there's a story there, *the* story of Shooting Star, and I'm going to be the one to tell it. What turned this indie-pop band into a primal rock phenomenon?"

I feel a cold hard fist in my stomach. "Life happened. And it took us a while to write the new stuff—"

"Took *you* a while," Vanessa interrupts. "You wrote both the recent albums."

I just shrug.

"Come on, Adam! *Collateral Damage* is your record. It's a masterpiece. You should be proud of it. And I just know the story behind it, behind your band, is your story, too. A huge shift like this, from collaborative indie quartet to star-driven emotional punk powerhouse—it's all on you. I mean you alone were the one up at the Grammys accepting the award for Best Song. What did that feel like?"

Like shit. "In case you forgot, the whole band won Best New Artist. And that was more than a year ago."

She nods. "Look, I'm not trying to diss anybody or reopen wounds. I'm just trying to understand the shift. In sound. In lyrics. In band dynamics." She gives me a knowing look. "All signs point to you being the catalyst."

"There's no catalyst. We just tinkered with our sound. Happens all the time. Like Dylan going electric. Like Liz Phair going commercial. But people tend to freak out when something diverges from their expectations."

"I just know there's something more to it," Vanessa continues, pushing forward against the table so hard that it shoves into my gut and I have to physically push it back.

"Well, you've obviously got your theory, so don't let the truth get in the way."

Her eyes flash for a quick second and I think I've pissed her off, but then she puts her hands up. Her nails are bitten down. "Actually, you want to know my theory?" she drawls.

Not particularly. "Lay it on me."

"I talked to some people you went to high school with."

I feel my entire body freeze up, soft matter hardening into lead. It takes extreme concentration to lift the glass to my lips and pretend to take a sip.

"I didn't realize that you went to the same high school as Mia Hall," she says lightly. "You know her? The cellist? She's starting to get a lot of buzz in that world. Or whatever the equivalent of buzz is in classical music. Perhaps hum."

The glass shakes in my hand. I have to use my other hand to help lower it to the table to keep from spilling all over myself. *All the people who really know what actually had happened back then aren't talking,* I remind myself. *Rumors, even true ones, are like flames: Stifle the oxygen and they sputter and die.*

"Our high school had a good arts program. It was kind of a breeding ground for musicians," I explain.

"That makes sense," Vanessa says, nodding. "There's a vague rumor that you and Mia were a couple in high school. Which was funny because I'd never read about it anywhere and it certainly seems noteworthy."

An image of Mia flashes before my eyes. Seventeen years old, those dark eyes full of love, intensity, fear, music, sex, magic, grief. Her freezing hands. My own freezing hands, now still grasping the glass of ice water.

"It would be noteworthy if it were true," I say, forcing my voice into an even tone. I take another gulp of water and signal the waiter for another beer. It's my third, the dessert course of my liquid lunch.

"So it's not?" She sounds skeptical.

"Wishful thinking," I reply. "We knew each other casually from school."

"Yeah, I couldn't get anyone who really knew either of you to corroborate it. But then I got a hold of an old yearbook and there's a sweet shot of the two of you. You look pretty coupley. The thing is, there's no name with the photo, just a caption. So unless you know what Mia looks like, you might miss it."

Thank you, Kim Schein: Mia's best friend, yearbook queen, paparazzo. We hadn't wanted that picture used, but Kim had snuck it in by not listing our names with it, just that stupid nickname.

"Groovy and the Geek?" Vanessa asks. "You guys even had a handle."

"You're using high school yearbooks as your source? What next? Wikipedia?"

"You're hardly a reliable source. You said you knew each other 'casually.'"

"Look, the truth is we maybe hooked up for a few weeks, right when those pictures got taken. But, hey, I dated a lot of girls in high school." I give her my best playboy smirk.

"So you haven't seen her since school then?"

"Not since she left for college," I say. That part, at least, is true.

"So how come when I interviewed the rest of your bandmates, they went all no comment when I asked about her?" she asks, eyeing me hard.

Because whatever else has gone wrong with us, we're still loyal. About that. I force myself to speak out loud: "Because there's nothing to tell. I think people like you like the sitcom aspect of, you know, two well-known musicians from the same high school being a couple."

"People like me?" Vanessa asks.

Vultures. Bloodsuckers. Soul-stealers. "Reporters," I say. "You're fond of fairy tales."

"Well, who isn't?" Vanessa says. "Although that woman's life has been anything but a fairy tale. She lost her whole family in a car crash."

Vanessa mock shudders the way you do when you talk about someone's misfortunes that have nothing to do with you, that don't touch you, and never will. I've never hit a woman in my life, but for one minute I want to punch her in the face, give her a taste of the pain she's so casually describing. But I hold it together and she carries on, clueless. "Speaking of fairy tales, are you and Bryn Shraeder having a baby? I keep seeing her in all the tabloids' bump watches."

"No," I reply. "Not that I know of." I'm damn sure Vanessa knows that Bryn is off-limits, but if talking about Bryn's supposed pregnancy will distract her, then I'll do it.

"*Not that you know of*? You're still together, right?"

God, the hunger in her eyes. For all her talk of writing definitive surveys, for all her investigative skills, she's no different from all the other hack journalists and stalker photographers, dying to be the first to deliver a big scoop, either on a birth: *Is It Twins for Adam and Bryn?* Or a death: *Bryn Tells Her Wilde Man: "It's Quits!"* Neither story is true, but some weeks I see both of them on the covers of different gossip rags at the same time.

I think of the house in L.A. that Bryn and I share. Or coinhabit. I can't remember the last time the two of us were there together at the same time for more than a week. She makes two, three films a year, and she just started her own production company. So between shooting and promoting her films and chasing down properties to produce, and me being in the studio and on tour, we seem to be on opposing schedules.

"Yep, Bryn and I are still together," I tell Vanessa. "And she's not pregnant. She's just into those peasant tops these days, so everyone always assumes it's to hide a belly. It's not."

Truth be told, I sometimes wonder if Bryn wears those tops on purpose, to court the bump watch as a way to tempt fate. She *seriously* wants a kid. Even though publicly, Bryn is twenty-four, in reality, she's twenty-eight and she claims her clock is ticking and all that. But I'm twenty-one, and Bryn and I have only been together a year. And I don't care if Bryn says that I have an old soul and have been through a lifetime already. Even if I were forty-one, and Bryn and I had just celebrated twenty years together, I wouldn't want a kid with her.

"Will she be joining you on the tour?"

At the mere mention of the tour, I feel my throat start to close up. The tour is sixty-seven nights long. *Sixty-seven*. I mentally pat for my pill bottle, grow calmer knowing it's there, but am smarter than to sneak one in front of Vanessa.

"Huh?" I ask.

"Is Bryn going to come meet you on the tour at all?"

I imagine Bryn on tour, with her stylists, her Pilates instructors, her latest raw-foods diet. "Maybe."

"How do you like living in Los Angeles?" Vanessa asks. "You don't seem like the SoCal type."

"It's a dry heat," I reply.

"What?"

"Nothing. A joke."

"Oh. Right." Vanessa eyes me skeptically. I no longer read interviews about myself, but when I used to, words like *inscrutable* were often used. And *arrogant*. Is that really how people see me?

Thankfully, our allotted hour is up. She closes her notebook and calls for the check. I catch Aldous's relieved-looking eyes to let him know we're wrapping up.

"It was nice meeting you, Adam," she says.

"Yeah, you too," I lie.

"I gotta say, you're a puzzle." She smiles and her teeth gleam an unnatural white. "But I like puzzles. Like your lyrics, all those grisly images on *Collateral Damage*. And the lyrics on the new record, also very cryptic. You know some critics question whether *Blood-*

SuckerSunshine can match the intensity of *Collateral Damage*. . . ."

I know what's coming. I've heard this before. It's this thing that reporters do. Reference other critics' opinions as a backhanded way to espouse their own. And I know what she's *really* asking, even if she doesn't: *How does it feel that the only worthy thing you ever created came from the worst kind of loss?*

Suddenly, it's all too much. Bryn and the bump watch. Vanessa with my high school yearbook. The idea that nothing's sacred. Everything's fodder. That my life belongs to anyone but me. Sixty-seven nights. *Sixty-seven, sixty-seven.* I push the table hard so that glasses of water and beer go clattering into her lap.

"What the—?"

"This interview's over," I growl.

"I know that. Why are you freaking out on me?"

"Because you're nothing but a vulture! This has fuck all to do with music. It's about picking everything apart."

Vanessa's eyes dance as she fumbles for her recorder. Before she has a chance to turn it back on, I pick it up and slam it against the table, shattering it, and then dump it into a glass of water for good measure. My hand is shaking and my heart is pounding and I feel the beginnings of a panic attack, the kind that makes me sure I'm about to die.

"What did you just do?" Vanessa screams. "I don't have a backup."

"Good."

"How am I supposed to write my article now?"

"You call *that* an article?"

"Yeah. Some of us have to work for a living, you prissy, temperamental ass—"

"Adam!" Aldous is at my side, laying a trio of hundred-dollar bills on the table. "For a new one," he says to Vanessa, before ushering me out of the restaurant and into a taxi. He throws another hundred-dollar bill at the driver after he balks at my lighting up. Aldous reaches into my pocket and grabs my prescription bottle, shakes a tablet into his hand, and says, "Open up," like some bearish mother.

He waits until we're a few blocks from my hotel, until I've sucked down two cigarettes in one continuous inhale and popped another anxiety pill. "What happened back there?"

I tell him. Her questions about the "black hole." Bryn. Mia.

"Don't worry. We can call *Shuffle*. Threaten to pull their exclusive if they don't put a different reporter on the piece. And maybe this gets into the tabloids or Gabber for a few days, but it's not much of a story. It'll blow over."

Aldous is saying all this stuff calmly, like, *hey, it's only rock 'n' roll*, but I can read the worry in his eyes.

"I can't, Aldous."

"Don't worry about it. You don't have to. It's just an article. It'll be handled."

"Not just that. I can't do it. Any of it."

Aldous, who I don't think has slept a full night since he toured with Aerosmith, allows himself to look exhausted for a few seconds. Then he goes back to manager mode. "You've just got pretour burnout. Happens to the best of 'em," he assures me. "Once you get on the road, in front of the crowds, start to feel the love, the adrenaline, the music, you'll be energized. I mean, hell, you'll be fried for sure, but happy-fried. And come November, when this is over, you can go veg out on an island somewhere where nobody knows who you are, where nobody gives a shit about Shooting Star. Or wild Adam Wilde."

November? It's August now. That's three months. And the tour is sixty-seven nights. *Sixty-seven*. I repeat it in my head like a mantra, except it does the opposite of what a mantra's supposed to do. It makes me want to grab fistfuls of my hair and yank.

And how do I tell Aldous, how do I tell any of them, that the music, the adrenaline, *the love*, all the things that mitigate how hard this has become, all of that's gone? All that's left is this vortex. And I'm right on the edge of it.

My entire body is shaking. I'm losing it. A day might be just twenty-four hours but sometimes getting through just one seems as impossible as scaling Everest.

TWO

Needle and thread, flesh and bone
Spit and sinew, heartbreak is home
Your suture lines sparkle like diamonds
Bright stars to light my confinement

"STITCH"
COLLATERAL DAMAGE, TRACK 7

Aldous leaves me in front of my hotel. "Look, man, I think you just need some time to chill. So, listen: I'm gonna clear the schedule for the rest of the day and cancel your meetings tomorrow. Your flight to London's not till seven; you don't have to be at the airport till five." He glances at his phone. "That's more than twenty-four hours to do whatever you want to. I promise you, you'll feel so much better. Just go be free."

Aldous is peering at me with a look of calculated concern. He's my friend, but I'm also his responsibility. "I'm gonna change my flight," he announces. "I'll fly with you tomorrow."

I'm embarrassed by how grateful I am. Flying Upper Class with the band is no great shakes. We all tend to stay plugged into our own luxury pods, but at least when I fly with them, I'm not alone. When I fly alone, who knows who I'll be seated next to? I once had a Japanese businessman who didn't stop talking to me at all during a ten-hour flight. I'd wanted to be moved but hadn't wanted to seem like the kind of rock-star prick who'd ask to be moved, so I'd sat there, nodding my head, not understanding half of what he was saying. But worse yet are the times when I'm truly alone for those long-haul flights.

I know Aldous has lots to do in London. More to the point, missing tomorrow's meeting with the rest of the band and the video director will be one more little earthquake. But whatever. There are too many fault lines to count now. Besides, nobody blames Aldous; they blame me.

So, it's a huge imposition to let Aldous spend an extra day in New York. But I still accept his offer, even as I downplay his generosity by muttering, "Okay."

"Cool. You clear your head. I'll leave you alone, won't even call. Want me to pick you up here or meet you at the airport?" The rest of the band is staying downtown.

We've gotten into the habit of staying in separate hotels since the last tour, and Aldous diplomatically alternates between staying at my hotel and theirs. This time he's with them.

"Airport. I'll meet you in the lounge," I tell him.

"Okay then. I'll order you a car for four. Until then, just chill." He gives me a half handshake, half hug and then he's back inside the cab, zooming off to his next order of business, probably mending the fences that I've thrashed today.

I go around to the service entrance and make my way to my hotel room. I take a shower, ponder going back to sleep. But these days, sleep eludes me even with a medicine cabinet full of psychopharmacological assistance. From the eighteenth-story windows, I can see the afternoon sun bathing the city in a warm glow, making New York feel cozy somehow, but making the suite feel claustrophobic and hot. I throw on a clean pair of jeans and my lucky black T-shirt. I wanted to reserve this shirt for tomorrow when I leave for the tour, but I feel like I need some luck right now, so it's gonna have to pull double duty.

I turn on my iPhone. There are fifty-nine new email messages and seventeen new voice mails, including several from the label's now-certainly irate publicist and a bunch from Bryn, asking how it went in the studio and with the interview. I could call her, but what's the point? If I tell her about Vanessa LeGrande, she'll get all upset with me for losing my "public face" in front of a reporter. She's trying to train me out of that bad habit. She says every time I lose it in front of the press, I only whet their appetites for more. "Give them a dull public face, Adam, and they'll stop writing so much about you," she constantly advises me. The thing is, I have a feeling if I told Bryn which question set me off, she'd probably lose her public face, too.

I think about what Aldous said about getting away from it all, and I turn off the phone and toss it on the nightstand. Then I grab my hat, shades, my pills, and wallet and am out the door. I turn up Columbus, making my way toward Central Park. A fire truck barrels by, its sirens whining. *Scratch your head or you'll be dead.* I don't even remember where I learned that childhood rhyme or the dictum that demanded you scratch your head every time you heard a siren, lest the next siren be for you. But I do know when I started doing it, and now it's become second nature. Still, in a place like Manhattan, where the sirens are always blaring, it can become exhausting to keep up.

It's early evening now and the aggressive heat has mellowed, and it's like everyone senses that it's safe to go out because they're mobbing the place: spreading out picnics on the lawn, pushing jogging strollers up the paths, floating in canoes along the lily-padded lake.

Much as I like seeing all the people doing their thing, it all makes me feel exposed. I don't get how other people in the public eye do it. Sometimes I see pictures of Brad Pitt with his gaggle of kids in Central Park, just playing on swings, and clearly he was followed by paparazzi but he still looks like he's having a normal day with his family. Or maybe not. Pictures can be pretty deceptive.

Thinking about all this and passing happy people enjoying a summer evening, I start to feel like a moving target, even though I have my cap pulled low and my shades are on and I'm without Bryn. When Bryn and I are together, it's almost impossible to fly under the radar. I'm seized with this paranoia, not even so much that I'll get photographed or hounded by a mob of autograph seekers—though I really don't want to deal with that right now—but that I'll be mocked as the only person in the entire park who's alone, even though this obviously isn't the case. But still, I feel like any second people will start pointing, making fun of me.

So, this is how it's become? This is what *I've* become? A walking contradiction? I'm surrounded by people and feel alone. I claim to crave a bit of normalcy but now that I have some, it's like I don't know what to do with it, don't know how to be a normal person anymore.

I wander toward the Ramble, where the only people I'm likely to bump into are the kind who don't want to be found. I buy a couple of hot dogs and down them in a few bites, and it's only then that I realize I haven't eaten all day, which makes me think about lunch—and the Vanessa LeGrande debacle.

What happened back there? I mean, you've been known to get testy with reporters, but that was just an amateur-hour move, I tell myself.

I'm just tired, I justify. *Overtaxed.* I think of the tour and it's like the mossy ground next to me opens up and starts whirring.

Sixty-seven nights. I try to rationalize it. *Sixty-seven nights is nothing.* I try to divide up the number, to fractionalize it, to do something to make it smaller, but nothing divides evenly into sixty-seven. So I break it up. Fourteen countries, thirty-nine cities, a few hundred hours on a tour bus. But the math just makes the whirring go faster and I start to feel dizzy. I grab hold of the tree trunk and run my hand against the bark, which reminds me of Oregon and makes the earth at least close up for the time being.

I can't help but think about how, when I was younger, I'd read about the legions of artists who imploded—

Morrison, Joplin, Cobain, Hendrix. They disgusted me. *They got what they wanted and then what did they do? Drugged themselves to oblivion. Or shot their heads off. What a bunch of assholes.*

Well, take a look at yourself now. You're no junkie but you're not much better.

I would change if I could, but so far, ordering myself to shut up and enjoy the ride hasn't had much of an impact. If the people around me knew how I feel, they'd laugh at me. No, that's not true. Bryn wouldn't laugh. She'd be baffled by my inability to bask in what I've worked so hard to accomplish.

But have I worked so hard? There's this assumption among my family, Bryn, the rest of the band—well, at least there used to be among those guys—that I somehow deserve all this, that the acclaim and wealth is payback. I've never really bought that. Karma's not like a bank. Make a deposit, take a withdrawal. But more and more, I *am* starting to suspect that all this *is* payback for something—only not the good kind.

I reach for a cigarette, but my pack's empty. I stand up and dust off my jeans and make my way out of the park. The sun is starting to dip to the west, a bright blaring ball tilting toward the Hudson and leaving a collage of peach and purple streaks across the sky. It really is pretty and for a second I force myself to admire it.

I turn south on Seventh, stop at a deli, grab some smokes, and then head downtown. I'll go back to the hotel, get some room service, maybe fall asleep early for once. Outside Carnegie Hall, taxis are pulling up, dropping off people for tonight's performances. An old woman in pearls and heels teeters out of a taxi, her stooped-over companion in a tux holding onto her elbow. Watching them stumble off together, I feel something in my chest lurch. *Look at the sunset*, I tell myself. *Look at something with beauty.* But when I look back up at the sky, the streaks have darkened to the color of a bruise.

Prissy, temperamental asshole. That's what the reporter was calling me. She was a piece of work, but on that particular point, she was speaking the truth.

My gaze returns to earth and when it does, it's *her* eyes I see. Not the way I used to see them—around every corner, behind my own closed lids at the start of each day. Not in the way I used to imagine them in the eyes of every other girl I laid on top of. No, this time it really is her eyes. A photo of her, dressed in black, a cello leaning against one shoulder like a tired child. Her hair is up in one of those buns that seem to be a requisite for classical musicians. She used to wear it up like that for recitals and chamber music concerts, but with little pieces hanging down, to soften the severity of the look. There are no tendrils in this photo. I peer closer at the sign. YOUNG CONCERT SERIES PRESENTS MIA HALL.

A few months ago, Liz broke the unspoken embargo on all things Mia and mailed me a clip from the magazine *All About Us*. *I thought you should see this,* was scrawled on a sticky note. It was an article titled "Twenty Under 20," featuring upcoming "wunderkinds." There was a page on Mia, including a picture I could barely bring myself to glance at, and an article about her, that after a few rounds of deep breathing, I only managed to skim. The piece called her the "heir apparent to Yo-Yo Ma." In spite of myself, I'd smiled at that. Mia used to say that people who had no idea about the cello always described cellists as the next Yo-Yo Ma because he was their single point of reference. "What about Jacqueline Du Pré?" she'd always asked, referring to her own idol, a talented and tempestuous cellist who'd been stricken with multiple sclerosis at the age of twenty-eight and died about fifteen years later.

The *All About Us* article called Mia's playing "otherworldly" and then very graphically described the car accident that had killed her parents and little brother more than three years ago. That had surprised me. Mia hadn't been one to talk about that, to fish for sympathy points. But when I'd managed to make myself skim the piece again, I'd realized that it was a write-around, quotes taken from old newspaper accounts, but nothing directly from Mia herself.

I'd held onto the clipping for a few days, occasionally taking it out to glance over it. Having the thing in my wallet felt a little bit like carrying around a vial of plutonium. And for sure if Bryn caught me with an article about Mia there'd be explosions of the nuclear variety. So after a few more days, I threw it away and forced myself to forget it.

Now, I try to summon the details, to recall if it said anything about Mia leaving Juilliard or playing recitals at Carnegie Hall.

I look up again. Her eyes are still there, still staring at me. And I just know with as much certainty as I know anything in this world that she's playing tonight. I know even before I consult the date on the poster and see that the performance is for August thirteenth.

And before I know what I'm doing, before I can argue myself out of it, rationalize what a *terrible* idea this is, I'm walking toward the box office. *I don't want to see her*, I tell myself. *I won't see her. I only want to hear her.* The box office sign says that tonight is sold out. I could announce who I am or put in a call to my hotel's concierge or Aldous and probably get a ticket, but instead I leave it to fate. I present myself as an anonymous, if underdressed, young man and ask if there are any seats left.

"In fact, we're just releasing the rush tickets. I have a rear mezzanine, side. It's not the ideal view, but it's all that's left," the girl behind the glass window tells me.

"I'm not here for the view," I reply.

"I always think that, too," the girl says, laughing. "But people get particular about these kinds of things. That'll be twenty-five dollars."

I throw down my credit card and enter the cool, dim theater. I slide into my seat and close my eyes, remembering the last time I went to a cello concert somewhere this fancy. Five years ago, on our first date. Just as I did that night, I feel this mad rush of anticipation, even though I know that unlike that night, tonight I won't kiss her. Or touch her. Or even see her up close.

Tonight, I'll listen. And that'll be enough.

THREE

Mia woke up after four days, but we didn't tell her until the sixth day. It didn't matter because she seemed to already know. We sat around her hospital bed in the ICU, her taciturn grandfather having drawn the short straw, I guess, because he was the one chosen to break the news that her parents, Kat and Denny, had been killed instantly in the car crash that had landed her here. And that her little brother, Teddy, had died in the emergency room of the local hospital where he and Mia had been brought to before Mia was evacuated to Portland.

Nobody knew the cause of the crash. Did Mia have any memory of it?

Mia just lay there, blinking her eyes and holding onto my hand, digging her nails in so tightly it seemed like she'd never let me go. She shook her head and quietly said "no, no, no," over and over again, but without tears, and I wasn't sure if she was answering her grandfather's question or just negating the whole situation. *No!*

But then the social worker stepped in, taking over in her no-nonsense way. She told Mia about the operations she'd undergone so far, "triage, really, just to get you stable, and you're doing remarkably well," and then talked about the surgeries that she'd likely be facing in the coming months: First a surgery to reset the bone in her left leg with metal rods. Then another surgery a week or so after that, to harvest skin from the thigh of her uninjured leg. Then another to graft that skin onto the messed-up leg. Those two procedures, unfortunately, would leave some "nasty scars." But the injuries on her face, at least, could vanish completely with cosmetic surgery after a year. "Once you're through your nonelective surgeries, provided there aren't any complications—no infections from the splenectomy, no pneumonia, no problems with your lungs—we'll get you out of the hospital and into rehab," the social worker said. "Physical and occupational, speech and whatever else you need. We'll assess where you are in a few days." I was dizzy from this litany, but Mia seemed to hang on her every word, to pay more attention to the details of her surgeries than to the news of her family.

Later that afternoon, the social worker took the rest of us aside. We—Mia's grandparents and me—had been worried about Mia's reaction, or her lack of one. We'd expected screaming, hair pulling, something explosive, to match the horror of the news, to match our *own* grief. Her eerie quiet had all of us thinking the same thing: brain damage.

"No, that's not it," the social worker quickly reassured. "The brain is a fragile instrument and we may not know for a few weeks what specific regions have been affected, but young people are so very resilient and right now her neurologists are quite optimistic. Her motor control is generally good. Her language faculties don't seem too affected. She has weakness in her right side and her balance is off. If that's the extent of her brain injury, then she is fortunate."

We all cringed at that word. *Fortunate.* But the social worker looked at our faces. "*Very* fortunate because all of that is reversible. As for that reaction back there," she said, gesturing toward the ICU, "that is a typical response to such extreme psychological trauma. The brain can only handle so much, so it filters in a bit at a time, digests slowly. She'll take it all in, but she'll need help." Then she'd told us about the stages of grief, loaded us up with pamphlets on post-traumatic stress disorder, and recommended a grief counselor at the hospital for Mia to see. "It might not be a bad idea for the rest of you, too," she'd said.

We'd ignored her. Mia's grandparents weren't the therapy types. And as for me, I had Mia's rehabilitation to worry about, not my own.

The next round of surgeries started almost immediately, which I found cruel. Mia had just come back from the brink of it, only to be told her family was dead, and now she had to go under the knife again. Couldn't they cut the girl a break? But the social worker had explained that the sooner Mia's leg was fixed, the sooner Mia would be mobile, and the sooner she could really start to heal. So her femur was set with pins; skin grafts were taken. And with speed that made me breathless, she was discharged from the hospital and dispatched to a rehab center, which looked like a condo complex, with flat paths crisscrossing the grounds, which were just beginning to bloom with spring flowers when Mia arrived.

She'd been there less than a week, a determined, teeth-gritted terrifying week, when the envelope came.

Juilliard. It had been so many things to me before. A foregone conclusion. A point of pride. A rival. And then I'd just forgotten about it. I think we all had. But life was churning outside Mia's rehab center, and somewhere out there in the world, that other Mia—the one who had two parents, a brother, and a fully working body—still continued to exist. And in that other world, some judges had listened to Mia play a few months earlier and had gone on processing her application, and it had gone through the various motions until a final judgment was made, and that final judgment was before us now. Mia's grandmother had been too nervous to open the envelope, so she waited for me and Mia's grandfather before she sliced into it with a mother-of-pearl letter opener.

Mia got in. Had there ever been any question?

We all thought the acceptance would be good for her, a bright spot on an otherwise bleak horizon.

"And I've already spoken to the dean of admissions and explained your situation, and they've said you can put off starting for a year, two if you need," Mia's grandmother had said as she'd presented Mia with the news and the generous scholarship that had accompanied the acceptance. Juilliard had actually suggested the deferral, wanting to make sure that Mia was able to play up to the school's rigorous standards, if she chose to attend.

"No," Mia had said from the center's depressing common room in that dead-flat voice she had spoken in since the accident. None of us was quite sure whether this was from emotional trauma or if this was Mia's affect now, her newly rearranged brain's way of speaking. In spite of the social worker's continued reassurances, in spite of her therapists' evaluations that she was making solid progress, we still worried. We discussed these things in hushed tones after we left her alone on the nights that I couldn't con myself into staying over.

"Well, don't be hasty," her grandmother had replied. "The world might look different in a year or two. You might still want to go."

Mia's grandmother had thought Mia was refusing Juilliard. But I knew better. I knew *Mia* better. It was the deferral she was refusing.

Her grandmother argued with Mia. September was five months away. Too soon. And she had a point. Mia's leg was still in one of those boot casts, and she was just starting to walk again. She couldn't open a jar because her right hand was so weak, and she would often blank on the names of simple things, like scissors. All of which the therapists said was to be expected and would likely pass—in good time. But five months? That wasn't long.

Mia asked for her cello that afternoon. Her grandmother had frowned, worried that this foolishness would waylay Mia's recovery. But I jumped out of my chair and ran to my car and was back with the cello by the time the sun set.

After that, the cello became her therapy: physical, emotional, mental. The doctors were amazed at Mia's upper-body strength—what her old music teacher Professor Christie had called her "cello body," broad shoulders, muscular arms—and how her playing brought that strength back, which made the weakness in her right arm go away and strengthened her injured leg. It helped with the dizziness. Mia closed her eyes as she played, and she claimed that this, along with grounding her two feet on the floor, helped her balance. Through playing, Mia revealed the lapses she tried to hide in everyday conversation. If she wanted a Coke but couldn't remember the word for it, she'd cover up and just ask for orange juice. But with cello, she would be honest about the fact that she remembered a Bach suite she'd been working on a few months ago but not a simple étude she'd learned as a child; although once Professor Christie, who came down once a week to work with her, showed it to her, she'd pick it right up. This gave the speech therapists and neurologists clues as to the hopscotch way her brain had been impacted, and they tailored their therapies accordingly.

But mostly, the cello improved her mood. It gave her

something to do every day. She stopped speaking in the monotone and started to talk like Mia again, at least when she was talking about music. Her therapists altered her rehabilitation plan, allowing her to spend more time practicing. "We don't really get how music heals the brain," one of her neurologists told me one afternoon as he listened to her play to a group of patients in the common room, "but we know that it does. Just look at Mia."

She left the rehab center after four weeks, two weeks ahead of schedule. She could walk with a cane, open a jar of peanut butter, and play the hell out of Beethoven.

⌐⌐

That article, the "Twenty Under 20" thing from *All About Us* that Liz showed me, I do remember one thing about it. I remember the not-just-implied but overtly stated connection between Mia's "tragedy" and her "otherworldly" playing. And I remember how that pissed me off. Because there was something insulting in that. As if the only way to explain her talent was to credit some supernatural force. Like what'd they think, that her dead family was inhabiting her body and playing a celestial choir through her fingers?

But the thing was, there *was* something otherworldly that happened. And I know because I was there. I witnessed it: I saw how Mia went from being a very talented player to something altogether different. In the space of five months, something magical and grotesque transformed her. So, yes, it was all related to her "tragedy," but Mia was the one doing the heavy lifting. She always had been.

∽

She left for Juilliard the day after Labor Day. I drove her to the airport. She kissed me good-bye. She told me that she loved me more than life itself. Then she stepped through security.

She never came back.

FOUR

The bow is so old, its horsehair is glue
Sent to the factory, just like me and like you
So how come they stayed your execution?
The audience roars its standing ovation

"DUST"
COLLATERAL DAMAGE, TRACK 9

When the lights come up after the concert, I feel drained, lugubrious, as though my blood has been secreted out of me and replaced with tar. After the applause dies down, the people around me stand up, they talk about the concert, about the beauty of the Bach, the mournfulness of the Elgar, the risk—that paid off—of throwing in the contemporary John Cage piece. But it's the Dvořák that's eating up all the oxygen in the room, and I can understand why.

When Mia used to play her cello, her concentration was always written all over her body: a crease folded across her forehead. Her lips, pursed so tightly they sometimes lost all their color, as if all her blood was requisitioned to her hands.

There was a little bit of that happening with the earlier pieces tonight. But when she got to the Dvořák, the final piece of her recital, something came over her. I don't know if she hit her groove or if this was her signature piece, but instead of hunching over her cello, her body seemed to expand, to bloom, and the music filled the open spaces around it like a flowering vine. Her strokes were broad and happy and bold, and the sound that filled the auditorium seemed to channel this pure emotion, like the very intention of the composer was spiraling through the room. And the look on her face, with her eyes upward, a small smile playing on her lips, I don't know how to describe it without sounding like one of these clichéd magazine articles, but she seemed so at one with the music. Or maybe just happy. I guess I always knew she was capable of this level of artistry, but witnessing it fucking blew me away. Me and everyone else in that auditorium, judging by the thunderous applause she got.

The houselights are up now, bright and bouncing off the blond wood chairs and the geometric wall panels, making the floor start to swim. I sink back down into the nearest chair and try not to think about the Dvořák—or the other things: the way she wiped her hand on her skirt in between pieces, the way she cocked her head in time to some invisible orchestra, all gestures that are way too familiar to me.

Grasping onto the chair in front of me for balance, I stand up again. I make sure my legs are working and the ground isn't spinning and then will one leg to follow the other toward the exit. I am shattered, exhausted. All I want to do now is go back to my hotel to down a couple of Ambien or Lunesta or Xanax or whatever's in my medicine cabinet—and end this day. I want to go to sleep and wake up and have this all be over.

"Excuse me, Mr. Wilde."

I normally have a thing about enclosed spaces, but if there is one place in the city where I'd expect the safety of anonymity, it's Carnegie Hall for a classical concert. All through the concert and intermission, no one gave me a second glance, except a pair of old biddies who I think were mostly just dismayed by my jeans. But this guy is about my age; he's an usher, the only person within fifty feet under the age of thirty-five, the only person around here likely to own a Shooting Star album.

I'm reaching into my pocket for a pen that I don't

have. The usher looks embarrassed, shaking his head and his hands simultaneously. "No, no, Mr. Wilde. I'm not asking for an autograph." He lowers his voice. "It's actually against the rules, could get me fired."

"Oh," I say, chastened, confused. For a second I wonder if I'm about to get dressed-down for dressing down.

The usher says: "Ms. Hall would like you to come backstage."

It's noisy with the after-show hubbub, so for a second I assume I've misheard him. I think he says that *she* wants me backstage. But that can't be right. He must be talking about *the* hall, not *Mia* Hall.

But before I can get him to clarify, he's leading me by the elbow back toward the staircase and down to the main lobby and through a small door beside the stage and through a maze of corridors, the walls lined with framed sheet music. And I'm allowing myself to be led; it's like the time when I was ten years old and was sent to the principal's office for throwing a water balloon in class, and all I could do was follow Mrs. Linden down the hallways and wonder what awaited me behind the main office doors. I have that same feeling. That I'm in trouble for something, that Aldous didn't really give me the evening off and I'm about to be reamed out for missing a photo shoot or pissing off a reporter or being the antisocial lone wolf in danger of breaking up the band.

And so I don't really process it, don't let myself hear it or believe it or think about it until the usher leads me to a small room and opens the door and closes it, and suddenly she's there. Really there. A flesh-and-blood person, not a specter.

My first impulse is not to grab her or kiss her or yell at her. I simply want to touch her cheek, still flushed from the night's performance. I want to cut through the space that separates us, measured in feet—not miles, not continents, not years—and to take a callused finger to her face. I want to touch her to make sure it's really her, not one of those dreams I had so often after she left when I'd see her as clear as day, be ready to kiss her or take her to me only to wake up with Mia just beyond reach.

But I can't touch her. This is a privilege that's been revoked. Against my will, but still. Speaking of will, I have to mentally hold my arm in place, to keep the trembling from turning it into a jackhammer.

The floor is spinning, the vortex is calling, and I'm itching for one of my pills, but there's no reaching for one now. I take some calming breaths to preempt a panic attack. I work my jaw in a vain attempt to get my mouth to say some words. I feel like I'm alone on a stage, no band, no equipment, no memory of any of our songs, being watched by a million people. I feel like an hour has gone by as I stand here in front of Mia Hall, speechless as a newborn.

The first time we ever met in high school, I spoke first. I asked Mia what cello piece she'd just played. A simple question that started everything.

This time, it's Mia who asks the question: "Is it really you?" And her voice, it's exactly the same. I don't know why I'd expect it to be different except that everything's different now.

Her voice jolts me back to reality. Back to the reality of the past three years. There are so many things that demand to be said. *Where did you go? Do you ever think about me? You've ruined me. Are you okay?* But of course, I can't say any of that.

I start to feel my heart pound and a ringing in my ears, and I'm about to lose it. But strangely, just when the panic starts to peak, some survival instinct kicks in, the one that allows me to step onto a stage in front of thousands of strangers. A calm steals over me as I retreat from myself, pushing me into the background and letting that other person take over. "In the flesh," I respond in kind. Like it's the most normal thing in the world for me to be at her concert and for her to have beckoned me into her sanctum. "Good concert," I add because it seems like the thing to say. It also happens to be true.

"Thank you," she says. Then she cringes. "I just, I can't believe you're *here*."

I think of the three-year restraining order she basically took out on me, which I violated tonight. *But you called me down*, I want to say. "Yeah. I guess they'll let any old riffraff in Carnegie Hall," I joke. In my nervousness, though, the quip comes out surly.

She smooths her hands on the fabric of her skirt. She's already changed out of her formal black gown into a long, flowy skirt and a sleeveless shirt. She shakes her head, tilts her face toward mine, all conspiratorial. "Not really. No punks allowed. Didn't you see the warning on the marquee? I'm surprised you didn't get arrested just for setting foot in the lobby."

I know she's trying to return my bad joke with one of her own and part of me is thankful for that, and thankful to see a glimmer of her old sense of humor. But another part, the churlish part, wants to remind her of all of the chamber music concerts, string quartets, and recitals I once sat through. Because of her. With her. "How'd you know I was here?" I ask.

"Are you kidding? Adam Wilde in Zankel Hall. At the intermission, the entire backstage crew was buzzing about it. Apparently, a lot of Shooting Star fans work at Carnegie Hall."

"I thought I was being incognito," I say. To her feet. The only way to survive this conversation is to have it with Mia's sandals. Her toenails are painted pale pink.

"You? Impossible," she replies. "So, how are you?"

How am I? Are you for real? I force my eyes upward and look at Mia for the first time. She's still beautiful. Not in an obvious Vanessa LeGrande or Bryn Shraeder kind of way. In a quiet way that's always been devastating to me. Her hair, long and dark, is down now, swimming damply against her bare shoulders, which are still milky white and covered with the constellation of freckles that I used to kiss. The scar on her left shoulder, the one that used to be an angry red welt, is silvery pink now. Almost like the latest rage in tattoo accessories. Almost pretty.

Mia's eyes reach out to meet mine, and for a second I fear that my facade will fall apart. I look away.

"Oh, you know? Good. Busy," I answer.

"Right. Of course. Busy. Are you on tour?"

"Yep. Off to London tomorrow."

"Oh. I'm off to Japan tomorrow."

Opposite directions, I think and am surprised when Mia actually says it out loud. "Opposite directions." The words just hang out there, ominous. Suddenly, I feel the vortex begin to churn again. It's going to swallow us both if I don't get away. "Well, I should probably go." I hear the calm person impersonating Adam Wilde say from what sounds like several feet away.

I think I see something darken her expression, but I can't really tell because every part of my body is undulating, and I swear I might just come inside-out right here. But as I'm losing it, that other Adam is still functioning. He's reaching out his hand toward Mia even though the thought of me giving Mia Hall a business handshake is maybe one of the saddest things I've ever imagined.

Mia looks down at my outstretched hand, opens her mouth to say something, and then just sighs. Her face hardens into a mask as she reaches out her own hand to take mine.

The tremor in my hand has become so normal, so nonstop, that it's generally imperceptible to me. But as soon as my fingers close around Mia's, the thing I notice is that it stops and suddenly it goes quiet, like when the squall of feedback is suddenly cut when someone switches off an amp. And I could linger here forever.

Except this is a handshake, nothing more. And in a few seconds my hand is at my side and it's like I've transferred a little of my crazy to Mia because it looks like her own hand is trembling. But I can't be sure because I'm drifting away on a fast current.

And the next thing I know, I hear the door to her dressing room click behind me, leaving me out here on the rapids and Mia back there on the shore.

FIVE

I know it's really cheesy—crass even—to compare my being dumped to the accident that killed Mia's family, but I can't help it. Because for me, at any rate, the aftermath felt exactly the same. For the first few weeks, I'd wake up in a fog of disbelief. *That didn't really happen, did it? Oh, fuck, it did.* Then I'd be doubled over. Fist to the gut. It took a few weeks for it all to sink in. But unlike with the accident—when I had to be there, be present, help, be the person to lean on—after she left, I was all alone. There was nobody to step up to the plate for. So

I just let everything fall away and then everything just stopped.

I moved home, back to my parents' place. Just grabbed a pile of stuff from my room at the House of Rock and left. Left everything. School. The band. My life. A sudden and wordless departure. I balled up in my boy bed. I was worried that everyone would bang down the door and force me to explain myself. But that's the thing with death. The whisper of its descent travels fast and wide, and people must've known I'd become a corpse because nobody even came to view the body. Well, except relentless Liz, who stopped by once a week to drop off a CD mix of whatever new music she was loving, which she cheerfully stacked on top of the untouched CD she'd left the week before.

My parents seemed baffled by my return. But then, bafflement was pretty typical where I was concerned. My dad had been a logger, and then when that industry went belly-up he'd gotten a job on the line at an electronics plant. My mom worked for the university catering department. They were one another's second marriages, their first marital forays both disastrous and childless and never discussed; I only found out about them from an aunt and uncle when I was ten. They had me when they were older, and I'd apparently come as a surprise. And my mom liked to say that everything that I'd done—from my mere existence to becoming a musician, to falling in love with a girl like Mia, to going to college, to having the band become so popular, to dropping out of college, to dropping out of the band—was a surprise, too. They accepted my return home with no questions. Mom brought me little trays of food and coffee to my room, like I was a prisoner.

For three months, I lay in my childhood bed, wishing myself as comatose as Mia had been. That had to be easier than this. My sense of shame finally roused me. I was nineteen years old, a college dropout, living in my parents' house, unemployed, a layabout, a cliché. My parents had been cool about the whole thing, but the reek of my pathetic was starting to make me sick. Finally, right after the New Year, I asked my father if there were any jobs at the plant.

"You sure this is what you want?" he'd asked me. It wasn't what I wanted. But I couldn't have what I wanted. I'd just shrugged. I'd heard him and my mom arguing about it, her trying to get him to talk me out of it. "Don't you want more than that for him?" I heard her shout-whisper from downstairs. "Don't you want him back in school at the very least?"

"It's not about what I want," he'd answered.

So he asked around human resources, got me an interview, and a week later, I began work in the data-entry department. From six thirty in the morning to three thirty in the afternoon, I would sit in a windowless room, plugging in numbers that had no meaning to me.

On my first day of work, my mother got up early to make me a huge breakfast I couldn't eat and a pot of coffee that wasn't nearly strong enough. She stood over me in her ratty pink bathrobe, a worried expression on her face. When I got up to leave, she shook her head at me.

"What?" I asked.

"You working at the plant," she said, staring at me solemnly. "*This* doesn't surprise me. *This* is what I would've expected from a son of mine." I couldn't tell if the bitterness in her voice was meant for her or me.

The job sucked, but whatever. It was brainless. I came home and slept all afternoon and then woke up and read and dozed from ten o'clock at night until five in the morning, when it was time to get up for work. The schedule was out of sync with the living world, which was fine by me

A few weeks earlier, around Christmas, I'd still held a candle of hope. Christmas was when Mia had initially planned to come home. The ticket she'd bought for New York was a round-trip, and the return date was

December nineteenth. Though I knew it was foolish, I somehow thought she'd come see me, she'd offer some explanation—or, better yet, a massive apology. Or we'd find that this had all been some huge and horrible misunderstanding. She'd been emailing me daily but they hadn't gotten through, and she'd show up at my door, livid about my not having returned her emails, the way she used to get pissed off at me for silly things, like how nice I was, or was not, to her friends.

But December came and went, a monotony of gray, of muted Christmas carols coming from downstairs. I stayed in bed.

It wasn't until February that I got a visitor home from a back East college.

"Adam, Adam, you have a guest," my mom said, gently rapping at my door. It was around dinnertime and I was sacked out, the middle of the night to me. In my haze, I thought it was Mia. I bolted upright but saw from my mother's pained expression that she knew she was delivering disappointing news. "It's Kim!" she said with forced joviality.

Kim? I hadn't heard from Mia's best friend since August, not since she'd taken off for school in Boston. And all at once, it hit me that her silence was as much a betrayal as Mia's. Kim and I had never been buddies when Mia and I were together. At least not before the accident. But after, we'd been soldered somehow. I hadn't realized that Mia and Kim were a package deal, one with the other. Lose one, lose the other. But then, how else would it be?

But now, here was Kim. Had Mia sent her as some sort of an emissary? Kim was smiling awkwardly, hugging herself against the damp night. "Hey," she said. "You're hard to find."

"I'm where I've always been," I said, kicking off the covers. Kim, seeing my boxers, turned away until I'd pulled on a pair of jeans. I reached for a pack of cigarettes. I'd started smoking a few weeks before. Everyone at the plant seemed to. It was the only reason to take a break. Kim's eyes widened in surprise, like I'd just pulled out a Glock. I put the cigarettes back down without lighting up.

"I thought you'd be at the House of Rock, so I went there. I saw Liz and Sarah. They fed me dinner. It was nice to see them." She stopped and appraised my room. The rumpled, sour blankets, the closed shades. "Did I wake you?"

"I'm on a weird schedule."

"Yeah. Your mom told me. *Data entry?*" She didn't bother to try to mask her surprise.

I was in no mood for small talk or condescension. "So, what's up, Kim?"

She shrugged. "Nothing. I'm in town for break. We all went to Jersey to see my grandparents for Hanukkah, so this is the first time I've been back and I wanted to stop and say hi."

Kim looked nervous. But she also looked concerned. It was an expression I recognized well. The one that said *I* was the patient now. In the distant night I heard a siren. Reflexively, I scratched my head.

"Do you still see her?" I asked.

"What?" Kim's voice chirped in surprise.

I stared at her. And slowly repeated the question. "Do you still see Mia?"

"Y—Yes," Kim stumbled. "I mean, not a lot. We're both busy with school, and New York and Boston are four hours apart. But yes. Of course."

Of course. It was the certainty that did it. That made something murderous rise up in me. I was glad there was nothing heavy within reaching distance.

"Does she know you're here?"

"No. I came as your friend."

"As *my* friend?"

Kim blanched from the sarcasm in my voice, but that girl was always tougher than she seemed. She didn't back down or leave. *"Yes,"* she whispered.

"Tell me, then, *friend*. Did Mia, *your* friend, your BFF, did she tell you why she dumped me? Without a word? Did she happen to mention that to you at all? Or didn't I come up?"

"Adam, please . . ." Kim's voice was an entreaty.

"No, please, Kim. Please, because I haven't got a clue."

Kim took a deep breath and then straightened her posture. I could practically see the resolve stiffening up her spine, vertebra by vertebra, the lines of loyalty being drawn. "I didn't come here to talk about Mia. I came here to see you, and I don't think I should discuss Mia with you or vice versa."

She'd adopted the tone of a social worker, an impartial third party, and I wanted to smack her for it. For all of it. Instead, I just exploded. "Then what the fuck are you doing here? What good are you then? Who are you to me? Without her, who are you? You're nothing! A nobody!"

Kim stumbled back, but when she looked up, instead of looking angry, she looked at me full of tenderness. It made me want to throttle her even more. "Adam—" she began.

"Get the hell out of here," I growled. "I don't want to see you again!"

The thing with Kim was, you didn't have to tell her twice. She left without another word.

That night, instead of sleeping, instead of reading, I paced my room for four hours. As I walked back and forth, pushing permanent indentations into the tread of my parents' cheap shag carpeting, I felt something febrile growing inside of me. It felt alive and inevitable, the way a puke with a nasty hangover sometimes is. I felt it itching its way through my body, begging for release, until it finally came tearing out of me with such force that first I punched my wall, and then, when that didn't hurt enough, my window. The shards of glass sliced into my knuckles with a satisfying ache followed by the cold blast of a February night. The shock seemed to wake something slumbering deep within me.

Because that was the night I picked up my guitar for the first time in a year.

And that was the night I started writing songs again.

Within two weeks, I'd written more than ten new songs. Within a month, Shooting Star was back together and playing them. Within two months, we'd signed with a major label. Within four months, we were recording *Collateral Damage*, comprised of fifteen of the songs I'd written from the chasm of my childhood bedroom. Within a year, *Collateral Damage* was on the

Billboard charts and Shooting Star was on the cover of national magazines.

It's occurred to me since that I owe Kim either an apology or a thank-you. Maybe both. But by the time I came to this realization, it seemed like things were too far gone to do anything about it. And, the truth is, I still don't know what I'd say to her.

SIX

I'll be your mess, you be mine
That was the deal that we had signed
I bought a hazmat suit to clean up your waste
Gas masks, gloves, to keep us safe
But now I'm alone in an empty room
Staring down immaculate doom

"MESSY"

<u>**COLLATERAL DAMAGE, TRACK 2**</u>

When I get onto the street, my hands are quaking and my insides feel like they're staging a coup. I reach for my pills, but the bottle is empty. *Fuck!* Aldous must've fed me the last one in the cab. Do I have more at the hotel? I've got to get some before tomorrow's flight. I grab for my phone and remember that I left it back at the hotel in some boneheaded attempt to disconnect.

People are swarming around and their gazes are lingering a little too long on me. I can't deal with being recognized right now. I can't deal with anything. I don't want this. I don't want *any* of this.

I just want out. Out of my existence. I find myself wishing that a lot lately. Not be dead. Or kill myself. Or any of that kind of stupid shit. It's more that I can't help thinking that if I'd never been born in the first place, I wouldn't be facing those sixty-seven nights, I wouldn't be right here, right now, having just endured that conversation with her. *It's your own fault for coming tonight*, I tell myself. *You should've left well enough alone.*

I light a cigarette and hope that will steady me enough to walk back to the hotel where I'll call Aldous and get everything straightened out and maybe even sleep a few hours and get this disastrous day behind me once and for all.

"You should quit."

Her voice jars me. But it also somehow calms me. I look up. There's Mia, face flushed, but also, oddly, smiling. She's breathing hard, like she's been running. Maybe she gets chased by fans, too. I imagine that old couple in the tux and pearls tottering after her.

I don't even have time to feel embarrassed because *Mia is here again*, standing in front of me like when we still shared the same space and time and bumping into each other, though always a happy coincidence, was nothing unusual, not the slightest bit extraordinary. For a second I think of that line in *Casablanca* when Bogart says: Of all the gin joints in the world, she has to walk into mine. But then I remind myself that I walked into *her* gin joint.

Mia covers the final few feet between us slowly, like I'm a cagey cat that needs to be brought in. She eyes the cigarette in my hand. "Since when do you smoke?" she asks. And it's like the years between us are gone, and Mia has forgotten that she no longer has the right to get on my case.

Even if in this instance it's deserved. Once upon a time, I'd been adamantly straightedge where nicotine was concerned. "I know. It's a cliché," I admit.

She eyes me, the cigarette. "Can I have one?"

"You?" When Mia was like six or something, she'd read some kid's book about a girl who got her dad to quit smoking and then she'd decided to lobby her mom, an on-again-off-again-smoker, to quit. It had taken Mia months to prevail upon Kat, but prevail she did. By the time I met them, Kat didn't smoke at all. Mia's dad, Denny, puffed on a pipe, but that seemed mostly for show. "*You* smoke now?" I ask her.

"No," Mia replies. "But I just had a really intense experience and I'm told cigarettes calm your nerves."

The intensity of a concert—it sometimes left me pent up and edgy. "I feel that way after shows sometimes," I say, nodding.

I shake out a cigarette for her; her hand is still trembling, so I keep missing the tip of the cigarette with my lighter. For a second I imagine grabbing her wrist to hold her steady. But I don't. I just chase the cigarette until the flame flashes across her eyes and lights the tip. She inhales and exhales, coughs a little. "I'm not talking about the concert, Adam," she says before taking another labored drag. "I'm talking about *you*."

Little pinpricks fire-cracker up and down my body. *Just calm down*, I tell myself. *You just make her nervous, showing up all out of the blue like that*. Still, I'm flattered that I matter—even if it's just enough to scare her.

We smoke in silence for a while. And then I hear something gurgle. Mia shakes her head in dismay and looks down at her stomach. "Remember how I used to get before concerts?"

Back in the day, Mia would get too nervous to eat before shows, so afterward she was usually ravenous. Back then, we'd go eat Mexican food at our favorite joint or hit a diner out on the highway for French fries with gravy and pie—Mia's dream meal. "How long since your last meal?" I ask.

Mia peers at me again and stubs out her half-smoked cigarette. She shakes her head. "Zankel Hall? I haven't eaten for days. My stomach was rumbling all through the performance. I was sure even people in the balcony seats could hear it."

"Nope. Just the cello."

"That's a relief. I think."

We stand there in silence for a second. Her stomach gurgles again. "Fries and pie still the optimal meal?" I ask. I picture her in a booth back in our place in Oregon, waving her fork around, as she critiqued her own performance.

"Not pie. Not in New York. The diner pies are such disappointments. The fruit's almost always canned. And marionberry does not exist here. How is it possible that a fruit simply ceases to exist from one coast to another?"

How is it possible that a boyfriend ceases to exist from one day to another? "Couldn't tell you."

"But the French fries are good." She gives me a hopeful half smile.

"I like French fries," I say. *I like French fries?* I sound like a slow child in a made-for-TV movie.

Her eyes flutter up to meet mine. "Are you hungry?" she asks.

Am I ever.

⁓

I follow her across Fifty-seventh Street and then down Ninth Avenue. She walks quickly—without even a faint hint of the limp she had when she left—and purposefully, like New Yorkers do, pointing out landmarks here and there like a professional tour guide. It occurs to me I don't even know if she still lives here or if tonight was just a tour date.

You could just ask her, I tell myself. *It's a normal enough question.*

Yeah, but it's so normal that it's weird that I have to ask.

Well you've got to say something to her.

But just as I'm getting up the nerve, Beethoven's Ninth starts chiming from her bag. Mia stops her NYC monologue, reaches in for her cell phone, looks at the screen, and winces.

"Bad news?"

She shakes her head and gives a look so pained it has to be practiced. "No. But I have to take this."

She flips open the phone. "Hello. I know. Please calm down. I know. Look, can you just hold on one second?" She turns to me, her voice all smooth and professional now. "I know this is unbearably rude, but can you just give me five minutes?"

I get it. She just played a big show. She's got people calling. But even so, and in spite of the mask of apology she's wearing, I feel like a groupie being asked to wait in the back of the bus until the rock star's ready. But like the groupies always do, I acquiesce. The rock star is Mia. What else am I gonna do?

"Thank you," she says.

I let Mia walk a few paces ahead of me, to give her some privacy, but I still catch snippets of her end of the conversation. *I know it was important to you. To us. I promise I'll make it up to everyone.* She doesn't mention *me* once. In fact she seems to have forgotten about me back here entirely.

Which would be okay except that she's also oblivious to the commotion that my presence is creating along Ninth Avenue, which is full of bars and people loitering and smoking in front of them. People who double take as they recognize me, and yank out their cell phones and digital cameras to snap pictures.

I vaguely wonder if any of the shots will make it onto Gabber or one of the tabloids. It would be a dream for Vanessa LeGrande. And a nightmare with Bryn. Bryn is jealous enough of Mia as it is, even though she's never met her; she only knows about her. Even though she knows I haven't seen Mia in years, Bryn still complains: "It's hard competing with a ghost." As if Bryn Shraeder has to compete with anyone.

"Adam? Adam Wilde?" It's a real paparazzo with a telephoto lens about a half block away. "Yo, Adam. Can we get a shot? Just one shot," he calls.

Sometimes that works. Give them one minute of your face and they leave. But more often than not, it's like killing one bee and inviting the swarm's wrath.

"Yo, Adam. Where's Bryn?"

I put on my glasses, speed up, though it's too late for that. I stop walking and step out on to Ninth Avenue, which is clogged with taxis. Mia just keeps walking down the block, yapping away into her cell phone. The old Mia hated cell phones, hated people who talked on them in public, who dismissed one person's company to take a phone call from someone else. The old Mia would never have uttered the phrase *unbearably rude*.

I wonder if I should let her keep going. The thought of just jumping into a cab and being back at my hotel by the time she figures out I'm not behind her anymore gives me a certain gritty satisfaction. Let her do the wondering for a change.

But the cabs are all occupied, and, as if the scent of my distress has suddenly reached her, Mia swivels back around to see me, to see the photographer approaching me, brandishing his cameras like machetes. She looks back on to Ninth Avenue at the sea of cars. *Just go on, go on ahead*, I silently tell her. *Get your picture taken with me and your life becomes fodder for the mill. Just keep moving.*

But Mia's striding toward me, grabbing me by the wrist and, even though she's a foot shorter and sixty pounds lighter than me, I suddenly feel safe, safer in her custody than I do in any bouncer's. She walks right into the crowded avenue, stopping traffic just by holding up her other hand. A path opens for us, like we're the Israelites crossing the Red Sea. As soon as we're on the opposite curb, that opening disappears as the cabs all roar toward a green light, leaving my paparazzo stalker on the other side of the street. "It's near impossible to get a cab now," Mia tells me. "All the Broadway shows just let out."

"I've got about two minutes on that guy. Even if I get into a cab, he's gonna follow on foot in this traffic."

"Don't worry. He can't follow where we're going."

She jogs through the crowds, down the avenue, simultaneously pushing me ahead of her and shielding me like a defensive linebacker. She turns off on to a dark street full of tenement buildings. About halfway down the block, the cityscape of brick apartments abruptly gives way to a low area full of trees that's surrounded by a tall iron fence with a heavy-duty lock for which Mia magically produces the key. With a clank, the lock pops open. "In you go," she tells me, pointing to a hedge and a gazebo behind it. "Duck in the gazebo. I'll lock up."

I do as she says and a minute later she's back at my side. It's dark in here, the only light the soft glow of a nearby street lamp. Mia puts a finger to her lips and motions for me to crouch down.

"Where the hell did he go?" I hear someone call from the street.

"He went this way," says a woman, her voice thick with a New York accent. "I swear to ya."

"Well then, where is he?"

"What about that park?" the woman asks.

The clatter of the gate echoes through the garden. "It's locked," he says. In the darkness, I see Mia grin.

"Maybe he jumped over."

"It's like ten feet high," the guy replies. "You don't just leap over something like that."

"D'ya think he has superhuman strength?" the woman replies. "Ya could go inside and check for him."

"And rip my new Armani pants on the fence? A man has his limits. And it looks empty in there. He probably caught a cab. Which we should do. I got sources texting that Timberlake's at the Breslin."

I hear the sound of footsteps retreating and stay quiet for a while longer just to be safe. Mia breaks the silence.

"D'ya think he has superhuman strength?" she asks in a pitch-perfect imitation. Then she starts to laugh.

"I'm not gonna rip my new Armani pants," I reply. "A man has his limits."

Mia laughs even harder. The tension in my gut eases. I almost smile.

After her laughter dies down, she stands up, wipes the dirt from her backside, and sits down on the bench in the gazebo. I do the same. "That must happen to you all the time."

I shrug. "It's worse in New York and L.A. And London. But it's everywhere now. Even fans sell their pics to the tabloids."

"Everyone's in on the game, huh?" she says. Now this sounds more like the Mia I once knew, not like a Classical Cellist with a lofty vocabulary and one of those pan-Euro accents like Madonna's.

"Everyone wants their cut," I say. "You get used to it."

"You get used to a lot of things," Mia acknowledges.

I nod in the darkness. My eyes have adjusted so I can see that the garden is pretty big, an expanse of grass bisected by brick paths and ringed by flower beds. Every now and then, a tiny light flashes in the air. "Are those fireflies?" I ask.

"Yes."

"In the middle of the city?"

"Right. It used to amaze me, too. But if there's a patch of green, those little guys will find it and light it up. They only come for a few weeks a year. I always wonder where they go the rest of the time."

I ponder that. "Maybe they're still here, but just don't have anything to light up about."

"Could be. The insect version of seasonal affective disorder, though the buggers should try living in Oregon if they really want to know what a depressing winter is like."

"How'd you get the key to this place?" I ask. "Do you have to live around here?"

Mia shakes her head, then nods. "Yes, you do have to live in the area to get a key, but I don't. The key belongs to Ernesto Castorel. Or did belong to. When he was a guest conductor at the Philharmonic, he lived nearby and the garden key came with his sublet. I was having roommate issues at the time, which is a repeating theme in my life, so I wound up crashing at his place a lot, and after he left, I 'accidentally' took the key."

I don't know why I should feel so sucker-punched. *You've been with so many girls since Mia you've lost count*, I reason with myself. *It's not like you've been languishing in celibacy. You think she has?*

"Have you ever seen him conduct?" she asks me. "He always reminded me of you."

Except for tonight, I haven't so much as listened to classical music since you left. "I have no idea who you're talking about."

"Castorel? Oh, he's incredible. He came from the slums of Venezuela, and through this program that helps street kids by teaching them to play musical instruments, he wound up becoming a conductor at sixteen. He was the conductor of the Prague Philharmonic at twenty-four, and now he's the artistic director for the Chicago Symphony Orchestra and runs that very same program in Venezuela that gave him his start. He sort of breathes music. Same as you."

Who says I breathe music? Who says I even breathe? "Wow," I say, trying to push back against the jealousy I have no right to.

Mia looks up, suddenly embarrassed. "Sorry. I forget sometimes that the entire world isn't up on the minutiae of classical music. He's pretty famous in our world."

Yeah, well my *girlfriend is* really *famous in the rest of the world*, I think. But does she even know about Bryn and me? You'd have to have your head buried beneath a mountain not to have heard about us. Or you'd have to intentionally be avoiding any news of me. Or maybe you'd just have to be a classical cellist who doesn't read tabloids. "He sounds *swell*," I say.

Even Mia doesn't miss the sarcasm. "Not famous, like you, I mean," she says, her gushiness petering into awkwardness.

I don't answer. For a few seconds there's no sound, save for the river of traffic on the street. And then Mia's stomach gurgles again, reminding us that we've been waylaid in this garden. That we're actually on our way someplace else.

SEVEN

In a weird twisted way, Bryn and I met because of Mia. Well, one degree of separation, I guess. It was really because of the singer-songwriter Brooke Vega. Shooting Star had been slated to open for Brooke's former band, Bikini, the day of Mia's accident. When I hadn't been allowed to visit Mia in the ICU, Brooke had come to the hospital to try to create a diversion. She hadn't been successful. And that had been the last I'd seen of Brooke until the crazy time after *Collateral Damage* went double platinum.

Shooting Star was in L.A. for the MTV Movie

Awards. One of our previously recorded but never released songs had been put on the sound track for the movie *Hello, Killer* and was nominated for Best Song. We didn't win.

It didn't matter. The MTV Awards were just the latest in a string of ceremonies, and it had been a bumper crop in terms of awards. Just a few months earlier we'd picked up our Grammys for Best New Artist and Song of the Year for "Animate."

It was weird. You'd think that a platinum record, a pair of Grammys, a couple of VMAs would make your world, but the more it all piled on, the more the scene was making my skin crawl. There were the girls, the drugs, the ass-kissing, plus the hype—the constant hype. People I didn't know—and not groupies, but industry people—rushing up to me like they were my longtime friends, kissing me on both cheeks, calling me "babe," slipping business cards into my hand, whispering about movie roles or ads for Japanese beer, one-day shoots that would pay a million bucks.

I couldn't handle it, which was why once we'd finished doing our bit for the Movie Awards, I'd ducked out of the Gibson Amphitheater to the smokers' area. I was planning my escape when I saw Brooke Vega striding toward me. Behind her was a pretty, vaguely familiar-looking girl with long black hair and green eyes the size of dinner plates.

"Adam Wilde as I live and breathe," Brooke said, embracing me in a dervish hug. Brooke had recently gone solo and her debut album, *Kiss This*, had been racking up awards, too, so we'd been bumping into each other a lot at the various ceremonies. "Adam, this is Bryn Shraeder, but you probably know her as the fox nominated for The Best Kiss Award. Did you catch her fabulous smooch in *The Way Girls Fall*?"

I shook my head. "Sorry."

"I lost to a vampire-werewolf kiss. Girl-on-girl action doesn't have quite the same impact it used to," Bryn deadpanned.

"You were robbed!" Brooke interjected. "Both of you. It's a cryin' shame. But I'll leave you to lick your wounds or just get acquainted. I've got to get back and present. Adam, see you around, I hope. You should come to L.A. more often. You could use some color." She sauntered off, winking at Bryn.

We stood there in silence for a second. I offered a cigarette to Bryn. She shook her head, then looked at me with those eyes of hers, so unnervingly green. "That was a setup, in case you were wondering."

"Yeah, I was, sort of."

She shrugged, not in the least embarrassed. "I told Brooke I thought you were intriguing, so she took matters into her own hands. She and I, we're alike that way."

"I see."

"Does that bother you?"

"Why would it?"

"It would bother a lot of guys out here. Actors tend to be really insecure. Or gay."

"I'm not from here."

She smiled at that. Then she looked at my jacket. "You going AWOL or something?"

"You think they'll send the dogs on me?"

"Maybe, but it's L.A., so they'll be teeny-tiny Chihuahuas all trussed up in designer bags, so how much damage can they do. You want company?"

"Really? You don't have to stay and mourn your best-kiss loss?"

She looked me squarely in the eye, like she got the joke I was making and was in on it, too. Which I appreciated. "I prefer to celebrate or commiserate my kissing in private."

The only plan I had was to return to my hotel in the limo we had waiting. So instead I went with Bryn. She gave her driver the night off and grabbed the keys to her hulking SUV and drove us down the hill from Universal City toward the coast.

We cruised along the Pacific Coast Highway to a beach north of the city called Point Dume. We stopped on the way for a bottle of wine and some takeout sushi. By the time we reached the beach, a fog had descended over the inky water.

"June gloom," Bryn said, shivering in her short little green-and-black off-the-shoulder dress. "Never fails to freeze me."

"Don't you have a sweater or something?" I asked.

"It didn't complete the look."

"Here." I handed her my jacket.

She raised her eyebrows in surprise. "A gentleman."

We sat on the beach, sharing the wine straight out of the bottle. She told me about the film she'd recently wrapped and the one she was leaving to start shooting the following month. And she was trying to decide between one of two scripts to produce for the company she was starting.

"So you're a fundamentally lazy person?" I asked.

She laughed. "I grew up in this armpit town in Arizona, where all my life my mom told me how pretty I was, how I should be a model, an actress. She never even let me play outside in the sun—in Arizona!—because she didn't want me to mess up my skin. It was like all I had going for me was a pretty face." She turned to stare at me, and I could see the intelligence in her eyes, which were set, admittedly, in a very pretty face. "But fine, whatever, my face was the ticket out of there. But now Hollywood's the same way. Everyone has me pegged as an ingenue, another pretty face. But I know better. So if I want to prove I have a brain, if I want to play in the sunshine, so to speak, it's up to me to find the project that breaks me out. I feel like I'll be better positioned to do that if I'm a producer, too. It's all about control, really. I want to control everything, I guess."

"Yeah, but some things you can't control, no matter how hard you try."

Bryn stared out at the dark horizon, dug her bare toes into the cool sand. "I know," she said quietly. She turned to me. "I'm really sorry about your girlfriend. Mia, right?"

I coughed on the wine. That wasn't a name I was expecting to hear right now.

"I'm sorry. It's just when I asked Brooke about you, she told me how you two met. She wasn't gossiping or anything. But she was there, at the hospital, so she knew."

My heart thundered in my chest. I just nodded.

"My dad left when I was seven. It was the worst thing that ever happened to me," Bryn continued. "So I can't imagine losing someone like that."

I nodded again, swigged at the wine. "I'm sorry," I managed to say.

She nodded slightly in acknowledgment. "But at least they all died together. I mean that's got to be a blessing in a way. I know I wouldn't have wanted to wake up if the rest of my family had died."

The wine came sputtering out of my mouth, through my nose. It took me a few moments to regain my breath and my power of speech. When I did, I told Bryn that Mia wasn't dead. She'd survived the crash, had made a full recovery.

Bryn looked genuinely horrified, so much so that I felt sorry for her instead of for myself. "Lord, Adam. I'm so mortified. I just sort of assumed. Brooke said she'd never heard boo about Mia again and I would've come to the same conclusion. Shooting Star kind of disappears and then *Collateral Damage*, I mean, the lyrics are just so full of pain and anger and betrayal at being left behind. . . ."

"Yep," I said.

Then Bryn looked at me, the green of her eyes reflecting in the moonlight. And I could tell that she understood it all, without my having to say a word. Not having to explain, that felt like the biggest relief. "Oh, Adam. That's even worse in a way, isn't it?"

When Bryn said that, uttered out loud the thing that

to my never-ending shame I sometimes felt, I'd fallen in love with her a little bit. And I'd thought that was enough. That this implicit understanding and those first stirrings would bloom until my feelings for Bryn were as consuming as my love for Mia had once been.

I went back to Bryn's house that night. And all that spring I visited her on set up in Vancouver, then in Chicago, then in Budapest. Anything to get out of Oregon, away from the awkwardness that had formed like a thick pane of aquarium glass between me and the rest of the band. When she returned to L.A. that summer, she suggested I move into her Hollywood Hills house. "There's a guesthouse out back that I never use that we could turn into your studio."

The idea of getting out of Oregon, away from the rest of the band, from all that history, a fresh start, a house full of windows and light, a future with Bryn—it had felt so right at the time.

So that's how I became one half of a celebrity couple. Now I get my picture snapped with Bryn as we do stuff as mundane as grab a coffee from Starbucks or take a walk through Runyon Canyon.

I should be happy. I should be grateful. But the problem is, I never can get away from feeling that my fame isn't about me; it's about them. *Collateral Damage* was written with Mia's blood on my hands, and that was the record that launched me. And when I became really famous, it was for being with Bryn, so it had less to do with the music I was making than the girl I was with.

And the girl. She's great. Any guy would kill to be with her, would be proud to knock her up.

Except even at the start, when we were in that can't-get-enough-of-you phase, there was like some invisible wall between us. At first I tried to take it down, but it took so much effort to even make cracks. And then I got tired of trying. Then I justified it. *This was just how adult relationships were, how love felt once you had a few battle scars.*

Maybe that's why I can't let myself enjoy what we have. Why, in the middle of the night when I can't sleep, I go outside to listen to the lapping of the pool filter and obsess about the shit about Bryn that drives me crazy. Even as I'm doing it, I'm aware that it's minor league—the way she sleeps with a BlackBerry next to her pillow, the way she works out hours a day and catalogs every little thing she eats, the way she refuses to deviate from a plan or a schedule. And I know that there's plenty of great stuff to balance out the bad. She's generous as an oil baron and loyal as a pit bull.

I know I'm not easy to live with. Bryn tells me I'm withdrawn, evasive, cold. She accuses me—depending on her mood—of being jealous of her career, of being with her by accident, of cheating on her. It's not true. I haven't touched a groupie since we've been together; I haven't wanted to.

I always tell her that part of the problem is that we're hardly ever in the same place. If I'm not recording or touring, then Bryn's on location or off on one of her endless press junkets. What I don't tell her is that I can't imagine us being together more of the time. Because it's not like when we're in the same room everything's so great.

Sometimes, after Bryn's had a couple of glasses of wine, she'll claim that Mia's what's between us. "Why don't you just go back to your ghost?" she'll say. "I'm tired of competing with her."

"Nobody can compete with you," I tell her, kissing her on the forehead. And I'm not lying. Nobody *can* compete with Bryn. And then I tell her it's not Mia; it's not any girl. Bryn and I live in a bubble, a spotlight, a pressure cooker. It would be hard on any couple.

But I think we both know I'm lying. And the truth is, there isn't any avoiding Mia's ghost. Bryn and I wouldn't even be together if it weren't for her. In that twisted, incestuous way of fate, Mia's a part of our history, and we're among the shards of her legacy.

EIGHT

The clothes are packed off to Goodwill
I said my good-byes up on that hill
The house is empty, the furniture sold
Soon your smells will decay to mold
Don't know why I bother calling, ain't nobody answering
Don't know why I bother singing, ain't nobody listening

"DISCONNECT"

COLLATERAL DAMAGE, TRACK 10

Ever hear the one about that dog that spent its life chasing cars and finally caught one—and had no idea what to do with it?

I'm that dog.

Because here I am, alone with Mia Hall, something I've fantasized about now for more than three years, and it's like, now what?

We're at the diner that was apparently her destination, some random place way over on the west side of town. "It has a parking lot," Mia tells me when we arrive.

"Uh-huh," is all I can think to answer.

"I'd never seen a Manhattan restaurant with a parking lot before, which is why I first stopped in. Then I noticed that all the cabbies ate here and cabbies are usually excellent judges of good food, but then I wasn't sure because there *is* a parking lot, and free parking is a hotter commodity than good, cheap food."

Mia's babbling now. And I'm thinking: *Are we really talking about parking? When neither of us, as far as I can tell, owns a car here.* I'm hit again by how I don't know anything about her anymore, not the smallest detail.

The host takes us to a booth and Mia suddenly grimaces. "I shouldn't have brought you here. You probably never eat in places like this anymore."

She's right, actually, not because I prefer darkened, overpriced, exclusive eateries but because those are the ones I get taken to and those are the ones I generally get left alone in. But this place is full of old grizzled New Yorkers and cabbies, no one who'd recognize me. "No, this place is good," I say.

We sit down in a booth by the window, next to the vaunted parking lot. Two seconds later, a short, squat hairy guy is upon us. "Maestro," he calls to Mia. "Long time no see."

"Hi, Stavros."

Stavros plops down our menus and turns to me. He

raises a bushy eyebrow. "So, you finally bring your boyfriend for us to meet!"

Mia goes scarlet and, even though there's something insulting in her being so embarrassed by being tagged as my girlfriend, there's something comforting in seeing her blush. This uncomfortable girl is more like the person I knew, the kind who would never have hushed conversations on cell phones.

"He's an old friend," Mia says.

Old friend? Is that a demotion or a promotion?

"Old friend, huh? You never come in here with anyone before. Pretty, talented girl like you. Euphemia!" he bellows. "Come out here. The maestro has a fellow!"

Mia's face has practically turned purple. When she looks up, she mouths: "The wife."

Out of the kitchen trundles the female equivalent of Stavros, a short, square-shaped woman with a face full of makeup, half of which seems to have melted onto her jowly neck. She wipes her hands on her greasy white apron and smiles at Mia, showing off a gold tooth. "I knew it!" she exclaims. "I knew you had a boyfriend you were hiding. Pretty girl like you. Now I see why you don't want to date my Georgie."

Mia purses her lips and raises her eyebrow at me; she gives Euphemia a faux-guilty smile. *Caught me.*

"Now, come on, leave them be," Stavros interjects, swatting Euphemia on the hip and edging in front of her. "Maestro, you want your usual?"

Mia nods.

"And your boyfriend?"

Mia actually cringes, and the silence at the table lengthens like dead air you still sometimes hear on college radio stations. "I'll have a burger, fries, and a beer," I say finally.

"Marvelous," Stavros says, clapping his hands together like I've just given him the cure for cancer. "Cheeseburger Deluxe. Side of onion rings. Your young man is too skinny. Just like you."

"You'll never have healthy kids if you don't put some meat on your bones," Euphemia adds.

Mia cradles her head in her hands, as though she's literally trying to disappear into her own body. After they leave, she peeks up. "God, that was, just, awkward. Clearly, they didn't recognize you."

"But they knew who *you* were. Wouldn't have pegged them as classical music buffs." Then I look down at my jeans, my black T-shirt, my beat-up sneakers. Once upon a time I'd been a classical music fan, too, so there's no telling.

Mia laughs. "Oh, they're not. Euphemia knows me from playing in the subway."

"You busked in the subway? Times that tough?" And then I realize what I just said and want to hit rewind. You don't ask someone like Mia if times are tough, even though I knew, financially, they weren't. Denny had taken out a supplemental life insurance policy in addition to the one he had through the teachers' union and that had left Mia pretty comfortable, although no one knew about the second policy right away. It was one of the reasons that, after the accident, a bunch of the musicians in town had played a series of benefit concerts and raised close to five thousand dollars for Mia's Juilliard fund. The outpouring had moved her grandparents—and me, too—but it had infuriated Mia. She'd refused to take the donation, calling it blood money, and when her grandfather had suggested that accepting other people's generosity was itself an act of generosity that might help people in the community feel better, she'd scoffed that it wasn't her job to make other people feel better.

But Mia just smiles. "It was a blast. And surprisingly lucrative. Euphemia saw me and when I came here to eat, she remembered me from the Columbus Circle station. She proudly informed me that she'd put a whole dollar into my case."

Mia's phone rings. We both stop to listen to the tinny melody. Beethoven plays on and on.

"Are you going to get that?" I ask.

She shakes her head, looking vaguely guilty.

No sooner does the ringing stop then it pipes up again.

"You're popular tonight."

"Not so much popular as in trouble. I was supposed to be at this dinner after the concert. Lots of bigwigs. Agents. Donors. I'm pretty sure that's either a Juilliard professor, someone from Young Concert Artists, or my management calling to yell at me."

"Or Ernesto?" I say as lightly as humanly possible. Because Stavros and Euphemia may have been on to something about Mia having some fancy-pants boy-friend—one that she doesn't drag into Greek diners. He just isn't me.

Mia looks uncomfortable again. "Could be."

"If you have people to talk to, or, you know, business to attend to, don't let me stand in your way."

"No. I should just turn this off." She reaches into her bag and powers down the phone.

Stavros comes by with an iced coffee for Mia and a Budweiser for me and leaves another awkward pause in his wake.

"So," I begin.

"So," Mia repeats.

"So, you have a usual at this place. This like your regular spot?"

"I come for the spanakopita and nagging. It's close to campus, so I used to come here a lot."

Used to? For like the twentieth time tonight, I do the math. It's been three years since Mia left for Juilliard. That would make her a senior this fall. But she's playing Carnegie Hall? She has management? I'm suddenly wishing I'd paid more attention to that article.

"Why not anymore?" My frustration echoes through the din.

Mia's face prickles up to attention, and a little caterpillar of anxiety bunches up above the bridge of her nose. "What?" she says quickly.

"Aren't you *still* in school?"

"Oh, that," she says, relief unfurling her brow. "I should've explained it before. I graduated in the spring. Juilliard has a three-year-degree option for . . ."

"Virtuosos." I mean it as a compliment, but my annoyance at not having the baseball card on Mia Hall—the stats, highlights, career bests—turns it bitter.

"Gifted students," Mia corrects, almost apologetically. "I graduated early so I can start touring sooner. Now, actually. It all starts now."

"Oh."

We sit there in an awkward silence until Stavros arrives with the food. I didn't think I was hungry when we ordered, but as soon as I smell the burger, my stomach starts rumbling. I realize all I've eaten today is a couple of hot dogs. Stavros lays down a bunch of plates in front of Mia, a salad, a spinach pie, French fries, rice pudding.

"*That's* your regular?" I ask.

"I told you. I haven't eaten in two days. And you know how I much I can put away. Or knew, I mean . . ."

"You need anything, Maestro, you just holler."

"Thanks, Stavros."

After he leaves, we both kill a few minutes drowning our fries and the conversation in ketchup.

"So . . ." I begin.

"So . . ." she repeats. Then: "How's everyone. The rest of the band?"

"Good."

"Where are they tonight?"

"London. Or on their way."

Mia cocks her head to the side. "I thought you said you were going tomorrow."

"Yeah, well, I had to tie up some loose ends. Logistics and all that. So I'm here an extra day."

"Well that's lucky."

"*What?*"

"I mean . . . fortunate, because otherwise we wouldn't have bumped into each other."

I look at her. Is she serious? Ten minutes ago she

looked like she was about to have a coronary at the mere *possibility* of being my girlfriend, and now she's saying it's lucky I stalked her tonight. Or is this merely the polite small talk portion of the evening?

"And how's Liz? Is she still with Sarah?"

Oh, it is *the small talk interlude.* "Oh yeah, going strong. They want to get married and have this big debate about whether to do it in a legal state like Iowa or wait for Oregon to legalize. All that trouble to tie the knot." I shake my head in disbelief.

"What, you don't want to get married?" she asks, a hint of challenge in her voice.

It's actually kind of hard to return her stare, but I force myself. "Never," I say.

"Oh," she says, sounding almost relieved.

Don't panic, Mia. I wasn't gonna propose.

"And you? Still in Oregon?" she asks.

"Nope. I'm in L.A. now."

"Another rain refugee flees south."

"Yeah, something like that." No need to tell her how the novelty of being able to eat dinner outside in February wore off quickly, and how now the lack of seasons seems fundamentally wrong. I'm like the opposite of those people who need to sit under sunlamps in the gloom of winter. In the middle of L.A.'s sunny non-winter, I need to sit in a dark closet to feel right. "I moved my parents down, too. The heat's better for my dad's arthritis."

"Yeah, Gramps's arthritis is pretty bad, too. In his hip."

Arthritis? Could this be any more like a Christmas-card update: *And Billy finished swimming lessons, and Todd knocked up his girlfriend, and Aunt Louise had her bunions removed.*

"Oh, that sucks," I say.

"You know how he is. He's all stoic about it. In fact, he and Gran are gearing up to do a lot of traveling to visit me on the road, got themselves new passports. Gran even found a horticulture student to look after her orchids when she's away."

"So how are your gran's orchids?" I ask. *Excellent. We've moved on to flowers now.*

"Still winning prizes, so I guess they must be doing well." Mia looks down. "I haven't seen her greenhouse in a while. I haven't been back there since I came out here."

I'm both surprised by this—and not. It's like I knew it already, even though I thought that once I skipped town, Mia might return. Once again, I've overestimated my importance.

"You should look them up sometime," she says. "They'd be so happy to hear from you, to hear about how well you're doing."

"How *well* I'm doing?"

When I look up at her, she's peering at me from under a waterfall of hair, shaking her head in wonder. "Yeah, Adam, how *amazing* you're doing. I mean, you did it. You're a rock star!"

Rock star. The words are so full of smoke and mirrors that it's impossible to find a real person behind them. But I *am* a rock star. I have the bank account of a rock star and the platinum records of a rock star and the girlfriend of a rock star. But I fucking hate that term, and hearing Mia pin it on me ups the level of my loathing to a new stratosphere.

"Do you have any pictures of the rest of the band?" she asks. "On your phone or something?"

"Yeah, pictures. I have a ton on my phone, but it's back at the hotel." Total bullshit but she'll never know. And if it's pictures she wants, I can just get her a copy of *Spin* at a corner newsstand.

"I have some pictures. Mine are actual paper pictures because my phone is so ancient. I think I have some of Gran and Gramps, and oh, a great one of Henry and Willow. They brought their kids to visit me at the Marlboro Festival last summer," she tells me. "Beatrix, or Trixie as they call her, remember their little girl? She's five now. And they had another baby, a little boy, Theo, named for Teddy."

At the mention of Teddy's name, my gut seizes up. In the calculus of feelings, you never really know how one person's absence will affect you more than another's. I loved Mia's parents, but I could somehow accept their deaths. They'd gone too soon, but in the right order—parent before child—though, not, I supposed, from the perspective of Mia's grandparents. But somehow I *still* can't wrap my head around Teddy staying eight years old forever. Every year I get older, I think about how old Teddy would be, too. He'd be almost twelve now, and I see him in the face of every zitty adolescent boy who comes to our shows or begs an autograph.

I never told Mia about how much losing Teddy gutted me back when we were together, so there's no way I'm gonna tell her now. I've lost my right to discuss such things. I've relinquished—or been relieved of—my seat at the Hall family table.

"I took the picture last summer, so it's a little old, but you get the idea of how everyone looks."

"Oh, that's okay."

But Mia's already rooting through her bag. "Henry still looks the same, like an overgrown kid. Where is my wallet?" She heaves the bag onto the table.

"I don't want to see your pictures!" My voice is as sharp as ice cracking, as loud as a parent's reprimand.

Mia stops her digging. "Oh. Okay." She looks chastened, slapped down. She zips her bag and slides it back into the booth, and in the process, knocks over my bottle of beer. She starts frantically grabbing at napkins from the dispenser to sop up the brew, like there's battery acid leaking over the table. "Damn!" she says.

"It's no big deal."

"It is. I've made a huge mess," Mia says breathlessly.

"You got most of it. Just call your buddy over and he'll get the rest."

She continues to clean maniacally until she's emptied the napkin dispenser and used up every dry paper product in the vicinity. She balls up the soiled napkins and I think she's about to go at the tabletop with her bare arm, and I'm watching the whole thing, slightly perplexed. Until Mia runs out of gas. She stops, hangs her head. Then she looks up at me with those eyes of hers. "I'm sorry."

I know the cool thing to do is say it's okay, it's no big deal, I didn't even get beer on me. But all of a sudden I'm not sure we're talking about beer, and if we're *not* talking about beer, if Mia's issuing some stealth apology . . .

What are you sorry about, Mia?

Even if I could bring myself to ask that—which I

can't—she's jumping out of the booth and running to-ward the bathroom to clean the beer off herself like she's Lady Macbeth.

She's gone for a while, and as I wait the ambiguity she left in the booth curdles its way into the deepest part of me. Because I've imagined a lot of scenarios over the last three years. Most of them versions of this all being some kind of Huge Mistake, a giant misunderstanding. And a lot of my fantasies involve the ways in which Mia grovels for my forgiveness. Apologizes for returning my love with the cruelty of her silence. For acting as though two years of life—those two years of *our* lives—amount to nothing.

But I always stop short of the fantasy of her apolo-gizing for leaving. Because even though she might not know it, she just did what I told her she could do.

NINE

There were signs. Probably more of them than I ever caught, even after the fact. But I missed them all. Maybe because I wasn't looking for them. I was too busy checking over my shoulder at the fire I'd just come through to pay much attention to the thousand-foot cliff looming in front of me.

When Mia had decided to go to Juilliard that fall, and when by late that spring it became clear that she'd be able to, I'd said I'd go with her to New York. She'd just given me this look, *no way*. "That was never on the table before," she said, "so why should it be now?"

Because before you were a whole person but now you don't have a spleen. Or parents. Because New York might swallow you alive, I'd thought. I didn't say anything.

"It's time for both of us to get back to our lives," she continued. I'd only been at the university part-time before but had just stopped going after the accident and now had a term's worth of incompletes. Mia hadn't been back to school, either. She'd missed too much of it, and now she worked with a tutor to finish up her senior year classes so she could graduate and go to Juilliard on time. It was more going through the motions. Her teachers would pass her even if she never turned in another assignment.

"And what about the band?" she asked. "I know they're all waiting on you." Also true. Just before the accident, we'd recorded a self-titled record on Smiling Simon, a Seattle-based independent label. The album had come out at the beginning of the summer, and even though we hadn't toured to support it, the CD had been selling up a storm, getting tons of play on college radio stations. As a result, Shooting Star now had major labels circling, all interested in signing a band that existed only in theory. "Your poor guitar is practically dying of neglect," she said with a sad smile. It hadn't been out of its case since our aborted opening act for Bikini.

So, I agreed to the long-distance thing. In part

because there was no arguing with Mia. In part because I really didn't want to quit Shooting Star. But also, I was kind of cocky about the distance. I mean, before I'd been worried about what the continental divide would do to us. But *now*? What the hell could twenty-five hundred miles do to us now? And besides, Kim had accepted a spot at NYU, a few miles downtown from Juilliard. She'd keep an eye on Mia.

Except, then Kim made a last-minute change and switched to Brandeis in Boston. I was furious about this. After the accident, we frequently had little chats about Mia's progress and passed along pertinent info to her grandparents. We kept our talks secret, knowing Mia would've killed us had she thought we were conspiring. But Kim and I, we were like co-captains of Team Mia. If I couldn't move to New York with Mia, I felt Kim had a responsibility to stay near her.

I stewed about this for a while until one hot July night about a month before she and Mia were due to leave. Kim had come over to Mia's grandparents house to watch DVDs with us. Mia had gone to bed early so it was just the two of us finishing some pretentious foreign movie. Kim kept trying to talk to me about Mia, how well she was doing, and was jabbering over the film like a noisy parrot. I finally told her to shut up. Her eyes narrowed and she started gathering her stuff. "I know what you're upset about and it's not this lame movie, so why don't you just yell at me about it already and get it over with," she said. Then she'd burst out crying. I'd never seen Kim cry, full-on like this, not even at the memorial service, so I'd immediately felt like crap and apologized and sort of awkwardly hugged her.

After she'd finished sniveling, she'd dried her eyes and explained how Mia had made her choose Brandeis. "I mean, it's where I really want to go. After so long in Goyoregon, I really wanted to be at a Jewish school, but NYU was fine, and New York is plenty Jewish. But, she was fierce on this. She said she didn't want 'any more babysitting.' Those were her exact words. She swore that if I went to NYU, she'd know it was because we'd hatched a plan to keep an eye on her. She said she'd cut ties with me. I told her I didn't believe her, but she had a look in her eye I'd never seen. She was serious. So I did it. Do you know how many strings I had to pull to get my spot back this late in the game? Plus, I lost my tuition deposit at NYU. But whatever, it made Mia happy and not a lot does these days." Kim smiled ruefully. "So I'm not sure why it's making me feel so miserable. Guilt, I guess. Religious hazard." Then she'd started crying again.

Pretty loud sign. I guess I had my fingers in my ears.

But the end, when it finally came, was quiet.

Mia went to New York. I moved back to the House of Rock. I went back to school. The world didn't end. For the first couple of weeks, Mia and I sent each other these epic emails. Hers were all about New York, her classes, music, school. Mine were all about our record-label meetings. Liz had scheduled a bunch of gigs for us around Thanksgiving—and we had some serious practicing to do before then, given that I hadn't picked up a guitar in months—but, at Mike's insistence, we were seeing to business first. We were traveling to Seattle and L.A. and meeting label execs. Some A&R guys from New York were coming out to Oregon to see us. I told Mia about the promises they made, how each of them said they'd hone our sound and launch us to superstardom. All of us in the band tried to keep it in check, but it was hard not to inhale their stardust.

Mia and I also had a phone call check-in every night before she went to bed. She was usually pretty wiped so the conversations were short; a chance to hear one another's voice, to say *I love you* in real time.

One night about three weeks into the semester, I was a little late calling because we were meeting one of the A&R reps for dinner at Le Pigeon in Portland and everything ran a little late. When my call went to voice mail, I figured she'd already gone to sleep.

But the next day, there was no email from her. "Sorry I was late. U pissed @ me?" I texted her.

"No," she texted right back. And I was relieved.

But that night, I called on time, and that call went right to voice mail. And the next day, the email from Mia was a terse two sentences, something about orchestra getting very intense. So I justified it. Things were starting to heat up. She was at Juilliard, after all. Her cello didn't have WiFi. And this was Mia, the girl known to practice eight hours a day.

But then I started calling at different times, waking up early so I could get her before classes, calling during her dinnertime. And my calls kept going to voice mail, never getting returned. She didn't return my texts either. I was still getting emails, but not every day, and even though *my* emails were full of increasingly desperate questions—"Why aren't you picking up your cell?" "Did you lose it? Are you okay?"—her responses glossed right over everything. She just claimed to be busy.

I decided to go visit her grandparents. I'd pretty much lived with them for five months while Mia was recovering and had promised to visit frequently but I'd reneged on that. I found it hard to be in that drafty old house with its photo gallery of ghosts—a wedding portrait of Denny and Kat, a gut-wrenching shot of twelve-year-old Mia reading to Teddy on her lap—without Mia beside me. But with Mia's contact dwindling, I needed answers.

The first time I went that fall, Mia's grandmother talked my ear off about the state of her garden and then went out to her greenhouse, leaving me to sit in the kitchen with her grandfather. He brewed us a strong pot of coffee. We didn't say much, so all you could hear was the crackling of the woodstove. He just looked at me in that quiet sad way that made me inexplicably want to kneel at the foot of his chair and put my head in his lap.

I went back a couple more times, even after Mia had cut off contact with me completely, and it was always like that. I felt kind of bad pretending that I was there on social calls when really I was hoping for some news, some explanation. No, what I was *really* hoping for was not to be the odd man out. I wanted them to say: "Mia has stopped calling us. Has she been in touch with you?" But, of course, that never happened because that never *would* happen.

The thing was, I didn't need any confirmation from Mia's grandparents. I knew from that second night when my call went to voice mail, that it was the end of the line for me.

Because hadn't I told her? Hadn't I stood over her

body and promised her that I'd do anything if she stayed, even if it meant letting her go? The fact that she'd been in a coma when I'd said this, hadn't woken up for another three days, that neither of us had ever mentioned what I'd said—that seemed almost irrelevant. I'd brought this on myself.

The thing I can't wrap my head around is *how* she did it. I've never dumped a girl with such brutality. Even back when I did the groupie thing, I'd always escort the girl du jour out of my hotel room or limo or whatever, give her a chaste kiss on the cheek and a "Thanks, that was a lot of fun," or something with a similar note of finality in it. And that was a *groupie*. Mia and I had been together for more than two years, and yes, it was a high-school romance, but it was still the kind of romance where I thought we were trying to find a way to make it forever, the kind that, had we met five years later and had she not been some cello prodigy and had I not been in a band on the rise—or had our lives not been ripped apart by all this—I was pretty sure it would've been.

I've come to realize there's a world of difference between knowing something happened, even knowing why it happened, and believing it. Because when she cut off contact, yeah, I *knew* what had happened. But it took me a long, long time to believe it.

Some days, I *still* don't quite believe it.

TEN

Barrel of the gun, rounds one two three
She says I have to pick: choose you, or choose me
Metal to the temple, the explosion is deafening
Lick the blood that covers me
She's the last one standing

"ROULETTE"
COLLATERAL DAMAGE, TRACK 11

After we leave the diner, I start to feel nervous. Because we bumped into each other. We did the polite thing and stuck around to catch up, so what's left except our good-byes? But I'm not ready for that. I'm pretty sure there's not going to be another postscript with Mia, and I'm gonna have to live on the fumes of tonight for the rest of my life, so I'd like a little more to show for it than parking lots and arthritis and aborted apologies.

Which is why every block we walk that Mia doesn't hail a cab or make excuses and say good night feels like a stay of execution. In the sound of my footsteps slapping against the pavement, I can almost hear the word, *reprieve, reprieve,* echo through the city streets.

We walk in silence down a much-quieter, much-scummier stretch of Ninth Avenue. Underneath a dank overpass, a bunch of homeless guys camp out. One asks for some spare change. I toss him a ten. A bus goes by, blasting a cloud of diesel exhaust.

Mia points across the street. "That's the Port Authority Bus Terminal," she says.

I just nod, not sure if we're going to discuss bus stations with the same amount of detail we did parking lots, or if she's planning on sending me away.

"There's a bowling alley inside," she tells me.

"In the bus station?"

"Crazy right?!" Mia exclaims, suddenly all animated. "I couldn't believe it when I found it either. I was coming home from visiting Kim in Boston late one night and got lost on the way out and there it was. It reminded me of Easter egg hunts. Do you remember how Teddy and I used to get about those?"

I remember how *Mia* used to get. She'd been a sucker for any holiday that had a candy association—especially making it fun for Teddy. One Easter she'd painstakingly hand-colored hard-boiled eggs and hidden them all over the yard for Teddy's hunt the next morning. But then it poured all night and all her colorful eggs had turned a mottled gray. Mia had been tearfully disappointed, but Teddy had practically peed himself with excitement—the eggs, he declared, weren't Easter eggs; they were *dinosaur* eggs.

"Yeah, I remember," I say.

"Everyone loves New York City for all these different reasons. The culture. The mix of people. The pace. The food. But for me, it's like one epic Easter egg hunt. You're always finding these little surprises around every corner. Like that garden. Like a bowling alley in a giant bus depot. You know—" She stops.

"What?"

She shakes her head. "You probably have something going tonight. A club. An entourage to meet."

I roll my eyes. "I don't do entourage, Mia." It comes out harder than I intended.

"I didn't mean it as an insult. I just assumed all rock stars, celebrities, traveled with packs."

"Stop assuming. I'm still me." *Sort of.*

She looks surprised. "Okay. So you don't have anywhere you need to be?"

I shake my head.

"It's late. Do you need to get to sleep?"

"I don't do much of that these days. I can sleep on the plane."

"So . . ." Mia kicks away a piece of trash with her

toe, and I realize *she's still nervous.* "Let's go on an urban Easter egg hunt." She pauses, searches my face to see if I know what she's talking about, and of course I know exactly what she's talking about. "I'll show you all the secret corners of the city that I love so much."

"Why?" I ask her. And then as soon as I ask the question, I want to kick myself. *You got your reprieve, now shut up!* But part of me does want to know. If I'm unclear why I went to her concert tonight, I'm thoroughly confused as to why she called me to her, why I'm still here.

"Because I'd like to show you," she says simply. I stare at her, waiting for her to elaborate. Her brows knit as she tries to explain. Then she seems to give up. She just shrugs. After a minute she tries again: "Also, I'm not exactly leaving New York, but I sort of am. I go to Japan tomorrow to do two concerts there and then one in Korea. And after that I come back to New York for a week and then I really start touring. I'll be on the road for maybe forty weeks a year, so . . ."

"Not much time for egg hunting?"

"Something like that."

"So this would be like your farewell tour?" *Of New York? Of me?*

A little late for me.

"That's one way of looking at it, I suppose," Mia replies.

I pause, as though I'm actually considering this, as though I'm weighing my options, as though the RSVP to her invitation is in question. Then I shrug, put on a good show, "Sure, why not?"

But I'm still a little iffy about the bus station, so I put on my shades and cap before we go inside. Mia leads me through an orange-tiled hall, the aroma of pine disinfectant not quite masking the smell of piss, and up a series of escalators, past shuttered newsstands and fast-food restaurants, up more escalators to a neon sign blaring LEISURE TIME BOWL.

"Here we are," she says shyly, proudly. "After I found it by accident, I made a habit of peeking in any time I was in the station. And then I started coming here just to hang out. Sometimes I sit at the bar and order nachos and watch people bowl."

"Why not bowl yourself?"

Mia tilts her head to the side, then taps her elbow.

Ahh, her elbow. Her Achilles' heel. One of the few parts of her body that, it seemed, hadn't been hurt in the accident, hadn't been encased in plaster or put together with pins or stitches or touched by skin grafts. But when she'd started playing cello again in that mad attempt to catch up with herself, her elbow had started to hurt. X-rays were taken. MRIs done. The doctors couldn't find anything wrong, told her it might be a bad bruise or a contused nerve, and suggested she ease off the practicing, which had set Mia off. She said if she couldn't play, she had nothing left. *What about me?* I remember thinking, but never saying. Anyhow, she'd ignored the doctors and played through the pain and either it had gotten better or she'd gotten used to it.

"I tried to get some people from Juilliard to come down a few times, but they weren't into it. But it doesn't matter," she tells me. "It's the *place* I love. How it's totally secreted away up here. I don't need to bowl to appreciate it."

So your Garden-of-Eden boyfriend is too highbrow for greasy diners and bowling alleys, huh?

Mia and I used to go bowling, sometimes the two of us, other times with her whole family. Kat and Denny had been big bowlers, part of Denny's whole retro thing. Even Teddy could hit an eighty. *Like it or not, Mia Hall, you have a bit of grunge twined into your DNA, thanks to your family. And, maybe, thanks to me.*

"We could go bowling now," I suggest.

Mia smiles at the offer. Then taps her elbow again. She shakes her head.

"You don't have to bowl," I explain. "I'll bowl. You can watch. Just for you to get the whole effect. Or I can even bowl for both of us. It seems like you should have one game here. This being your farewell tour."

"You'd do that for me?" And it's the surprise in her voice that gets to me.

"Yeah, why not? I haven't been bowling in ages." This isn't entirely true. Bryn and I went bowling a few months ago for some charity thing. We paid twenty thousand bucks to rent a lane for an hour for some worthy cause and then we didn't even bowl; just drank champagne while Bryn schmoozed. I mean who drinks champagne at a bowling alley?

Inside Leisure Time, it smells like beer—and wax and hot dogs and shoe disinfectant. It's what a bowling alley should smell like. The lanes are full of an unusually unattractive grouping of New Yorkers who actually seem to be bowling for the sake of bowling. They don't look twice at us; they don't even look once at us. I book us a lane and rent us each a pair of shoes. Full treatment here.

Mia's practically giddy as she tries hers on, doing a little soft-shoe as she selects a ladies' pink eight-pounder for me to bowl with on her behalf.

"What about names?" Mia asks.

Back in the day, we always went for musicians; she'd choose an old-school punk female singer and I'd pick a male classical musician. Joan and Frederic. Or Debbie and Ludwig.

"You pick," I say, because I'm not exactly sure how

much of the past we're supposed to be reliving. Until I see the names she inputs. And then I almost fall over. *Kat* and *Denny*.

When she sees my expression she looks embarrassed. "They liked to bowl, too," she hastily explains, quickly changing the names to Pat and Lenny. "How's that?" she asks a little too cheerfully

Two letters away from morbid, I think. My hand is shaking again as I step up to the lane with "Pat's" pink ball, which might explain why I only knock down eight pins. Mia doesn't care. She squeals with delight. "A spare will be mine," she yells. Then catches her outburst and looks down at her feet. "Thanks for renting me the shoes. Nice touch."

"No problem."

"How come nobody recognizes you here?" she asks.

"It's a context thing."

"Maybe you can take off your sunglasses. It's kind of hard talking to you in them."

I forgot that I still had them on and feel stupid for it, and stupid for having to wear them in the first place. I take them off.

"Better," Mia says. "I don't get why classical musicians think bowling is white trash. It's so fun."

I don't know why this little Juilliard-snobs-versus-the-rest-of-us should make me feel a little digging thrill, but it does. I knock down the remaining two of Mia's pins. She cheers, loudly.

"Did you like it? Juilliard?" I ask. "Was it everything you thought it'd be?"

"No," she says, and again, I feel this strange sense of victory. Until she elaborates. "It was more."

"Oh."

"Didn't start out that way, though. It was pretty rocky at first."

"That's not surprising, you know, all things considered."

"That was the problem. 'All things considered.' Too many things considered. When I first got there, it was like everywhere else; people were very considerate. My roommate was so considerate that she couldn't look at me without crying."

The Over-Empathizer—her I remember. I got cut off a few weeks into her.

"All my roommates were drama queens. I changed so many times the first year before I finally moved out of the dorms. Do you know I've lived in eleven different places here? I think that must be some kind of record."

"Consider it practice for being on the road."

"Do you like being on the road?"

"No."

"Really? Getting to see all those different countries. I would've thought you'd love that."

"All I get to see is the hotel and the venue and the blur of the countryside from the window of a tour bus."

"Don't you *ever* sightsee?"

The band does. They go out on these private VIP tours, hit the Rome Colosseum before it's open to the public and things like that. I could tag along, but it would mean going with the band, so I just wind up holed up in my hotel. "There's not usually time," I lie. "So you were saying, you had roommate issues."

"Yeah," Mia continues. "Sympathy overload. It was like that with everyone, including the faculty, who were all kind of nervous around me, when it should've been the opposite. It's kind of a rite of passage when you first take orchestra to have your playing deconstructed— basically picked apart—in front of everyone. And it happened to everybody. Except me. It was like I was invisible. Nobody dared critique me. And trust me, it wasn't because my playing was so great."

"Maybe it was," I say. I edge closer, dry my hands over the blower.

"No. It wasn't. One of the courses you have to take when you first start is String Quartet Survey. And one of the profs is this guy Lemsky. He's a bigwig in the department. Russian. Imagine every cruel stereotype you can think of, that's him. Mean, shriveled-up little man. Straight out of Dostoyevsky. My dad would've loved him. After a few weeks, I get called into his office. This is not usually a happy sign.

"He's sitting behind this messy wooden desk, with papers and sheet music piled high. And he starts telling me about his family. Jews in the Ukraine. Lived through pogroms. Then through World War II. Then he says, 'Everyone has hardship in their life. Everyone has pain. The faculty here will coddle you because of what you went through. I, however, am of the opinion if we do that, that car crash might as well have killed you, too, because we will smother your talent. Do you want us to do that?'

"And, I didn't know how to respond, so I just stood there. And then he *yelled* at me: '*Do you? Do you want us to smother you?*' And I manage to eke out a 'no.' And he says, 'Good.' Then he picks up his baton and sort of flicks me out with it."

I can think of places I'd like to stick that guy's baton. I grab my ball and hurl it down the lane. It hits the pin formation with a satisfying thwack; the pins go flying in every direction, like little humans fleeing Godzilla. When I get back to Mia, I'm calmer.

"Nice one," she says at the same time I say, "Your professor sounds like a dick!"

"True, he's not the most socially graced. And I was freaked out at the time, but looking back I think that was one of the most important days of my life. Because he was the first person who didn't just give me a pass."

I turn, glad to have a reason to walk away from her so she can't see the look on my face. I throw her pink ball down the lane, but the torque is off and it veers to the right. I get seven down and the remaining three are split. I only pick off one more on my next go. To even things up, I purposely blow *my* next frame, knocking down six pins.

"So, a few days later, in orchestra," Mia continues, "my glissando gets taken apart, and not very kindly." She grins, awash in happy memories of her humiliation.

"Nothing like a public flogging."

"Right!? It was great. It was like the best therapy in the world."

I look at her. "Therapy" was once a forbidden word. Mia had been assigned a grief counselor in the hospital and rehab but had refused to continue seeing anyone once she'd come home, something Kim and I had argued against. But Mia had claimed that talking about her dead family an hour a week wasn't therapeutic.

"Once that happened, it was like everyone else on the

faculty relaxed around me," she tells me. "Lemsky rode me extra hard. No time off. No life that wasn't cello. Summers I played festivals. Aspen. Then Marlboro. Then Lemsky and Ernesto both pushed me to audition for the Young Concert Artists program, which was insane. It makes getting into Juilliard look like a cakewalk. But I did it. And I got in. That's why I was at Carnegie tonight. Twenty-year-olds don't normally play recitals at Zankel Hall. And that's just thrown all these doors wide open. I have management now. I have agents interested in me. And that's why Lemsky pushed for early graduation. He said I was ready to start touring, though I don't know if he's right."

"From what I heard tonight, he's right."

Her face is suddenly so eager, so young, it almost hurts. "Do you really think so? I've been playing recitals and festivals, but this will be different. This will be me on my own, or soloing for a few nights with an orchestra or a quartet or a chamber music ensemble." She shakes her head. "Some days I think I should just find a permanent position in an orchestra, have some continuity. Like you have with the band. It has to be such a comfort to always be with Liz, Mike, and Fitzy." The stage changes, but the players stay the same.

I think of the band, on an airplane as we speak, speeding across the Atlantic—an ocean, the least of the things, dividing us now. And then I think of Mia, of the way she played the Dvořák, of what all the people in the theater were saying after she left the stage. "No, you shouldn't do that. That would be a waste of your talent."

"Now *you* sound like Lemsky."

"Great."

Mia laughs. "Oh, I know he comes across as such a hard-ass, but I suspect deep down he's doing this because he thinks by giving me a shot at a career, he'll help fill some void."

Mia stops and turns to me, her eyes dead on mine, searching, reaching. "But he doesn't have to give me the career. That's not what fills the void. You understand that, right? You always understood that."

Suddenly, all the shit from the day comes ricocheting back—Vanessa and Bryn and the bump watches and *Shuffle* and the looming sixty-seven days of separate hotels and awkward silences and playing shows with a band behind me that no longer has my back.

And it's like, Mia, don't you get it? The *music* is the void. And you're the reason why.

ELEVEN

Shooting Star had always been a band with a code—feelings first, business second—so I hadn't given the band much thought, hadn't considered their feelings, or their resentments, about my extended leave. I figured they'd get my absence without my having to explain.

After I came out of my haze and wrote those first ten songs, I called Liz, who organized a band dinner/meeting. During dinner, we sat around the Club Table—so named because Liz had taken this fugly 1970s wooden dining table we'd found on the curb and covered it with band flyers and about a thousand layers of lacquer to resemble the inside of a club. First, I apologized for going MIA. Then I pulled out my laptop and played them recordings of the new stuff I'd been writing. Liz's and Fitzy's eyes went wide. They dangled vegetable lasagna in front of their mouths as they listened to track after track: "Bridge," "Dust," "Stitch," "Roulette," "Animate."

"Dude, we thought you were just packing it in, working some crap-ass job and pining, but you've been *productive*," Fitzy exclaimed. "This shit rocks."

Liz nodded. "It does. And it's beautiful, too. It must have been cathartic," she said, reaching over to squeeze my hand. "I'd love to read the lyrics. Do you have them on your computer?"

"Scrawled on paper at home. I'll transcribe them and email them to you."

"Home? Isn't this home?" Liz asked. "Your room is an untouched museum. Why don't you move back?"

"Not much to move. Unless you sold my stuff."

"We tried. Too dusty. No takers," Fitzy said. "We've been using your bed as a hat rack, though." Fitzy shot me a wiseass grin. I'd made the mistake of telling him how I'd thought I was turning into my dead grandfather, with all his weird superstitions, like his vehement belief that hats on beds bring bad luck.

"Don't worry, we'll burn sage," Liz said. Clearly Fitzy had alerted the media.

"So, what, that's it?" Mike said, tapping his nails against my laptop.

"Dude, that's ten songs," Fitzy said, a piece of spinach in his giant grin. "Ten insanely good songs. That's practically an album. We already have enough to go into the studio."

"Those are just the ones that are done," I interrupted. "I've got at least ten more coming. I don't know what's going on, but they're just kinda flowing out of me right now, like they're already written and recorded and someone just pressed *play*. I'm getting it all out as fast I can."

"Obey the muse," Liz said. "She's a fickle mistress."

"I'm not talking about the songs," Mike said. "We don't even know if there will be any album. If any of the labels will still want us. We had all this forward momentum and he basically killed it."

"He didn't kill anything," Liz said. "For one, it's only been a few months, and second of all, our Smiling Simon album has been ripping up the indie charts, getting tons of play on the college stations. And I've been working the college angle pretty well," Liz continued, "with interviews and all, to keep the embers burning."

"And dude, 'Perfect World' has even crossed over; it's getting play on satellite radio stations," Fitzy said. "I'm sure all those A&R guys will be happy to see us, shitting bricks to hear this."

"You don't know," Mike said. "They have their trends. Quotas. The outfits they want. And my point is, he"—he jabbed a finger at me—"ditches the band without a word and just waltzes back like it's no big deal."

Mike had a point, but it wasn't like I held anyone back. "Look, I'm sorry. We all go off the cliff sometimes. But you could've replaced me if you'd wanted to. Gotten a new guitar player and your major-label deal."

By the quick look that passed among the three of them, I could see that this option had been discussed, and likely vetoed by Liz. Shooting Star was a democratic outfit; we'd always made decisions together. But when it came down to it, the band was Liz's. She started it and recruited me to play guitar after seeing me play around town. Then she'd lassoed Fitzy and Mike, so ultimately a personnel change would've been her call. Maybe this was why Mike had started playing gigs with another drummer under the name of Ranch Hand.

"Mike, I don't get what you want out of this," Fitzy said. "Do you want a box of chocolates? Do you want Adam to get you a nice bouquet to say sorry?"

"Piss off, Fitz," Mike said.

"I'll buy you flowers," I offered. "Yellow roses. I believe those symbolize friendship. Whatever it takes, I'll do what I'm told."

"Will that make it good?" Fitzy continued. "Because what the fuck, man? We have these amazing songs. I wish I'd written those songs. But Adam did. He came through. And we have him back. So maybe now we can get back to making kick-ass music and see where it takes us. And maybe, you know, let our kid get a little joy back in his life. So, dude. Bygones."

⟳

Mike's worries turned out to be unfounded. Some of the major labels that had been courting us in the fall had cooled on us, but a handful were still interested, and when we sent them the demos of the songs that would become *Collateral Damage* they went ballistic, and we were signed and in the studio with Gus before we knew it.

And for a while, things were good. Fitzy and Liz were both right. Recording *Collateral Damage* was cathartic. And there was joy. Working with Gus was intense; he brought out the noise in us, told us not to be scared of our raw power, and we all ran with it. And it was cool being up in Seattle recording and staying in a corporate apartment and feeling like The Shit. Everything seemed good.

Not long after the record came out, the tour started. A five-month slog through North America, Europe, and Asia that, at the outset, seemed like the most exciting thing in the world. And in the beginning, it was. But it was also grueling. And soon I was tired all the time. And lonely. There was a lot of empty time in which to miss her. I kind of holed away in my hotel rooms, the backs of tour buses. I pushed everyone away. Even Liz. Especially Liz. She wasn't stupid; she knew what was going on—and why. And she wasn't some fragile flower, either. She kept after me. So I burrowed, until, I guess, she got tired of trying to dig me out.

As the tour went on, the album just started going haywire. Platinum. Then double-platinum. The tour dates sold out, so our promoters added additional ones to meet demand. The merchandising deals were everywhere. Shooting Star T-shirts, caps, posters, stickers, even a special-edition Shooting Star telescope. Suddenly, the press was all over us. Interviews all the time, which was flattering at first. People cared enough about us to read what we had to say.

But a weird thing started to happen in interviews. The reporter would sit the band down together, ask some perfunctory questions to us all, and then turn the microphone or camera on me. And I tried to open it up to the rest of the band. That's when reporters started requesting interviews with just me, a request I uniformly turned down, until it suddenly became impossible for us to do interviews any other way.

About four months into the tour, we were in Rome. *Rolling Stone* had sent a reporter to spend a few days with us. One night, after a show, we were closing the hotel bar. It was a pretty mellow scene and we were sitting around, decompressing, pounding grappa. But then the reporter starts firing away with all these heavy-duty questions. All to me. I mean, there were about a dozen of us in there—me, Liz, Fitzy, Mike, Aldous, some roadies, some groupies—but this guy was acting like I was the only person in the room. "Adam, do you see *Collateral Damage* as having a single narrative? If so, can you elaborate on it?" "Adam, do think this record represents your growth as a songwriter?" "Adam, you've mentioned in other interviews you don't want to go down 'that dark rock star path,' but how do you keep from suffocating on your own fumes?"

Mike just lost it. "You hijacked the band!" he screamed at me, like it was just the two of us in a room, like there wasn't a reporter right there. "This isn't just the Adam Wilde Show, you know. We're a band. A unit. There are four of us. Or did you forget that, on your way down the 'dark rock star path?'"

Mike turned to the reporter. "You wanna know

about the illustrious Adam Wilde? I've got some choice details. Like our rock star over here has to do this crazy voodoo shit before each show and is such a prima donna that if you whistle backstage before a show he has a tantrum because of the bad luck—"

"Mike, come on," Liz interrupted sharply. "All artists have their rituals."

The reporter, meanwhile, was scribbling away, eating all this up until Aldous diplomatically said that everyone was tired and shooed everyone but the band out of the bar and tried to get me and Mike to make nice. But then Mike just let loose for round two of insults, telling me what a spotlight-hogging asshole I'd become. I looked over at Liz to come to my defense again, but she was staring intently at her drink. So I turned to Fitzy, but he just shook his head. "I never thought I'd be the one to say this, but grow up, you two." Then he left. I looked pleadingly at Liz. She looked sympathetic, but tired. "Mike, you were out of line in there," she said flatly. But then she turned to me and shook her head. "But, Adam, come on. You've got to try to see it from his perspective. From *all* of ours. It's tough to be big about this, especially when you've retreated from us. I get why you have, but that doesn't make it any easier."

All of them—they were all against me. I waved my hands in surrender. I ran out of the bar, strangely close to tears. In the lobby, this Italian model named Rafaella, who'd been hanging with us, was waiting for a taxi. She smiled when she saw me. When her taxi came, she gestured with her head, inviting me inside. And I went. The next day, I checked into a different hotel from the band.

The story hit RollingStone.com almost immediately and the tabloids a few days later. Our label freaked, as did our tour promoters, all of whom warned of the various forms of hell there would be to pay if we didn't honor our concert commitments. Aldous flew in a professional mediator to talk to me and Mike. She was useless. Her genius idea, a legacy that continues to this day, is what Fitzy refers to as "The Divorce." I would continue to stay at one hotel for the remainder of the tour, the rest of the band at another. And our publicists decided it was safer to keep me and Mike separate in interviews, so now reporters often talk to me solo. Yeah, those changes have helped a lot!

When I got back from the *Collateral Damage* tour, I almost quit the band. I moved out of the house I'd been sharing with Fitzy in Portland and into my own place. I avoided those guys. I was angry, but also ashamed. I wasn't sure how, but I'd clearly ruined everything. I might've just let the run end there, but Liz stopped by my new place one afternoon and asked me to just give it a few months' breathing space and see how I felt. "Anyone would be going a little nuts after the couple years we've had, especially the couple of years you've had," she'd said, which was about as much as we acknowledged Mia. "I'm not asking you to do anything. I'm just asking you to *not* do anything and see how you feel in a few months."

Then the album started winning all these awards, and then I met Bryn and moved to L.A. and didn't have to deal with them much, so I just wound up getting sucked in for another round.

Bryn's the only person who knows how close to the edge that tour pushed me, and how badly I've been dreading this upcoming one. "Cut them loose," is her solution. She thinks I have some sort of guilt complex, coming from humble origins and all, and that's why I won't go solo. "Look, I get it. It's hard to accept that you deserve the acclaim, but you do. You write all the songs and most of the music and that's why you get all the attention," she tells me. "*You're* the talent! Not just some pretty face. If this were a movie, you'd be the twenty-million-dollar star and they'd be the supporting players, but instead you all get an equal split," she says. "You don't need them. Especially with all the grief they give you."

But it's not about the money. It never has been. And

going solo doesn't seem like much of a solution. It would just be out of the frying pan and into the fire. And there'd still be touring to contend with, the thought of which has been making me physically sick.

"Why don't you call Dr. Weisbluth?" Bryn suggested on the phone from Toronto, where she was wrapping her latest film. Weisbluth's the psychopharmacologist the label had hooked me up with a few months earlier. "See if he can give you something a little stronger. And when you get back, we need to have a sit-down with Brooke and seriously talk about you going solo. But you *have* to get through this tour. You'll blow your reputation otherwise."

There are worse things to blow than your reputation, aren't there? That's what I thought. But I didn't say it. I just called Weisbluth, got some more scripts, and steeled myself for the tour. I guess Bryn understood, like I understood, like everyone who knew me understood, that in spite of his bad-boy rep, Adam Wilde does as he's told.

TWELVE

There's a piece of lead where my heart should beat
Doctor said too dangerous to take out
You'd better just leave it be
Body grew back around it, a miracle, praise be
Now, if only I could get through airport security

"BULLET"

<u>**COLLATERAL DAMAGE**</u>, **TRACK 12**

Mia doesn't tell me what the next destination is. Says because it's her secret New York tour, it should be a secret and then proceeds to lead me out of Port Authority down, down, down into a warren of subway tunnels.

And I follow her. Even though I don't like secrets, even though I think that Mia and I have *enough* secrets between the two of us at this point, and even though the subway is like the culmination of all my fears. Enclosed spaces. Lots of people. No escape. I sort of mention this to her, but she throws back what I said earlier in the bowling alley about context. "Who's going to be expecting Adam Wilde on the subway at three in the morning? Without an entourage?" She gives me a joking smile. "Besides, it should be dead at this hour. And in my New York, I always take the train."

When we reach the Times Square subway station, the place is so crowded that it might as well be five P.M. on a Thursday. My warning bell starts to ping. Even more so once we get to the thronged platform. I stiffen and back toward one of the pillars. Mia gives me a look. "This is a bad idea," I mumble, but my worries are drowned out by the oncoming train.

"The trains don't run often at night, so it must be that everyone's been waiting for a while," Mia shouts over the clatter. "But here comes one now, so look, everything's fine."

When we get on the N, we both see that Mia's wrong. The car's packed with people. Drunk people.

I feel the itchiness of eyes on me. I know I'm out of pills, but I need a cigarette. *Now.* I reach for my pack.

"You can't smoke on the train," Mia whispers.

"I need to."

"It's illegal."

"I don't care." If I get arrested, at least I'd be in the safety of police custody.

Suddenly, she goes all Vulcan. "If the purpose is to not call attention to yourself, don't you think that perhaps lighting up is counterproductive?" She pulls me into a corner. "It's fine," she croons, and I half expect her to caress my neck like she used to do when I'd get tense. "We'll just hang out here. If it doesn't empty out at Thirty-fourth Street, we'll get off."

At Thirty-fourth, a bunch of people do get off, and I feel a little better. At Fourteenth more people get off. But then suddenly at Canal, our car fills up with a group of hipsters. I angle myself into the far end of the train, near the conductor's booth, so my back is to the riders.

It's hard for most people to understand how freaked out I get by large crowds in small contained spaces now. I think it would be hard for the me of three years ago to understand. But that me never had the experience of minding his own business at a small record shop in Minneapolis when one guy recognized me and shouted out my name and it was like watching popcorn kernels in hot oil: First one went, then another, then an explosion of them, until all these sedate record-store slackers suddenly became a mob, surrounding me, then tackling me. I couldn't breathe. I couldn't move.

It sucks because I like the fans when I meet them individually, I do. But get a group of them together and this swarm instinct takes over and they seem to forget that you're a mere mortal: flesh and bone, bruisable and scareable.

But we seem okay in the corner. Until I make the fatal mistake of doing just one final check over my shoulder to make sure no one's looking at me. And in that little quarter second, it happens. I catch someone's eye. I feel the recognition ignite like a match. I can almost smell the phosphorus in the air. Then everything seems to happen in slow motion. First, I hear it. It goes unnaturally quiet. And then there's a low buzz as the news travels. I hear my name, in stage whispers, move across the noisy train. I see elbows nudged. Cell phones reached for, bags grabbed, forces rallied, legs shuffling. None of this takes longer than a few seconds, but it's always agonizing, like the moments when a first punch is thrown but hasn't yet connected. One guy with a beard is preparing to step out of his seat, opening his mouth to call my name. I know he means me no harm, but once he outs me, the whole train will be on me. Thirty seconds till all hell breaks loose.

I grab Mia's arm and yank.

"Oww!"

I have the door between subway cars open and we're pushing into the next car.

"What are you doing?" she says, flailing behind me

I'm not listening. I'm pulling her into another car then another until the train slows into a station and then I'm tugging her out of the train, onto the platform, up the stairs, taking them two at a time, some part of my brain vaguely warning me that I'm being too rough but the other part not giving a shit. Once up on the street, I pull her along for a few blocks until I'm sure no one is following us. Then I stop.

"Are you *trying* to get us killed?" she yells.

I feel a bolt of guilt shoot through me. But I throw the bolt right back at her.

"Well, what about you? Are you trying to get me attacked by a mob?"

I look down and realize that I'm still holding her hand. Mia looks, too. I let go.

"What mob, Adam?" she asks softly.

She's talking to me like I'm a crazy person now. Just like Aldous talks to me when I have one of my panic attacks. But at least Aldous would never accuse me of fantasizing a fan attack. He's seen it happen too many times.

"I got recognized down there," I mutter, walking away from her.

Mia hesitates for a second, then skitters to catch up. "Nobody knew it was you."

Her ignorance—the *luxury* of that ignorance!

"The whole car knew it was me."

"What are you talking about, Adam?"

"What am I talking about? I'm talking about having

photographers camped out in front of my house. I'm talking about not having gone record shopping in almost two years. I'm talking about not being able to take a walk without feeling like a deer on the opening day of hunting season. I'm talking about every time I have a cold, it showing up in a tabloid as a coke habit."

I look at her there in the shadows of the shut-down city, her hair falling onto her face, and I can see her trying to figure out if I've lost it. And I have to fight the urge to take her by the shoulders and slam her against a shuttered building until we feel the vibrations ringing through both of us. Because I suddenly want to hear her bones rattle. I want to feel the softness of her flesh give, to hear her gasp as my hip bone jams into her. I want to yank her head back until her neck is exposed. I want to rip my hands through her hair until her breath is labored. I want to make her cry and then lick up the tears. And then I want to take my mouth to hers, to devour her alive, to transmit all the things she can't understand.

"This is bullshit! Where the hell are you taking me anyway?" The adrenaline thrumming through me turns my voice into a growl.

Mia looks taken aback. "I told you. I'm taking you to my secret New York haunts."

"Yeah, well, I'm a little over secrets. Do you mind

telling me where we're going. Is that too much to fucking ask?"

"Christ, Adam, when did you become such a . . ."

Egomaniac? Asshole? Narcissist? I could fill in the blank with a million words. They've all been said before.

". . . guy?" Mia finishes.

For a second, I almost laugh. *Guy*? That's the best she's got? It reminds me of the story my parents tell about me, how when I was a little kid and would get angry, I'd get so worked up and then curse them out by going "You, you, you . . . *piston*!" like it was the worst thing ever.

But then I remember something else, an old conversation Mia and I had late one night. She and Kim had this habit of categorizing everything into diametric categories, and Mia was always announcing a new one. One day she told me that they'd decided that my gender was divvied into two neat piles—Men and Guys. Basically, all the saints of the world: Men. The jerks, the players, the wet T-shirt contest aficionados? They were Guys. Back then, I was a Man.

So I'm a Guy now? A Guy! I allow my hurt to show for half a second. Mia's looking at me with confusion, but not remembering a thing.

Whoever said that the past isn't dead had it backward. It's the future that's already dead, already played out.

This whole night has been a mistake. It's not going to let me rewind. Or unmake the mistakes I've made. Or the promises I've made. Or have her back. Or have me back.

Something's changed in Mia's face. Some type of recognition has clicked on. Because she's explaining herself, how she called me a guy because guys always need to know the plan, the directions, and how she's taking me on the Staten Island Ferry, which isn't really a secret but it's something few Manhattanites ever do, which is a shame because there's this amazing view of the Statue of Liberty and on top of that, the ferry is free and nothing in New York is free, but if I'm worried about crowds we can forget it, but we can also just check it out and if it's not empty—and she's pretty sure it will be this time of night—we can get right back off before it leaves.

And I have no idea if she remembered that conversation about the Man/Guy distinction or not, but it doesn't really matter anymore. Because she's right. I *am* a Guy now. And I can peg the precise night I turned into one.

THIRTEEN

The groupies started showing up right away. Or maybe they'd always been there and I just hadn't noticed. But as soon as we started touring, they were buzzing about like hummingbirds dipping their beaks into spring flowers.

One of the first things we did after we signed with the label was hire Aldous to manage us. *Collateral Damage* was due to come out in September, and the label planned a modest tour in the late fall, but Aldous had different ideas.

"You guys need to get your sea legs back," Aldous

said when we finished mixing the album. "You need to get back on the road."

So right as the album came out, Aldous booked us a series of ten tour dates up and down the West Coast, in clubs we'd played in before, to reconnect with our fan base—or to remind them that we still existed—and to get comfortable playing in front of an audience again.

The label rented us a nice Econoline van, tricked out with a bed in the back, and a trailer to haul our gear, but other than that when we set out, it didn't feel that different from the shows we'd always played.

It was completely different.

For one, right away and for whatever reason, "Animate" was breaking out as a hit single. Even over the course of the two-week tour, its momentum was building and as that happened, you could feel it in every consecutive show we played. They went from well-attended to packed to sold-out to lines around the corner to fire marshals showing up. All in a matter of two weeks.

And the energy. It was like a live wire, like everyone at the shows knew we were right there on the verge and they wanted to be a part of it, a part of our history. It was like we were all in on this secret together. Maybe that's why these were the best, most frenetic, rocking shows we'd ever played—tons of stage diving and people shouting along to the songs, even though nobody had heard any of our new stuff before. And I felt pretty good, pretty vindicated because even though it was just a matter of pure luck that things had gone this way, *I* hadn't blown it for the band after all.

The groupies just seemed part of this wave of energy, this growing swell of fandom. At first, I didn't even think of them as groupies because a lot of the girls I'd known vaguely from the scene. Except whereas before they'd been friendly, now they were brazen in their flirting. After one of our first shows in San Francisco, this hipster chick named Viv who I'd known for a few years came backstage. She had glossy black hair and wiry arms covered in a daisy chain of tattoos. She gave me a huge hug and then a kiss on the mouth. She hung by my side all night long, her hand resting on the small of my back.

At that point, I'd been out of commission for well over a year. Mia and I, well, she'd been in the hospital, then in rehab, and even if she hadn't been covered in stitches, plaster, and pressure bandages, there was no way. All those fantasies about sexy hospital sponge baths are a joke; there is no place *less* of a turn-on than a hospital. The smell alone is one of putrefaction—the opposite of desire.

When she'd come home, it had been to a downstairs room that had been her gran's sewing room, which we'd turned into Mia's bedroom. I'd slept on a nearby couch in the living room. There were spare rooms on the second floor, but Mia, who was still walking with a cane, couldn't handle the stairs at first, and I hadn't wanted to be even that far away.

Even though I was spending every night at Mia's, I'd never officially moved out of the House of Rock, and one night, a few months after Mia had come back to her grandparents', she'd suggested we go there. After dinner with Liz and Sarah, Mia had tugged me up to my room. The minute the door clicked shut behind us, she'd pounced on me, kissing me with her mouth wide open, like she was trying to swallow me whole. I'd been taken aback at first, freaked out by this sudden ardor, worried that it was going to hurt her, and also, not really wanting to look at the stubbly red scar on her thigh where the skin had been taken for her graft or to bang against the snakeskin-like scar on her other leg, even though she kept that one covered with a pressure bandage.

But as she'd kissed me, my body had begun waking up to her, and with it, my mind had gone, too. We'd laid down on my futon. But then, right as things had gotten going, she'd started crying. I couldn't tell at first because the little sobs had sounded just the same as the little moans she'd been giving off moments before. But soon, they'd grown in intensity, something awful and animal coming from deep within her. I'd asked if I'd hurt her, but she'd said that wasn't it and asked me to leave the room. When she'd come out fully dressed, she'd asked to go home.

She'd tried to start things up with me once more after that. A summer night a few weeks before she'd left for Juilliard. Her grandparents had gone away to visit her aunt Diane, so we'd had the house to ourselves for the night, and Mia had suggested we sleep in one of the upstairs bedrooms since by then the stairs were no longer a problem for her. It had been hot. We'd opened the windows and kicked off the antique quilt and just gotten under the sheet. I remember feeling all self-conscious, sharing a bed with her after all that time. So I'd grabbed a book for myself and propped up a row of pillows for Mia to bolster her leg against, like she liked to at night.

"I'm not ready to sleep," she'd said, running a finger down my bare arm.

She'd leaned in to kiss me. Not the usual dry peck on the lips but a deep, rich, exploring kiss. I'd started to kiss her back. But then I'd remembered that night at the House of Rock, the sound of her animal keening, the look of fear in her eyes when she'd come out of the bedroom. *No way* was I sending her down that wormhole again. No way was *I* going down that wormhole again.

That night in San Francisco, though, with Viv's hand playing on the small of my back, I was raring to go. I spent the night with her at her apartment, and she came with me the next morning to have breakfast with the band before we took off for our next stop. "Call me next time you're in town," she whispered in my ear as we parted ways.

"Back on the horse, my man," Fitzy said, high-fiving me as we piloted the van south.

"Yeah, congratulations," Liz said, a little sadly. "Just don't rub it in." Sarah had recently finished law school and was working for a human rights organization. No more dropping everything to be Liz's plus-one on tours anymore.

"Just because you and Mikey are all tied down, don't come sobbing to us," Fitzy said. "Tour time is playtime, right, Wilde Man?"

"Wilde Man?" Liz asked. "Is that how it's gonna be?"

"No," I said.

"Hey, if the name fits . . ." Fitzy said. "Good thing I hit Fred Meyer for the economy box of condoms before we left."

In L.A., there was another girl waiting. And in San Diego, another. But none of it felt skeevy. Ellie, the girl in L.A. was an old friend, and Laina, the one in San Diego, was a grad student—smart and sexy and older. Nobody had any illusions that these flings were leading to grand romance.

It wasn't until our second-to-last gig that I met a girl whose name I never did catch. I noticed her from the stage. She locked eyes on me the entire set and wouldn't stop staring. It was weirding me out but also building me up. I mean she was practically undressing me with her eyes. You couldn't help but feel powerful and turned on, and it felt good to be so obviously wanted again.

Our label was throwing us a CD-release party after the show, invitation only. I didn't expect to see her there. But after a few hours, there she was, striding up to me in an outfit that was half hooker, half supermodel: skirt cut up to there, boots that could double as military-grade weaponry.

She marched right up to me and announced in a not-too-quiet voice: "I've come all the way from England to fuck you." And with that, she grabbed my hand and led me out the door and to her hotel room.

The next morning was awkward like none of the morning afters had been. I did a walk of shame to the bathroom, quickly dressed and tried to slip out, but she was right there, packed and ready to go. "What are you doing?" I asked.

"Coming with you?" she said, as though it was obvious.

"Coming with me where?"

"To Portland, love."

Portland was our last show and a sort of homecoming as we'd all be basing there now. Not in a communal House of Rock anymore. Liz and Sarah were getting their own place. Mike was moving in with his girlfriend. And Fitzy and I were renting a house together. But we were all still in the same area, within walking distance to one another and the rehearsal space we now rented.

"We're in a van. Not a tour bus," I told her, looking down at my Converse. "And Portland's the last show, a kind of friends-and-family thing. You shouldn't come." *And you are not my love.*

She frowned and I'd slunk out the door, thinking that was the last of it. But when I showed up to sound check in Portland, she was there, waiting for me in the Satyricon. I told her to leave, not very nicely. It was along the lines of: *There's a name for this and it's called stalking.* I was a dick, I know, but I was tired. I'd asked her not to come. And she was freaking me out in a big way. Not just her. Four girls in two weeks was doing my head in. I needed to be alone.

"Piss off, Adam. You're not even a bloody rock star

yet, so stop acting like such a self-important wanker. And you weren't even that good." This she shouted in front of everyone.

So I had the roadies throw her out. She left screaming insults about me, my sexual prowess, my ego.

"Wilde Man, indeed," Liz said, raising an eyebrow.

"Yeah," I said, feeling like the opposite of a wild man, actually wanting to sneak into a room and hide. I didn't know it yet, but once the real tour started—the one our label sent us on after the album went haywire, a five-month slog of sold-out shows and groupies galore—all I'd wanted to do was hide. Given my isolationist tendencies, you'd think I'd have learned to stay away from the freebie affection on such constant offer. But after shows, I craved connection. I craved skin—the taste of another woman's sweat. If it couldn't be *hers*, well, then anyone's would do . . . for a few hours. But I'd learned one lesson—no more overnight guests.

So, that night in Seattle may have been the first time I became a guy. But it wasn't the last.

FOURTEEN

The boogeyman sleeps on your side of the bed
Whispers in my ear: "Better off dead."
Fills my dreams with sirens and lights of regret
Kisses me gently when I wake up in a sweat

"BOO!"

COLLATERAL DAMAGE, TRACK 3

I go with Mia to the ferry anyway. Because what else am I going to do? Throw a tantrum because she hasn't kept an up-to-date catalog of every conversation we've ever had. *It's called moving on.*

And she's right about the ferry being dead. At four thirty in the morning, not a lot of demand for Staten Island. There are maybe a dozen people sprawled out in the downstairs deck. One trio of late-night stragglers is sacked out on a bench, rehashing the evening, but as we pass them, one of the girls lifts her head and stares at me. Then she asks her friend, "Dude, is that Adam Wilde?"

The friend laughs. "Yeah. And next to him is Britney Spears. Why the hell would Adam Wilde be on the Staten Island Ferry?"

I'm asking myself the same question.

But this is apparently one of Mia's things, and this is her farewell-to-New-York-even-though-I'm-not-actually-leaving tour. So I follow her upstairs to the bow of the boat near the railing.

As we pull away from New York, the skyline recedes behind us and the Hudson River opens up to one side, the harbor to the other. It's peaceful out here on the water, quiet except for a pair of hopeful seagulls following in our wake, squawking for food, I guess, or maybe just some company in the night. I start to relax in spite of myself.

And after a few minutes, we're close to the Statue of Liberty. She's all spotlit in the night, and her torch is also illuminated, like there's really a flame in there, welcoming the huddled masses. *Yo, lady, here I am.*

I've never been to the Statue of Liberty. Too many crowds. Aldous once invited me on a private helicopter tour, but I don't do choppers. But now that she's right here, I can see why this is on Mia's list. In pictures, the statue always looks kind of grim, determined, But up close, she's softer. She has a look on her face, like she knows something you don't.

"You're smiling," Mia says to me.

And I realize I am. Maybe it's being granted a special pass to do something I thought was off-limits. Or maybe the statue's look is contagious.

"It's nice," Mia says. "I haven't seen it in a while."

"It's funny," I reply, "because I was just thinking about her." I gesture toward the statue. "It's like she has some kind of secret. The secret to life."

Mia looks up. "Yeah. I see what you mean."

I blow air out my lips. "*I* could really use that secret."

Mia tilts her head out over the railing. "Yeah? So ask her for it."

"Ask her?"

"She's right there. No one's here. No tourists crawling around her feet like little ants. Ask her for her secret."

"I'm not going to ask her."

"You want me to do it? I will, but it's your question, so I think you should do the honors."

"You make a habit of talking to statues?"

"Yes. And pigeons. Now, are you going to ask?"

I look at Mia. She's got her arms crossed across her chest, a little impatient. I turn back to the railing. "Um. Statue? Oh, Statue of Liberty," I call out quietly. No one is around, but this is still really embarrassing.

"Louder," Mia prods.

What the hell. "Hey, excuse me," I call out, "what's your secret?"

We both cock our ears out over the water, as though we expect an answer to come racing back.

"What did she say?" Mia asks.

"Liberty."

"Liberty," Mia repeats, nodding in agreement. "No, wait, I think there's more. Hang on." She leans out over the railing, widening her eyes. "*Hmm. Hmm.* Aha." She turns to me. "Apparently, she isn't wearing any underwear under her robes, and with the bay breeze, it provides a certain *frisson*."

"Lady Liberty's going commando," I say. "That is *so* French!"

Mia cracks up at that. "Do you think she ever flashes the tourists?"

"No way! Why do you think she has that private little look on her face? All those red-state puritans coming by the boatload, never once suspecting that Old Libs hasn't got panties on. She's probably sporting a Brazilian."

"Okay, I need to lose that visual," Mia groans. "And might I remind you that we're from a red state— sort of."

"Oregon's a divided state," I reply. "Rednecks to the east, hippies to the west."

"Speaking of hippies, and going commando . . ."

"Oh, no. Now that's a visual I really don't need."

"Mammary Liberation Day!" Mia crows, referring to some sixties holdover in our town. Once a year a bunch of women spend the day topless to protest the inequity that it's legal for men to go shirtless, but not women. They do it in the summer, but Oregon being Oregon, half the time, it's still freezing, so there was a lot of aging puckered flesh. Mia's mom had always threatened to march; her dad had always bribed her with a dinner out at a fancy restaurant not to.

"Keep Your Class B Misdemeanor off My B Cups," Mia says, quoting one of the movement's more ridiculous slogans between gasps of laughter. "That makes no sense. If you're baring your boobs, why a bra?"

"Sense? It was some stoner hippie idea. And you're looking for logic?"

"Mammary Liberation Day," Mia says, wiping away the tears. "Good old Oregon! That was a lifetime ago."

And it was. So the remark shouldn't feel like a slap. But it does. "How come you never went back?" I ask. It's not really Oregon's abandonment I want explained, but it seems safer to hide under the big green blanket of our state.

"Why should I?" Mia asks, keeping her gaze steady over the water.

"I don't know. The people there."

"The people there can come here."

"To visit them. Your family. At the . . ." *Oh, shit, what am I saying?*

"You mean the graves?"

I just nod.

"Actually, they're the reason I don't go back."

I nod my head. "Too painful."

Mia laughs. A real and genuine laugh, a sound about as expected as a car alarm in a rain forest. "No, it's not like that at all." She shakes her head. "Do you honestly think that where you're buried has any bearing on where your spirit lives?"

Where your spirit lives?

"Do you want to know where my family's spirits live?"

I suddenly feel like I'm talking to a spirit. The ghost of rational Mia.

"They're here," she says, tapping her chest. "And here," she says, touching her temple. "I hear them all the time."

I have no idea what to say. Were we not just making fun of all the New Agey hippie types in our town two minutes ago?

But Mia's not kidding anymore. She frowns deeply, swivels away. "Never mind."

"No. I'm sorry."

"No, I get it. I sound like a Rainbow Warrior. A freak. A Looney Tune."

"Actually, you sound like your gran."

She stares at me. "If I tell you, you'll call the guys with the straitjackets."

"I left my phone at the hotel."

"Right."

"Also, we're on a boat."

"Good point."

"And if by chance they do show up, I'll just offer myself up. So, what, do they, like, haunt you?"

She takes a deep breath and her shoulders slump as if she's setting down a heavy load. She beckons me over to one of the empty benches. I sit down next to her.

"'Haunt' is not the right word for it. Haunt makes it sound bad, unwelcome. But I do hear them. All the time."

"Oh."

"Not just hear their voices, like the memory of them," she goes on. "I can hear them talk to me. Like now. In real time. About my life."

I must give her a weird look, because she blushes. "I know. I hear dead people. But it's not like *that*. Like remember that crazy homeless woman who used to wander around the college campus claiming she heard voices broadcast to her shopping cart?" I nod. Mia stops for a minute.

"At least I don't *think* it's like that," she says. "Maybe it is. Maybe I am nuts and just don't think I am because crazy people never think they're crazy, right? But I really *do* hear them. Whether it's some kind of angel force like Gran believes, and they're up in some heaven on a direct line to me, or whether it's just the them I've stored inside me, I don't know. And I don't know if it even matters. What matters is that they're with me. All the time. And I *know* I sound like a crazy person, mumbling to myself sometimes, but I'm just talking to Mom about what skirt to buy or to Dad about a recital I'm nervous about or to Teddy about a movie I've seen.

"And I can hear them answer me. Like they're right there in the room with me. Like they never really went away. And here's what's really weird: I couldn't hear them back in Oregon. After the accident, it was like their voices were receding. I thought I was going to totally lose the ability to remember what they even sounded like. But once I got away, I could hear them all the time. That's why I don't want to go back. Well, one of the reasons. I'm scared I'll lose the connection, so to speak."

"Can you hear them now?"

She pauses, listens, nods.

"What are they saying?"

"They're saying it's so good to see you, Adam."

I know she's sort of joking, but the thought that they can see me, keep tabs on me, know what I've done these last three years, it makes me actually shudder in the warm night.

Mia sees me shudder, looks down. "I know, it's crazy. It's why I've never told anyone this. Not Ernesto. Not even Kim."

No, I want to tell her. *You got it wrong. It's not crazy at all.* I think of all the voices that clatter around in my head, voices that I'm pretty sure are just some older, or younger, or just *better* versions of me. There have been times—when things have been really bleak—that I've tried to summon *her*, to have *her* answer me back, but it never works. I just get me. If I want her voice, I have to rely on memories. At least I have plenty of those.

I can't imagine what it would be like to have had her company in my head—the comfort that would've brought. To know that she's had *them* with her all this time, it makes me glad. It also makes me understand why, of the two of us, she seems like the sane one.

FIFTEEN

I'm pretty sure that when babies are born in Oregon, they leave the hospital with birth certificates—and teeny-tiny sleeping bags. Everyone in the state camps. The hippies and the rednecks. The hunters and the tree huggers. Rich people. Poor people. Even rock musicians. *Especially* rock musicians. Our band had perfected the art of punk-rock camping, throwing a bunch of crap into the van with, like, an hour's notice and just driving out into the mountains, where we'd drink beer, burn food, jam on our instruments around the campfire, and sack out under the open sky. Sometimes, on tour, back in the early hardscrabble days, we'd even camp as an alternative to crashing in another crowded, roach-infested rock 'n' roll house.

I don't know if it's because no matter where you live, the wilderness is never that far off, but it just seemed like everyone in Oregon camped.

Everyone, that was, except for Mia Hall.

"I sleep in beds," was what Mia told me the first time I invited her to go camping for a weekend. To which I'd offered to bring one of those blow-up air mattresses, but she'd still refused. Kat had overheard me trying to persuade Mia and had laughed.

"Good luck with that, Adam," she'd said. "Denny and I took Mia camping when she was a baby. We planned to spend a week at the coast, but she screamed for two days straight and we had to come home. She's allergic to camping."

"It's true," Mia had said.

"I'll go," Teddy had offered. "I only ever get to go camp in the backyard."

"Gramps takes you out every month," Denny had replied. "And I take you. You just don't get to go camping with all of us as a *family*." He'd given Mia a look. She'd just rolled her eyes back at him.

So it shocked me when Mia agreed to go camping. It was the summer before her senior year of high school and my first year of college, and we'd hardly seen each other. Things with the band had really started heating up, so I'd been touring for a lot of that summer, and Mia had been away at her band camp and then visiting relatives. She must've been really missing me. It was the only explanation I could imagine for her relenting.

I knew better than to rely on the punk-rock mode of camping. So I borrowed a tent. And one of those foam things to sleep on. And I packed a cooler full of food. I wanted to make everything okay, though to be honest, I wasn't really clear on why Mia was so averse to camping in the first place—she was not a prissy chick, not by a long shot; this was a girl who liked to play midnight basketball—so I had no idea if the creature comforts would help.

When I went to pick her up, her whole family came down to see us off, like we were heading off on a cross-country road trip instead of a twenty-four-hour jaunt. Kat waved me over.

"What'd you pack, for food?" she asked.

"Sandwiches. Fruit. For tonight, hamburgers, baked beans, s'mores. I'm trying for the authentic camping experience."

Kat nodded, all serious. "Good, though you might want to feed her the s'mores first if she gets cranky.

Also, I packed you some provisions." She handed me a half-gallon Ziploc. "In case of emergency, break glass."

"What's all this stuff?"

"Now and Laters. Starburst. Pixie Stix. If she gets too bitchy, just feed her this crap. As long as the sugar high is in effect, you and the wildlife should be safe."

"Well, thanks."

Kat shook her head "You're a braver man than I. Good luck."

"Yeah, you'll need it," Denny replied. Then he and Kat locked eyes for a second and started cracking up.

～

There were plenty of great camping spots within an hour's drive, but I wanted to take us somewhere a little more special, so I wound us deep into the mountains, to this place up an old logging road I'd been to a lot as a kid. When I pulled off the road, onto a dirt path, Mia asked: "Where's the campground?"

"Campgrounds are for tourists. We free camp."

"Free camp?" Her voice rose in alarm.

"Relax, Mia. My dad used to log around here. I know these roads. And if you're worried about showers and stuff—"

"I don't care about the showers."

"Good, because we have our own private pool." I turned off my car and showed Mia the spot. It was right alongside the river, where a small inlet of water pooled calm and crystal clear. The view in all directions was unfettered, nothing but pine trees and mountains, like a giant postcard advertising OREGON!

"It's pretty," Mia admitted, grudgingly.

"Wait till you see the view from the top of the ridge. You up for a walk?"

Mia nodded. I grabbed some sandwiches and waters and two packs of watermelon Now and Laters and we traipsed up the trail, hung out for a while, read our books under a tree. By the time we got back down, it was twilight.

"I'd better get the tent up," I said.

"You need some help?"

"No. You're the guest. You relax. Read your book or something."

"If you say so."

I dumped the borrowed tent pieces on the ground and started to hook up the poles. Except the tent was one of those newfangled ones, where all the poles are in one giant puzzle piece, not like the simple pup tents I'd grown up assembling. After half an hour, I was still struggling with it. The sun was dipping behind the mountains, and Mia had put down her book. She was watching me, a bemused little smile on her face.

"Enjoying this?" I asked, perspiring in the evening chill.

"Definitely. Had I known this was what it would be like, I would've agreed to come ages ago."

"I'm glad you find it so amusing."

"Oh, I do. But are you sure you wouldn't like some help? You'll need me to hold a flashlight if this takes much longer."

I sighed. Held my hands up in surrender. "I'm being bested by a piece of sporting goods."

"Does your opponent have instructions?"

"It probably did at some point."

She shook her head, stood up, grabbed the top of the tent. "Okay, you take this end. I'll do this end. I think the long part loops over the top here."

Ten minutes later we had the tent set up and staked down. I collected some rocks and some kindling for a fire pit and got a campfire going with the firewood I'd brought. I cooked us burgers in a pan over the fire and baked beans directly in the can.

"I'm impressed," Mia said.

"So you like camping?"

"I didn't say that," she said, but she was smiling.

It was only later, after we'd had dinner and s'mores and washed our dishes in the moonlit river and I'd played some guitar around the campfire as Mia sipped tea and chowed through a pack of Starburst, that I finally understood Mia's issue with camping.

It was maybe ten o'clock, but in camping time, that's like two in the morning. We got into our tent, snuggled into the double sleeping bag. I pulled Mia to me. "Wanna know the best part about camping?"

I felt her whole body tense up—but not in the good way. "What was that?" she whispered.

"What was what?"

"I heard something," she said.

"It was probably just an animal," I said.

She flicked on the flashlight. "How do you know that?"

I took the flashlight and shined it on her. Her eyes were huge. "You're scared?"

She looked down and—barely—nodded her head.

"The only thing you need to worry about out here is bears and they're only interested in the food, which is why we put it all away in the car," I reassured her.

"I'm not scared of bears," Mia said disdainfully.

"Then what is it?"

"I, I just feel like such a sitting target out here."

"Sitting target for who?"

"I don't know, people with guns. All those hunters."

"That's ridiculous. Half of Oregon hunts. My whole family hunts. They hunt animals, not campers."

"I know," she said in a small voice. "It's not really that, either. I just feel . . . defenseless. It's just, I don't know, the world feels so big when you're out in the wide open. It's like you don't have a place in it when you don't have a home."

"Your place is right here," I whispered, laying her down and hugging her close.

She snuggled into me. "I know." She sighed. "What a freak! The granddaughter of a retired Forest Service biologist who's scared of camping."

"That's just the half of it. You're a classical cellist whose parents are old punk rockers. You're a *total* freak. But you're *my* freak."

We lay there in silence for a while. Mia clicked off the flashlight and scooted closer to me. "Did you hunt as a kid?" she whispered. "I've never heard you mention it."

"I used to go out with my dad," I murmured back. Even though we were the only people within miles, something about the night demanded we speak in hushed tones. "He always said when I was twelve I'd get a rifle for my birthday and he'd teach me to shoot. But when I was maybe nine, I went out with some older cousins and one of them loaned me his rifle. And it must've been beginner's luck or something because I shot a rabbit. My cousins were all going crazy. Rabbits are small and quick and hard for even seasoned hunters to kill, and I'd hit one on my first try. They went to get it so we could bring it back to show everyone and maybe stuff it for a trophy. But when I saw it all bloody, I just started crying. Then I started screaming that we had to take it to a vet, but of course it was dead. I wouldn't let them bring it back. I made them bury it in the forest. When my dad heard, he told me that the point of hunting was to take some sustenance from the animal, whether we eat it or skin it or something, otherwise it was a waste of a life. But I think he knew I wasn't cut out for it because when I turned twelve, I didn't get a rifle; I got a guitar."

"You never told me that before," Mia said.

"Guess I didn't want to blow my punk-rock credibility."

"I would think that would cement it," she said.

"Nah. But I'm emocore all the way, so it works."

A warm silence hung in the tent. Outside, I could hear the low hoot of an owl echo in the night. Mia nudged me in the ribs. "You're such a softy!"

"This from the girl who's scared of camping!"

She chuckled. I pulled her closer to me, wanting to eradicate any distance between our bodies. I pushed her hair off her neck and nuzzled my face there. "Now you owe me an embarrassing story from your childhood," I murmured into her ear.

"All my embarrassing stories are still happening," she replied.

"There must be one I don't know."

She was silent for a while. Then she said: "Butterflies."

"Butterflies?"

"I was terrified of butterflies."

"What is it with you and nature?"

She shook with silent laughter. "I know," she said. "And can there be a less-threatening creature than a butterfly? They only live, like, two weeks. But I used to freak any time I saw one. My parents did everything they could to desensitize me: bought me books on butterflies, clothes with butterflies, put up butterfly posters in my room. But nothing worked."

"Were you like attacked by a gang of monarchs?" I asked.

"No," she said. "Gran had this theory behind my phobia. She said it was because one day I was going to have to go through a metamorphosis like a caterpillar transforming into a butterfly and that scared me, so butterflies scared me."

"That sounds like your gran. How'd you get over your fear?"

"I don't know. I just decided not to be scared of them anymore and then one day I wasn't."

"Fake it till you make it."

"Something like that."

"You could try that with camping."

"Do I have to?"

"Nah, but I'm glad you came."

She'd turned to face me. It was almost pitch-black in the tent but I could see her dark eyes shining. "Me too. But do we have to go to sleep? Can we just stay like this for a while?"

"All night long if you want. We'll tell our secrets to the dark."

"Okay."

"So let's hear another one of your irrational fears."

Mia grasped me by the arms and pulled herself in to my chest, like she was burrowing her body into mine. "I'm scared of losing you," she said in the faintest of voices.

I pushed her away so I could see her face and kissed the top of her forehead. "I said 'irrational' fears. Because that's not gonna happen."

"It still scares me," she murmured. But then she went on to list other random things that freaked her out and I did the same, and we kept whispering to each other, telling stories from our childhoods, deep, deep into the night until finally Mia forgot to be scared and fell asleep.

The weather turned cool a few weeks later, and that winter was when Mia had her accident. So that actually turned out to be the last time I went camping. But even if it weren't, I still think it would be the best trip of my life. Whenever I remember it, I just picture our tent, a little ship glowing in the night, the sounds of Mia's and my whispers escaping like musical notes, floating out on a moonlit sea.

SIXTEEN

You crossed the water, left me ashore
It killed me enough, but you wanted more
You blew up the bridge, a mad terrorist
Waved from your side, threw me a kiss
I started to follow but realized too late
There was nothing but air underneath my feet

"BRIDGE"
<u>**COLLATERAL DAMAGE**</u>**, TRACK 4**

Fingers of light are starting to pry open the night sky. Soon the sun will rise and a new day will inarguably begin. A day in which I'm leaving for London. And Mia for Tokyo. I feel the countdown of the clock ticking like a time bomb.

We're on the Brooklyn Bridge now, and though Mia hasn't said so specifically, I feel like this must be the last stop. I mean, we're leaving Manhattan—and not a round-trip like our cruise out to Staten Island and back was. And also, Mia has decided, I guess, that since she's pulled some confessionals, it's my turn. About halfway across the bridge, she stops suddenly and turns to me.

"So what's up with you and the band?" she asks.

There's a warm wind blowing, but I suddenly feel cold. "What do you mean, 'what's up?'"

Mia shrugs. "Something's up. I can tell. You've hardly talked about them all night. You guys used to be inseparable, and now you don't even live in the same state. And why didn't you go to London together?"

"I told you, logistics."

"What was so important that they couldn't have waited one night for you?"

"I had to, to do some stuff. Go into the studio and lay down a few guitar tracks."

Mia eyes me skeptically. "But you're on tour for a new album. Why are you even recording?"

"A promo version of one of our singles. More of this," I say, frowning as I rub my fingers together in a money-money motion.

"But wouldn't you be recording together?"

I shake my head. "It doesn't really work like that anymore. And besides, I had to do an interview with *Shuffle.*"

"An interview? Not with the band? Just with you? That's what I don't get."

I think back to the day before. To Vanessa LeGrande. And out of the blue, I'm recalling the lyrics to "Bridge," and wondering if maybe discussing this with Mia Hall above the dark waters of the East River isn't such a hot idea. At least it isn't Friday the thirteenth anymore.

"Yeah. That's kinda how it works these days, too," I say.

"Why do they only want just you? What do they want to know about?"

I really don't want to talk about this. But Mia's like a bloodhound, tracking a scent, and I know her well enough to know that I can either throw her a piece of bloody meat, or let her sniff her way to the real pile of stinking corpses. I go for the diversion.

"Actually, that part's kinda interesting. The reporter, she asked about you."

"What?" Mia swivels around to face me.

"She was interviewing me and asked about you. About us. About high school." The look of shock on Mia's face, I savor it. I think about what she said earlier, about her life in Oregon being a lifetime ago. *Well, maybe not such a lifetime ago!* "That's the first time that's happened. Kinda strange coincidence, all things considered."

"I don't believe in coincidences anymore."

"I didn't tell her anything, but she'd gotten a hold of

the old *Cougar* yearbook. The one with our picture—Groovy and the Geek."

Mia shakes her head. "Yeah, I *so* loved that nickname."

"Don't worry. I didn't say anything. And for good measure, I smashed her recorder. Destroyed all evidence."

"Not *all* the evidence." She stares at me. "The *Cougar* lives on. I'm sure Kim will be delighted to know her early work may turn up in a national magazine." She shakes her head and chuckles. "Once Kim gets you in her shutter, you're stuck forever. So it was pointless to destroy that reporter's recorder."

"I know. I just sort of lost it. She was this very provocative person, and she was trying to get a rise out of me with all these insults-disguised-as-compliments."

Mia nods knowingly. "I get that, too. It's the worst! 'I was fascinated by the Shostakovich you played tonight. So much more subdued than the Bach,' she says in a snooty voice. 'Translation: The Shostakovich sucked.'"

I can't imagine the Shostakovich ever sucking, but I won't deny us this common ground.

"So what did she want to know about me?"

"She had plans to do this big exposé, I guess, on what makes Shooting Star tick. And she went digging around our hometown and talked to people we went to high

school with. And they told her about us . . . about the
. . . about what we were. And about you and what
happened . . ." I trail off. I look down at the river, at a
passing barge, which, judging by its smell, is carrying
garbage.

"And what really happened?" Mia asks.

I'm not sure if this is a rhetorical question, so I force
my own voice into a jokey drawl. "Yeah, that's what I'm
still trying to figure out."

It occurs to me that this is maybe the most honest
thing I've said all night, but the way I've said it trans-
forms it into a lie.

"You know, my manager warned me that the accident might get a lot of attention as my profile went up,
but I didn't think that the connection to you would be
an issue. I mean, I did in the beginning. I sort of waited
for someone to look me up—ghosts of girlfriends past—
but I guess I wasn't interesting enough compared to
your other, um, attachments."

She thinks *that's* why none of the hacks have pestered
her, because she's not as interesting as Bryn, who I guess
she *does* know about. If only she knew how the band's
inner circle has bent over backward to keep her name
out of things, to not touch the bruise that blooms at the
mere mention of her. That right at this very moment
there are riders in interview contracts that dictate whole

swaths of forbidden conversational topics that, though they don't name her specifically, are all about obliterating her from the record. Protecting her. And me.

"I guess high school really is ancient history," she concludes.

Ancient history? Have you really relegated us to the trash heap of the Dumb High-School Romance? And if that's the case, why the hell can't I do the same?

"Yeah, well you plus me, we're like MTV plus Lifetime," I say, with as much jauntiness as I can muster. "In other words, shark bait."

She sighs. "Oh, well. I suppose even sharks have to eat."

"What's that supposed to mean?"

"It's just, I don't particularly want my family history dragged through the public eye, but if that's the price to be paid for doing what you love, I guess I'll pay it."

And we're back to this. The notion that music can make it all worthwhile—I'd *like* to believe. I just don't. I'm not even sure that I ever did. It isn't the *music* that makes me want to wake up every day and take another breath. I turn away from her toward the dark water below.

"What if it's not what you love?" I mumble, but my voice gets lost in the wind and the traffic. But at least I've said it out loud. I've done that much.

I need a cigarette. I lean against the railing and look uptown toward a trio of bridges. Mia comes to stand beside me as I'm fumbling to get my lighter to work.

"You should quit," she says, touching me gently on the shoulder.

For a second, I think she means the band. That she heard what I said before and is telling me to quit Shooting Star, leave the whole music industry. I keep waiting for someone to advise me to quit the music business, but no one ever does. Then I remember how earlier tonight, she told me the same thing, right before she bummed a cigarette. "It's not so easy," I say.

"Bullshit," Mia says with a self-righteousness that instantly recalls her mother, Kat, who wore her certitude like a beat-up leather jacket and who had a mouth on her that could make a roadie blush. "Quitting's not hard. *Deciding* to quit is hard. Once you make that mental leap, the rest is easy."

"Really? Was that how you quit me?"

And just like that, without thinking, without saying it in my head first, without arguing with myself for days, it's out there.

"So," she says, as if speaking to an audience under the bridge. "He finally says it."

"Was I not supposed to? Am I just supposed to let this whole night go without talking about what you did?"

"*No*," she says softly.

"So why? Why did you go? Was it because of the voices?"

She shakes her head. "It wasn't the voices."

"Then what? What was it?" I hear the desperation in my own voice now.

"It was lots of things. Like how you couldn't be yourself around me."

"What are you talking about?"

"You stopped talking to me."

"That's absurd, Mia. I talked to you all the time!"

"You talked to me, but you didn't. I could see you having these two-sided conversations. The things you wanted to say to me. And the words that actually came out."

I think of all the dual conversations I have. With everyone. Is *that* when it started? "Well, you weren't exactly easy to talk to," I shoot back. "Anything I said was the wrong thing."

She looks at me with a sad smile. "I know. It wasn't just you. It was you plus me. It was us."

I just shake my head. "It's not true."

"Yes it is. But don't feel bad. Everyone walked on eggshells around me. But with you, it was painful that you couldn't be real with me. I mean, you barely even touched me."

As if to reinforce the point, she places two fingers on the inside of my wrist. Were smoke to rise and the imprints of her two fingers branded onto me, I wouldn't be the least bit surprised. I have to pull away just to steady myself.

"You were healing," is my pathetic reply. "And if I recall, when we did try, you freaked."

"Once," she says. "Once."

"All I wanted was for you to be okay. All I wanted was to help you. I would've done *anything*."

She drops her chin to her chest. "Yes, I know. You wanted to rescue me."

"Damn, Mia. You say that like it's a bad thing."

She looks up at me. The sympathy is still in her eyes, but there's something else now, too: a fierceness; it slices up my anger and reconstitutes it as dread.

"You were so busy trying to be my savior that you left me all alone," she says. "I know you were trying to help, but it just felt, at the time, like you were pushing me away, keeping things from me for my own good and making me more of a victim. Ernesto says that people's good intentions can wind up putting us in boxes as confining as coffins."

"Ernesto? What the hell does he know about it?"

Mia traces the gap between the wooden boardwalk planks with her toe. "A lot, actually. His parents were killed when he was eight. He was raised by his grandparents."

I know what I'm supposed to feel is sympathy. But the rage just washes over me. "What, is there some *club*?" I ask, my voice starting to crack. "A grief club that I can't join?"

I expect her to tell me no. Or that I'm a member. After all, I lost them, too. Except even back then, it had been different, like there'd been a barrier. That's the thing you never expect about grieving, what a competition it is. Because no matter how important they'd been to me, no matter how *sorry* people told me they were, Denny and Kat and Teddy weren't my family, and suddenly that distinction had mattered.

Apparently, it still does. Because Mia stops and considers my question. "Maybe not a grief club. But a guilt club. From being left behind."

Oh, don't talk to me about guilt! My blood runs thick with it. On the bridge, now I feel tears coming. The only way to keep them at bay is to find the anger that's sustained me and push back with it. "But you could've at least told me," I say, my voice rising to a shout. "Instead of dropping me like a one-night stand, you could've had the decency to break up with me instead of leaving me wondering for three years. . . ."

"I didn't plan it," she says, her own pitch rising. "I

didn't get on that plane thinking we'd split up. You were *everything* to me. Even as it was happening, I didn't believe it was happening. But it was. Just being here, being away, it was all so much easier in a way I didn't anticipate. In a way I didn't think my life could be anymore. It was a huge relief."

I think of all the girls whose backs I couldn't wait to see in retreat. How once their sound and smell and voices were gone, I felt my whole body exhale. A lot of the time Bryn falls into this category. *That's how my absence felt to Mia?*

"I planned to tell you," she continues, the words coming out in a breathless jumble now, "but at first I was so confused. I didn't even know what was happening, only that I was feeling better *without* you and how could I explain that *to* you? And then time went by, you didn't call me, when you didn't pursue it, I just figured that you, *you* of all people, you understood. I knew I was being a chickenshit. But I thought . . ." Mia stumbles for a second then regains her composure. "I thought I was allowed that. And that you understood it. I mean you seemed to. You wrote: 'She says I have to pick: Choose you, or choose me. She's the last one standing.' I don't know. When I heard 'Roulette' I just thought you *did* understand. That you were angry, but you knew. I had to choose *me*."

"*That's* your excuse for dropping me without a word? There's cowardly, Mia. And then there's cruel! Is that who you've become?"

"Maybe it was who I needed to be for a while," she cries. "And I'm sorry. I know I should've contacted you. Should've explained. But you weren't all that accessible."

"Oh, bullshit, Mia. I'm inaccessible to most people. But you? Two phone calls and you could've tracked me down."

"It didn't feel that way," she said. "You were this . . ." she trails off, miming an explosion, the same as Vanessa LeGrande had done earlier in the day. "Phenomenon. Not a person anymore."

"That's such a load of crap and you should know it. And besides, that was more than a year after you left. *A year.* A year in which I was curled up into a ball of misery at my parents' house, Mia. Or did you forget that phone number, too?"

"No." Mia's voice is flat. "But I couldn't call you at first."

"Why?" I yell. "Why not?"

Mia faces me now. The wind is whipping her hair this way and that so she looks like some kind of mystical sorceress, beautiful, powerful, and scary at the same time. She shakes her head and starts to turn away.

Oh, no! We've come this far over the bridge. She can

blow the damn thing up if she wants to. But not without telling me everything. I grab her, turn her to face me. "Why not? Tell me. You owe me this!"

She looks at me, square in the eye. Taking aim. And then she pulls the trigger. "Because I hated you."

The wind, the noise, it all just goes quiet for a second, and I'm left with a dull ringing in my ear, like after a show, like after a heart monitor goes to flatline.

"Hated me? Why?"

"You made me stay." She says it quietly, and it almost gets lost in the wind and the traffic and I'm not sure I heard her. But then she repeats it louder this time. "You made me stay!"

And there it is. A hollow blown through my heart, confirming what some part of me has always known.

She knows.

The electricity in the air has changed; it's like you can smell the ions dancing. "I still wake up every single morning and for a second I forget that I don't have my family anymore," she tells me. "And then I remember. Do you know what that's like? Over and over again. It would've been so much easier . . ." And suddenly her calm facade cracks and she begins to cry.

"Please," I hold up my hands. "Please don't . . ."

"No, you're right. You have to let me say this, Adam! You have to hear it. It would've been easier to die. It's not that I want to be dead now. I don't. I have a lot in my life that I get satisfaction from, that I love. But some days, especially in the beginning, it was so hard. And I couldn't help but think that it would've been so much simpler to go with the rest of them. But you—you asked me to stay. You *begged* me to stay. You stood over me and you made a promise to me, as sacred as any vow. And I can understand why you're angry, but you can't blame me. You can't hate me for taking your word."

Mia's sobbing now. I'm wracked with shame because I brought her to this.

And suddenly, I get it. I understand why she summoned me to her at the theater, why she came after me once I left her dressing room. *This* is what the farewell tour is really all about—Mia completing the severance she began three years ago.

Letting go. Everyone talks about it like it's the easiest thing. Unfurl your fingers one by one until your hand is open. But my hand has been clenched into a fist for three years now; it's frozen shut. All of me is frozen shut. And about to shut down completely.

I stare down at the water. A minute ago it was calm and glassy but now it's like the river is opening up, churning, a violent whirlpool. It's that vortex, threatening to swallow me whole. I'm going to drown in it, with nobody, *nobody* in the murk with me.

I've blamed her for all of this, for leaving, for ruining me. And maybe that was the seed of it, but from that one little seed grew this tumor of a flowering plant. And *I'm* the one who nurtures it. I water it. I care for it. I nibble from its poison berries. I let it wrap around my neck, choking the air right out of me. I've done that. All by myself. All to myself.

I look at the river. It's like the waves are fifty feet high, snapping at me now, trying to pull me over the bridge into the waters below.

"I can't do this anymore!" I yell as the carnivorous waves come for me.

Again, I scream, *"I can't do this anymore!"* I'm yelling to the waves and to Liz and Fitzy and Mike and Aldous, to our record executives and to Bryn and Vanessa and the paparazzi and the girls in the U Mich sweatshirts and the scenesters on the subway and everyone who wants a piece of me when there aren't enough pieces to go around. But mostly I'm yelling it to myself.

"I CAN'T DO THIS ANYMORE!" I scream louder than I've ever screamed in my life, so loud my breath is knocking down trees in Manhattan, I'm sure of it. And as I battle with invisible waves and imaginary vortexes and demons that are all too real and of my own making, I actually feel something in my chest open, a feeling so intense it's like my heart's about to burst. And I just let it. I just let it out.

When I look up, the river is a river again. And my hands, which had been gripping the railing of the bridge so tight that my knuckles had gone white, have loosened.

Mia is walking away, walking toward the other end of the bridge. Without me.

I get it now.

I have to make good on my promise. To let her go. To really let her go. To let us both go.

SEVENTEEN

I started playing in my first band, Infinity 89, when I was fourteen years old. Our first show was at a house party near the college campus. All three of us in the band—me on guitar, my friend Nate on bass, and his older brother Jonah on drums—sucked. None of us had been playing for long, and after the gig we found out that Jonah had bribed the host of the party to let us play. It's a little-known fact that Adam Wilde's first foray into playing rock music in front of an audience might never have happened had Jonah Hamilton not pitched in for a keg.

The keg turned out to be the best thing about that show. We were so nervous that we turned the amps up too loud, creating a frenzy of feedback that made the neighbors complain, and then we overcompensated by playing so low that we couldn't hear one another's instruments.

What I could hear in the pauses between songs was the sound of the party: the din of beer bottles clinking, of mindless chatter, of people laughing, and, I swear, in the back room of the house, people watching *American Idol*. The point is, I could hear all this because our band was so crappy that no one bothered to acknowledge that we were playing. We weren't worth cheering. We were too bad to even boo. We were simply ignored. When we finished playing, the party carried on as if we'd never gone on.

We got better. Never great, but better. And never good enough to play anything but house parties. Then Jonah went off to college, and Nate and I were left without a drummer, and that was the end of Infinity 89.

Thus began my brief stint as a lone singer-songwriter about town, playing in coffeehouses, mostly. Doing the café circuit was marginally better than the house parties. With just me and a guitar, I didn't need to up the volume that much, and people in the audience were mostly respectful. But as I played, I was still distracted by the sounds of things other than the music: the hiss of the cappuccino maker, the intellectual college students' hushed conversations about Important Things, the giggles of girls. After the show, the giggles grew louder as the girls came up to me to talk, to ask me about my inspiration, to offer me mix CDs they'd made, and sometimes to offer other things.

One girl was different. She had ropy muscled arms and a fierce look in her eyes. The first time she spoke to me she said only: "You're wasted."

"Nope. Sober as a stone," I replied.

"Not that kind of wasted," she said, arching her pierced eyebrow. "You're wasted on acoustic. I saw you play before in that terrible band of yours, but you were really good, even for a child such as yourself."

"Thanks. I think."

"You're welcome. I'm not here for flattery. I'm here for recruitment."

"Sorry. I'm a pacifist."

"Funny! I'm a dyke, one who likes to ask and tell, so I'm also ill-suited for the military. No, I'm putting together a band. I think you're an outrageously talented guitar player so I'm here to rob the cradle, artistically speaking."

I was barely sixteen years old and a little bit intimidated by this ballsy chick, but I'd said why not. "Who else is in the band?"

"Me on drums. You on guitar."

"And?"

"Those are the most important parts, don't you think? Fantastic drummers and singing guitar players don't grow on trees, not even in Oregon. Don't worry, I'll fill in the blanks. I'm Liz by the way." She stuck out her hand. It was crusted with calluses, always a good sign on a drummer.

Within a month, Liz had drafted Fitzy and Mike, and we'd christened ourselves Shooting Star and started writing songs together. A month after that, we had our first gig. It was another house party, but nothing like the ones I'd played with Infinity 89. Right from the get-go, something was different. When I slashed out my first chord, it was like turning off a light. Everything just fell silent. We had people's attention and we kept it. In the empty space between songs, people cheered and then got quiet, anticipating our next song. Over time, they'd start shouting requests. After a while, they got to know our lyrics so well that they'd sing along, which was handy when I spaced a lyric.

Pretty soon, we moved on to playing in bigger clubs. I could sometimes make out bar sounds in the background—the clink of glasses, the shouts of orders to a bartender. I also started to hear people scream my name for the first time. "Adam!" "Over here!" A lot of those voices belonged to girls.

The girls I mostly ignored. At this point, I'd started obsessing about a girl who never came to our shows but who I'd seen playing cello at school. And when Mia had become my girlfriend, and then started coming to my shows—and to my surprise, seemed to actually enjoy, if not the gigs, then at least our music—I sometimes listened for her. I wanted to hear her voice calling out my name, even though I knew that was something she'd never do. She was a reluctant plus-one. She tended to hang backstage and watch me with a solemn intensity. Even when she loosened up enough to sometimes watch the show like a normal person, from the audience, she remained pretty reserved. But still, I listened for the sound of her voice. It never seemed to matter that I didn't hear it. Listening for her was half the fun.

As the band got bigger and the shows got bigger, the cheers just grew louder. And then for a while, it all went quiet. There was no music. No band. No fans. No Mia.

When it came back—the music, the gigs, the crowds—it all sounded different. Even during that two-week tour right on the heels of *Collateral Damage*'s release, I could tell how much had changed just by how different everything sounded. The wall of sound as we played enveloped the band, almost as if we were playing in a bubble made of nothing other than our own noise. And in between the songs, there was this screaming and shrieking. Soon, much sooner than I ever could've imagined, we were playing these enormous venues: arenas and stadiums, to more than fifteen thousand fans.

At these venues, there are just so many people, and so much sound, that it's almost impossible to differentiate a specific voice. All I hear, aside from our own instruments now blaring out of the most powerful speakers available, is that wild scream from the crowd when we're backstage and the lights go down right before we go out. And once we're onstage, the constant shrieking of the crowd melds so it sounds like the furious howl of a hurricane; some nights I swear I can feel the breath of those fifteen thousand screams.

I don't like this sound. I find the monolithic nature of it disorienting. For a few gigs, we traded our wedge monitors for in-ear pieces. It was perfect sound, as though we were in the studio, the roar of the crowd blocked off. But that was even worse in a way. I feel so disconnected from the crowds as it is, by the distance between them and us, a distance separated by a vast expanse of stage and an army of security keeping fans from bounding up to touch us or stage-dive the way they used to. But more than that, I don't like that it's so hard to hear any one single voice break through. I dunno. Maybe I'm still listening for that one voice.

Every so often during a show, though, as me or Mike pause to retune our guitars or someone takes a swig from a bottle of water, I'll pause and strain to pick out a voice from the crowd. And every so often, I can. Can hear someone shouting for a specific song or screaming *I love you!* Or chanting my name.

As I stand here on the Brooklyn Bridge I'm thinking about those stadium shows, of their hurricane wail of white noise. Because all I can hear now is a roaring in my head, a wordless howl as Mia disappears and I try to let her.

But there's something else, too. A small voice trying to break through, to puncture the roar of nothingness. And the voice grows stronger and stronger, and it's *my* voice this time and it's asking a question: *How does she know?*

EIGHTEEN

Are you happy in your misery?
Resting peaceful in desolation?
It's the final tie that binds us
The sole source of my consolation

"BLUE"

COLLATERAL DAMAGE, TRACK 6

Mia's gone.

The bridge looks like a ghost ship from another time even as it fills up with the most twenty-first-century kind of people, early-morning joggers.

And me, alone again.

But I'm still standing. I'm still breathing. And somehow, I'm okay.

But still the question is gaining momentum and volume: *How does she know?* Because I never told anyone what I asked of her. Not the nurses. Not the grandparents. Not Kim. And not Mia. So how does she know?

*If you stay, I'll do whatever you want. I'll quit the band,
go with you to New York. But if you need me to go away, I'll
do that, too. Maybe coming back to your old life would just be
too painful, maybe it'd be easier for you to erase us. And that
would suck, but I'd do it. I can lose you like that if I don't lose
you today. I'll let you go. If you stay.*

That was my vow. And it's been my secret. My burden. My shame. That I asked her to stay. That she listened. Because after I promised her what I promised
her, and played her a Yo-Yo Ma cello piece, it had
seemed as if she *had* heard. She'd squeezed my hand
and I'd thought it was going to be like in the movies, but all she'd done was squeeze. And stayed unconscious. But that squeeze had turned out to be her first
voluntary muscle movement; it was followed by more
squeezes, then by her eyes opening for a flutter or two,
and then longer. One of the nurses had explained that
Mia's brain was like a baby bird, trying to poke its way
out of an eggshell, and that squeeze was the beginning
of an emergence that went on for a few days until she
woke up and asked for water.

Whenever she talked about the accident, Mia said the
entire week was a blur. She didn't remember a thing.
And I wasn't about to tell her about the promise I'd
made. A promise that in the end, I was forced to keep.

But *she knew*.

No wonder she hates me.

In a weird way, it's a relief. I'm so tired of carrying this secret around. I'm so tired of feeling bad for making her live and feeling angry at her for living without me and feeling like a hypocrite for the whole mess.

I stand there on the bridge for a while, letting her get away, and then I walk the remaining few hundred feet to the ramp down. I've seen dozens of taxis pass by on the roadway below, so even though I have no clue where I am, I'm pretty sure I'll find a cab to bring me back to my hotel. But when I get down the ramp, I'm in a plaza area, not where the car traffic lets out. I flag down a jogger, a middle-aged guy chugging off the bridge, and ask where I can get a taxi, and he points me toward a bunch of buildings. "There's usually a queue on weekdays. I don't know about weekends, but I'm sure you'll find a cab somewhere."

He's wearing an iPod and has pulled out the earbuds to talk to me, but the music is still playing. And it's Fugazi. The guy is running to Fugazi, the very tail end of "Smallpox Champion." Then the song clicks over and it's "Wild Horses" by the Rolling Stones. And the music, it's like, I dunno, fresh bread on an empty stomach or a woodstove on a frigid day. It's reaching out of the earbuds and beckoning me.

The guy keeps looking at me. "Are you Adam Wilde?

From Shooting Star?" he asks. Not at all fanlike, just curious.

It takes a lot of effort to stop listening to the music and give him my attention. "Yeah." I reach out my hand.

"I don't mean to be rude," he says after we shake, "but what are you doing walking around Brooklyn at six thirty on a Saturday morning? Are you lost or something?"

"No, I'm not lost. Not anymore anyway."

Mick Jagger is crooning away and I practically have to bite my lip to keep from singing along. It used to be I never went anywhere without my tunes. And then it was like everything else, take it or leave it. But now I'll take it. Now I *need* it. "Can I ask you for an insanely huge and just plain insane favor?" I ask.

"Okaaay?"

"Can I borrow your iPod? Just for the day? If you give me your name and address, I'll have it messengered over to you. I promise you'll have it back by tomorrow's run."

He shakes his head, laughs. "One butt-crack-of-dawn run a weekend is enough for me, but yeah, you can borrow it. The buzzer on my building doesn't work, so just deliver it to Nick at the Southside Café on Sixth Avenue in Brooklyn. I'm in there every morning."

"Nick. Southside Café. Sixth Avenue. Brooklyn. I won't forget. I promise."

"I believe you," he says, spooling the wires. "I'm afraid you won't find any Shooting Star on there."

"Better yet. I'll have this back to you by tonight."

"Don't worry about it," he says. "Battery was fully charged when I left so you should be good for at least . . . an hour. The thing's a dinosaur." He chuckles softly. Then he takes off running, tossing a wave at me without looking back.

I plug myself into the iPod; it's truly battered. I make a note to get him a new one when I return this one. I scroll through his collection—everything from Charlie Parker to Minutemen to Yo La Tengo. He's got all these playlists. I choose one titled Good Songs. And when the piano riff at the start of the New Pornographers' "Challengers" kicks in, I know I've put myself in good hands. Next up is some Andrew Bird, followed by a kick-ass Billy Bragg and Wilco song I haven't heard in years and then Sufjan Stevens's "Chicago," which is a song I used to love but had to stop listening to because it always made me feel too stirred up. But now it's just right. It's like a cool bath after a fever sweat, helping to soothe the itch of all those unanswerable questions I just can't be tormenting myself with anymore.

I spin the volume up all the way, so it's blasting even

my battle-worn eardrums. That, along with the racket of downtown Brooklyn waking up—metal grates grinding and buses chugging—is pretty damn loud. So when a voice pierces the din, I almost don't hear it. But there it is, the voice I've been listening for all these years.

"Adam!" it screams.

I don't believe it at first. I turn off Sufjan. I look around. And then there she is, in front of me now, her face streaked with tears. Saying my name again, like it's the first word I've ever heard.

I let go. I truly did. But there she is. Right in front of me.

"I thought I'd lost you. I went back and looked for you on the bridge but I didn't see you and I figured you'd walked back to the Manhattan side and I got this dumb idea that I could beat you over in a cab and ambush you on the other side. I know this is selfish. I heard what you said up there on the bridge, but we can't leave it like that. *I* can't. Not again. We have to say good-bye differently. Bet—"

"Mia?" I interrupt. My voice is a question mark and a caress. It stops her babbling cold. "How did you know?"

The question is out of the blue. Yet she seems to know exactly what I'm asking about. "Oh. That," she says. "That's complicated."

I start to back away from her. I have no right to ask

her, and she isn't under any obligation to tell me. "It's okay. We're good now. *I'm* good now."

"No, Adam, stop," Mia says.

I stop.

"I want to tell you. I *need* to tell you everything. I just think I need some coffee before I can get it together enough to explain."

She leads me out of downtown into a historic district to a bakery on a cobblestoned street. Its windows are darkened, the door locked, by all signs the place is closed. But Mia knocks and within a minute a bushy-haired man with flour clinging to his unruly beard swings open the door and shouts *bonjour* to Mia and kisses her on both cheeks. Mia introduces me to Hassan, who disappears into the bakery, leaving the door open so that the warm aroma of butter and vanilla waft into the morning air. He returns with two large cups of coffee and a brown paper bag, already staining dark with butter. She hands me my coffee, and I open it to see it's steaming and black just like I like it.

It's morning now. We find a bench on the Brooklyn Heights Promenade, another one of Mia's favorite New York spots, she tells me. It's right on the East River, with Manhattan so close you can almost touch it. We sit in companionable silence, sipping our coffee, eating Hassan's still-warm croissants. And it feels so good, so like old times that part of me would like to just click a magic stopwatch, exist in this moment forever. Except there are no magic stopwatches and there are questions that need to be answered. Mia, however, seems in no rush. She sips, she chews, she looks out at the city. Finally, when she's drained her coffee, she turns to me.

"I didn't lie before when I said I didn't remember anything about the accident or after," she begins. "But then I did start remembering things. Not exactly remembering, but hearing details of things and having them feel intensely familiar. I told myself it was because I'd heard the stories over and over, but that wasn't it.

"Fast-forward about a year and a half. I'm on my seventh or eighth therapist."

"So you *are* in therapy?"

She gives me a cockeyed look. "Of course I am. I used to go through shrinks like shoes. They all told me the same thing."

"Which is?"

"That I was *angry*. That I was *angry* the accident happened. That I was *angry* I was the only survivor. That I was *angry* at you." She turns to me with an apologetic grimace. "The other stuff all made sense, but *you* I didn't get. I mean, why you? But I was. I could feel how . . ." she trails off for a second, "furious I was," she finishes quietly. "There were all the obvious reasons, how you withdrew from me, how much the accident changed us. But it didn't add up to this *lethal* fury I suddenly felt once I got away. I think really, somewhere in me, I must've known all along that you asked me to stay—way before I actually remembered it. Does that make *any* sense?"

No. Yes. I don't know. "None of this makes *sense*," I say.

"I know. So, I was angry with you. I didn't know why. I was angry with the world. I did know why. I hated all my therapists for being useless. I was this little ball of self-destructive fury, and none of them could do anything but tell me that I was a little ball of self-destructive fury. Until I found Nancy, not one of them helped me as much as my Juilliard profs did. I mean, hello! I *knew* I was angry. Tell me what to *do* with the anger, please. Anyhow, Ernesto suggested hypnotherapy. It helped him quit smoking, I guess." She elbows me in the ribs.

Of course Mr. Perfect wouldn't smoke. And of course, he'd be the one who helped Mia unearth the reason she hates me.

"It was kind of risky," Mia continues. "Hypnosis tends to unlock hidden memories. Some trauma is just too much for the conscious mind to handle and you have to go in through a back door to access it. So I reluctantly submitted to a few sessions. It wasn't what I thought it would be. No swinging amulet, no metronome. It was more like those guided imagery exercises they'd sometimes have us do at camp. At first, nothing happened, and then I went to Vermont for the summer and quit.

"But a few weeks later, I started to get these flashes. Random flashes. Like I could remember a surgery, could actually hear the specific music the doctors played in the operating room. I thought about calling them to ask if what I remembered was true, but so much time had passed I doubted they'd remember. Besides, I didn't really feel like I needed to ask them. My dad used to say that when I was born I looked so totally familiar to him, he was overwhelmed with this feeling that he'd known me all his life, which was funny, considering how little I looked like him or Mom. But when I had my first memories, I felt that same certainty, that they were real and mine. I didn't put the pieces together fully until I was working on a cello piece—a lot of memories seem to hit when I'm playing—anyhow, it was Gershwin, *Andante con moto e poco rubato*."

I open my mouth to say something, but at first nothing comes out. "I played you that," I finally say.

"I know." She doesn't seem surprised by my confirmation.

I lean forward, put my head between my knees, and take deep breaths. I feel Mia's hand gently touch the back of my neck.

"Adam?" Her voice is tentative. "There's more. And here's where it gets a little freaky. It makes a certain sense to me that my mind somehow recorded the things that were happening around my body while I was unconscious. But there are other things, other memories. . . ."

"Like what?" My voice is a whisper.

"Most of it is hazy, but I have certain strong memories of things I couldn't know because I wasn't there. I have this one memory. It's of you. It's dark out. And you're standing outside the hospital entrance under the floodlights, waiting to come see me. You're wearing your leather jacket, and looking up. Like you're looking for me. Did you do that?"

Mia cups my chin up and lifts my face, this time apparently seeking some affirmation that this moment was real. I want to tell her that she's right, but I've completely lost the ability to speak. My expression, however, seems to offer the validation she's after. She nods her head slightly. "How? How, Adam? How could I know that?"

I'm not sure if the question's rhetorical or if she thinks I have a clue to her metaphysical mystery. And I'm in

209

no state to answer either way because I'm crying. I don't realize it till I taste the salt against my lips. I can't remember the last time I've cried but, once I accept the mortification of sniveling like a baby, the floodgates open and I'm sobbing now, in front of Mia. In front of the whole damn world.

NINETEEN

The first time I ever saw Mia Hall was six years ago. Our high school had this arts program and if you chose music as your elective, you could take music classes or opt for independent study to practice in the studios. Mia and I both went for the independent study.

I'd seen her playing her cello a couple of times but nothing had really registered. I mean she was cute and all, but, not exactly my type. She was a classical musician. I was a rock guy. Oil and water and all that.

I didn't really notice her until the day I saw her *not* playing. She was just sitting in one of the soundproof practice booths, her cello resting gently against her knees, her bow poised a few inches above the bridge. Her eyes were closed and her brow was a little furrowed. She was so still, it seemed like she'd taken a brief vacation from her body. And even though she wasn't moving, even though her eyes were closed, I somehow knew that she was listening to music then, was grabbing the notes from the silence, like a squirrel gathering acorns for the winter, before she got down to the business of playing. I stood there, suddenly riveted by her, until she seemed to wake up and start playing with this intense concentration. When she finally looked at me, I hustled away.

After that, I became kind of fascinated by her and by what I guessed was her ability to hear music in the silence. Back then, I'd wanted to be able to do that, too. So I took to watching her play, and though I told myself the reason for my attention was because she was as dedicated a musician as I was and that she was cute, the truth was that I also wanted to understand what she heard in the silence.

During all the time we were together, I don't think I ever found out. But once I was with her, I didn't need to. We were both music-obsessed, each in our own way. If we didn't entirely understand the other person's obsession, it didn't matter, because we understood our own.

I know the exact moment Mia is talking about. Kim and I had driven to the hospital in Sarah's pink Dodge Dart. I don't remember asking Liz's girlfriend to borrow her car. I don't remember driving it. I don't remember piloting the car up into the hills where the hospital is or how I even knew the way. Just that one minute I was in a theater in downtown Portland, sound-checking for that night's show when Kim showed up to deliver the awful news. And the next minute I was standing outside the hospital.

What Mia inexplicably remembers, it's sort of the first pinpoint of clarity in that whole petri-dish blur between hearing the news and arriving at the trauma center. Kim and I had just parked the car and I'd walked out of the garage ahead of her. I'd needed a couple of seconds to gather my strength, to steel myself for what I was about to face. And I'd remembered looking at the hulking hospital building and wondering if Mia was somewhere in there, and feeling a heart-in-throat panic that she'd died in the time it had taken Kim to fetch me. But then I'd felt this wave of something, not really hope, not really relief, but just a sort of knowledge that Mia was still in there. And that had been enough to pull me through the doors.

They say that things happen for a reason, but I don't know that I buy that. I don't know that I'll ever see a reason for what happened to Kat, Denny, and Teddy that day. But it took forever to get in to see Mia. I got turned away from the ICU by Mia's nurses, and then Kim and I devised this whole plan to sneak in. I don't think I realized it at the time, but I think in a weird way, I was probably stalling. I was gathering my strength. I didn't want to lose it in front of her. I guess part of me somehow knew that Mia, deep in her coma, would be able to tell.

Of course, I ended up losing it in front of her anyway. When I finally saw her the first time, I almost blew chunks. Her skin looked like tissue paper. Her eyes were covered with tape. Tubes ran in and out of every part of her body, pumping liquids and blood in and draining some scary-ass shit out. I'm ashamed to say it, but when I first came in, I wanted to run away.

But I couldn't. I wouldn't. So instead, I just focused on the part of her that still looked remotely like Mia— her hands. There were monitors stuck to her fingers, but they still looked like her hands. I touched the fingertips of her left hand, which felt worn and smooth, like old leather. I ran my fingers across the nubby calluses of her thumbs. Her hands were freezing, just like they always were, so I warmed them, just like I always did.

And it was while warming her hands that I thought about how lucky it was that they looked okay. Because without hands, there'd be no music and without music, she'd have lost everything. And I remember thinking that somehow Mia had to realize that, too. That she needed to be reminded that she had the music to come back to. I ran out of the ICU, part of me fearing that I might never see her alive again, but somehow knowing that I had to do this one thing. When I came back, I played her the Yo-Yo Ma.

And that's also when I made her the promise. The promise that she's held me to.

I did the right thing. I know it now. I must've always known, but it's been so hard to see through all my anger. And it's okay if she's angry. It's even okay if she hates me. It was selfish what I asked her to do, even if it wound up being the most unselfish thing I've ever done. The most unselfish thing I'll have to *keep* doing.

But I'd do it again. I know that now. I'd make that promise a thousand times over and lose her a thousand times over to have heard her play last night or to see her in the morning sunlight. Or even without that. Just to know that she's somewhere out there. Alive.

Mia watches me lose my shit all over the Promenade. She bears witness as the fissures open up, the lava leaking out, this great explosion of what, I guess to her, must look like grief.

But I'm not crying out of grief. I'm crying out of gratitude.

TWENTY

Someone wake me when it's over
When the evening silence softens golden
Just lay me on a bed of clover
Oh, I need help with this burden

"HUSH"
COLLATERAL DAMAGE, TRACK 13

When I get a grip over myself and calm down, my limbs feel like they're made of dead wood. My eyes start to droop. I just drank a huge cup of insanely strong coffee, and it might as well have been laced with sleeping pills. I could lie down right here on this bench. I turn to Mia. I tell her I need to sleep

"My place is a few blocks away," she says. "You can crash there."

I have that floppy calm that follows a cry. I haven't felt this way since I was a child, a sensitive kid, who would scream at some injustice or another until, all cried out, my mother would tuck me into bed. I picture Mia, tucking me into a single boy's bed, pulling the Buzz Lightyear sheets up to my chin.

It's full-on morning now. People are awake and out and about. As we walk, the quiet residential area gives way to a commercial strip, full of boutiques, cafés, and the hipsters who frequent them. I'm recognized. But I don't bother with any subterfuge—no sunglasses, no cap. I don't try to hide at all. Mia weaves among the growing crowds and then turns off onto a leafy side street full of brownstones and brick buildings. She stops in front of a small redbrick carriage house. "Home sweet home. It's a sublet from a professional violinist who's with the Vienna Philharmonic now. I've been here a record nine months!"

I follow her into the most compact house I've ever seen. The first floor consists of little more than a living room and kitchen with a sliding-glass door leading out to a garden that's twice as deep as the house. There's a white sectional couch, and she motions for me to lie down on it. I kick off my shoes and flop onto one of the sections, sinking into the plush cushions. Mia lifts my head, places a pillow underneath it, and a soft blanket over me, tucking me in just as I'd hoped she would.

I listen for the sound of her footsteps on the stairs

up to what must be the bedroom, but instead, I feel a slight bounce in the upholstery as Mia takes up a position on the other end of the couch. She rustles her legs together a few times. Her feet are only inches away from my own. Then she lets out a long sigh and her breathing slows into a rhythmic pattern. She's asleep. Within minutes, so am I.

When I wake up, light is flooding the apartment, and I feel so refreshed that for a second I'm sure I've slept for ten hours and have missed my flight. But a quick glance at the kitchen clock shows me it's just before two o'clock, still Saturday. I've only been asleep for a few hours, and I have to meet Aldous at the airport at five.

Mia's still asleep, breathing deeply and almost snoring. I watch her there for a while. She looks so peaceful and so familiar. Even before I became the insomniac I am now, I always had problems falling asleep at night, whereas Mia would read a book for five minutes, roll onto her side, and be gone. A strand of hair has fallen onto her face and it gets sucked into her mouth and back out again with each inhalation and exhalation. Without even thinking I lean over and move the strand away, my finger accidentally brushing her lips. It feels so natural, so much like the last three years haven't passed, that I'm almost tempted to stroke her cheeks, her chin, her forehead.

Almost. But not quite. It's like I'm seeing Mia through a prism and she's mostly the girl I knew but something has changed, the angles are off, and so now, the idea of me touching a sleeping Mia isn't sweet or romantic. It's stalkerish.

I straighten up and stretch out my limbs. I'm about to wake her—but can't quite bring myself to. Instead, I walk around her house. I was so out of it when we came in a few hours ago, I didn't really take it in. Now that I do, I see that it looks oddly like the house Mia grew up in. There's the same mismatched jumble of pictures on the wall—a Velvet Elvis, a 1955 poster advertising the World Series between the Brooklyn Dodgers and the New York Yankees—and the same decorative touches, like chili-pepper lights festooning the doorways.

And photos, they're everywhere, hanging on the walls, covering every inch of counter and shelf space. Hundreds of photos of her family, including what seem to be the photos that once hung in her old house. There's Kat and Denny's wedding portrait; a shot of Denny in a spiked leather jacket holding a tiny baby Mia in one of his hands; eight-year-old Mia, a giant grin on her face, clutching her cello; Mia and Kat holding a red-faced Teddy, minutes after he was born. There's even that heartbreaking shot of Mia reading to Teddy, the one that I could never bear to look at at Mia's grandparents', though somehow here, in Mia's place, it doesn't give me that same kick in the gut.

I walk through the small kitchen, and there's a veritable gallery of shots of Mia's grandparents in front of a plethora of orchestra pits, of Mia's aunts and uncles and cousins hiking through Oregon mountains or lifting up pints of ale. There are a jumble of shots of Henry and Willow and Trixie and the little boy who must be Theo. There are pictures of Kim and Mia from high school and one of the two of them posing on top of the Empire State Building—a jolting reminder that their relationship wasn't truncated, they have a history of which I know nothing. There's another picture of Kim, wearing a flak jacket, her hair tangled and down and blowing in a dusty wind.

There are pictures of musicians in formal wear, holding flutes of champagne. Of a bright-eyed man in a tux with a mass of wild curls holding a baton, and the same guy conducting a bunch of ratty-looking kids, and then him again, next to a gorgeous black woman, kissing a not-ratty-looking kid. This must be Ernesto.

I wander into the back garden for my wake-up smoke. I pat my pockets, but all I find there is my wallet, my sunglasses, the borrowed iPod, and the usual assortment of guitar picks that always seem to live on me. Then I remember that I must have left my cigarettes on the bridge. No smokes. No pills. I guess today is the banner day for quitting bad habits.

I come back inside and take another look around. This isn't the house I expected. From all her talk of moving, I'd imagined a place full of boxes, something impersonal and antiseptic. And despite what she'd said about spirits, I wouldn't have guessed that she'd surround herself so snugly with her ghosts.

Except for my ghost. There's not a single picture of me, even though Kat included me in so many of the family shots; she'd even hung a framed photo of me and Mia and Teddy in Halloween costumes above their old living-room mantel, a place of honor in the Hall home. But not here. There are none of the silly shots Mia and I used to take of each other and of ourselves, kissing or mugging while one of us held the camera at arm's length. I loved those pictures. They always cut off half a head or were obscured by someone's finger, but they seemed to capture something true.

I'm not offended. Earlier, I might've been. But I get it now. Whatever place I held in Mia's life, in Mia's heart, was irrevocably altered that day in the hospital three and a half years ago.

Closure. I loathe that word. Shrinks love it. Bryn loves it. She says that I've never had *closure* with Mia.

"More than five million people have bought and listened to my closure," is my standard reply.

Standing here, in this quiet house where I can hear the birds chirping out back, I think I'm kind of getting the concept of closure. It's no big dramatic before-after. It's more like that melancholy feeling you get at the end of a really good vacation. Something special is ending, and you're sad, but you can't be that sad because, hey, it was good while it lasted, and there'll be other vacations, other good times. But they won't be with Mia—or with Bryn.

I glance at the clock. I need to get back to Manhattan, pack up my stuff, reply to the most urgent of the emails that have no doubt piled up, and get myself to the airport. I'll need to get a cab out of here, and before that I'll need to wake Mia up and say a proper goodbye.

I decide to make coffee. The smell of it alone used to rouse her. On the mornings I used to sleep at her house, sometimes I woke up early to hang with Teddy. After I let her sleep to a decent hour, I'd take the percolator right into her room and waft it around until she lifted her head from the pillow, her eyes all dreamy and soft.

I go into the kitchen and instinctively seem to know where everything is, as though this is my kitchen and

I've made coffee here a thousand times before. The metal percolator is in the cabinet above the sink. The coffee in a jar on the freezer door. I spoon the rich, dark powder into the chamber atop the percolator, then fill it with water and put it on the stove. The hissing sound fills the air, followed by the rich aroma. I can almost see it, like a cartoon cloud, floating across the room, prodding Mia awake.

And sure enough, before the whole pot is brewed, she's stretching out on the couch, gulping a bit for air like she does when she's waking up. When she sees me in her kitchen, she looks momentarily confused. I can't tell if it's because I'm bustling around like a housewife or just because I'm here in the first place. Then I remember what she said about her daily wake-up call of loss. "Are you remembering it all over again?" I ask the question. Out loud. Because I want to know and because she asked me to ask.

"No," she says. "Not this morning." She yawns, then stretches again. "I thought I dreamed last night. Then I smelled coffee."

"Sorry," I mutter.

She's smiling as she kicks off her blanket. "Do you really think that if you don't mention my family I'll forget them?"

"No," I admit. "I guess not."

"And as you can see, I'm not trying to forget." Mia motions to the photos.

"I was looking at those. Pretty impressive gallery you've got. Of everyone."

"Thanks. They keep me company."

I look at the pictures, imagining that one day Mia's own children will fill more of her frames, creating a new family for her, a continuing generation that I won't be a part of.

"I know they're just pictures," she continues, "but some days they really help me get up in the morning. Well, them, and coffee."

Ahh, the coffee. I go to the kitchen and open the cabinets where I know the cups will be, though I'm a little startled to find that even these are the same collection of 1950s and 60s ceramic mugs that I've used so many times before; amazed that she's hauled them from dorm to dorm, from apartment to apartment. I look around for my favorite mug, the one with the dancing coffeepots on it, and am so damn happy to find it's still here. It's almost like having my picture on the wall, too. A little piece of me still exists, even if the larger part of me can't.

I pour myself a cup, then pour Mia's, adding a dash of half-and-half, like she takes it.

"I like the pictures," I say. "Keeps things interesting."

Mia nods, blows ripples into her coffee.

"And I miss them, too," I say. "Every day."

She looks surprised at that. Not that I miss them, but, I guess by my admitting it, finally. She nods solemnly. "I know," she says.

She walks around the room, running her fingers lightly along the picture frames. "I'm running out of space," she says. "I had to put up a bunch of Kim's recent shots in the bathroom. Have you talked to her lately?"

She must know what I did to Kim. "No."

"Really? Then you don't know about the *scandale*?"

I shake my head.

"She dropped out of college last year. When the war flared up in Afghanistan, Kim decided, screw it, I want to be a photographer and the best education is in the field. So she just took her cameras and off she went. She started selling all these shots to the AP and the *New York Times*. She cruises around in one of those burkas and hides all her photographic equipment underneath the robes and then whips them off to get her shot."

"I'll bet Mrs. Schein loves that." Kim's mom was notoriously overprotective. The last I'd heard of her, she was having a freak-out that Kim was going to school across the country, which, Kim had said, was precisely the point.

Mia laughs. "At first, Kim told her family she was just

taking a semester off, but now she's getting really successful so she's officially dropped out, and Mrs. Schein has officially had a nervous breakdown. And then there's the fact that Kim's a nice Jewish girl in a very Muslim country." Mia blows on her coffee and sips. "But, on the other hand, now Kim gets her stuff in the *New York Times,* and she just got a feature assignment for *National Geographic*, so it gives Mrs. Schein some bragging ammo."

"Hard for a mother to resist," I say.

"She's a big Shooting Star fan, you know?"

"Mrs. Schein? I always had her pegged as more hip-hop."

Mia grins. "No. She's into death metal. Hard core. *Kim.* She saw you guys play in Bangkok. Said it poured rain and you played right through it."

"She was at that show? I wish she would've come backstage, said hi," I say, even though I know why she wouldn't have. Still, she came to the show. She must have forgiven me a little bit.

"I told her the same thing. But she had to leave right away. She was supposed to be in Bangkok for some R & R, but that rain you were playing in was actually a cyclone somewhere else and she had to run off and cover it. She's a very badass shutterbabe these days."

I think of Kim chasing Taliban insurgents and ducking flying trees. It's surprisingly easy to imagine. "It's funny," I begin.

"What is?" Mia asks.

"Kim being a war photographer. All Danger Girl."

"Yeah, it's a laugh riot."

"That's not how I meant. It's just: Kim. You. Me. We all came from this nowhere town in Oregon, and look at us. All three of us have gone to, well, extremes. You gotta admit, it's kind of weird."

"It's not weird at all," Mia says, shaking out a bowl of cornflakes. "We were all forged in the crucible. Now come on, have some cereal."

I'm not hungry. I'm not even sure I can eat a single cornflake, but I sit down because my place at the Hall family table has just been restored.

Time has a weight to it, and right now I can feel it heavy over me. It's almost three o'clock. Another day is half over and tonight I leave for the tour. I hear the clicking of the antique clock on Mia's wall. I let the minutes go by longer than I should before I finally speak.

"We both have our flights. I should probably get moving," I say. My voice sounds faraway but I feel weirdly calm. "Are there taxis around here?"

"No, we get back and forth to Manhattan by river raft," she jokes. "You can call a car," she adds after a moment.

I stand up, make my way toward the kitchen counter where Mia's phone sits. "What's the number?" I ask.

"Seven-one-eight," Mia begins. Then she interrupts herself. "Wait."

At first I think she has to pause to recall the number, but I see her eyes, at once unsure and imploring.

"There's one last thing," she continues, her voice hesitant. "Something I have that really belongs to you."

"My Wipers T-shirt?"

She shakes her head. "That's long gone, I'm afraid. Come on. It's upstairs."

I follow her up the creaking steps. At the top of the narrow landing to my right I can see her bedroom with its slanted ceilings. To my left is a closed door. Mia opens it, revealing a small studio. In the corner is a cabinet with a keypad. Mia punches in a code and the door opens.

When I see what she pulls out of the cabinet, at first I'm like, *Oh, right, my guitar.* Because here in Mia's little house in Brooklyn is my old electric guitar, my Les Paul Junior. The guitar I bought at a pawnshop with my pizza-delivery earnings when I was a teenager. It's the guitar I used to record all of our stuff leading up to, and including, *Collateral Damage*. It's the guitar I auctioned off for charity and have regretted doing so ever since.

It's sitting in its old case, with my old Fugazi and K Records stickers, with the stickers from Mia's dad's old band, even. Everything is the same, the strap, the dent from when I'd dropped it off a stage. Even the dust smells familiar.

And I'm just taking it all in, so it's a few seconds before it really hits me. This is *my* guitar. *Mia* has my guitar. Mia is the one who *bought* my guitar for some exorbitant sum, which means that Mia knew it was up for auction. I look around the room. Among the sheet music and cello paraphernalia is a pile of magazines, my face peeking out from the covers. And then I remember something back on the bridge, Mia justifying why she left me by reciting the lyrics to "Roulette."

And suddenly, it's like I've been wearing earplugs all night and they've fallen out, and everything that was muffled is now clear. But also so loud and jarring.

Mia has my guitar. It's such a straightforward thing and yet I don't know that I would've been more surprised had Teddy popped out of the closet. I feel faint. I sit down. Mia stands right in front of me, holding my guitar by the neck, offering it back to me.

"You?" is all I can manage to choke out.

"Always me," she replies softly, bashfully. "Who else?"

My brain has vacated my body. My speech is reduced to the barest of basics. "But . . . why?"

"Somebody had to save it from the Hard Rock Café," Mia says with a laugh. But I can hear the potholes in her voice, too.

"But . . ." I grasp for the words like a drowning man reaching for floating debris," . . . you said you *hated* me?"

Mia lets out a long, deep sigh. "I know. I needed someone to hate, and you're the one I love the most, so it fell to you."

She's holding out the guitar, nudging it toward me. She wants me to take it, but I couldn't lift a cotton ball right now.

She keeps staring, keeps offering.

"But what about Ernesto?"

A look of puzzlement flits across her face, followed by amusement. "He's my mentor, Adam. My friend. He's *married*." She looks down for a beat. When her gaze returns, her amusement has hardened into defensiveness. "Besides, why should you care?"

Go back to your ghost, I hear Bryn telling me. But she has it wrong. *Bryn* is the one who's been living with the ghost—the specter of a man who never stopped loving someone else.

"There never would've been a Bryn if you hadn't decided you needed to hate me," I reply.

Mia takes this one square on the chin. "I don't hate you. I don't think I ever really did. It was just anger. And once I faced it head-on, once I understood it, it dissipated." She looks down, takes a deep breath, and exhales a tornado. "I know I owe you some kind of an apology; I've been trying to get it out all night but it's like those words—apology, sorry—are too measly for what you deserve." She shakes her head. "I know what I did to you was so wrong, but at the time it also felt so necessary to my survival. I don't know if those two things can both be true but that's how it was. If it's any comfort, after a while, when it didn't feel necessary anymore, when it felt hugely wrong, all I was left with was the magnitude of my mistake, of my missing you. And I had to watch you from this distance, watch you achieve your dreams, live what seemed like this perfect life."

"It's *not* perfect," I say.

"I get that *now*, but how was I supposed to know? You were so very, very far from me. And I'd accepted that. Accepted that as my punishment for what I'd done. And then . . ." she trails off.

"What?"

She takes a gulp of air and grimaces. "And then Adam Wilde shows up at Carnegie Hall on the biggest night of my career, and it felt like more than a coincidence. It felt like a gift. From them. For my first recital ever, they gave me a cello. And for this one, they gave me you."

Every hair on my body stands on end, my whole body alert with a chill.

She hastily wipes tears from her eyes with the back of her hand and takes a deep breath. "Here, are you going to take this thing or what? I haven't tuned it for a while."

I used to have dreams like this. Mia back from the not-dead, in front of me, alive to me. But it got so even in the dreams I knew they were unreal and could anticipate the blare of my alarm, so I'm kind of listening now, waiting for the alarm to go off. But it doesn't. And when I close my fingers around the guitar, the wood and strings are solid and root me to the earth. They wake me up. And she's still here.

And she's looking at me, at my guitar, and at her cello and at the clock on the windowsill. And I see what she wants, and it's the same thing I've wanted for years now but I can't believe that after all this time, and now that we're out of time, she's asking for it. But still, I give a little nod. She plugs in the guitar, tosses me the cord, and turns on the amp.

"Can you give me an E?" I ask. Mia plucks her cello's

E string. I tune from that and then I strum an A-minor, and as the chord bounces off the walls, I feel that dash of electricity shimmy up my spine in a way it hasn't done for a long, long time.

I look at Mia. She's sitting across from me, her cello between her legs. Her eyes are closed and I can tell she's doing that thing, listening for something in the silence. Then all at once, Mia seems to have heard what she needs to hear. Her eyes are open and on me again, like they never left. She picks up her bow, gestures toward my guitar with a slight tilt of her head. "Are you ready?" she asks.

There are so many things I'd like to tell her, top among them is that I've always been ready. But instead, I turn up the amp, fish a pick out of my pocket, and just say yes.

TWENTY-ONE

We play for what seems like hours, days, years. Or maybe it's seconds. I can't even tell anymore. We speed up, then slow down, we scream our instruments. We grow serious. We laugh. We grow quiet. Then loud. My heart is pounding, my blood is grooving, my whole body is thrumming as I'm remembering: *Concert* doesn't mean standing up like a target in front of thousands of strangers. It means coming together. It means harmony.

When we finally pause, I'm sweating and Mia's panting hard, like she's just sprinted for miles. We sit there in silence, the sound of our rapid breaths slowing in tandem, the beats of our hearts steadying. I look at the clock. It's past five. Mia follows my gaze. She lays down her bow.

"What now?" she asks.

"Schubert? Ramones?" I say, though I know she's not taking requests. But all I can think to do is keep playing because for the first time in a long time there's nothing more I want to do. And I'm scared of what happens when the music ends.

Mia gestures to the digital clock flashing ominously from the windowsill. "I don't think you'll make your flight."

I shrug. Never mind the fact that there are at least ten other flights to London tonight alone. "Can you make yours?"

"I don't *want* to make mine," she says shyly. "I have a spare day before the recitals begin. I can leave tomorrow."

All of a sudden, I picture Aldous pacing in Virgin's departure lounge, wondering where the hell I am, calling a cell phone that's still sitting on some hotel nightstand. I think of Bryn, out in L.A., unaware of an earthquake going down here in New York that's sending a tsunami her way. And I realize that before there's a next, there's a now that needs attending to. "I need to make some phone calls," I tell Mia. "To my manager, who's waiting for me . . . and to Bryn."

"Oh, right, of course," she says, her face falling as she rushes to stand up, almost toppling her cello in her fluster. "The phone's downstairs. And I should call Tokyo, except I'm pretty sure it's the middle of the night, so I'll just email and call later. And my travel agent—"

"Mia," I interrupt.

"What?"

"We'll figure this out."

"Really?" She doesn't look so sure.

I nod, though my own heart is pounding and the puzzle pieces are whirling as Mia places the cordless phone in my hand. I go into her garden where it's private and peaceful in the afternoon light, the summer cicadas chirping up a storm. Aldous picks up on the first ring and the minute I hear his voice and start talking, reassuring him that I'm okay, the plans start coming out of my mouth as though long, long contemplated. I explain that I'm not coming to London now, that I'm not making any music video, or doing any interviews, but that I'll be in England for the kickoff of our European tour and that I'll play every single one of those shows. The rest of the plan that's formulating in my head—part of which already solidified in some nebulous way last night on the bridge—I keep to myself, but I think Aldous senses it.

I can't see Aldous so I can't know if he blinks or flinches or looks surprised, but he doesn't miss a beat. "You'll honor all your tour commitments?" he repeats.

"Yep."

"What am I supposed to say to the band?"

"They can make the video without me if they want. I'll see them at the Guildford Festival," I say referring to the big music festival in England that we're headlining to kick off our tour. "And I'll explain everything then."

"Where you gonna be in the meantime? If anyone needs you."

"Tell anyone not to need me," I answer.

The next call is harder. I wish I hadn't chosen today to give up smoking. Instead, I do the deep breathing exercises like the doctors showed me and just dial. A journey of a thousand miles starts with ten digits, right?

"I thought that might be you," Bryn says when she hears my voice. "Did you lose your phone again? Where are you?"

"I'm in New York still. In Brooklyn." I pause, "With Mia."

Stone silence fills the line and I fill that silence with a monologue that's what? . . . I don't know: a running explanation of the night that happened by accident, an acknowledgment that things never were right between us, right the way she wanted them to be, and as a result, I've been a dick of a boyfriend. I tell her I hope she'll do better with the next guy.

"Yeah, I wouldn't worry about that," she says with an attempt at a cackle, but it doesn't quite come out that way. There's a long pause. I'm waiting for her tirade, her recriminations, all the things I have coming. But she doesn't say anything.

"Are you still there?" I ask.

"Yeah, I'm thinking."

"About what?"

"I'm thinking about whether I'd rather she'd have died."

"Jesus, Bryn!"

"Oh, shut up! You don't get to be the outraged one. Not right now. And the answer's no. I don't wish her dead." She pauses. "Not so sure about you, though." Then she hangs up.

I stand there, still clutching the phone to my ear, taking in Bryn's last words, wondering if there might've been a shred of absolution in her hostility. I don't know if it matters because as I smell the cooling air, I feel release and relief wash over me.

After a while, I look up. Mia's standing at the sliding-glass door, awaiting the all clear. I give her a dazed wave and she slowly makes her way to the bricked patio where I'm standing, still holding the phone. She grabs hold of the top of the phone, like it's a relay baton, about to be passed off. "Is everything okay?" she asks.

"I'm freed, shall we say, from my previous commitments."

"Of the tour?" She sounds surprised.

I shake my head. "Not the tour. But all the crap leading up to it. And my other, um, entanglements."

"Oh."

We both just stand there for a while, grinning like goofballs, still grasping the cordless. Finally, I let it go and then gently detach the receiver from her grasp and place it on the iron table, never releasing my grip of her hand.

I run my thumb over the calluses on her thumb and up and down the bony ridge of her knuckles and wrist. It's at once so natural and such a privilege. This is *Mia* I'm touching. And she's *allowing* it. Not just allowing it, but closing her eyes and leaning into it.

"Is this real. Am I allowed to hold this hand?" I ask, bringing it up to my stubbly cheek.

Mia's smile is melting chocolate. It's a kick-ass guitar solo. It's everything good in this world. *"Mmmm,"* she answers.

I pull her to me. A thousand suns rise from my chest. "Am I allowed to do *this*?" I ask, taking both of her arms in mine and slow-dancing her around the yard.

Her entire face is smiling now. "You're allowed," she murmurs.

I run my hands up and down her bare arms. I spin her around the planters, bursting with fragrant flowers. I bury my head into her hair and breathe the smell of her, of the New York City night that's seared into her. I follow her gaze upward, to the heavens.

"So, do you think they're watching us?" I ask as I give the scar on her shoulder the slightest of kisses and feel arrows of heat shoot through every part of me.

"Who?" Mia asks, leaning into me, shivering slightly.

"Your family. You seem to think they keep tabs on you. You think they can see this?" I loop my arms around her waist and kiss her right behind her ear, the way that used to drive her crazy, the way that, judging by the sharp intake of breath and the nails that dig into my side, still does. It occurs to me that there's seemingly something creepy in my line of questioning, but it doesn't feel that way. Last night, the thought of her family knowing my actions shamed me, but now, it's not like I want them to see *this*, but I want them to *know* about it, about us.

"I like to think they'd give me some privacy," she

says, opening up like a sunflower to the kisses I'm planting on her jaw. "But my neighbors can definitely see this." She runs her hand through my hair and it's like she electrocuted my scalp—if electrocution felt so good.

"Howdy, neighbor," I say, tracing lazy circles around the base of her clavicle with my finger.

Her hands dip under my T-shirt, my dirty, stinky, thank-you lucky black T-shirt. Her touch isn't so gentle anymore. It's probing, the fingertips starting to tap out a Morse code of urgency. "If this goes on much longer, my neighbors are going to get a show," she whispers.

"We are performers, after all," I reply, slipping my hands under her shirt and running them up the length of her long torso then back down again. Our skins reach outward, like magnets, long deprived of their opposite charge.

I run my finger along her neck, her jawline, and then cup her chin in my hand. And stop. We stand there for a moment, staring at each other, savoring it. And then all at once, we slam together. Mia's legs are off the ground, wrapped around my waist, her hands digging in my hair, my hands tangled in hers. And our lips. There isn't enough skin, enough spit, enough time, for the lost years that our lips are trying to make up for as they find each other. We kiss. The electric current switches to high. The lights throughout all of Brooklyn must be surging.

"Inside!" Mia half orders, half begs, and with her legs still wrapped around me, I carry her back into her tiny home, back to the couch where only hours before we'd slept, separately together.

This time we're wide awake. And all together.

We fall asleep, waking in the middle of the night, ravenous. We order takeout. Eat it upstairs in her bed. It's all like a dream, only the most incredible part is waking up at dawn. With Mia. I see her sleeping form there and feel as happy as I've ever been. I pull her to me and fall back asleep.

But when I wake again a few hours later, Mia's sitting on a chair under the window, her legs wrapped in a tight ball, her body covered in an old afghan that her gran crocheted. And she looks miserable, and the fear that lands like a grenade in my gut is almost as bad as anything I've ever feared with her. And that's saying a lot. All I can think is: *I can't lose you again. It really* will *kill me this time.*

"What's wrong?" I ask, before I lose the nerve to ask it and do something dumb like walk away before my heart gets truly incinerated.

"I was just thinking about high school," Mia says sadly.

"That would put anyone in a foul mood."

Mia doesn't take the bait. She doesn't laugh. She slumps in the chair. "I was thinking about how we're in the same boat all over again. When I was on my way to Juilliard and you were on your way to, well, where you are now." She looks down, twists the yarn from the blanket around her finger until the skin at the tip goes white. "Except we had more time back then to worry about it. And now we have a day, or had a day. Last night was amazing but it was just one night. I really do have to leave for Japan in like seven hours. And you have the band. Your tour." She presses against her eyes with the heels of her hands.

"Mia, stop!" My voice bounces off her bedroom walls. "We are *not* in high school anymore!"

She looks at me, a question hanging in the air.

"Look, my tour doesn't start for another week."

A feather of hope starts to float across the space between us.

"And you know, I was thinking I was craving some sushi."

Her smile is sad and rueful, not exactly what I was going for. "You'd come to Japan with me?" she asks.

"I'm already there."

"I would love that. But then what—I mean I know

244

we can figure something out, but I'm going to be on the road so much and . . . ?"

How can it be so unclear to her when it's like the fingers on my hand to me? "I'll be your plus-one," I tell her. "Your groupie. Your roadie. Your whatever. Wherever you go, I go. If you want that. If you don't, I understand."

"No, I want that. Trust me, I want it. But how would that work? With your schedule? With the band?"

I pause. Saying it out loud will finally make it true. "There is no more band. For me, at least, I'm done. After this tour, I'm finished."

"No!" Mia shakes her head with such force, the long strands of her hair thwack the wall behind her. The determined look on her face is one I recognize all too well, and I feel my stomach bottom out. "You can't do that for me," she adds, her voice softening. "I won't take any more free passes."

"Free passes?"

"For the last three years, everyone, except maybe the Juilliard faculty, has given me a free pass. Worse yet, I gave myself a free pass, and that didn't help me at all. I don't want to be that person, who just takes things. I've taken enough from you. I won't let you throw away the thing you love so much to be my caretaker or porter."

"That's just it," I murmur. "I've sort of fallen out of love with music."

"Because of me," Mia says mournfully.

"Because of life," I reply. "I'll always play music. I may even record again, but right now I just need some blank time with my guitar to remember why I got into music in the first place. I'm leaving the band whether you're part of the equation or not. And as for caretaking, if anything, *I'm* the one who needs it. *I'm* the one with the baggage."

I try to make it sound like a joke, but Mia always could see right through my bullshit; the last twenty-four hours have proven that.

She looks at me with those laser beam eyes of hers. "You know, I thought about that a lot these last couple of years," she says in a choked voice. "About who was there for *you*. Who held your hand while you grieved for all that *you'd* lost?"

Mia's words rattle something loose in me and suddenly there are tears all over my damn face again. I haven't cried in three years and now this is like the second time in as many days.

"*It's my turn to see you through*," she whispers, coming back to me and wrapping me in her blanket as I lose my shit all over again. She holds me until I recover my Y chromosome. Then she turns to me, a slightly faraway look in her eyes. "Your festival's next Saturday, right?" she asks.

I nod.

"I have the two recitals in Japan and one in Korea on Thursday, so I could be out of there by Friday, and you gain a day back when you travel west. And I don't have to be at my next engagement in Chicago for another week after that. So if we flew directly from Seoul to London."

"What are you saying?"

She looks so shy when she asks it, as if there's a snowball's chance in hell that I'd ever say no, as if this isn't what I've always wanted.

"Can I come to the festival with you?"

TWENTY-TWO

"How come I never get to go to any concerts?" Teddy asked.

We were all sitting around the table, Mia, Kat, Denny, Teddy, and me, the third child, who'd taken to eating over. You couldn't blame me. Denny was a way better cook than my mom.

"What's that, Little Man?" Denny asked, spooning a portion of mashed potatoes onto Teddy's plate next to the grilled salmon and the spinach that Teddy had tried—unsuccessfully—to refuse.

"I was looking at the old photo albums. And Mia got

to go to all these concerts all the time. When she was a baby, even. And I never even got to go to one. And I'm practically eight."

"You just turned seven five months ago." Kat guffawed.

"Still. Mia went before she could walk. It's not fair!"

"And who ever told you that life was fair?" Kat asked, raising an eyebrow. "Certainly not me. I am a follower of the School of Hard Knocks."

Teddy turned toward an easier target. "Dad?"

"Mia went to concerts because they were my shows, Teddy. It was our family time."

"And you *do* go to concerts," Mia said. "You come to my recitals."

Teddy looked as disgusted as he had when Denny had served him the spinach. "That doesn't count. I want to go to loud concerts and wear the Mufflers." The Mufflers were the giant headphones Mia had worn as a little kid when she'd been taken to Denny's old band's shows. He'd been in a punk band, a very loud punk band.

"The Mufflers have been retired, I'm afraid," Denny said. Mia's dad had long since quit his band. He now was a middle-school teacher who wore vintage suits and smoked pipes.

"You could come to one of my shows," I said, forking a piece of salmon.

Everyone at the table stopped eating and looked at me, the adult members of the Hall family each giving me a different disapproving look. Denny just looked tired at the can of worms I'd opened. Kat looked annoyed for the subversion of her parental authority. And Mia—who, for whatever reason, had this giant church-state wall between her family and my band—was shooting daggers. Only Teddy—up on his knees in his chair, clapping—was still on my team.

"Teddy can't stay up that late," Kat said.

"You let Mia stay up that late when she was little," Teddy shot back.

"*We* can't stay up that late," Denny said wearily.

"And I don't think it's appropriate," Mia huffed.

Immediately, I felt the familiar annoyance in my gut. Because this was the thing I never understood. On one hand, music was this common bond between Mia and me, and me being an all-rock guy *had* to be part of her attraction. And we both knew that the common ground we'd found at her family's house—where we hung out all the time—made it like a haven for us. But she'd all but banned her family from my shows. In the year we'd been together, they'd never been. Even though Denny and Kat had hinted that they'd like to come, Mia was always making up excuses why this show or that was not the right time.

"Appropriate? Did you just say that it's not 'appropriate' for Teddy to come to my show?" I asked, trying to keep my voice level.

"Yes, I did." She couldn't have sounded more defensive or snippy if she'd tried.

Kat and Denny flashed each other a look. Whatever annoyance they'd had with me had turned to sympathy. They knew what Mia's disapproval felt like.

"Okay, first off, you're sixteen. You're not a librarian. So you're not allowed to say 'appropriate.' And second of all, why the hell isn't it?"

"All right, Teddy," Kat said, scooping up Teddy's dinner plate. "You can eat in the living room in front of the TV."

"No way, I want to watch this!"

"SpongeBob?" Denny offered, pulling him by the elbow.

"By the way," I said to Denny and Kat, "the show I was thinking of is this big festival coming up on the coast next month. It'll be during the day, on a weekend, and outside, so not as loud. That's why I thought it'd be cool for Teddy. For all of you, actually."

Kat's expression softened. She nodded. "That does sound fun." Then she gestured to Mia as if to say: *But you've got bigger fish to fry.*

The three of them shuffled out of the kitchen. Mia

was slunk all the way down in her chair, looking both guilty and like there was no way in hell she was going to give an inch.

"What's your problem?" I demanded. "What's your hang-up with your family and my band? Do you think we suck so badly?"

"No, of course not!"

"Do you resent me and your dad talking music all the time?"

"No, I don't mind the rock-talk."

"So, what is it, Mia?"

The tiniest rebel teardrops formed in the edges of her eyes and she angrily swatted them away.

"What? What *is* the matter?" I asked, softening. Mia wasn't prone to crocodile tears, or to any tears, really.

She shook her head. Lips sealed shut.

"Will you just tell me? It can't be worse than what I'm thinking, which is that you're ashamed of Shooting Star because you think we reek to holy hell."

She shook her head again. "You know that's not true. It's just," she paused, as if weighing some big decision. Then she sighed. "The band. When you're with the band, I already have to share you with everyone. I don't want to add my family to that pot, too." Then she lost the battle and started to cry.

All my annoyance melted. "You dumb-ass," I crooned,

kissing her on the forehead. "You don't share me. You own me."

~

Mia relented. Her whole family came to the festival. It was a fantastic weekend, twenty Northwest bands, not a rain cloud in sight. The whole thing went down in infamy, spawning a live recorded CD and a series of festivals that continue to this day.

Teddy had insisted on wearing the Mufflers, so Kat had spent an hour grumbling and digging through boxes in the basement until she'd found them.

Mia generally liked to hang backstage at shows but when Shooting Star played, she was right in front of the stage, just clear of the mosh pit, dancing with Teddy the whole time.

TWENTY-THREE

First you inspect me
Then you dissect me
Then you reject me
I wait for the day
That you'll resurrect me

"ANIMATE"
COLLATERAL DAMAGE, TRACK 1

When our flight lands in London, it's pissing down rain, so it feels like home to both of us. It's five in the afternoon when we get in. We're due in Guildford that evening. We play the next night. Then it's countdown till total freedom. Mia and I have worked out a schedule for the next three months while I'm touring and she's touring, breaks here and there where we can overlap, visit, see each other. It's not going to be delightful, but compared to the last three years, it'll still feel like heaven.

It's past eight when we get to the hotel. I've asked Aldous to book me at the same place as the rest of the band, not just for the festival but the duration of the tour. Whatever their feelings are going to be about my leaving Shooting Star, sleeping two miles away ain't gonna minimize them. I haven't mentioned Mia to Aldous or anyone, and miraculously, we've managed to keep her name out of the tabloids so far. No one seems to know that I'd spent the last week in Asia with her. Everyone was too busy buzzing about Bryn's new love interest, some Australian actor.

There's a note at the front desk informing me that the band is having a private dinner in the atrium and asking me to join them. I suddenly feel like I'm being led to my execution and after the fifteen-hour trip from Seoul would like nothing more than to shower first, just maybe see them tomorrow. But Mia has her hand on my side. "No, you should go."

"You come, too?" I feel bad asking her. She just played three intensely amazing and crazily well-received concerts in Japan and Korea and then flew halfway around the world and directly into my psychodrama. But all of this will be bearable if she's with me.

"Are you sure?" she asks. "I don't want to intrude."

"Trust me, if anyone's intruding, it's me."

The bellman grabs our stuff to take to our room, and

the concierge leads us across the lobby. The hotel is in an old castle, but it's been taken over with rockers and a bunch of different musicians nod and "hey" me, but I'm too nervous right now to respond. The concierge leads us to a dimly lit atrium. The band's all in there, along with a giant buffet serving a traditional English roast.

Liz turns around first. Things haven't been the same between the two of us since that *Collateral Damage* tour, but the look she gives me now, I don't know how to describe it: Like I'm her biggest disappointment in life, but she tries to rise above it, to tamp it down, to act all casual, like I'm just one of the fans, one of the hangers-on, one of the many people who want something from her that she's not obliged to give. "Adam," she says with a curt nod.

"Liz," I begin cautiously.

"Hey, asshole! Nice of you to join us!" Fitzy's irrepressible voice is both sarcastic and welcoming, like he just can't decide which way to go.

Mike doesn't say anything. He just pretends I don't exist.

And then I feel the brush of Mia's shoulder as she steps out from behind me. "Hi, guys," she says.

Liz's face goes completely blank for a moment. Like she doesn't know who Mia is. Then she looks scared, like she's just seen a ghost. Then my strong, tough, butchy drummer—her lower lip starts to tremble, and then her face crumples. "Mia?" she asks, her voice quavering. "Mia?" she asks louder this time. "Mia!" she says, the tears streaming down her face right before she tackles my girl in a hug.

When she's released her, she holds Mia at arm's length and looks at her and then back at me and then back at Mia. "Mia?" she shouts, both asking and answering her own question. Then she turns to me. And if I'm not forgiven, then at least I'm understood.

⌒

The rain keeps up throughout the next day. "Lovely English summer we're having," everyone jokes. It's become my habit to barricade myself at these types of giant festivals, but realizing that this is probably my last one for a while, at least as a participant, I slip inside the grounds, listen to some of the bands on the side stages, catch up with some old friends and acquaintances, and even talk to a couple of rock reporters. I'm careful not to mention the breakup of the band. That'll come out in time, and I'll let everyone else decide how to release this news. I do, however, briefly comment on Bryn's and my split, which is all over the tabloids anyhow. Asked about my new mystery woman, I simply say "no comment." I know this will *all* come out soon enough, and while

I want to spare Mia the circus, I don't care if the whole world knows we're together.

By the time our nine P.M. slot rolls around, the rain has subsided to a soft mist that seems to dance in the late summer twilight. The crowd has long since accepted the slosh. There's mud everywhere and people are rolling around in it like it's Woodstock or something.

Before the set, the band was nervous. Festivals do that to us. A bigger ante than regular concerts, even stadium shows—festivals have exponentially larger crowds, and crowds that include our musician peers. Except tonight, I'm calm. My chips are all cashed out. There's nothing to lose. Or maybe I've already lost it and found it, and whatever else there might be to lose, it's got nothing to do with what's on this stage. Which might explain why I'm having such a good time out here, pounding through our new songs on my old Les Paul Junior, another piece of history brought back from the dead. Liz did a double take when she saw me pull it out of its old case. "I thought you got rid of that thing," she'd said.

"Yeah, me too," I'd replied, tossing off a private smile at Mia.

We race through the new album and then throw in some bones from *Collateral Damage* and before I know it, we're almost at the end of the set. I look down at the set list that's duct-taped to the front of the stage.

Scrawled there in Liz's block lettering is the last song before we leave for the inevitable encore. "Animate." Our anthem, our old producer Gus Allen, called it. The angstiest screed on *Collateral Damage*, critics called it. Probably our biggest hit of all. It's a huge crowd-pleaser on tours because of the chorus, which audiences love to chant.

It's also one of the few songs we've ever done with any kind of production, a strings section of violins right at the top of the recorded track, though we don't have those for the live version. So as we launch into it, it's not that rolling howl of the crowd's excitement that I hear, but the sound of her cello playing in my head. For a second, I have this vision of just the two of us in some anonymous hotel room somewhere dickering around, her on her cello, me on my guitar, playing this song I wrote for her. And shit, if that doesn't make me so damn happy.

I sing the song with all I've got. Then we get to the chorus: *Hate me. Devastate me. Annihilate me. Re-create me. Re-create me. Won't you, won't you, won't you re-create me.*

On the album, the chorus is repeated over and over, a rasp of fury and loss, and it's become a thing during shows for me to stop singing and turn the mic out toward the audience and let them take over. So I turn the mic toward the fields, and the crowd just goes insane, singing my song, chanting my plea.

I leave them at it and I take a little walk around the stage. The rest of the band sees what's going on so they just keep repping the chorus. When I get closer to the side of the stage, I see her there, where she always felt most comfortable, though for the foreseeable future, she'll be the one out here in the spotlight, and I'll be the one in the wings, and that feels right, too.

The audience keeps singing, keeps making my case, and I just keep strumming until I get close enough to see her eyes. And then I start singing the chorus. Right to her. And she smiles at me, and it's like we're the only two people out here, the only ones who know what's happening. Which is that this song we're all singing together is being rewritten. It's no longer an angry plea shouted to the void. Right here, on this stage, in front of eighty thousand people, it's becoming something else.

This is our new vow.

SHUFFLE

Evolution of a Rock Star

After a three-year hiatus, Shooting Star's Adam Wilde changes up again with a most unexpected solo album.

Former Shooting Star front man Adam Wilde returns to the music scene with both a whisper and a roar with his debut solo album, *Prepare for Landing*. Wilde, once one of the most recognizable names in rock music, chose to quietly release his first album in almost three years with little fanfare and zero publicity on Minneapolis-based independent label Extrascape. But there's no keeping this record from roaring, though not in the ways we've come to expect from Wilde. *Prepare for Landing* represents a huge departure—musically, lyrically, instrumentally, fundamentally—from the onslaught of heavy guitar, firepower, ballast emotion of Wilde's earlier songwriting on Shooting Star's megahit albums, *Collateral Damage* and *BloodSuckerSunshine*. This is a much quieter album, so much so that it's tempting to look backward, to the more jangly, poppy early Shooting Star recordings. But looking to Wilde's past misses this point. This album is nothing if not a sign of evolution.

After abruptly leaving Shooting Star three years ago,

Wilde has all but disappeared from the public eye, but *Prepare for Landing* gives listeners a sense of just how busy the man has been. Perhaps it is the influence of renowned cellist Mia Hall, with whom Wilde has been romantically linked since leaving Shooting Star; but Wilde has both deepened as a songwriter and expanded himself from a guitar player to a multi-instrumentalist, on a par with a Sufjan Stevens or an Andrew Bird. Whereas Shooting Star records were all about heavy guitar riffs mixed with pounding percussives, *Prepare for Landing's* softer tenor allows for the other instruments—Wilde shows up on everything from mandolin to sitar to theremin—to pipe through, giving the album a romantic, dreamy, ethereal feel. Yes, Adam Wilde, ethereal. Who'da thunk it? But the title track, "Prepare for Landing," announces how much things have changed: echoy guitar and a moody piano lend the track a romantic nostalgic flavor. The mandolin on "Happy Birthday" gives that song a necessary soulful note that perfectly balances out its elegiac lyrics: *Another day, another year, to light the candles, without you here.*

But if you strip away all the instruments and the lo-fi sound, you can still see the Adam Wilde DNA at work. Wilde has retained his ability to write extremely catchy hooks, albeit this time around it might be with a banjo riff instead of a guitar, as in the hauntingly beautiful love song "Kaleidoscope Eyes."

Shooting Star fans hoping for a rehash of all the *Sturm und Drang* of the earlier records may be disappointed by Wilde's elegant, nuanced recording but for those listeners who, like Wilde himself, have perhaps matured in the intervening years, this album is a masterpiece.

"PREPARE FOR LANDING"

The seat belt sign is illuminated
The flight attendants beyond frustrated
The passengers are drunk and frayed
A baby's screaming in seat 16A

Another flight from here to where?
Crammed in a sardine can with not enough air
We're on the map, I know that much
But the directions I really need are in your touch

Prepare for landing, says the captain
As the plane arcs down to the looming horizon
Ushering us onto some foreign soil
I touch the ground, and see your smile

Up and down, and down and up
Cokespritebeerpretzelspeanuts
As we careen through empty sky
It feels like nothing but you and I

Prepare for landing, says the captain
Out the window, the sun is setting
Hand in mine, you give a squeeze
You're all the home I'll ever need

"HAPPY BIRTHDAY"

PREPARE FOR LANDING, TRACK 4

Another day, another year
To light the candles, without you here
It's still the day that you were born
She says we laugh as we mourn

Nothing, she tells me, is ever really gone
Not you, not me, not him, it all just rolls along
An object never disappears without any trace
In its absence, there still exists a kind of negative space
Fill it up, she says, with love, with song, with candles on a cake
Light the darkness, take my hand, it will all be okay

So happy birthday, happy birthday, happy birthday, we sing
Then plunge our fingers into cake with neon sweet frosting
Hands slick with sugar icing, we feed each other cake
Like a wedding we'll have someday, the family we create

Nothing, she tells me, is ever really gone
Not you, not me, not them, so long as we carry on
So light a candle, take a breath, blow deep now, blow strong
Because after darkness, there always comes the dawn

"WITH THESE HANDS"

PREPARE FOR LANDING, TRACK 9

I want to build you a house
With these hands
I want to cut down the trees
I want to hew the wood smooth
Till my own calluses grow huge

I want to build you a jewel box
With these hands
And fill it with all kinds of treasure
Not diamond or rubies or
*   emeralds or gold*
But lost things harder to measure

I want to build you a woodstove
With these hands
To keep your own hands warm
I'd fuel it with maple and oak and alder
And stoke it with the heat of my love

I want to build you a house
With these hands
A place of wood, light, and music
There'll be room for me, for you,
*   for our future, too*
And of course all the ghosts in the attic

I want to build you a house
With these hands
Oh, I want to build you a house
With these hands
I want to build you a house
With these hands
Because you've already
*   made me a home*

"KALEIDOSCOPE EYES"

PREPARE FOR LANDING, TRACK 2

Sometimes her eyes rage sorrow
Sometimes her eyes bathe love
Sometimes her eyes are a fist
Sheathed in a boxer's glove

Sometimes I'm scared to look
Afraid of the stories they'll tell
Afraid that in those eyes
Is a return ticket to hell

Sometimes her eyes grow flowers
Bursting with sweet perfume
Sometimes her eyes are fire
And I'm yearning to be consumed

Sometimes I'm scared to look
Afraid that her eyes are a dream
And if I look too closely
None of this will be as it seems

Sometimes her eyes bathe sorrow
Sometimes her eyes rage love
Sometimes her eyes are a caress
Soft as a velvet glove

Sometimes I'm scared to look
Afraid that I might trespass
But every time I lift my eyes to hers
Those eyes, they always say yes
Your eyes always say yes

PLAYLIST

As in *If I Stay*, music plays a big role in *Where She Went*, though Adam's relationship to music has changed quite drastically from the first book. I don't think I referenced that many songs—except maybe classical pieces—in this book, until about two-thirds of the way through when Adam's feelings about music change, suddenly and drastically. That said, music always inspires me when I write. So here is a *Where She Went* playlist, comprised of tunes inspired by Mia and Adam's journey through New York City as well as songs mentioned in the story.

1. Cello Suite no. 1 (Prelude) Johann Sebastian Bach
2. "Take the Skinheads Bowling" Camper Van Beethoven
3. "I Am a Scientist" Guided By Voices
4. "My My Metrocard" Le Tigre
5. "Challengers" The New Pornographers
6. Three Preludes George Gershwin
7. "Bluebird of Happiness" Mojave 3
8. "Chicago" Sufjan Stevens
9. "Smallpox Champion" Fugazi
10. "Wild Horses" The Rolling Stones
11. "Scythian Empires" Andrew Bird
12. "Airline to Heaven" Billy Bragg & Wilco

ACKNOWLEDGMENTS

It is customary in these types of things for writers to thank their editors and agents separately. But when I think of my writing career, I often imagine myself flanked by my editor, Julie Strauss-Gabel, and my agent, Sarah Burnes. These two fiercely intelligent book warriors are both so integral to the creation and guidance of my work that it's hard to separate them. Sarah advises, advocates, and helps me keep things in perspective. Julie's greatest gift is that she gives me the key to unlock my stories. The two of them are my twin pillars.

But, as the saying goes, it takes a village. And in Julie's case, that village consists of many, many dedicated people at the Penguin Young Readers Group. I will save some trees and not list them all but suffice it to say, there are dozens of people in the sales, marketing, publicity, design, online, and production departments to whom I am deeply—and daily—grateful. Shout-outs must go to Don Weisberg, Lauri Hornik, Lisa Yoskowitz, and Allison Verost, who is equal parts publicist, therapist, and friend.

Sarah's village at The Gernert Company includes Rebecca Gardner, Logan Garrison, Will Roberts, and the formidable Courtney Gatewood, who, for someone bent on world domination, is remarkably nice.

Thank you to Alisa Weilerstein, for inspiring me, as well as giving up some of her precious free time to help me understand the career trajectory for a young professional cellist. Thank you Lynn Eastes, trauma coordinator at OHSU, for offering insights into what Mia's recovery and rehabilitation process might look like. Thank you to Sean Smith for an insider's view into the film industry (and a million other things). Anything I got right in regard to these details is because of these people. Anything I got wrong is because of me.

Thank you to the Edna St. Vincent Millay Society for the generous use of one of my all-time favorite sonnets, "Love is not all: it is not meat nor drink." Many of Edna St. Vincent Millay's poems are incredibly romantic and yet still kind of edgy all these years later. I only included the second half of this sonnet in the book; you should all go look up the full sonnet.

Thank you to my readers at all stages: Jana Banin, Tamara Glenny, Marjorie Ingall, Tamar Schamhart, and Courtney Sheinmel for just the right mix of encouragement and critique.

Thank you to my other village—my neighborhood community—for pitching in with my kids and generally having my back. Isabel Kyriacou and Gretchen Sonju, I am forever in your debt!

Thank you to the entire Christie Family for their enduring grace and generosity.

Thank you to Greg and Diane Rios for continuing on this journey with us.

Thank you to my family, the Formans, Schamharts, and Tuckers, for your cheerleading and cheer. Extra thanks to my sister for hand-selling my books to half the population of Seattle.

Thank you to my daughters: Denbele, who arrived in our family about midway through the writing of this book, and if she ever thought it was weird that her new mom occasionally seemed to channel an angsty twenty-one-year-old guy, never let that dent her ebullience. And to Willa, who inadvertently supplied me with so many of the book's fictional band/movie/character names in a way that only a four/five-year-old can. I should probably raise your allowance.

Thank you to my husband, Nick, for your not-so-gentle critiques that always force me to up my game. For your sublime playlists that bring music into my life (and books). For supplying me with all the little band details. And for being the reason I can't seem to stop writing love stories about guitar players.

And finally, thank you to the booksellers, librarians, teachers, and bloggers. For helping books take flight.

DISCUSSION QUESTIONS

• *Where She Went* picks up three years after Mia decided to stay. Do you think this time lapse matters? Would the story have worked if it took place one or even two years later? Why or why not?

• The chapters in this novel alternate between Adam's current life and his relationship with Mia both pre- and post-accident. How did this storytelling tactic enhance your understanding of their breakup?

• When the story opens, Adam's band is famous, but he struggles internally on account of his breakup with Mia. In what ways did this breakup change his life? Were any of them for the good?

• Adam and Mia's breakup was a very quiet affair. Why was this so devastating to Adam? Discuss any signs of an impending breakup you saw in the flashbacks. Do you understand why Mia acted that way?

• Do you think Mia could have broken up with Adam face-to-face? Show how the intensity of their relationship in combination with the accident might have influenced her choice.

• Were you shocked to discover Mia and Adam had broken up at the beginning of the novel? It could be argued the breakup was necessary for both to completely heal. Do you believe this? Explain your reasons.

• Compare and contrast Adam's and Mia's current lives. Does Mia seem happy with her life in New York? Is there anything in her story that would make you think otherwise?

• Consider the way Adam treats the people in his life: Bryn, his band mates, his manager, his parents, and even Kim. Were there different choices he could have made to end up on a different path? Would you have stuck by a friend going through the same thing or moved on?

• Did Mia have a right to be angry with Adam? What did you think of her revelation to him? Do you agree with her anger?

• Mia says, "For my first recital ever, they gave me a cello. And for this one, they gave me you." How do you feel about the way Mia discusses her family? What is Adam's reaction?

• Explain the significance of Adam's guitar and the circumstances surrounding it.

• *If I Stay* had themes of sacrifice and choice. What are the main themes of *Where She Went*? Can you identify the way they play out for both characters?

• Do you consider Mia and Adam's relationship stronger on account of their history? Why or why not? What does the future holds for Adam and Mia?

Read on for a sneak peek of JUST ONE DAY . . .

'Sweepingly romantic, this book is a living, breathing memory of the whirlwind of emotions that go hand in hand with falling in love' *Sugarscape*

All the world's a stage,
And all the men and women merely players:
They have their exits and their entrances;
And one man in his time plays many parts....
From William Shakespeare's *As You Like It*

PART ONE

One Day

One

*W*hat if Shakespeare had it wrong?

To be, or not to be: that is the question. That's from Hamlet's—maybe Shakespeare's—most famous soliloquy. I had to memorize the whole speech for sophomore English, and I can still remember every word. I didn't give it much thought back then. I just wanted to get all the words right and collect my A. But what if Shakespeare—and Hamlet—were asking the wrong question? What if the real question is not whether *to* be, but *how* to be?

The thing is, I don't know if I would have asked myself that question—*how* to be—if it wasn't for *Hamlet*. Maybe I would have gone along being the Allyson Healey I had been. Doing just what I was supposed to do, which, in this case, was going to see *Hamlet*.

— — —

"God, it's so hot. I thought it wasn't supposed to get this hot in England." My friend Melanie loops her blond hair into a bun and fans her sweaty neck. "What time are they opening the doors, anyhow?"

I look over at Ms. Foley, who Melanie and pretty much the rest of our group has christened Our Fearless Leader behind her back. But she is talking to Todd, one of the history grad students co-leading the trip, probably telling him off for something or other. In the Teen Tours! Cultural Extravaganza brochure that my parents presented to me upon my high school graduation two months ago, the Todd-like graduate students were called "historical consultants" and were meant to bolster the "educational value" of the Teen Tours! But so far, Todd has been more valuable in bolstering the hangovers, taking everyone out drinking almost every night. I'm sure tonight everyone else will go extra wild. It is, after all, our last stop, Stratford-upon-Avon, a city full of Culture! Which seems to translate into a disproportionate number of pubs named after Shakespeare and frequented by people in blaring white sneakers.

Ms. Foley is wearing her own snow-white sneakers—along with a pair of neatly pressed blue jeans and a Teen Tours! polo shirt—as she reprimands Todd. Sometimes, at night, when everyone else is out on the town, she will tell me she ought to call the head office on him. But she never seems to follow through. I think partly because when she scolds, he flirts. Even with Ms. Foley. Especially with Ms. Foley.

"I think it starts at seven," I say to Melanie. I look at my watch, another graduation present, thick gold, the back engraved *Going Places*. It weighs heavy against my sweaty wrist. "It's six thirty now."

"Geez, the Brits do love to line up. Or queue. Or whatever. They should take a lesson from the Italians, who just mob. Or maybe the Italians should take a lesson from the Brits." Melanie tugs on her miniskirt—her bandage skirt, she calls it—and adjusts her cami-top. "God, Rome. It feels like a year ago."

Rome? Was it six days ago? Or sixteen? All of Europe has become a blur of airports, buses, old buildings, and prix-fixe menus serving chicken in various kinds of sauce. When my parents gave me this trip as a big high-school graduation present, I was a little reluctant to go. But Mom had reassured me that she'd done her research. Teen Tours! was very well regarded, noted for its high-quality educational component, as well as the care that was taken of its students. I would be well looked after. "You'll never be alone," my parents had promised me. And, of course, Melanie was coming too.

And they were right. I know everyone else gives Ms. Foley crap for the eagle eye she keeps on us, but I appreciate how she is always doing a head count, even appreciate how she disapproves of the nightly jaunts to local bars, though most of us are of legal drinking age in Europe—not that anyone over here seems to care about such things anyway.

I don't go to the bars. I usually just go back to the hotel rooms Melanie and I share and watch TV. You can almost always find American movies, the same kinds of movies which, back at home, Melanie and I often watched together on weekends, in one of our rooms, with lots of popcorn.

"I'm roasting out here," Melanie moans. "It's like middle of the afternoon still."

I look up. The sun is hot, and the clouds race across the sky. I like how fast they go, nothing in their way. You can tell from the sky that England's an island. "At least it's not pouring like it was when we got here."

"Do you have a pony holder?" Melanie asks. "No, of course you don't. I bet you're loving your hair now."

My hand drifts to the back of my neck, which still feels strange, oddly exposed. The Teen Tour! had begun in London, and on the second afternoon, we'd had a few free hours for shopping, which I guess qualifies as culture. During that time, Melanie had convinced me to get my hair bobbed. It was all part of her precollege reinvention scheme, which she'd explained to me on the flight over: "No one at college will know that we were AP automatons. I mean, we're too pretty to just be brainiacs, and at college, everyone will be smart. So we can be cool *and* smart. Those two things will no longer be mutually exclusive."

For Melanie, this reinvention apparently meant the new heavy-on-skimp wardrobe she'd blown half her spending money on at Topshop, and the truncating of her name from Melanie to Mel—something I can't quite remember to do, no matter how many times she kicks me under the table. For me, I guess it meant the haircut she talked me into.

I'd freaked out when I'd seen myself. I've had long black hair and no bangs for as long as I can remember, and the girl staring back at me in the salon mirror didn't look like anything like me. At that point, we'd only been gone two days, but my stomach went hollow with homesickness. I wanted to be back in my bedroom at home, with my familiar peach walls, my collection of vintage alarm clocks. I'd wondered how I was ever going to handle college if I couldn't handle this.

But I've gotten used to the hair, and the homesickness has

mostly gone away, and even if it hasn't, the tour is ending. Tomorrow, almost everyone else is taking the coach straight to the airport to fly home. Melanie and I are catching a train down to London to stay with her cousin for three days. Melanie is talking about going back to the salon where I got my bob to get a pink streak in her hair, and we're going to see *Let It Be* in the West End. On Sunday, we fly home, and soon after that, we start college—me near Boston, Melanie in New York.

"Set Shakespeare free!"

I look up. A group of about a dozen people are coming up and down the line, handing out multicolored neon flyers. I can tell straightaway that they're not American—no bright white tennis shoes or cargo shorts in sight. They are all impossibly tall, and thin, and different looking, somehow. It's like even their bone structure is foreign.

"Oh, I'll take one of those." Melanie reaches out for a flyer and uses it to fan her neck.

"What's it say?" I ask her, looking at the group. Here in touristy Stratford-upon-Avon, they stand out like fire-orange poppies in a field of green.

Melanie looks at the flyer and wrinkles her nose. "Guerrilla Will?"

A girl with the kind of magenta streaks Melanie has been coveting comes up to us. "It's Shakespeare for the masses."

I peer at the card. It reads *Guerrilla Will. Shakespeare Without Borders. Shakespeare Unleashed. Shakespeare For Free. Shakespeare For All.*

"Shakespeare for free?" Melanie reads.

"Yeah," the magenta-haired girl says in accented English.

"Not for capitalist gain. How Shakespeare would've wanted it."

"You don't think he'd want to actually sell tickets and make money from his plays?" I'm not trying to be a smart-ass, but I remember that movie *Shakespeare in Love* and how he was always owing money to somebody or other.

The girl rolls her eyes, and I start to feel foolish. I look down. A shadow falls over me, momentarily blocking out the glare of the sun. And then I hear laughter. I look up. I can't see the person in front of me because he's backlit by the still-bright evening sun. But I can hear him.

"I think she's right," he says. "Being a starving artist is not so romantic, maybe, when you're actually starving."

I blink a few times. My eyes adjust, and I see that the guy is tall, maybe a full foot taller than I am, and thin. His hair is a hundred shades of blond, and his eyes so brown as to almost be black. I have to tilt my head up to look at him, and he's tilting his head down to look at me.

"But Shakespeare is dead; he's not collecting royalties from the grave. And we, we are alive." He opens his arms, as if to embrace the universe. "What are you seeing?"

"*Hamlet*," I say.

"Ah, *Hamlet*." His accent is so slight as to be almost imperceptible. "I think a night like this, you don't waste on tragedy." He looks at me, like it's a question. Then he smiles. "Or indoors. We are doing *Twelfth Night*. Outside." He hands me a flyer.

"We'll *think* about it," Melanie says in her coy voice.

The guy raises one shoulder and cocks his head toward it so his ear is almost touching his very angular shoulder blade. "What you will," he says, though he's looking at me. Then he saunters off to join the rest of his troupe.

Melanie watches them go. "Wow, why are they not on the Teen Tours! Cultural Extravaganza? That's some culture I could get into!"

I watch them leave, feeling a strange tug. "I've seen *Hamlet* before, you know."

Melanie looks at me, her eyebrows, which she has overly plucked into a thin line, raised. "Me too. It was on TV, but still . . ."

"We could go . . . to this. I mean, it would be different. A cultural experience, which is why our parents sent us on this tour."

Melanie laughs. "Look at you, getting all bad! But what about Our Fearless Leader? It looks like she's gearing up for one of her head counts."

"Well, the heat was really bothering you . . . " I begin.

Melanie looks at me for a second, then something clicks. She licks her lips, grins, and then crosses her eyes. "Oh, yeah. I totally have heatstroke." She turns to Paula, who's from Maine and is studiously reading a Fodor's guide. "Paula, I'm feeling so dizzy."

"It's way hot," Paula says, nodding sympathetically. "You should hydrate."

"I think I might faint or something. I'm seeing black spots."

"Don't pile it on," I whisper.

"It's good to build a case," Melanie whispers, enjoying this now. "Oh, I think I'm going to pass out."

"Ms. Foley," I call.

Ms. Foley looks up from ticking names off her roll-call sheet. She comes over, her face so full of concern, I feel bad for lying. "I think Melanie, I mean Mel, is getting heatstroke."

"Are you poorly? It shouldn't be much longer now. And it's lovely and cool inside the theater." Ms. Foley speaks in a strange hybrid of Britishisms with a Midwestern accent that everyone makes fun of because they think it's pretentious. But I think it's just that she's from Michigan and spends a lot of time in Europe.

"I feel like I'm going to puke." Melanie pushes on. "I would hate to do that inside the Swan Theatre."

Ms. Foley's face wrinkles in displeasure, though I can't tell if it is from the idea of Melanie barfing inside the Swan or using the word *puke* in such close proximity to the Royal Shakespeare Company. "Oh, dear. I'd better escort you back to the hotel."

"I can take her," I say.

"Really? Oh, no. I couldn't. You should see *Hamlet*."

"No, it's fine. I'll take her."

"No! It's my responsibility to take her. I simply couldn't burden you like that." I can see the argument she's having with herself play out over her pinched features.

"It's fine, Ms. Foley. I've seen *Hamlet* before, and the hotel is just over the square from here."

"Really? Oh, that would be lovely. Would you believe in all the years I've been doing this, I have never seen the Bard's *Hamlet* done by the RSC?"

Melanie gives a little moan for dramatic effect. I gently elbow her. I smile at Ms. Foley. "Well, then, you definitely shouldn't miss it."

She nods solemnly, as though we are discussing important business here, order of succession to the throne or something. Then she reaches for my hand. "It has been such a pleasure traveling with you, Allyson. I shall miss you. If only more young people today were like you. You are such a . . ." She pauses for a moment, searching for the right word. "Such a good girl."

"Thank you," I say automatically. But her compliment leaves me empty. I don't know if it's because that's the nicest thing she could think to say about me, or if it's because I'm not being such a good girl right now.

"Good girl, my ass." Melanie laughs once we are clear of the queue and she can give up her swooning act.

"Be quiet. I don't like pretending."

"Well, you're awfully good at it. You could have a promising acting career of your own, if you ask me."

"I don't ask you. Now, where is this place?" I look at the flyer. "Canal Basin? What is that?"

Melanie pulls out her phone, which, unlike my cell phone, works in Europe. She opens the map app. "It appears to be a basin by the canal."

A few minutes later, we arrive at a waterfront. It feels like a carnival, full of people hanging about. There are barges moored to the side of the water, different boats selling everything from ice cream to paintings. What there isn't is any kind of theater. Or stage. Or chairs. Or actors. I look at the flyer again.

"Maybe it's on the bridge?" Melanie asks.

We walk back over to the medieval arched bridge, but it's just more of the same: tourists like us, milling around in the hot night.

"They did say it was tonight?" Melanie asks.

I think of that one guy, his eyes so impossibly dark, specifically saying that *tonight* was too nice for tragedy. But when I look around, there's no play here, obviously. It was probably some kind of joke—fool the stupid tourist.

"Let's get an ice cream so the night's not a total write-off," I say.

We are queuing up for ice cream when we hear it, a hum of acoustic guitars and the echoey beat of bongo drums. My ears perk up, my sonar rises. I stand on a nearby bench to look around. It's not like a stage has magically appeared, but what has just materialized is a crowd, a pretty big one, under a stand of trees.

"I think it's starting," I say, grabbing Melanie's hand.

"But the ice cream," she complains.

"After," I say, yanking her toward the crowd.

"If music be the food of love, play on."

The guy playing Duke Orsino looks nothing like any Shakespearian actor I've ever seen, except maybe the movie version of *Romeo + Juliet* with Leonardo DiCaprio. He is tall, black, dreadlocked, and dressed like a glam rock-star in tight vinyl pants, pointy-toed shoes, and a sort of mesh tank top that shows off his ripped chest.

"Oh, we *so* made the right choice," Melanie whispers in my ear.

As Orsino gives his opening soliloquy to the sounds of the guitars and bongo drums, I feel a shiver go up my spine.

We watch the entire first act, chasing the actors around the waterfront. When they move, we move, which makes it feel like *we* are a part of the play. And maybe that's what makes it so different. Because I've seen Shakespeare before. School productions and a few plays at the Philadelphia Shakespeare Theatre. But it's always felt like listening to something in a foreign language I didn't know that well. I had to force myself to pay attention, and half the time, I wound up rereading the program over and over again, as if it would impart some deeper understanding.

This time, it clicks. It's like my ear attunes to the weird language and I'm sucked fully into the story, the same way I am when I watch a movie, so that I *feel* it. When Orsino pines for the cool Olivia, I feel that pang in my gut from all the times I've crushed on guys I was invisible to. And when Viola mourns her brother, I feel her loneliness. And when she falls for Orsino, who thinks she's a man, it's actually funny and also moving.

He doesn't show up until act two. He's playing Sebastian, Viola's twin brother, thought dead. Which makes a certain sense, because by the time he does arrive, I am beginning to think he never really existed, that I've merely conjured him.

As he races through the green, chased after by the ever-loyal Antonio, we chase after him. After a while, I work up my nerve. "Let's get closer," I say to Melanie. She grabs my hand, and we go to the front of the crowd right at the part where Olivia's clown comes for Sebastian and they argue before Sebastian sends him away. Right before he does, he seems to catch my eye for half a second.

As the hot day softens into twilight and I'm sucked deeper into the illusory world of Illyria, I feel like I've entered some weird otherworldly space, where anything can happen, where identities can be swapped like shoes. Where those thought dead are alive again. Where everyone gets their happily-ever-afters. I recognize it's kind of corny, but the air is soft and warm, and the trees are lush and full, and the crickets are singing, and it seems like, for once, maybe it can happen.

All too soon, the play is ending. Sebastian and Viola are reunited. Viola comes clean to Orsino that she's actually a girl, and of course he now wants to marry her. And Olivia realizes that Sebastian isn't the person she thought she married—but she doesn't care; she loves him anyway. The musicians are playing again as the clown gives the final soliloquy. And then the actors are out and bowing, each one doing something a little silly with his or her bow. One flips. One plays air guitar. When Sebastian bows, he scans the audience and stops dead on me. He smiles this funny little half smile, takes one of the prop coins out of his pocket, and flips it to me. It's pretty dark, and the coin is small, but I catch it, and people clap for me too, it now seems.

With the coin in my hand, I clap. I clap until my hands sting. I clap as if doing so can prolong the evening, can transform *Twelfth Night* into *Twenty-Fourth Night*. I clap so that I can hold on to this feeling. I clap because I know what will happen when I stop. It's the same thing that happens when I turn off a really good movie—one that I've lost myself to—which is that I'll be thrown back to my own reality and something hollow will settle in my chest. Sometimes, I'll watch a movie all over again just to recapture that feeling of being inside something real. Which, I know, doesn't make any sense.

But there's no restarting tonight. The crowd is dispersing; the actors drifting off. The only people left from the show are a couple of musicians passing around the donation hat. I reach into my wallet for a ten-pound note.

Melanie and I stand together in silence. "Whoa," she says.

"Yeah. Whoa," I say back.

"That was pretty cool. And I hate Shakespeare."

I nod.

"And was it me, or was that hot guy from the line earlier, the one who played Sebastian, was he totally checking us out?"

Us? But he threw *me* the coin. Or had I just been the one to catch it? Why wouldn't it have been Melanie with her blond hair and her camisole top that he'd been checking out? Mel 2.0, as she calls herself, so much more appealing than Allyson 1.0.

"I couldn't tell," I say.

"*And* he threw the coin at us! Nice catch, by the way. Maybe we should go find them. Go hang out with them or something."

"They're gone."

"Yeah, but those guys are still here." She gestures to the money collectors. "We could ask where they hang out."

I shake my head. "I doubt they want to hang out with stupid American teenagers."

"We're not stupid, and most of them didn't seem that much older than teenagers themselves."

"No. And besides, Ms. Foley might check in on us. We should get back to the room."

Melanie rolls her eyes. "Why do you always do this?"

"Do what?"

"Say no to everything. It's like you're averse to adventure."

"I don't always say no."

"Nine times out of ten. We're about to start college. Let's live a little."

"I live just plenty," I snap. "And besides, it never bothered you before."

Melanie and I have been best friends since her family moved two houses down from ours the summer before second grade. Since then, we've done everything together: we lost our teeth at the same time, we got our periods at the same time, even our boyfriends came in tandem. I started going out with Evan a few weeks after she started going out with Alex (who was Evan's best friend), though she and Alex broke up in January and Evan and I made it until April.

We've spent so much time together, we almost have a secret language of inside jokes and looks. We've fought plenty, of course. We're both only children, so sometimes we're like sisters. We once even broke a lamp in a tussle. But it's never been like this. I'm not even sure what *this* is, only that since we got on the tour, being with Melanie makes me feel like I'm losing a race I didn't even know I'd entered.

"I came out here tonight," I say, my voice brittle and defensive. "I lied to Ms. Foley so we could come."

"Right? And we've had so much fun! So why don't we keep it going?"

I shake my head.

She shuffles through her bag and pulls out her phone, scrolls through her texts. "*Hamlet* just let out too. Craig says that Todd's taken the gang to a pub called the Dirty Duck. I like the sound of that. Come out with us. It'll be a blast."

The thing is, I did go out with Melanie and everyone from the tour once, about a week into the trip. By this time, they'd already gone out a couple times. And even though Melanie had known these guys only a week—the same amount of time

I'd known them—she had all these inside jokes with them, jokes *I* didn't understand. I'd sat there around the crowded table, nursing a drink, feeling like the unlucky kid who had to start a new school midway into the year.

I look at my watch, which has slid all the way down my wrist. I slide it back up, so it covers the ugly red birthmark right on my pulse. "It's almost eleven, and we have to be up early tomorrow for our train. So if you don't mind, I'm going to take my adventure-averse self back to the room." With the huffiness in my voice, I sound just like my mom.

"Fine. I'll walk you back and then go to the pub."

"And what if Ms. Foley checks in on us?"

Melanie laughs. "Tell her I had heatstroke. And it's not hot anymore." She starts to walk up the slope back toward the bridge. "What? Are you waiting for something?"

I look back down toward the water, the barges, now emptying out from the evening rush. Trash collectors are out in force. The day is ending; it's not coming back.

"No, I'm not."